This book
MALICE MASTERPIECES 6
contains novellas
Twenty-Six through
Thirty
including:
METHODICAL MALICE
MALEVOLENT MALICE
MILITARIAL MALICE
MACHIAVELLIAN MALICE
MALEFIC MALICE

A K'Anne Meinel novel

Book 26 METHODICAL MALICE

Moving on after a long-term marriage ends is killer and finding and decorating a new home is not something Alice enjoys. She's becoming annoyed with the inconveniences caused by those who are surveilling her and her new life. She is methodically putting her life back together, but when she finally begins to get her things in order, life throws her a curve ball no one could have seen coming.

Book 27 MALEVOLENT MALICE

Alice's accident puts an immense strain on the family dynamic that no one could have anticipated. Its far-reaching impact will alter their family in more ways than one.

Book 28 MILITARIAL MALICE

Alice's unfinished business has caused her and her family a lot of unforeseen aggravation, and Alice seeks to make amends. But it seems life isn't finished with her yet. Just when Alice thinks they're about to be happy again, life throws her one more curve, and this one is a doozy!

Book 29 MACHIAVELLIAN MALICE

When your life is a mess, and you are surrounded by enemies, how do you combat the overwhelming odds against you? Alice and Kathy must face down more than health concerns; life concerns and a litany of grievances are stacked against them.

Book 30 MALEFIC MALICE

Lessons on how to piss off a lesbian serial killer:

1) Hit her in the head with the butt of a gun.
2) Treat her with disdain and underestimate her abilities.
3) Involve her family!

Alice awakens to discover she has been taken prisoner. Flashbacks are instantaneous, and when she realizes that Kathy and Emily are there too, she is compelled to return them to safety. Alice doesn't want her family involved in this part of her life. She isn't comfortable with them knowing, much less participating, after all her years of hard work to keep them in the dark.

Paybacks can be deadly for those who don't realize how truly gifted Alice is. Follow along as Alice continues to triumph at what she does so very well...

Also by K'Anne Meinel:

Novels in Paperback:

SHIPS *CompanionSHIP, FriendSHIP,*
RelationSHIP
Long Distance Romance
Children of Another Mother
Erotica
The Claim
Bikini's Are Dangerous
The Complete Series
Germanic
Malice Masterpieces 1
The First Five Books
Represented
Timed Romance
Malice Masterpieces 2
Books Six through Ten
The Journey Home
Out at the Inn
Shorts
Anthology Volume 1
Lawyered
Malice Masterpieces 3
Books Eleven through Fifteen
Blown Away
Blown Away
The Alternate Cover

Small Town Angel
Pirated Love
Doctored
Veil of Silence
Malice Masterpieces 4
Books Sixteen through Twenty
The Outsider
Pirated Heart
Recombinant Love
Survivors
Inn the Dog House
Flight
An Island Between Us
Malice Masterpieces 5
Books Twenty-One through Twenty-Five
Malice Masterpieces 6
Books Twenty-Six through Thirty
Beauty and the Beast

Vetted Series:
Vetted
Cavalcade (Prequel)
Pioneering (Prequel)
Vetted Further
Vetted Again

Novellas in Paperback:

Sapphic Surfer
Sapphic Cowgirl
Sapphic Cowboi
Mysterious Malice (Book 1)
Meticulous Malice (Book 2)
Mistaken Malice (Book 3)
Malicious Malice (Book 4)
Masterful Malice (Book 5)
Matrimonial Malice (Book 6)
Mourning Malice (Book 7)
Murderous Malice (Book 8)
Mental Malice (Book 9)
Menacing Malice (Book 10)
Minor Malice (Book 11)
Morally Malice (Book 12)
Morose Malice (Book 13)
Melancholy Malice (Book 14)
Mad Malice (Book 15)

Macabre Malice (Book 16)
Marinating Malice (Book 17)
Macerating Malice (Book 18)
Minacious Malice (Book 19)
Meddlesome Malice (Book 20)
Meandering Malice (Book 21)
Maniacal Malice (Book 22)
Sayyida
The Northwood Lodge
Monitoring Malice (Book 23)
Marked Malice (Book 24)
Shanghaied (Prequel)
Outback Born
Outback Bred
Outback Heritage
Outback Native
Outback Splendor

A K'Anne Meinel novel

Novellas in E-book:

Outback Escape (Prequel)
Mandating Malice (Book 25)
Methodical Malice (Book 26)
Malevolent Malice (Book 27)
Militarial Malice (Book 28)

Machiavellian Malice (Book 29)
Malefic Malice (Book 30)
Religious Experience
Lied

Pocket Paperbacks:

Mysterious Malice (Book 1)
Sapphic Surfer
Sapphic Cowgirl
Meticulous Malice (Book 2)
Mistaken Malice (Book 3)
Malicious Malice (Book 4)
Masterful Malice (Book 5)
Matrimonial Malice (Book 6)
Mourning Malice (Book 7)
Murderous Malice (Book 8)

Mental Malice (Book 9)
Menacing Malice (Book 10)
Minor Malice (Book 11)
Morally Malice (Book 12)
Morose Malice (Book 13)
Melancholy Malice (Book 14)
Mad Malice (Book 15)
Macabre Malice (Book 16)
Marinating Malice (Book 17)

In E-Book Format:
Short Stories

Fantasy
Wet & Wet Again
Family Night
Quickie ~ Against the Car
Quickie ~ Against the Wall
Quickie ~ Over the Couch
Mile High Club
Quickie ~ Under the Pier
Heel or Heal
Kiss
Family Night 2
Beach Dreams
Internet Dreamers
Snoggered

On the Parkway
Stable Affair
Kept
Stolen
Agitated
Love of my LIFE
Quickie in an Elevator,
GOING DOWN?
Into the Garden
The Book Case
The Other Women
Menage a WHAT?

Audiobooks

Doctored
Sapphic Surfer
The Rockhound
Cavalcade
Pioneering
To Love A Shooting Star
Mysterious Malice
Ghostly Love

Stable Affair
Sapphic Cowgirl
Love of my LIFE
The Book Case
Flight
Sayyida
Vetted

All Novels and Novellas in paperback are also available as e-books.

Videos

Biography of Books
Ships
Sapphic Surfer
Ghostly Love
Long Distance Romance
Germanic
Sensual Sapphic
Sapphic Cowgirl
Couples
Lie Next To Me

Sapphic Cowboi
Timed Romance
Readings (SHIPS)
Doctored
Veil of Silence
She's Coming (The Outsider short)
It's Coming (The Outsider short)
The Outsider
Vetted

Novels/Novellas in other Languages:

Sapphic Cowboi: Vaquera Safica (Spanish)
Sapphic Surfer: Surfista Safica (Spanish)
Sapphic Surfer: ケーアンヌ・マイネル (Japanese)
Doctored: A Doutora (Portuguese)
Doctored: La Doctora (Spanish)

LARGE Print Novels

SHIPS CompanionSHIP, FriendSHIP,
RelationSHIP
Erotica Volume 1
Long Distance Romance
Children of Another Mother
Bikini's Are Dangerous
The Complete Series

Malice Masterpieces
The First Five Books
To Love a Shooting Star
The Claim
Represented
Timed Romance

K'ANNE MEINEL

Malice Masterpieces

6

Books Twenty-Six through Thirty

ISBN-13: 978-1959436096

K'Anne Meinel is available for comments at KAnneMeinel@aim.com as well as on Facebook, Google +, or her blog @ http://kannemeinel.wordpress.com/ or on Twitter @ kannemeinelaim.com, or on her website @ www.kannemeinel.com if you would like to follow her to find out about stories and book's releases.

www.shadoepublishing.com

ShadoePublishing@gmail.com

Shadoe Publishing is a United States of America company

Cover by: K'Anne Meinel @ Shadoe Publishing
Edited by: Deb Amia, Grammar Queen

MALICE MASTERPIECES

6

Table of Contents:

METHODICAL MALICE Page 1
MALEVOLENT MALICE Page 59
MILITARIAL MALICE Page 119
MACHIAVELLIAN MALICE Page 191
MALEFIC MALICE Page 257

❦ METHODICAL MALICE ❦

BOOK 26

Moving on after a long-term marriage ends is killer and finding and decorating a new home is not something Alice enjoys. She's becoming annoyed with the inconveniences caused by those who are surveilling her and her new life. She is methodically putting her life back together, but when she finally begins to get her things in order, life throws her a curve ball no one could have seen coming.

Alice stared at Kathy in surprise. Why did she ask that question? Was she here to accuse Alice of causing Linda's death? "What do you want me to do about it?" she asked instead.

Kathy sighed gustily, obviously annoyed. She looked beyond Alice into the beach house and asked, "May I come in?"

Alice made a sweeping motion with her arm to indicate that her soon-to-be ex-wife was welcome to come in. She looked beyond Kathy at the Lexus parked in her driveway behind her Ferrari. The driveway was barely big enough for both cars and only if they were placed end to end. She glanced past them at the Pacific Coast Highway (PCH) where cars were speeding along a little too close for her comfort. Land was at such a premium down here in Malibu that they couldn't afford to waste any. She glanced farther along the busy road to the now familiar car that was always parked there and always watching. Different people manned the vehicle in six- to eight-hour shifts, but someone was always watching, ready to follow if Alice went out. They no longer made any attempt to hide their presence, and Alice's Ferrari certainly wasn't inconspicuous. Closing the door firmly, she made sure the automatic lock engaged before turning to look at her wife, who was closely examining the small but expensive house.

Kathy looked around the ground floor. It was an open floor plan from front to back, the entrance only about five feet long by three feet wide. It led to a stairwell that curved upstairs, or you could bypass the stairwell and go directly into the living room. There was a modern gas fireplace along the wall and a few windows, so Alice could see along that side of her house. Bookshelves stood empty on each side of the bank of windows, nothing placed on them yet. The living room led into the dining area, which was furnished with only a cold, sterile, little table. If you turned to the left, you would enter a small kitchen, then a laundry area, and beyond that was a bedroom, probably intended for a maid. The kitchen, dining room, and bedroom areas all had French doors that led onto a balcony overlooking Malibu beach, which stretched the entire length of the relatively small house. The beach was filled with people.

But there was no warm, welcoming feeling in this house; even to Alice it felt bare. The townhome she'd had in the marina when she met Kathy had been sterile and impeccably clean, but at least there was furniture to indicate that someone lived there. This was too glacial. It

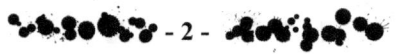

reminded Kathy of a four-star hotel room. At least in a five-star hotel they supplied a bit of warmth. This was functional but just barely.

"Pass muster?" Alice asked, her sardonic question making her lips quiver as she hid a smile while watching her wife gaze about the rather insignificant house.

"Did you hear what I asked?" Kathy asked, clearly still upset.

Alice nodded and asked, "Did you hear what I asked?"

Kathy sighed, allowing an exasperated sound to escape from her nose for effect.

Alice was amused. She knew how to push Kathy's buttons.

"Did you kill her?"

Alice's expression didn't change. "No, I didn't."

"Do you know–?" Kathy began and then stopped in alarm as Alice determinedly advanced on her and grabbed her arm to propel her outside. When she tried to fight Alice off, twisting her arm to release it, Alice grabbed her again in a body hug that locked their bodies firmly together.

Shocked, Kathy stood still as Alice whispered in her ear, "My place is bugged. Say nothing," then she danced them through the remainder of the room and onto the back deck. She released Kathy as soon as they were both outside and she'd closed the patio door, a set of sliders helping it move effortlessly despite the sand. She continued to walk across the deck, down the steps, and onto the beach below.

Kathy stared at the back of her wife's head for a moment. She was still startled by how that whisper had made her shiver, and the feel of Alice's arms around her was a welcome comfort. She hadn't expected that, or her own reaction. She rubbed her arms, the warmth dissipating quickly on this cool fall day. She followed Alice down the steps to the beach.

Alice turned, confronting Kathy. "You can't say stuff like that."

"It's not like I knew your place was bugged. Who–?" she began.

"I'm not sure yet, but I assume it's the Feds. After what I gave the CIA, I'm certain they want more information from me." She didn't mention the car that was parked out along the PCH all the time. Kathy didn't need to know about that.

"Can't you remove them?"

"I don't have the equipment yet."

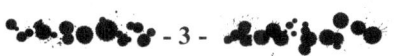

"Can you find out who–?" she began, and at Alice's expression the words died off. She realized she no longer had the right to ask about what happened in Alice's life.

"Look, I know you liked that woman and maybe even loved her–" Alice stopped, the pain of that statement hurt her, "but I didn't do what you asked, and I certainly am not going to investigate Linda's death."

"How do I know you aren't lying to me?"

"I don't lie to you, Kathy."

Kathy knew that was true. Alice might not tell her everything, but a direct question was always answered truthfully, at least Alice's version of the truth. She might be a killer, but she wasn't a liar. Kathy sighed again, exasperated as she looked away from her wife's startling and intriguing cat-like eyes. She looked back after a moment and asked, "Do you think it's legal for them to surveil you?"

Alice's eyebrow cocked in sardonic amusement at the question.

"Of course, it's not legal," Kathy sighed as she answered her own question, shrugged, and looked out at the fantastic view. She gestured at the house that was lacking in furniture and changed the subject. "Why haven't you decorated?"

Alice shrugged. "I didn't feel like it, and I didn't like the idea of having Sean draped on a couch." She shared a grin with her wife. Their son, a teenager with big feet, would stretch out on any surface and take it over. "Besides, I only needed a bedroom for me and furniture for them." Her head nodded back towards the house and somehow included the children.

Kathy nodded. Alice had taken very little when she left their house, just her clothes and a few items from their home in Palos Verdes. She'd been very amenable during the divorce negotiations, going so far as giving Kathy more than the half she had asked for and was legally entitled to. Kathy had wondered about that. She knew there was probably a lot more in hidden assets, but she wasn't going to be greedy when Alice was being so generous. She turned away from Alice's inquiring eyes again. They seemed to look in her soul, and right now, she didn't want Alice looking there. Kathy gazed out at the crowds gathered on the beach despite the cool fall day. The view was beautiful, and the location ideal, even if the house was small. "Nice view," she commented.

Alice agreed with her, turning at the deliberate distraction to look out over the sands. "Yeah, it's a nice spot," she responded.

"The kids like it," Kathy agreed, having heard all about their other mother's house in Malibu. Kathy was just surprised it wasn't more elaborate. She looked up at the second story, interested in what the rest of the house looked like.

"Would you like a tour?" Alice asked, knowing her wife was curious and itching to see it all. She'd gotten this place for a song, relatively speaking, as some new wave kid singer with too much money, a busy career, and no time to live in the house, had sold it off.

"That would be nice," she admitted.

"Just be careful what you say," the blonde reminded her, waiting a moment for Kathy to nod her agreement.

Kathy followed as Alice led the way up to the back deck that spanned the length of the small cracker box house.

Alice showed her the rest of the downstairs. She was thinking that space alone would have been enough, if Alice didn't need bedrooms for the children. It was awkward for both women as Alice showed her the rest of the house in silence. The awkwardness was a new thing, something they had never really experienced except on a few memorable occasions in their married life.

Kathy could see that both kids' bedrooms were neatly made, and she knew that neither Sean nor Emily would have left them in that condition. There wasn't much in the rooms other than basic furniture. Most of their things were kept at the house in Palos Verdes, where they had lived almost all their lives. Neither of them remembered the house at the marina. And that reminded her, "Kit is coming home this weekend."

Alice looked up as she exited the bathroom situated between the two kids' bedrooms. She was heading into the master bedroom that traversed almost the entire length of the back of the house and overlooked the beach. The master had its own private, rather elaborate bathroom, one of the main reasons she had bought this home. "I'd like to see her," Alice reminded her wife as she allowed her to walk into the bedroom.

"I'll make sure she knows that," Kathy said as she looked at the walk-in closet and the inviting bathroom with the jetted tub, separate shower, skylights, toilet, and bidet. She spotted something on the floor near the French patio doors on the far side of the king-sized bed. It was a nightgown, and it wasn't anything Alice would wear. Her heart twisted painfully as she realized Alice must already be seeing someone

else. She hardened her heart against that thought, knowing it was really none of her business. "She's declared her major."

"Oh, yeah?" Alice asked, intrigued. She had been aware of the exact moment when Kathy saw that nightgown, something she had deliberately left on the floor where it had been thrown. She carefully schooled her face not to smile at the game she was playing. She wasn't certain that the bugs that were listening in didn't also have video, but she would have to check that out soon. Inwardly, she sighed. If *they* would just leave her alone, she would leave them alone; however, who *they* were was yet to be determined.

Kathy turned to look at Alice, her back to the French doors. She had seen that the doors afforded Alice an even better view of Malibu Beach, the second story providing a grander perspective than any of the one-story homes. "You aren't going to like her choice."

"No?" Alice inquired, her eyebrow cocking in inquiry.

Kathy smiled slightly as she spoke with her wife, her child's second mother since she was eight years old. Alice had saved her then, had saved them both from a life she couldn't even contemplate now. "She's decided to go into law enforcement."

Kathy was surprised when Alice began to laugh. The blonde laughed so hard that tears ran from the corners of her eyes, and she wiped them away as she continued to chuckle.

"May I ask why that is so funny?"

"It's just ironic, don't you think?" Alice used the sleeve of her blouse to dry the tears, still sniggering.

Kathy had to smile as she nodded too. It *was* ironic, considering all the crimes Alice had committed over the years. Fortunately, their children didn't know, at least, *they didn't know much*, she mentally amended. She recalled that Emily knew a little more than she needed to and had asked a couple leading questions, obviously curious about what she had overheard and nearly spouting information in front of a cop. She remembered that Linda was the cop Emily had nearly said too much in front of, and she was now dead. She'd come here to ask Alice about that, at least that had been the premise of her visit. She made to move back through the room and go downstairs. "I'll tell her to stop by," Kathy promised as she reached the stairs. She glanced at the bare walls, the color a boring, muted off-white. "You really should decorate. Maybe get some furniture? A TV?" She noted the game set up in the room that was dedicated to Sean had a computer, and the

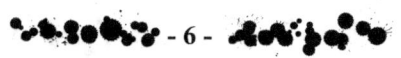

multi-colored light-up keyboard was apparently only for games. Alice's small office off the master bedroom didn't even have a desk, much less the many computers Alice had used so often in the past. It was curious to Kathy that there was no computer equipment after all this time since Alice had bought the house and moved in. There was no lived-in feeling to the place, and there was obviously no work being done here. What did Alice do with her days? Kathy remembered the nightgown and tried not to think of what Alice did with her nights. Then, she remembered that Alice didn't need to confine those activities to nights.

"Yeah, maybe Kit and the kids would like to help me?" she offered.

"I'll mention it. I'm sure Sean will try to talk you into more computer games," she commented wryly, knowing their son well. It was a good thing his grades were up to snuff, or those games would be locked up. She would stay on top of that.

"I think I have enough," she gestured through the open door of the boy's room where the elaborate gaming system was set up.

"Is that original?" Kathy asked, looking a second time. She'd missed it the first time she glanced in the room as she was focused more on the well-made bed. The computer games were stacked neatly on a table near a very wide monitor, and two gaming chairs allowed the users to lean back from the floor as they played. She saw now, there were several gaming consoles hooked up to multiple screens.

"The Nintendo?" Alice confirmed, grinning as she nodded at the game that came out in the 1980s. "Yeah, I kicked his ass on that. He is so used to the modern graphics and doodads that he never saw me coming in Super Mario Bros with all the hidden mushrooms and whatnots."

Kathy laughed. She'd forgotten that Alice liked that game. "But what about Duck Hunt?" she teased as she left the doorway and headed for the stairs once again.

"Oh, yeah. Em and I enjoyed that, and it annoyed Sean, so bonus," she teased back, knowing her son had been put out that his younger sister had beaten him at the hand-eye coordination of the simple game. The games he had now were so much more sophisticated, and a lot of them involved war, which simply didn't interest Alice as it might once have.

They proceeded down the stairs to the front door, and Kathy noted that the alarm system wasn't something Alice would have permitted in

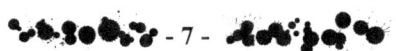

their own home. It didn't seem as sophisticated, but maybe she wasn't reading it right? Something was afoot here, and although she was curious about it, she wasn't going to ask. It wasn't her place, and while she still cared for Alice, it was obvious the blonde had moved on. She swallowed again, wondering who belonged to the nightgown upstairs.

"I'll tell Kit to give you a call when she's settled in the house, so you two can make plans," Kathy promised as she headed out to her blue Lexus. She glanced at the flashy Ferrari Alice now drove, something that had surprised her after all the Porsches the blonde had owned during their years together. She looked up in surprise and found a woman barring her way. Kathy looked at her curiously, wondering if this was the mysterious nightgown owner, then dismissing that thought immediately. This woman was not Alice's type. She was dressed very conservatively in a suit.

"Hello, Alice," the woman said, ignoring Kathy. She knew who Kathy was from the pictures they had of Alice's family. She was a nobody and a mouse compared to Alice Weaver. The suited woman still wondered what sort of woman could have held Alice Weaver's attention for all those years. There had to be something more to her if Alice had married her. She knew from their surveillance of Alice that a divorce had been filed. Several of their team wondered if they could use that to their benefit. After all, a wife couldn't testify against her spouse but an ex-wife could.

"Hello, Madelyn," Alice responded in an amused tone that irritated both Madelyn and Kathy. Kathy was curious to know who this was, and seeing that curiosity and being courteous, Alice introduced them. "Madelyn Korbel, this is my ex-wife, Kathy."

The two women eyed each other. Madelyn dismissed the mousy woman, and Kathy asked, "CIA?" in a tone that left them both with no doubt that she despised the acronym and the people behind it.

Madelyn was intrigued. Why would Alice's ex-wife care if she was with the CIA or not? She nodded, a bit coldly in agreement.

Kathy was feeling hurt by Alice referring to her as her ex-wife. The paperwork wasn't final yet. Her tone when she replied was perhaps a bit touchy.

"Whatcha want, Madelyn?" Alice asked, leaning against the wall of the house in a relaxed slouch and watching the two women. She was wondering if Madelyn frequently underestimated people. She could see how dismissive she was being of Kathy. If she only knew....

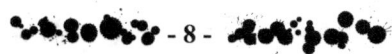

"Is there somewhere we could talk?" Madelyn asked, glancing at the beach house before them curiously.

Alice nodded and held her hand out to Kathy. "Maybe you should come back in for this?" she offered.

"This is private," Madelyn stated, glancing at the mousy woman again and reassessing her. Her tone brooked no argument, but Alice chose to ignore it.

"Yeah, but whether I tell her later or she hears it first-hand, she is going to want to know," Alice pointed out.

"You mean she knows–?"

Alice nodded. "I didn't keep anything from her."

Madelyn looked at the two women again. She was surprised and trying to hide it. It didn't pay to let your emotions or feelings show around people like this. She tried to shrug it off, acting as though it didn't matter as she followed Kathy into the house. She was looking about just as curiously as Kathy had and noting how bare things were.

"Let's go out on the deck," Alice offered. "Anyone want anything to drink?" she asked as she gestured towards the back door.

"This isn't something we want overheard," Madelyn warned as Alice went to get three glasses from the cupboard and the pitcher of lemonade she kept in the fridge.

"I understand that, Madelyn; however, I would prefer to go *out on the deck*," the blonde said meaningfully, staring Madelyn down until she caught on. It didn't take long for the CIA operative to begin glancing around. She wondered where the bugs could possibly be hidden. There wasn't much furniture or decorations to hide them.

When they were settled on the deck and sipping ice-cold lemonade with real lemon slices floating in the glasses, Madelyn settled back in her chair and sighed. The cool fall day here was still much warmer than back east. Langley often seemed cold, but perhaps, it was the buildings. Then, thinking about the work that went on there and the people, she realized it was probably the atmosphere of the place. She looked up at the sun, relishing what little warmth it provided.

"Going to sunbathe later?" Alice asked, the sarcasm obvious as she watched the eastern woman with her nose pointed towards the sun and her eyes closed.

"I wish I had the time," she admitted with a smile.

"I'm sure you would like to get down to business then," Alice hinted subtly.

Madelyn smiled. That was something she liked about Alice; she didn't bullshit around like so many people. "You knew they were going to want more," she began.

Alice nodded, an enigmatic smile hovering around her lips as she sipped delicately at her lemonade. "We had an agreement–" she started.

"And we intend to honor it. We do, however, need more from you."

"What's in it for me?"

"Alice, there are over a dozen Russian nationals from very prominent families that are dead, and we need to get information on them."

"I gave you a lot of that information," she pointed out dryly.

"And we need to know how you got that information and how much more you have."

"What has that got to do with me?"

They stared at each other. Alice was looking innocent. She'd had years of practice at that, and Madelyn's eyes narrowed as she watched the woman and wondered how she had gotten away with so much for so long. She'd seen a lot of the redacted reports…hell, she'd written many of them. Director Wolf had been frustrated to learn the complete reports weren't available to him as he'd assumed they would be since the redacted reports didn't tell him everything he needed to know about Alice Weaver. The FBI's paperwork was even worse than the CIA's, and it frustrated and intrigued the agents more than it should have. Alice Weaver seemed like an ordinary citizen, but the four-inch file on her led to various operations over the years where some of their players had disappeared. Some reports only implied that she was involved, and other reports blatantly stated her name, but her role in these affairs wasn't clear. There was much speculation and conjecture, but proof was non-existent in most of their information. There was nothing they could pin on her, especially after the latest release of information had absolved her from prosecution. Still, some of their best agents had been put on the job to *try*.

"Alice we both know there is more information–" she began, gesturing with her hand and feeling suddenly inadequate. It was just like when she first started out with the agency and people like Alice could have danced rings around her. She'd been so naive. Why Alice Weaver still make her feel that way after all these years…she had no idea.

"We do?" Alice toyed with her prey. Suddenly tired of the game, she asked, "Should I have Nia Toyomoto contact you?"

"Why would you need your lawyer?" she asked, suddenly alert. If Alice was lawyering up so quickly, there must be more…there had to be a lot more. She knew from several sources how close they had come to that information ending up on the evening news. The little bits that Alice had fed the press had put several prominent reporters on the trail, and it was up to the CIA to keep the press from away from the information for the sake of national security. Even now, deals were being cut with reporters, TV stations, and powerful men and women to keep the information away from the public.

"Do I? I was under the impression that I had immunity from prosecution?" she confirmed, and at Madelyn's reluctant nod she added, "I gave you plenty of information."

"That my teams are going over with a fine-tooth comb. You knew that."

Alice smiled congenially, taking another sip of her lemonade for effect. "And?"

"That's just the tip of the iceberg.…"

"Really?" Alice asked, sounding intrigued.

"What can I offer you as an incentive?"

"Nothing." Alice replied with a note of finality. She gestured to the expensive beach house they were sitting behind. "But you can call your dogs off."

"My dogs?" Madelyn asked, intrigued.

"Your people aren't watching my house and bugging me?"

"Not yet," she assured her, suddenly amused and yet…*not*. If someone had authorized surveillance on this woman, she wanted to know why and who. Alice was prickly enough as it was. If she thought she was being surveilled, it wouldn't bode well for those involved. *Maybe someone at the FBI…*her thoughts trailed off, but that should have been authorized by their joint task team, which she was heading up.

Alice tried to stare her down, but Madelyn was good at this game too, and she wouldn't be intimidated. She had answered honestly, and that seemed to ingratiate her to Alice. The blonde believed her but that led to the obvious question: Who was surveilling her? "You got a name for me yet?" she asked, changing the subject quickly before she became angry over this information.

"No," Madelyn admitted, quickly adding, "but I am working on it, and I hope to have it for you soon."

"That's not good enough, Madelyn," Alice said, her voice changing to a warning tone that they both knew the agent might want to heed.

"I understand, and I am working on it. At the same time, if you could–"

"Not another name. Not another tidbit of information," Alice assured her, draining her glass. "Turnabout is fair play. You know that."

Madelyn did know that, but she had had to try. Director Wolf and others didn't understand that you just didn't demand information from people like Alice Weaver. She amended that comment in her mind. *You didn't demand anything from Alice Weaver.* Already, they were trying to find a work-around to the immunity from prosecution paperwork. Those dead men that Alice had handed them were important Russian men. They were related in different ways: some through business and others through what they believed were mafia ties. "How do those men relate to the arms sale?" Madelyn asked. The agents were still trying to put the pieces of the puzzle together.

Alice just sat there with her empty glass in her hand and watched her prey. If Madelyn wanted more information from her, she was going to have to offer more. Getting the dismissal of prosecution from the federal government, the local police, and the IRS hadn't been easy, but it had worked out in her favor. The men she had given the authorities the extensive information on—Vashti Baltizar, Leonid Baltizar, Alexander or Xander Baltizar, the Bogomolov family, Filipov, and Kozlov—were very bad men. Their business ties had seemed obvious, and they were all part of The Assemblage, a crime syndicate of massive, international proportions. If the CIA hadn't discovered that yet with the information Alice had given them, they soon would.

Madelyn felt decidedly uncomfortable. Alice didn't often play games, but when she did, she played better than most people. Her games usually ended with someone dead, and Madelyn knew that the blonde hid her tracks very well. The redacted paperwork was filled with assumptions but few hard facts that showed Alice Weaver was a killer in the various cases Madelyn and others had worked on. In Madelyn's private thoughts, even the ones she dared to carefully word and put into writing, Alice was a serial killer of proportions they had never seen before, but Madelyn's opinions didn't matter in the greater scheme of things, and they didn't contribute to what she was trying to achieve.

"I'll be in town for a few days, if you want to talk to me," Madelyn told her, reaching into her suit for a card. She noted Alice shifted in her chair, prepared for any movement on Madelyn's part that might be construed as an attack. Only an experienced operative would note that minuscule shift in body movement that placed Alice in a position to defend herself. She admired that about the woman even as she unconsciously acknowledged her fear and how dangerous this woman really was. "That's my new cell number. You can call it anytime." Instead of handing her the card, she slid it across the table.

"Thank you," Alice said politely, not picking up the card as she watched Madelyn. She was polite, but she wasn't going to add anything to that statement and give her old acquaintance one iota more information. She was still owed some things, and until she got them, she wasn't giving away anything more.

Madelyn sighed inwardly. She had told Alice the truth. They were working on getting that name for her as promised, but with everything Alice had given them, their resources on the investigations were stretched thin. Still, she knew she better produce something and quickly.

Alice led her to the front door and closed it behind her when she left, returning quickly to the deck. Kathy was standing and asked, "What was that about?"

"A fishing expedition," she stated blandly, glancing at the embossed card curiously and putting it in her pocket for future use. She would call it at some point. She deserved information, and Madelyn knew what might happen if she had to wait much longer for it. The meeting, while relatively short, hadn't produced anything that was of use to the agent.

"I better be going," Kathy stated. She wondered why Alice had asked her to stay for that meeting. She was relieved to learn the woman wasn't anyone who was involved with her wife, but it concerned her that the CIA was still calling on her. "I'll have Kat call you," she reminded her.

"Thanks, I'd appreciate that," Alice responded, stopping outside the door to watch Kathy get in the Lexus and back out carefully into the parking lane, then merge smoothly onto the highway, the powerful engine of the Lexus making it look effortless. She waved and then pushed a button once she got inside, closing the gate this time. She had left it open earlier. She glanced only briefly at the car parked across the highway.

"She wouldn't give me anything," Madelyn confirmed as she talked on her car phone using her Bluetooth speaker.

"Then you have to squeeze her," Director Wolf told her.

Madelyn nearly laughed aloud in his ear. He underestimated Alice Weaver, and he had no idea who he was messing with. Alice Weaver pissed off and irritated was just what she didn't need. She hadn't missed the underlying menace in Alice's tone that told her she better find the person who had arranged things against Alice. She had to find a name, and it better be a good one, or Alice might direct her anger towards Madelyn. She didn't need that headache, and she'd really like to live a good, long life. Why had she come back to the agency...for this?

"We really need more out of her. This whole thing was handled sloppily. There should have been more time. You can't blackmail the CIA," he insisted.

And yet, Alice Weaver had blackmailed them, thought Madelyn, *and very handily*. Using the media, the unofficial fourth branch of the government, against the government had been brilliant, something she had admired about the prickly woman. She thought back to one of the many meetings they'd had in the last couple months since Alice had given them the memory card with the information on the Russian mafia members, oligarchs that unofficially ran the country.

"We should obtain warrants and raid this Alice Weaver's house," one agent had contended hotly at one of their many meetings on the subject.

"She's immune to that by our own paperwork," another defended her, perhaps admiringly, as he slapped at the letter that freed one Alice Weaver from prosecution in return for information she had supplied the CIA. The way the paperwork was worded, even the FBI, who they had shared information with, couldn't go after Alice.

"She can't possibly cuckhold us like this," another argued, feeling bitter that *anyone* could blackmail them.

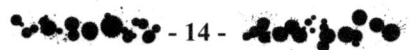

"Don't be too overconfident about our bureau's procedures," Madelyn reminded them. "There are reasons they are put into place for situations such as this.

"Your department is responsible for this," an FBI agent allowed to sit in on the meeting put in testily.

"Careful, there," Madelyn warned him. "We are responsible for this mess, and as we dig deeper, we are learning that some of it is of our own making. The FBI had some of this information," she gestured to the piles of data they had compiled, "but not to the extent we have been supplied," she indicated the mass of paperwork that had resulted from their investigation of the information Alice provided. It was being divided up by the names she gave them, and still there were gaping holes in it all, which they knew was due to other names being omitted. The odd footage they had seen of some sort of explosion in Kazakhstan was still not explained, but the pictures showing American weapons with the same Kazakhstan background were obvious. "Before pointing fingers and assigning blame, we should figure out who all these people are," she gestured to the bios they already had on each of the players, but these were still being added to as each one was investigated more thoroughly. They were hampered by these people being Russian citizens, and they had to rely on operatives working and living there as well as sleeper agents, who couldn't reveal where they were getting their information.

"There is exculpatory evidence–" began one agent, trying to get the conversation back to Alice's apparent involvement in the deaths of these men.

"We already know that Alice Weaver was held in prison with Sasha Brenhov. Of course, there will be fingerprints and other evidence, and some of it will have been planted by our Russian friends," another agent pointed out.

The endless debates over the evidence were frustrating to some and fascinating to others as they all worked to make sense of the information.

"We should go after Sasha Brenhov. She emerged unscathed from all of this," someone else put in. "Isn't she married to an American citizen?"

"No, they aren't married, but she did leave her assets to the woman. I hear that firm in New York is still straightening out the legal entanglements of that. Sasha Brenhov's assets are rather extensive."

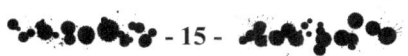

"She didn't lose anything due to her supposed death."

"You'll have a helluva time if you go after her without proof, and you will be swarmed by teams of lawyers. She's a Russian national, for Christ's sake!"

"There are errors in how the agency went about investigating Alice Weaver," the FBI agent pointed out, bringing them back to the point they were here to discuss.

"Are you trying to lay blame at our feet again?" Wolf asked as he came in, proving he had been listening to their endless debates regarding the investigation.

"No, sir, but there are procedures set in place to avoid–" he began.

"Then put them in your report," Wolf told the man, shutting him up. He handed Madelyn a pile of paperwork he had scooped up on his way through the computer department where they were still trying to figure out why they were having computer problems. They had determined the issues arrived at the same time as Alice Weaver's information, but they couldn't prove that she had planted a virus. This virus was completely different from the one wending its way through the various police departments in California. There was something insidious about all these security breaches. The FBI and the CIA had systems that prevented people from breaking in from the outside. There were certain parts that could not be accessed from external computer consoles, and yet, both agencies had hiccups in their systems that shouldn't be there. The computer geeks were working overtime trying to figure it out. Just when they fixed one glitch, another would pop up in some completely unrelated system. It was exasperating and made no sense. Things like this did not happen with their computer systems. "This one is a simple children's game," he indicated the report that showed some sort of Pac-Man game eating data within a financial program.

"This doesn't make sense," Madelyn murmured, looking at the readouts. It was a familiar and frustrating refrain from those involved in the investigation of the computer viruses.

"Are you sure she didn't plant–?" Wolf began, but Madelyn cut him off.

"I'm sure she planted something as a distraction, but your men already wiped those from the system," she pointed out.

"There has to be a way for us to get warrants and monitor her computer systems to get the information we need…" he began, just as

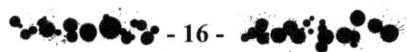

determined as the other agents on the teams to get more out of Alice Weaver and figure out if the virus they had found on her disk was planted deliberately.

"Yes, sir, but we have to prove intent, and it's just not here," another agent pointed out, waving to the paperwork. "We can monitor her. We don't need a judge to sign off on that, but what would that prove? She has money, that was proven by the IRS, but they can't go after it now."

"Wouldn't FISA (the Foreign Intelligence Surveillance Act) come into play since Russia is involved?" another agent asked.

"FISA is only used to target foreign spies and terrorists. Alice Weaver is an American citizen," Madelyn pointed out, proving she was paying attention to the many conversations going on around her. "Furthermore, we'd have to get a special court to grant approval to operate in secret and do wiretaps, and she's already protected by *that*," she indicated the paperwork that Alice had signed before she gave them the disk.

"But Sasha Brenhov is a Russian citizen," someone else pointed out.

"And Sasha doesn't live in the United States. We can investigate, and if we find she did something that affects America's interests, we could ask to have her extradited, but Russia will never approve that, and our own country wouldn't ask," Wolf pointed out. "However, compiling information on that businesswoman is a good idea."

And so, the debates continued for months as they sifted through all the fact and fiction they had gathered. One thing no one had noticed immediately was that each of the dead people, despite their power and seeming wealth while alive, had left behind no money on their deaths. Their families, if they had any, essentially inherited nothing. There was a money trail between the mafia members, but no one in the FBI or CIA realized that none of those people had any money left following their deaths and immediately prior to their sudden departures from this world.

"Madelyn do you think you might go out to Los Angeles and visit our offices there? You could talk to her and find out what these photos mean," Wolf asked, indicating the pictures that had obviously been taken from drones and showed the Kazakhstan landscape and American military equipment.

"Yes, I can do that, but you know she won't give us anything more. We still haven't fulfilled our agreement to her."

"How is that aspect of the investigation going?" he asked, not really caring if they ever satisfied their obligation to Alice Weaver. *Something about her–.*

"Still all dead ends," she told him, cutting off his thoughts, "but something stinks, and eventually, my people will figure it out." She knew she was obligated to keep him informed, and he would have to be told if her people eventually figured it out, but that didn't mean she wouldn't fulfil the terms of their agreement with Alice.

"Mom!" an exuberant, younger version of Kathy launched herself into Alice's welcoming arms.

"Wow! Look at you, all collegiate and shit," Alice said drolly when she had Kit at arm's length. The smile on Alice's features was genuine. She loved this kid, even if she wasn't blood. She'd endeared herself to the older woman's heart many years ago.

Kit grinned down at Alice. She had never realized how truly petite Alice was. She hadn't gained back all the weight she lost, and she looked…tired and quite a bit older. This worried the young woman briefly as she entered the beach house followed by her younger siblings.

"Mind if I go up to my room?" her son asked respectfully.

"Homework done?" Alice asked, knowing he only wanted to play on the computers. The games were top of the line, and she'd played them too. Ostensibly, she was using them to familiarize herself with the games, but she had used them to send a few messages that wouldn't be monitored, since she was so closely watched right now. She'd have to do something about that soon.

"Yes, Mom, and they don't assign homework over Thanksgiving," Sean reminded her as he started up the stairs.

Alice blinked. It was Thanksgiving already? How'd she missed that one? She looked at Emily, standing there and watching her. "We have got to decorate this place," the young girl instructed her, parroting her other mother.

"Why don't we all plan to go shopping on Saturday?" Alice asked, including Sean, who had just reached the top of the stairs.

"Can we get a TV?" he called down.

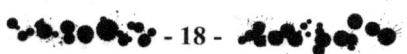

"Yes, for each room," she called back.

"Yay!" he said excitedly and hurried into his room to fire up the computer games. He would call his friends and ask them about the best TVs. He was certain they would have all the latest information he would need, and he was confident he could talk Alice into buying them.

"Why Saturday?" Emily asked as she watched Kit examining the sparse furnishings.

"Shopping on Black Friday would kill me," Alice told her blandly. "The deals will still be there Saturday, and you two can start shopping for Christmas." She put her arm around her daughter, hugging her close. "What are you going to get me?"

Emily chuckled appreciatively and looked again at Kit, who was watching them both now. She was amazed at how much her little sister was finally growing and how much her eye shape was becoming like Alice's. There was something different about Em's eye color though. It seemed to have changed since she was a child.

"Look at you two, like two peas in a pod. Hang on! I want a picture of this," Kit said, warning them to stand still while she held up her phone to snap a shot. When she had taken three pictures in rapid succession, she smiled down at the result. You could see the family resemblance in these two, and yet, when she stood next to Emily, Kit thought she looked just like her too. How the hell was that possible? She'd never considered how her birth mother, Kathy, had become pregnant with her siblings. Had she carried Alice's eggs? How the heck was it possible for Emily to look like both their mothers?

The three of them spent an enjoyable afternoon together, and Sean only came down to raid the refrigerator for food, lamenting loudly about the healthy stuff Alice had filled it with. They determined that Alice must come to dinner since Kathy had extended the offer. The women might be divorcing, but that didn't mean they weren't still a family. It was soothing to Alice's ears to listen to the girls chatting about college and life in general. Emily's ambitions weren't as defined as the older college student's yet. This was family. It was familiar, and she loved it.

She moved them outside after listening to Sean's complaints about 'no food' after his second and third excursions to the fridge for snacks, and he left them to their conversation.

"So, what's this I hear about law enforcement?" she smiled at Kit over the lemonade they were sipping. Emily had slipped down to the beach to check out who was about. She was looking for celebrities she could tell her friends she had seen. Both Sean and Emily's friends were salivating over an invite to their mom's new digs.

"Are you disappointed?" Kit asked, a little defensive.

"Nope, not in the least. Are you?" Alice asked, waiting for her response. She was a very patient cat and mouse player, much more so than this daughter, who was bound to her only by the bonds of love. She saw so much of Kathy in this young woman when she thought back to their college days. She'd had no romantic interest in Kathy at that time. Kathy had just been part of a group of young women that her sister hung out with.

"I'm excited about my courses again. It was becoming tedious," Kit admitted. "But that was good advice to get the basics out of the way. Now, I can concentrate on the fun courses. They aren't easy, but they are truly fascinating."

Alice smiled, showing off her new, neat, straight smile. Her teeth had been bad for so long after the torture and other hardships she endured, and she was pleased they were fixed now and no longer caused her pain. Going back to her Los Angeles dentist had proven to be a good idea. He fixed what others had changed about her smile. "Have you decided what area of law enforcement you are going into?" Alice asked carefully, not wishing to offend her daughter or cause her antennae to rise.

"I'm not going to be a cop," she said with a self-deprecating grin. "From what I've heard, I think this family has had enough of that." She waited a moment before adding, "I think I'll get my master's degree, so I can enter higher on the food chain wherever I land. Maybe Internal Affairs, so I can go after dirty cops."

Alice was surprised, and that didn't happen often. Kathy must have kept their daughter well informed...then she looked at her other daughter on the beach chatting with someone, and her eyes narrowed slightly. She thought maybe she knew who had kept Kit well informed. She only hoped that Emily never shared the whole story with anyone; that would be unfortunate. She looked back at Kit and something else occurred to her. With a master's in law enforcement and the ensuing courses, this kid, who studied hard, would probably get top grades and come to the attention of other law enforcement people. Suddenly, she wondered if Madelyn knew of Kit's plans. People might come calling from the FBI, the CIA, and other less desirable acronyms. That was the part that worried her. "That's a good idea," she said, not discouraging the young woman. She knew Kit had delayed declaring her major for as long as she could. Now, the master's program would keep her in school at least two more years. "Are you going to stay at Stanford?"

"I was thinking of transferring to Harvard for my master's," she informed Alice, watching her carefully for any sign of displeasure. For some reason, she had always wanted to please this woman. Alice had been extremely supportive of everything she wanted to do, not just financially but also providing emotional and informational support, anything Kit needed. She had to admit that meeting Alice had been the best thing that could have happened to her and her mother. Alice had provided them a level of financial stability they had never previously experienced. Even during the time her mother had been missing and was thought dead, Alice had been there for them all. Remembering her own brush with the insidious, she knew Alice had somehow protected her. She could see by the ravages on Alice's face and body that her time away from their family hadn't been pleasant, but she wouldn't pry. Just as she hadn't asked her mother why she was going through with the divorce while seemingly mourning the death of their marriage. It was obvious, at least to their children, that these two women loved each other.

"Want me to write letters?" Alice asked, not telling the young woman she could get her in with no effort at all. She was pleased that Kit wanted to go to her mother's and her alma mater.

"When I'm ready," she admitted. "I still have to get my bachelor's degree." She sighed inwardly, not sure why it had been so stressful to tell Alice her plans. Her mother hadn't objected in any way, and for that Kit was immensely relieved.

"Maybe I should consider Yale too? You know, have a back-up plan?" she teased Alice and enjoyed a good laugh at her mother's expense. She went on to talk about her roommates, and when she mentioned a guy named John, Alice's antennae perked up.

"How close are you and John becoming?" she asked casually…perhaps too casually.

"It's just a college thing for now," Kit admitted, sounding so grown up. "I told him I can't do serious. I want to get my degrees first."

Alice smiled slightly. *Atta girl*, she thought. "You still need to have fun," she pointed out. "Don't become so serious that you neglect your personal life away from academia." She felt like a hypocrite saying that. That was *exactly* what she wanted for their little girl, who was all grown up now. Still, her heart squeezed as she was reminded of Kathy at a younger age again when Kit smiled. *Study. Don't go out with guys. Get your degree and keep your nose to the grindstone*, is what she thought. Still, she had to be the parent, and encouraging her daughter to have a fully rounded life was the right thing to do. She sighed. She hated being a parent sometimes.

"Oh, I do," and Kit launched into stories of going to parties on beaches up in the San Francisco Bay area. Some of the stories were repeats of earlier stories she had told for Alice and Emily's benefit.

Alice had deliberately kept those conversations on tape in the house for the benefit of whoever was bugging her place. She reminded herself she would have to take care of that soon. She kept telling herself that there were a few things she had to take care of. It was *time*.

The visit was going well, and Alice was contemplating ordering pizza for everyone when Kit mentioned Emily's friend, Carmen. "I don't like that chick," Kit mentioned. "There is something insidious about her. She is always listening where she doesn't belong."

Alice's eyes narrowed slightly at this. It was odd to have someone else confirm her feelings. She had never liked that friend of Emily's either. She inwardly sighed, knowing she should have done something about it a while ago. She remembered meeting Carmen's parents, Sandi and Richard Pasternack. They were neighbors of theirs in Palos Verdes. They had triggered several red flags in her psyche. She couldn't discount the fact that Sandi worked for Sebastian. That on its own told her a lot about the woman, but it was the look in that woman's eyes that had set off all her alarms. That was something else she would have to investigate.

"Wasn't that girl one of the mean girls that Emily always complained about?" Kit mused, not expecting an answer.

Alice thought about that. The girl's attitude towards her sickly daughter had changed abruptly with Alice's return. Was that deliberate? Had her parents put her up to it? She remembered very well looking in Sandi Pasternack's eyes and seeing like for like. Then, seeing Sandi at Sebastian's house had been a shock to them both, which reminded her that she hadn't seen a death notice for Sebastian. She should visit him. God! What was wrong with her? She hadn't been taking care of business, and that would have to change. She looked out at the rapidly fading sunlight and saw her younger daughter heading back up the beach. She enjoyed the sight of her daughter's rapidly growing frame, which was finally filling out. It was as though Mother Nature was catching up for the times when she was so ill. Emily wasn't the skeleton she had been then, although she still needed to pack on some pounds. But then, so did Alice.

"Would you like me to order pizza? You can eat while we decide which stores to hit on Saturday?" Alice asked Kit.

"Sounds good. I want a vegan pizza please, if you don't mind?"

"Vegan? Since when?" Alice asked, amused.

"I love its cracker thin crust," she admitted. "Vegan or even vegetarian is healthier." She sounded sanctimonious, like a lot of college kids who thought of themselves as smarter than their parents.

Alice smiled. She'd have to agree. "I do recall a kid who once had extra meat on her meat lover's pizza," she pointed out as she reached for her phone. She already knew Sean's preferences for extra everything, and she would get a whole pie just for him and his voracious appetite. She could hear him on the video game upstairs as she hadn't bought headphones for it. As Emily walked up, she asked, "Em what do you want on your pizza?" just as Kit was enthusiastically denying her past love of meat lover's pizza.

"You know I love Hawaiian deep dish," Em said with a smile, showing the need for a bit of orthodontia in that smile. Alice made a mental note to discuss that with Kathy.

"There's a restaurant down here that adds pineapple and cherries on the pizza," Alice told her as she punched up the number on her phone.

"That doesn't sound…good," Emily stated hesitantly.

"Oh, it is. I promise," Alice told her as the person answered, and she placed orders for three pies plus plenty of soda and bread sticks. She had her credit card memorized, and the order was soon completed. "They'll be here within the hour," she informed her daughters.

"But cherries?" Emily whined, continuing the conversation now that her mother was off the phone.

"Remember how much you loved the ham at Easter with the pineapple and cherries your mom fastened to the sides with toothpicks?" Alice reminded the youth of those traditional meals Kathy had engineered. She was grateful for the memories and grateful that Kathy had given her a night alone with the children, even if Sean was glued to his video games and not really participating.

"Oh, yeah," she put in, suddenly brightening at the memory of that food and occasion. Pineapple on pizza had once seemed gross, but she had wanted to like the same things as Momma A, a moniker they had assigned to Alice years ago, and Alice liked Hawaiian pizza. Cherries didn't sound quite as gross now.

"You will love the pizza on the east coast if you like crackers for crusts," Alice continued, picking up where she'd left off in her conversation with Kit. They continued discussing food and the possibility of Kit going east for school at Harvard.

"Do you know what you want to be when you grow up?" Kit asked Emily.

"I hate the phrase 'when I grow up!' It isn't like you are so grown up." Emily stated to her older sister. "I've seen some adults that never grew up," she pointed out.

"Touché," Alice murmured, amused.

Kit laughed. "You do have a point."

"I don't know what I want to do yet." She looked at Alice and asked, "What do you want me to be?"

"Happy," Alice answered without any hesitation.

"No, really, Mom," she said, aggrieved. "What would you like me to become?"

Alice leaned forward and took her daughter's hand in her own, squeezing it slightly. As a woman known for not being very demonstrative, both her daughters were touched by this gesture in completely different ways. "I want you to be healthy and happy," she answered softly. "It's getting cold out here. Let's go inside. We can decide where we are going shopping and compose a list of what I need while we wait for our pizza."

Kit grinned ruefully, seeing how her actions had unnerved her mother, or so she imagined. Emily swelled with undisguised pride over what Alice said. The three of them went inside to wait for their pizza, and the two younger women started a list for Alice. It was going to be a very expensive weekend.

"Thank you for inviting me," Alice told Kathy as she helped put the trimmings on the table. They had inserted extra leaves in the table just

for this occasion. They'd already discussed Emily's orthodontia, and Kathy was going to arrange an appointment. Kathy was surprised that she hadn't noticed Emily's teeth, and she was pleased that Alice had consulted her.

"You're very welcome. We're still family," she admitted. Besides, she really liked seeing Alice there. It felt so right. "I hear you are all going shopping?" she asked, amused. Alice didn't like to shop. She liked to go in, get what she wanted without fuss, and get out. The girls' idea of shopping didn't match Alice's. "Are you taking Sean too?"

"He is welcome to come. I might need back-up…and muscles. Those girls can't lift," she confided in a conspiratorial whisper.

"I heard that," Emily put in as she brought a bowl of mashed potatoes to the table.

They all enjoyed a lively debate over the Thanksgiving dinner Kathy made, giving Mrs. Fernandez some well-deserved time off to spend with her own family. Besides, it made their housekeeper feel needed after the year of uncertainty they had all gone through in so many ways.

Sean agreed to go along for the shopping but only if he could drive. He planned on using the Rav4 to pick Alice up since the Ferrari would never hold all the purchases.

"I don't think the Rav4 can hold much more than us four passengers either," Alice pointed out, amused. She pointed to the two girls, including them in the conversation. Then, she looked at Kathy. "You want to come?"

"Oh, no. You aren't getting me involved in this. I'm going to stay home and enjoy the quiet."

Alice laughed, amused. She wasn't sure what Kathy was doing these days, and she missed that, but her wife's schedule was no longer any of her business.

They enjoyed some movies in the family movie room that night. The large screen, surround sound, and comfortable seating, was highly conducive to good movie viewing. Alice glanced at Kathy a couple times. It was not that long ago that she had confessed everything that happened to her in Russia right here in this room. She wondered if Kathy realized how much had changed in their lives since then, not all of it for the better.

"Hey, before I go," Alice said as she put on her coat to leave, "what happened when the police went through the house that last time? How did they not find the wall where I stored…" she began but lowered her voice in case any of the kids were listening. Emily had proven that they could be overheard.

"I'd used up the funds before you replaced them," Kathy pointed out. "Didn't you take your passports out?"

Alice realized she had and wondered why she hadn't thought of that. For some reason, she'd started to worry that the cops had copies of her fake passports. What the heck was wrong with her memory? She nodded stiffly. "If you need anything…" she said as Kathy saw her out to the Ferrari.

"No, we're good. All set," Kathy told her, regretting she had ever asked her wife to leave the house and filed for divorce, but it was too late now. The divorce was well on its way to being finalized. She thought that Portia, Andi, and Alice would all be upset if she asked to halt things now. She wasn't even sure Alice wanted the divorce stopped at this point. By the new year, she should be 'free,' but Kathy knew in her heart she would never really be free. There would always be something between them, and it was not just the children they shared. "Have fun shopping tomorrow," she said with a sardonic smile, knowing Alice would hate it. Alice waved as she drove the powerful car down the driveway and out through the gate. Glancing about the nearly fully restored estate, Kathy was grateful for the fact that Alice had sent those teams around to fix the damage caused by the front-end loaders, bulldozers, and other equipment while attempting to find evidence hidden on their grounds.

By the first week of December, Alice's house had a new look. It was filled with the latest furniture, fixtures, and electronics. She'd had the Geek Squad in to wire the TV and its components, including a DVD player that was beyond anything she felt she wanted to tackle. The sophistication of today's electronics was something she knew she was going to have to study up on. She felt in a funk over some of it, and that pissed her off. She sat down and read through the manuals, amazed by how far a simple TV had come over the years!

She wanted to get computers again but would wait until after she swept the house for bugs. She wanted to stop by her favorite stores without the children, but they made even more trips over to her house that week as the purchases were being delivered. She didn't mind though. She enjoyed her children. Kathy got an earful about the fantastic location of her house, the stars the children were certain they had seen, and all the new items Alice had purchased. She was almost sick of hearing about it. Kit returned to college, pleased to see her mothers were adjusting to their new lives, and she soon forgot her concerns over her mothers as she got back into the routine of her own life.

Alice knew she couldn't put some things off any longer, even with the tail that followed her to Palos Verdes time and again. She managed to lose them one day, so she diverted to Beverly Hills and watched as they whizzed by the hidden driveway she pulled into. Once she was sure she had lost them, she pulled out and headed for Sebastian's home. She ended up parking two blocks away as she had been refused entry at the gate just like last time. She made her way to his neighbor's property, jumped their gate, and then made her way around the perimeter, being careful not to trip the alarm or get caught in a frame when she saw a motion-activated camera. For a long time, she had been feeling like her skills were fogged up and muddled from her inactivity. She'd gone to the house in the valley for a workout, but her car was a bit too conspicuous for that and had attracted unwelcome attention. She seriously considered selling it, angry over her impulse buy.

"Alice," Sebastian gasped, barely able to get the word out when she suddenly appeared in his bedroom. That he was still alive after such a long time must be due to his doctor's vigilance. The man should have been dead months ago—between the cancer ravaging his body and the nurse that was killing him slowly and insidiously, gleefully taking pleasure in the pain caused by her administrations of meds. Maybe he was just imagining Alice there looking down on him like an avenging angel? "You're dead," he gasped, trying to remember if that was a dream or the truth. His hand crept to his chest where he felt his heart pounding.

"The rumors of my death have been greatly exaggerated," she told him with a grin. The smile told him that he was awake, and she was really there. "Sebastian you're alive," she stated unnecessarily, sorry to see the man so emaciated by a disease there was a cure for. Damned pharmaceutical companies and their greed!

"Is it really you?" he rasped, glancing beyond her looking for a halo, an unearthly glow, or something to indicate she had come from the beyond.

"I'm here, my friend. I'm sorry. I should have come sooner," she whispered, not wanting to bring her presence to anyone else's attention. Entering his house had been more difficult this time. They had learned from her last visit and installed more guards, monitors, and alarms. She'd had to fight against her own internal fog and really concentrate, looking for the innocent and seemingly innocuous patterns. It was the patterns that would give away the things that could catch her. She was grateful for that knowledge and vowed to train harder again. She needed to clear away her mental cobwebs.

"Kill me," she thought she heard him say. He reached out a claw-like hand, "Please?"

"You want me to kill you?" she heard herself whispering, suddenly feeling like something was clutching at her innards as she gazed upon her old friend and adversary.

"Yes, the pain of it. Nothing stops the pain, and that bitch!" he spat out the word 'bitch,' which sounded particularly nasty on his tongue, "is enjoying every moment."

"I'll take care of her for you," she promised, knowing immediately which bitch he meant.

"Will you kill me?" he pleaded.

Alice hesitated for a moment, and his eyes lowered in disappointment. "I came to visit an old friend, not to kill him," she tried to say. She was astonished to see he was still hanging on. She'd been certain her last visit would be the last time she saw him. She'd had to make certain he was gone though, as part of cleaning things up. She'd made a start, and it was important to her to methodically clean up her past, so she could begin her future, whatever it might be.

"Artum take care of your family? They safe?" he rasped out, making it hard for her to hear him despite the nearly silent room. There was one machine beeping regularly, but it was turned down low.

"No, Kathy refused his offer of help. Maybe it was all for the best?" Alice questioned honestly, seeing the flare of anger in the old man's eyes. That spark remained for just a moment before quickly fading; it required too much effort to sustain.

He sighed. He hadn't been obeyed, and Artum and his team would pay for that. He might be old and dying, but he would make sure that

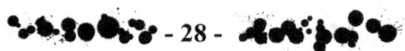

his orders were obeyed. Thoughts of what he would do faded as quickly as they formed. His mind was too befuddled by drugs, some prescribed by his doctor and some added for the amusement of a sadistic woman who enjoyed his pain. "Kill me?" he pleaded again, watching Alice.

"I would, Sebastian, you know I would, but it's not justified, and I've already got enough weighing on my soul. Also, you don't deserve it…" she looked at him sadly before adding a belated, "now."

"You got religion?" he started to laugh, which turned into a coughing fit.

Alice smiled widely. Her teeth were fixed now, and she was comfortable with her smile again. The idea of her going to a church, or following any organized religion, greatly amused her. "Anything else you need, my friend?" she asked, sad to see him in this condition. She glanced at the equipment setup and rose, readjusting the lines. She pulled the hose of one line from its drip, then reattached it in better order.

"Most is…taken," he said slowly, haltingly.

She waited for him to finish that sentence and then realized he had. "Pasternack?"

He nodded and said, "Some." He waited a moment, trying to gather his befuddled thoughts. "I got most of it diverted before he stole the rest. But his wife, she's something else," he added, his mind wandering again.

"Well, Sebastian, I can hear movement, and it won't be long before they discover me here. I wanted to see why you were still hanging on, you, old shyster," she teased, earning a glare from his fading eyes. She thought she saw a shadow in one of them. Perhaps it was cataracts. Still, it was obvious he could see her as his eyes followed her around the room.

"They will come," he said cryptically, but Alice didn't understand him. She frowned slightly, wondering what he meant.

"I should go before I get your people excited," she told him, touching his parchment-like hand, void of any fat below the skin. He was a skeleton.

"Avenge me," he whispered in goodbye, unable to summon the tears he wanted. He was simply too dehydrated to bother trying.

Alice looked at him once more before heading towards the door she had come through. She listened at the door momentarily before slipping out and going down the hallway to another door. She listened again and slipped through, just before footsteps on the stairs signaled someone was coming.

Artum looked down the hall and wondered where the guard outside Sebastian's bedroom had gotten to. Even the chair was missing, and that alarmed him. Slowly, he walked down the hall, listening carefully and looking through doors that were ajar, before he arrived at Sebastian's room. He cautiously opened the door, his hand on his gun, ready to pull and fire. He thought he saw something in the room and pulled his gun, leading with it as he opened the door wide, but all he found was the old man lying in his bed and looking up weakly at him.

Sebastian saw the gun coming through the door and hoped it was someone come to avenge some past crime he had committed. Instead, he was disappointed to recognize his nephew. Artum looked hale and hearty, like Sebastian had looked not too long ago, at least, that was how he saw himself in his mind. He gestured in a come-hither movement, reaching for his panic button at the same time. Before Artum even got across the room, they heard the running on the steps.

"Uncle?" he asked as he saw the button being pushed and then heard the quick steps on the stairs. Some of their men rushed into the room with guns drawn, and a few minutes later, the medical personal arrived.

Sebastian waved the medical people out, waited, and then gestured for the door to be closed. His men obeyed, although they looked at him curiously. They were glancing between Artum, who they knew was the favored heir apparent, and the man that paid their salaries. Sebastian pointed to the now closed door and raised an eyebrow inquiringly, prompting one of the men to open it and speak to the medical personnel hovering in the hall, including Sandi Pasternack. He commanded them all to go away.

Sebastian waited, his nephew and the men waited, and finally, he closed his eyes for a moment before gesturing them all to come closer. Weakly, he asked, "What happened to Alice Weaver's family?" It was too much! Between Alice's visit and this meeting, he was exhausted. He started to cough, and it took him some time to get it under control. He peed himself, the rich aroma of urine mixing with the smells of the stale air in the sickroom.

Sebastian pointed at a window, indicating someone should open it. Gently, he sipped water from a straw as Artum helped him to sit up.

He looked expectantly at his nephew. He might be old and absentminded, but he hadn't forgotten his question.

"You don't remember what I told you about that, Uncle?" Artum asked, surprised when the old man waved him to silence.

"You…told…me…nothing. Don't…lie!" he rasped, and they had to wait as another coughing fit took him. The men exchanged glances. The voice, while that of an old man, had still embodied its same commanding presence for a moment. Once he had the coughing under control, he fixed his nephew with a glare. "You will be fined for your incompetence," he managed to get out before he had to sip at the straw. The water made slurping sounds as its contents were depleted, and they waited while Artum filled the cup from the pitcher, the last of the water emptying into the cup.

"You, go and get–" began Artum, commanding one of the other men, but Sebastian waved him away.

"You…go," he countermanded, gesturing to his nephew. "Start paying penance NOW." He started to cough again, the wheezing in his chest making it hard to breathe as he hacked up phlegm and spit it into another cup. "Go!" he managed to get out before another wracking cough shook him. By now, Alice would surely have gotten away, and these incompetent fools would never know she was here. He watched as Artum took the pitcher and left the room. He fixed his eyes on the other men, unable to see them clearly but knowing their outlines. "He is to pay a penalty for disobeying my order," he got out weakly, laying back against his pillows. "Half a million," he gasped before taking a deep breath to continue and beginning to cough again. He lay there wheezing as he recovered, exhausted beyond reason. By the time Artum returned with a fresh pitcher, the condensation sending lines of moisture down the sides, Sebastian was nearly drifting off. He woke briefly to acknowledge his nephew as he filled the cup once again with cool, refreshing water. Sipping, he nodded again, thanking him without words. "Penalized…" he rasped at his nephew. "Disobeying…an…order." He waited, taking a deep breath. "Half…a…mill," he got out. He saw the brief flash of anger in Artum's eyes before he masked it and nodded, glancing at the other men. Sebastian's rheumy eyes followed the looks, and he saw only one of the men was Artum's. The others would make sure he was obeyed. He locked eyes with one of them, even if he couldn't really see the man, and the man nodded to show he would carry out Sebastian's order. He was loyal. Sebastian relaxed a little and waved them all away. He knew that he might not remember this order, but the men would. As the medical personnel returned, he saw Artum exchanging a look with the nurse, Pasternack was the name Alice had called her. His eyes narrowed as he began to drift off, beyond exhausted at his exertions.

The medical personal made sure he was comfortable, changing his pajamas and sheets before making sure his lines were still firmly attached. Sandi had no chance to administer her own deadly concoction, despite the temptation. She had seen the look in Artum's eyes and understood the command implicitly. There were men with the medical team looking on, and she didn't dare do anything that would arouse their suspicions.

Alice made her way out the open bedroom window, using the lattice fastened on that side of the house. She had no idea that Artum's personal team had rushed to Sebastian's room anticipating his death. They also happened to be his bodyguards, some of his best men, but they were loyal first to Sebastian and second to Artum. This diversion had helped her avoid detection as she retraced her steps to a tree and pulled herself up with some effort, her muscles not what they once were. She climbed across to another tree, then onto a wall, keeping herself plastered against it. Finally, she made her way over the wall and into the neighbor's yard, who didn't have quite as sophisticated a security setup as Sebastian. As she jogged back to her Ferrari, she thought about how she had been expecting for months to see a notice that Sebastian had died and how he had clung tenaciously to life. She could have killed him as he asked but leaving him alive might allow him to atone for sins she wasn't even aware of. She debated about going back and giving him compassionate leave of this world but decided she really did have enough on her own shoulders.

Two cars picked up her tail on the way home. She wondered how they had found her and realized there must be a tracking device on the expensive sports car. This angered her as she had none of her tools, but that would have to change. She parked carefully, backing into the driveway and watching as the gates closed and cut off the view to her curious onlookers. She walked back to those same gates to peer out the corners and saw the two cars settle into parking spaces. Since she was dressed for jogging, she went inside and used her keyless entry to go through the house and right out the back patio onto the beach. She jogged down half a city block and used a public access path back to the PCH before she began a leisurely stroll back to her home, keeping her eye out as the never-ending traffic whizzed by. She confirmed the two cars each held two people, one a sedan and the other a souped-up Audi. She supposed whoever was watching her needed to know their car could keep up to her Ferrari if she tried to get away. But she wasn't going to try and get away; she was going to let them follow her. She turned away, returned to the public path, and headed to her patio door. As she closed it, she didn't allow herself to react when she noticed the brief flash of light that turned from red to green on her new wall-mounted TV. What the heck? She went upstairs to wash off the sweat and change her clothes when another brief flash on the new TV in her bedroom alerted her that she was being observed. Closing the bathroom door, something she hadn't felt the need to do since the kids were little, she glanced around, feeling a little paranoid.

The next day, Alice was up bright and early. She packed a small bag with her back to the TV, so whoever was watching couldn't see what she was packing, then she picked it up and headed out to the Ferrari, revving it twice in the still, morning air. She hoped she didn't wake any of her neighbors knowing one of them was on TV, and the other was a long-time resident without any connections to Hollywood and its fleeting fame. Slowly, she backed down the driveway, and soon, she could see the tail cars. One of them had to make an illegal U-turn on the highway to follow her down the PCH. As she drove, she admired the beautiful scenery. There was brush growing along the hills and cliffs and the ocean on the other side, much of its beach filled with houses. Occasionally, there were breaks between the houses where the city hadn't allowed anything to be built, and there it was endless sand with blue-green water as far as the eye could see. She loved the beach, but she preferred Palos Verdes. As she headed up from the beach into Santa Monica, she made sure her followers saw where she was turning as she made her way back to her old home. Once there, she let herself in, parking in front of the garage and carrying her small pack with her inside the house.

"Hello?" she called out into the silence. Wasn't anyone home? She made her way from the garage door she had effortlessly opened, wondering why Kathy hadn't changed the locks, and headed up to the house itself.

"Hello?" she called again.

"Oh, hi, Mom," Emily answered, smiling to see her there.

"Where is everybody?" she asked, disappointed that Kathy wasn't here.

"Mom took Sean to get some sneakers. His big feet keep outgrowing–" began his little sister with a touch of avarice.

"Now, now," Alice wagged her finger at her daughter, admonishing her without saying more. Sean had been very supportive of Emily when she was ill. She wouldn't let her say bad things about him, even if he teased her mercilessly sometimes. "Do you know when they will be back?"

"They just left. Want me to call?"

"No, I was hoping your mother could drive me somewhere…" she said musingly, trying to reformulate her plan.

"Something wrong with the Ferrari?" the teen asked, sounding worried.

"No, but it's too conspicuous," she said in an aggrieved tone that made her daughter laugh. Alice suddenly focused on her daughter. "Do you know how to drive?"

"I'm not old enough, remember?"

"That's not what I asked," she stated, shaking her head. Sometimes teenagers could be rather dense. "I asked if you knew how to drive?"

"Well, I went out with Mom and Sean when he was learning, of course. I've watched you and Mom for ages. I couldn't drive a stick like your Ferrari, but I know I could manage an automatic, just not on the freeway," she mused as she considered the question.

"Good. Call your friend, and you can take me over there."

"Wait! What?" she asked, alarmed. "Which friend?"

"The Pasternack chick," Alice reminded her daughter. "You are going to drive me over there. We can use the Rav4, and we'll order an Uber from there."

"Wait, I don't understand…" began Emily, confused.

"Do you want to drive the Rav4 or not?" Alice asked, making it sound like she was about to change her mind.

"Of course, I do," the girl insisted stoutly.

"Well, then, let's go. Call your friend and tell her we are coming over. You can stay until the Uber gets there and then, you can drive the car back home before your Mom gets here. Okay?"

"Mom will be so mad–" she began.

"You can tell her it was all my idea, okay?" Alice interrupted.

"Okaaay," said the teen, unconvinced.

"Let's go then. Chop! Chop!" she said, clapping her hands in time with her words. She glanced around the house as her daughter ran to change out of her pajamas, get into something more suitable, and call Carmen. Em didn't know what was going on, but she was excited.

"So, what is going on?" Emily asked as they got into the Rav4, both putting on their seatbelts. She was excited to drive the small SUV.

"I was followed over here, and I don't wish to be followed. So, you are going to help me avoid these bozos and then, when I'm gone, you can return home."

"Okay, got that." She was extremely anxious as Alice pulled the handle to lay the seat nearly flat, and when that didn't work, she put it upright again.

"Hang on," Alice ordered when the teen went to put the garage door up with the automatic clicker attached between the sun visors. Alice climbed over the console to the back seat, pulling along the small duffel bag she had brought with her. She laid down on the back seat and said, "Okay, drive."

Nervously, Em pushed the button on the garage door opener, waiting until the garage door was completely open before starting up the car. She was very conscious of her mother lying on the backseat. Checking her mirrors, she slowly put the car in gear and applied the gas. The SUV jerked as it rolled backwards into the driveway. She pressed the garage door button again and waited for the door to close before putting the Rav4 into gear and slowly heading down the driveway. She felt exultant going down the driveway, and the sensors opened the gate as she approached when they recognized the car. As she drove through the gate, she saw the two cars that didn't belong in their neighborhood. Few, if any, of the neighbors parked on the street. Most, like her parents, had an estate with plenty of parking in the driveway. She made her way confidently over to the Pasternacks.

They didn't have a security gate, and she pulled into their driveway as though she did this all the time.

Alice sat up when the SUV stopped. She had felt her daughter's anxiety and was aware when her growing confidence had replaced it. "Good job," she stated. "Call me an Uber?"

"Your phone isn't working?" the teen asked as she turned off the Rav4.

"I don't want them to trace the call to my phone," she said as she took her phone out of her pocket and slipped it under the driver's seat from the back.

"Hey, what's going on?" Carmen asked, walking up to the driver's window and frowning in surprise at her friend. She was shocked to see Mrs. Weaver sitting in the backseat, acting as though they did this every day.

"Emily is practicing her driving, and she did pretty good," Alice said dryly. She examined her daughter's friend as Emily punched in the Pasternack's address on her Uber app.

Carmen looked at Alice then back at her friend. They all knew Emily was far too young to be practicing her driving skills. She didn't even have her temps, and she hadn't taken the class offered at the high school.

"Hang on," Emily told her friend, holding up her hand. "Where to from here?" she asked her mother, but Alice grabbed the phone to enter the address instead of replying. She was not willing to let Carmen hear the address where she was headed.

"She'll be going straight home once my ride gets here," she informed Carmen, eyeing the girl again and wondering why she didn't like her.

"Can I ride along?" Carmen asked eagerly.

"I don't think that's a good idea," Alice put in, negating the idea before they could even discuss it. Just what she needed—two girls joyriding in the neighborhood. "This was a one-time special deal for Emily," she stressed to her daughter, who got the hint right away.

Whatever was up with her mother, Emily didn't want to jeopardize it. She understood anything Alice did was to be kept under wraps. She had never told anyone what she overheard, and that had been difficult. The few times she had tried to discuss it with Kathy, she had been shut down. Alice had made it clear what her one mix-up could have cost them, and she didn't want that ever again. Keeping these secrets was costing her, but no one realized it at this point.

The Uber arrived quickly, and Alice grabbed her bag and got out. "Go right home," she warned Emily and slipped her a $20. "Later, when your mom gets home, order a pizza, and you and Carmen can share it," she said, including the neighbor girl with a smile. She waited until Emily nodded, waved goodbye to her friend, and drove off, before getting into the Uber. "Hey, thanks for the ride," she told the driver as they sped off behind Emily and the Rav4. She pretended to go through her bag at the last minute, so neither of the cars that had followed her to Palos Verdes saw her in the backseat of the SUV as they passed their location. She appreciated that the owner of the vehicle kept it very neat. She didn't speak as they drove through the streets on their way to the car rental place that she had entered in the Uber app. The Uber driver was surprised when she paid in cash, accustomed to the app depositing payment into her account. She took it gladly, briefly wondering how she might get around paying Uber for this odd customer, then realizing she would jeopardize her standing with them if she tried that.

"Alice Weaver has stopped by her wife's house in Palos Verdes."

"Has she left yet? Over."

"No, she's still there. The only activity was her daughter leaving the estate, but she didn't go far, just over to one of the neighbor's houses. Now, she's just sitting there."

There was a long wait, and another car came into the area, but they didn't pay it any attention as they were watching Kathy's house for the Ferrari. Just as they reported the Rav4 returning to the Weaver estate, someone had a thought....

"The daughter isn't of driving age," came over the walkie-talkie.

The two people in the sedan exchanged glances.

"Do you think Alice Weaver was in the back of that Rav4?" one asked the other.

"That's possible," the other one replied before picking up his walkie-talkie to report. "We believe Alice Weaver may have shaken our surveillance." He wasn't happy as he explained their suspicions to the person on the other end of the mic. They had spent weeks watching her Malibu home and had done some things that weren't legal.

They were ordered to watch the Palos Verdes home in case they were mistaken, and the Ferrari eventually emerged. It was several hours later when Kathy Weaver, not Alice Weaver, drove the Ferrari away from the estate, followed by Sean in the Rav4.

Alice rented a nice, little Toyota Camry. It was a sporty sedan, fast and nondescript. Driving up the 5 Freeway, she thought of the things she wanted to accomplish, and she hoped that Emily wouldn't tell Kathy too much too soon. She had things to take care of, and some of them were long overdue. Donning her first disguise at a rest stop before she got to Sacramento, she drove to her storage unit there. Once inside her unit, she jump-started the car stored there and left it running outside the unit while she talked to the owner of the facility, who happened to be manning the desk. Using the passport that matched her disguise, she closed her account. After so many years, the man was surprised, but he took her cash payment and shrugged it off. She'd been a good renter. He let her park her rental car while she took the sedan to a car wash and afterward, to a used car lot. She accepted a lot less money than she would have if it were any other car. Next, she bought a throw-away phone at a nearby store and ordered an Uber using an old email address that linked it to a bank account she rarely used. Once they dropped her at her rental car, she got in and slowly removed her disguise as she headed north.

The following day, she was in Portland doing the same thing with the Jeep she had stored there. She hated to get rid of it. Her little hidey-hole had so many uses, but this was all part of cleaning up some things. The different locks on both storage units told her that someone had been here. She suspected Kathy had figured out one location, and one could easily be traced to the other. Now, that was history as she sold the Jeep, again for less money than she would normally have accepted.

Driving south again, she enjoyed the scenery through Mount Shasta and wished she had the time to come here camping with the children. Her version of camping would have involved an RV and a few other luxuries, which would technically make it glamping, but she wasn't about to suggest anything until she talked to Kathy and discussed the children's schedules. It had begun to rain when she arrived back in Los Angeles, but that didn't prevent her from shopping at a few of the less than reputable stores she previously frequented, some she had taken Kathy to, and a few others she hadn't been introduced to. Alice stopped at a library and used their computers to do a lot of research. She spent the day there before returning the rental car. She had an Uber take her from the rental place to her home in Malibu, only to find her Ferrari in the driveway and a party in progress. There were cars parked in her driveway and all up and down the shoulders of the PCH.

"What the hell?" she murmured as she got out of the car. The many packages in her arms suddenly felt heavy as she observed the teenagers coming and going in her courtyard. They were acting as though they owned the house and property and looking at her curiously. Pushing past some, she stopped in the garage to put down her bags and continued into her house, looking for someone she recognized.

"Mom?" Sean asked when he saw his mother. He was surprised to see her. He had thought she would be gone all weekend. Kathy had brought the Ferrari home, and Sean and his friends had come over, ostensibly to use the beach and play video games. Someone had arrived with alcohol, and things were rapidly getting out of hand as word spread and more and more people came.

"Are you kidding me?" Alice asked him, remembering the party in Palos Verdes where she had been forced to throw several kids out.

"Mom, I just invited—"

"I don't care who you invited. Get them out of *my* home NOW!" The last word of that command came out in a roar as Alice went to a closet and removed a baseball bat, hefting it as she approached the TV in the living room. Some of the kids were watching videos on the seventy-two-inch screen Sean had talked her into buying, and others were dancing, the surround sound blasting in the beachside home. She had seen the red light on the TV quickly switch to green then turn off completely, and without hesitation, she began to smash the large-screen television.

"MOM!" Sean yelled, aghast. He turned to the friends he knew, shouting, "Get out! GET OUT NOW!" There was a mad exodus as Alice finished smashing that large-screen TV and began to push the mass of teenagers out of her way as she headed towards the stairs, beginning to work her way upstairs. "Mom NO!" Sean called, trying to follow her, but the press of bodies was hard to fight against, and she had already smashed the TV in his room, the TV in Em's room, and was advancing on her own room when he reached her. She smashed her TV too, stomping on it as it fell to the floor and ripping out the wires behind it. "Why, Mom?" he asked, feeling heartbroken at the devastation he had witnessed. He held his head and tears began to streak down his young face. He could hear the last of the guests encouraging others to get out of the house.

Alice looked up at her son. She was forced to look up because he was so much taller than she. Her heart wrenched seeing his tears. She glanced at the computer games that his friends had been playing on the big-screen TV she installed in his room, which now lay in tatters. She pulled his hands down and shook her head. He stared at her incredulously. Putting a finger to her lips, she gestured that they should go downstairs. Sean was hesitant at first, then curious, and he followed her. She led him to the garage where she had put several heavy bags and pulled out a couple gadgets. She soon had them working after inserting batteries, and using them, she found four bugs in her garage alone.

"What...?" he began but she put her finger to her lips again and shook her head to silence him.

She demonstrated how the gadget worked, and she showed him the bugs she'd found, again putting her finger to her lips. She mouthed, *"We are being monitored."* Staring wide-eyed, Sean nodded. Over the next two hours, they pulled dozens of innocuous-looking plaster plugs from her walls, putting the bugs they found beneath them all in baggies and placing them in the freezer.

Alice and Sean went over the house twice. Sean had used the weaker of the two devices she purchased, and she went over it one last time with her own hand-held monitor that was able to sense the electronics from these devices. She went over the smashed TVs, unhooking them from their wires but not before zooming in on the electronic eyes that had been installed in the new TVs. Equipped with internet streaming and facial recognition capabilities, they had made her vulnerable to intrusion by whoever was monitoring her.

"What the hell was that all about?" Sean finally asked after hours of silence while they pulled the bugs that were cleverly hidden beneath the plaster in her walls and inside the TVs. His heart wept over the loss of the huge TVs. He had thought Alice was just pissed off over the party, and he had never seen her that angry before.

"These next-generation smart TVs and devices run some pretty sophisticated software. With my internet connection and the integrated sensors," she indicated those she had pulled from the TVs to examine, "like these microphones, they can watch whoever is in the house. I noticed last week that the red signal, which I hadn't turned on, was coming on seemingly at will and turning green sporadically, and I realized someone was watching me through the TVs."

"Even when you were alone or getting dressed? What about in my room?" he asked, outraged.

"Possibly. What'd you do that I might not want to know about?" she asked.

"I changed my clothes..." he began, suddenly realizing the implications of this spyware as he surveyed all the equipment Alice had shown him. "What else can they do?" he asked in an attempt to change the subject. He didn't want Alice to know about the girlfriend he had in here before the party began. They'd taken the Ferrari out for a spin as well as some other things he didn't think any mother should know about.

"They can change channels, adjust the volume, cyberstalk us, and record us."

He stared at the electronics, horrified and wondering if he was about to be blackmailed by some unknown watcher. "How long–?" he began, remembering how excited he had been to get these things and now, they were smashed, and Alice was cleaning up the mess.

"Help me clean this up," she indicated the electronics and glass on the floor. She'd sent the message she intended. Whoever had bypassed the manufacturer or Geek Squad's install had gotten more than they intended on their end. The bonus was, she had frightened Sean's friends, and they wouldn't be partying at her home again anytime soon. "We can discuss your punishment for driving my Ferrari."

"How did you–?" he began, but she interrupted him and placed a damaged TV by the door.

"You just told me," she answered dryly, shaking her head at how easy it was to fool her son.

They brought the three TVs down from upstairs and placed them up against the first one. Alice had Sean vacuum up the glass and small plastic pieces from both floors as she installed new security features, things that only she would touch during installation. It was quite late when a phone on the counter rang. Alice realized it was her own cell phone and answered it.

"Is Sean with you?" Kathy asked as soon as Alice said hello.

"Yes, he's cleaning his room as punishment," she said dryly.

"Punishment?"

"For the party I walked in on when I got home this afternoon. Thanks for putting the Ferrari in the driveway and bringing my phone back."

"What the heck was up with that? Why did–?"

"We have to talk about that in person, you know what I mean?" she cautioned, certain that her phone was bugged, or she was still being listened to by some other method. She decided it was about time she figured out who *they* were.

Kathy sighed. She had been hoping that with the divorce they would be done with such things, but she had to admit she'd enjoyed driving Alice's Ferrari. It was a hot, little sports car, but she hadn't imagined that Sean would go back to party when he followed her and gave her a ride home. She needed to talk to Alice about having Uber pick her up here at the house, and she didn't know that Emily had driven the Rav4 yet. "I guess I'll talk to you about it tomorrow when you drop Sean off?"

"I'll do that," she promised, wondering if Kathy really wanted to know. She went back to opening her many packages.

"A new computer?" Sean asked when he finished vacuuming. There had been a lot of small glass shards but only because Alice had hit the TVs so violently and so many times. He'd vacuumed thoroughly, running the vacuum one way and then the other in all the rooms, and he had emptied the cannister in the garbage several times. He knew a shoddy job would earn his mother's ire, and right now, he was certain he didn't want to face that again.

"A network," she corrected, pulling another laptop from the bag. "I need to get a desktop too."

"Setting up your old system?" he asked. He had always admired the system on her desks in the old house. He hadn't understood it, and he had been too young to touch it, but it always looked impressive.

"Yeah, I thought I should get back into investing. It will give me something to do and keep my days busy." Also, she needed to do research. Only certain programs would do that for her, and she needed

dedicated systems for that. But she didn't share that information with her son; he didn't need to know.

"Can I come with you when you get the desktop?"

Alice glanced up at her tall, sturdy son. "I was thinking about asking your mom to go with me, so we could discuss your punishment for this unplanned party and driving my car without permission."

"I thought cleaning up the mess was–?"

"You thought cleaning up was your full punishment? C'mon, Sean. You really thought you would get off that easy?" She fixed him with a look that had him squirming slightly.

"I guess not," he answered lamely, looking down to get away from her penetrating stare and shuffling his feet uncomfortably. "Do you realize how many of my friends are going to tell people you're mental after that little display," he gestured to the four TV corpses leaning against the wall near the front door.

"Good! Then they won't mess with me, especially when I'm swinging a bat," she smiled to show she was teasing and saw him grin ruefully. He knew she loved him, but the display of temper he had seen had been impressive. He didn't care what people thought of his mom. He was just grateful she was back in their lives. "How about I replace the TVs, and you help me program the new ones, so no one can do that again?" she gestured to the pile of electronics she had pulled from the TVs that was all garbage now.

"You're going to buy new TVs?" he asked, surprised. He liked that idea. It had been fun buying the first new ones and seeing the latest technology.

"Yeah, but if they need to backorder any of them, I'm not buying them. Either they give me what is on hand in their warehouse, or I'm passing."

He thought about it for a second before nodding. "We'll need Mom's car or the Rav4," he warned her.

"That's why I thought I'd ask your mom to come. Maybe I should get a more practical SUV?" she wondered aloud, looking up from the two laptops she was setting up. One laptop was already set to go, and she could use the router to hook it up to the internet. She wanted an intranet in the house too, one that intruders couldn't get into. She also had a few programs to install but would wait until Sean wasn't around.

"You'd buy another car?" he asked eagerly, hoping to get one for himself eventually. He'd hinted many times, but his mothers had

ignored him. He knew they could afford it, but he wasn't going to push, especially now, while punishment was on the table.

"Yeah, I'm thinking the Ferrari is fun but too impractical. I love your mom's Lexus, but again, that's a sports car and not roomy enough to haul things," she said as she considered her options and supplied information when the screen requested it. "You better get some sleep. We'll take you home tomorrow," she told him.

"Okay. Good night, Mom," he said, giving her a kiss on the cheek, so he could get a glimpse at the two screens of her laptop. One was still loading things.

Alice knew her children well, which was why she hadn't pulled out programs they were better off not knowing about. Hell, she hadn't even bought some of them yet.

"What the hell is going on?" Kathy asked as they drove the Rav4 instead of her much-preferred Lexus. Alice had explained there simply wasn't enough room in the Lexus for what she wanted to purchase. They'd decided not to take Sean as they needed to talk in private.

"I honestly don't know yet, but I'm taking steps to find out," Alice responded, telling her wife what she had found in the plaster of the walls and in the TVs. She was going to have to stop at the hardware store for supplies to repair the damage of the various holes in her walls. It had been a slick job, and she wanted to keep going over the whole place but knew her obsessive behavior wouldn't net anything more.

They went to the house in Malibu and loaded up the damaged TVs, tying the seventy-two-inchers to the top of the Rav4 since they wouldn't fit inside, then taking them all to the dump. She was unhappy to learn she had to pay an electronics fee to dispose of them.

"What did you do to those?" Kathy asked, and Alice described the performance she had put on for the sake of the teenagers who were partying at her house. She'd already fielded several phone calls from concerned parents and quickly made her point that the kids shouldn't have been partying unsupervised in her house without permission. By asking if it was their child that brought the liquor, Alice had quickly ended several of those angry phone calls. Knowing Alice, Kathy was quite certain that the tales weren't overly exaggerated, and she was

certain that being unapologetic would serve them well against these parents.

"So, are the listening devices anything like the ones Linda planted?"

"No, these are much more sophisticated. They put them in the nail holes of the plaster, so they looked like they belonged there. I didn't notice because they probably used quick-drying cement and then painted. I have no idea when they did all that, and we just bought the TVs, so I don't even know if it's the same people that bugged them or if it's the government."

"But you are immune from prosecution!" Kathy said, naively.

"For past deeds, not future ones," Alice pointed out.

"What about me and the kids? Are we safe?"

Alice quickly waved around the device she had brought along to use in the car, then she and Kathy headed off to get rid of the TVs and buy a new desktop computer, several monitors, and four new televisions. The store tried to arrange for delivery when the seventy-two-inch TVs didn't fit in the car, but Alice refused delivery. She also declined to purchase the first two TVs she had chosen, which were out of stock. She wouldn't buy anything that wasn't readily available. With Christmas approaching, the stores were really limited as to what stock they had on hand, unless she wanted to wait. Alice wouldn't wait, preferring to be thought of as a difficult customer. They drove away with a full load, choosing alternate TVs and strapping one to the top of the car, although the store didn't recommend laying it flat.

"Careful," Kathy winced as they went over one those infernal dips on the sides of each road and water splashed up the sides of the car. It had stopped raining, and Alice was anxious to get this load to her house and start installing it by herself. That was the only way she could be certain that no other additions were made to her new purchases.

"I just don't want to be caught in the rain with that strapped to the roof," Alice said, pointing to the box she could just barely see through the sunroof. She was certain it wasn't good for the nice TV to be lying on its back, but she hoped the styrofoam they used to pack those things would keep it from getting damaged. The store staff had repeatedly tried to convince her to allow them to deliver it. She'd bought a lot from them the past few days, so they were eager to please, but she expressed her impatience and insisted she didn't want to wait. What she really didn't want was to give someone an opportunity to install more surveillance equipment. Already, her phone had picked up someone looking around the outside the house a bit too long for her comfort. The new equipment she had methodically installed was already working, sending her notifications over the program she had installed on her phone and Bluetoothing the information there.

"Is it the government?" Kathy murmured, surveying the wet hillsides that had been inundated by El Nino and the storms it generated.

"Probably, but I think there is more at work here than just that. I must start doing my homework," Alice answered. She glanced at Kathy as she drove, wondering why she was pursuing this divorce. They still got along well, and the anger had passed. Here she was helping Alice decorate her new home in Malibu.

Kathy started to ask if Alice needed any help but swallowed the words before they emerged, not wanting to get involved. She had to learn to turn that off. After all their years together, it was second nature, and she really did want to help Alice, but she had to learn to stop. That wasn't going to be easy.

Kathy helped Alice carry her boxes into the house. They took the TVs out of the large boxes one by one and hung them up. Alice could wire them herself but hanging them was tough because they were too unwieldy.

"How do you know they won't bug these too?" Kathy asked.

"I already looked it up. Smart TVs have security settings. You can change the default network passwords that the manufacturer set up." She gestured with the channel changer she was inserting batteries into. "There is also a way to disable the microphones and cameras. If that doesn't work, this should," she said as she took some electrical tape and covered the camera on the seventy-two-inch TV. They shared a grin. It was barely noticeable on the TV and such a simple fix.

Kathy left while Alice was installing software updates on her new TVs. She never saw when Alice hauled the boxes for her new monitors and computer into her office to set them up, completely forgetting that she didn't even have a desk yet. She sighed. Asking Kathy to help her again went against her grain, so she looked online with the laptop to find what she wanted and arranged next-day delivery. She spent her time constructively. The TVs were the simplest to set up, followed by the computers and the programs she needed to install. They were nothing that normal people would use, but they were things that someone in Alice's line of work required. She began her research over the next few days, allowing only one interruption by the desk delivery people. Once the desk was set up, she placed her new computers on it strategically, so she could still enjoy the view of the expensive real estate she had purchased with her new beach home.

During her research, Alice read that Sebastian had died. Saddened, she read the obituary closely again and realized she could still attend the funeral if she stopped what she was doing immediately and changed. While setting up the computers, she had made changes to the programming and customized the setup, so it worked only for her. The dummy laptop would be a little easier to use for the unknowing. It was a good fake out should anyone with any knowledge of encrypted software try to get on. She had known it was just a matter of time before her old computers would eventually be broken into, but in these computers, the software, and even the hardware, was so much more sophisticated.

Driving the Ferrari with her tails following, she was annoyed enough that she decided to make it difficult for them to tag along. As she made her way to the funeral home, she maneuvered through traffic as though people and their cars were merely a minor inconvenience, the powerful engine easily powering up as she applied pressure to the gas pedal. Arriving at the funeral home, she realized she had a reprieve from them for maybe a few minutes. She saw several of Sebastian's men including Artum, his nephew. One she especially remembered was looking just like the hood she remembered. Wearing black sweats to a funeral was a stereotype, if ever she saw one. He was pathetic when he tried to look menacing with his thick gold chains hanging down the front V of his track suit.

"Artum," Alice said kindly, her expensive suit showing off her new, slimmer figure. Alice had gotten a haircut, and her spikes were something she enjoyed now with her hair shaped into an elegant style.

"Alice," he responded, leaning down to shake her hand and bestow a kiss on her cheek. She smelled of some heavenly perfume.

"I am sorry for your loss. He was quite a man," she stated as she glanced beyond the line of men accepting condolences, most of whom she did not know and who were obviously there as a show of strength behind Artum.

Artum looked from the petite blonde to his uncle's casket and nodded. His uncle had cost him half a million dollars in penance for not guarding this woman's family properly. He already knew the money had been placed out of his reach, but he didn't know where. Pasternack was searching but hadn't found it yet. He glanced at his men, noting the attention a few of them were paying the older woman. He wondered if any of them had heard the stories his uncle told him. He didn't know if he quite believed them, but it didn't pay to totally ignore what his uncle said. He had a lot of work to do in the coming weeks as he secured his place in this world, especially now that he had his hands on his uncle's holdings. He appreciated that Alice had come to pay her respects, that spoke well of her. He glanced around at the others attending the viewing, some out of fear and others out of genuine respect.

Alice glanced around the room, not intending to stay for the service. As she started to make her way through the throng of well-wishers, she spotted the Pasternacks waiting in the line that had formed. She didn't know why, but they grated on her nerves. Richard nodded cordially, recognizing her as their former neighbor. He had planned to purchase their estate when it went into foreclosure with the IRS, but that had somehow been thwarted, and he wondered how and why. She recognized Sandi on a basic level that they both apparently recognized. Sandi stared at Alice coldly, and then, much to their mutual chagrin, she smiled. Alice returned her smile ever so slightly, realizing it was a feral challenge of some sort.

"Find it," he ordered the banker, wondering where the rest of his uncle's money had gone. Some of it seemed to have vanished into thin air, and he needed funds to enact the changes he wanted to see in the organization he had inherited. Dismissing the banker, he turned to his men and called them in individually, so they could report on their own small pieces of the pie and the monies they were earning for his organization.

"You aren't producing, Ignat," he said formally, knowing the man hated his full and proper name and preferred to be called 'Iggy.' "You either start bringing me more or your failures will be called into account," he indicated the accounting books he had been going over.

Iggy shifted. He was uncomfortable in the track suit he was wearing today. It concealed some of his bulk, but most of it was fat because he was essentially lazy. "I produce," he protested, taking it personally since he had also been called on the carpet for dressing inappropriately at the funeral. He had thought the track suit in black was suitable, and it was brand new. Apparently, these Americans wanted him to wear suits, but he hated how constricting a tie felt.

"Are you arguing with me, Ignat?" Artum asked menacingly, no longer the associate under the thumb of his uncle but very much in command.

"No. Sir," he added belatedly, realizing that Artum could order his death with very little effort.

"Good, then there is hope you are listening," the man said derisively. "You better find some merchandise to bring in soon. You have two weeks."

"Only two?" he began to whine but stopped himself. At the same instant he realized it was Christmas and people would have a lot of new gadgets that he and his men could steal. "Yes, sir. Two weeks," he corrected himself before Artum could chastise him for his tone. "I'll have it."

"Good," Artum said dismissively, never seeing the resentment burning in the eyes of his subordinate.

"Hello?" Alice answered her phone, surprised that Kathy had called. She'd been so involved in her research and new computer setup that she had barely eaten, much less communicated with anyone in the past few days. She'd only stopped to go to Sebastian's funeral. That had been a well-needed break, and she was grateful because it gave her footage of those trying to get into her house while she was gone. She was now looking into who these people were and hoping to trace them back to their employers. Photo imaging software was so much better than it had been just a few years ago. Her scanner, the camera shots, and a few clicks of the button, sent them searching through massive databases. Already, she had identified four of her followers and was now tracing their employers. She was also finding out who owned the cars and hacking into one of those two employers' networks. Hacking the networks without a trace was the key because it gave her so much more information than she needed.

"We never decided what Sean's punishment should be regarding the party and driving the Ferrari?" Kathy began, feeling nervous about asking Alice to Christmas. It really wasn't something she wanted to do, but the kids deserved a normal holiday for a change and excluding Alice wouldn't solve anything.

"I was thinking about that," Alice told her. She had done nothing of the kind, but she didn't feel she had to tell Kathy the whole truth anymore. "We should tell him the truck we were going to buy him for Christmas was returned, and he won't get one until graduation IF he keeps up his grades."

"Oh, that's diabolical," Kathy admired. Then in almost the same breath she asked, "You didn't buy him one, did you?"

"No, did you?" Alice asked, suddenly amused.

"No, but were you going to?"

"I hadn't really thought of it, although I didn't miss one of his hints. Now, if he thinks he blew it, he'll probably keep himself in line until graduation next year."

"Good point," Kathy laughed. She had wanted to buy him a truck, something he would have really liked showing off to his football buddies and his other geeky friends. It would really devastate him to learn that he lost it. "Should I tell him, or would you like the honors?"

"Maybe we shouldn't be this mean," Alice reconsidered. She'd said it on impulse and perhaps it was too harsh.

"Tell you what, go pick up one of those Hot Wheel trucks, and we'll give him that. We'll tell him that we decided not to give him the real thing because of his irresponsibility, but if he keeps his nose clean between now and graduation, he will get the real thing."

"And when should we do this?" Alice asked, amused.

"Well, I was calling to invite you to Christmas. I think the kids should have as normal a holiday as possible, and I want to have it here," she answered, holding her breath to hear what Alice thought.

"Okaaay," she drawled out, wondering at this.

"But we can punish Sean as soon as you want. Why don't you come to dinner tonight, and we'll tell him then?"

"Something to look forward to," Alice murmured into the phone quietly.

"What was that?" Kathy asked, not quite hearing her.

"Do you want me to bring anything besides the toy truck?" Alice asked, louder this time.

"Nope, I have the fixings for a roast. I'll put that in, and you can be here by five?"

"Sounds good," Alice said as she rang off, wondering if they were being too harsh on Sean. She'd already heard from Emily that people at school had been talking about her and calling her mental for her reaction to a *little* party. Emily had gotten into trouble at school for loudly defending her mother over the incident.

Alice finished up her work and showered, looking at her hair and deciding she needed more mousse for this style. She really liked the spikey look these days. The sun here at the beach, on the days it wasn't rainy from the winter storms, were bleaching her hair a pleasant shade of blonde.

Stopping at a store she knew would carry toy cars and trucks, she found the one her son wanted—a red Chevrolet Avalanche. She wrapped it up and brought it with her to the Palos Verdes estate. She missed living here. The quiet and the space made it feel like home. She felt much more comfortable there since she'd had years to make it their own. She didn't have that in Malibu, but she accepted her circumstances. She would make it her home…eventually. Things were what they were. She slipped the wrapped package to Kathy, who put it on Sean's plate before dinner.

"Did you get me this?" he asked excitedly as he opened the package and saw it was an exact replica of the vehicle he wanted.

"No, Sean. That's what you lost this Christmas," Alice told him, looking him straight in the eye and waiting for him to look away from her direct gaze.

"We decided that the truck Momma A bought you for Christmas had to go back," Kathy told him, using the moniker the kids had assigned to Alice. "You're too irresponsible to handle one of your own yet." Kathy always tried to present a united front to their children.

Emily's mouth gaped open as she watched her moms punish her brother.

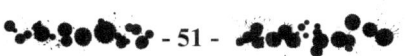

"But–" he began to argue.

"Just be glad I didn't sue any of those children's parents for trespassing," Alice warned. "California has some interesting laws," she added, as though just making conversation with her family.

"If you keep your grades up and don't screw up like this again, we'll revisit the idea of your own vehicle when you graduate high school," Kathy told him, and he looked up at her, furious.

"That's a year and a half away! It was only a party, for Christ's sake!"

"You watch your mouth when you're speaking to your mother!" Alice roared, standing up. Kathy put her hand on Alice's arm to calm her, knowing she would take their son on physically, if she had to.

Sean stared defiantly at both his parents before looking down at his plate and seeing the reminder of his mistake sitting there in its plastic container. He'd wanted an Avalanche for a while now, had really been hoping for it, but he would have settled for a sports car. "It's not like we can't afford–" he began, using arguments he had heard from his friends.

"Really? You have an abundance of cash?" Alice asked him, still standing and looking at the fine young man that was her son. She was wondering if his defiance was going to continue.

"We have trust funds…" he began, looking up.

"You've been listening to the wrong people," Kathy put in, suddenly sounding angry. "You do not have any money. You *don't* work. You go to school, and your allowance is all the money you have."

"It's not like you can't afford–" he began again, hotly.

"Neither can you," Alice finished for him, her voice sarcastic.

He looked up at the tone and realized that defying his moms wouldn't get him the truck he coveted. The fact that they said they might discuss a vehicle when he graduated did give him hope. "How am I supposed to get to my football practice and–"

"How have you been getting there now?" Alice asked as she sat down. Kathy's hand released her arm as she fussed with a napkin to cover her embarrassment over having touched her wife.

"The bus and friends," he answered, sounding sullen.

"Then you will continue to do that, and make sure you aren't a piker—contribute to their gas tanks."

He was angry and started to get up.

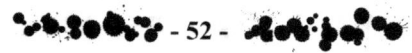

"Where are you going?" Alice asked him. "Your mother made a delicious dinner, and even if you don't eat it, you'll sit here while we enjoy it." Something in her tone told him not to leave the table. He wasn't afraid of Alice, but he had seen her whip that one football player's butt, and the smashing of those TVs was still fresh in his mind. Maybe his friends were right? Maybe Alice was mental?

Dinner was rather tense, but Alice ignored the tension as she enjoyed the food Kathy had prepared for her. Kathy insisted she stay for dessert, a sullen Sean eating only half the food he normally inhaled. His metabolism as a growing young man and football player burned off almost all he ate as soon as he put it into his system.

"Can we play some family games?" Emily asked hopefully after dinner when they had all chipped in to clean the table and get the dishes into the dishwasher.

"May I go to my room?" Sean asked politely, and his mothers took pity on him. Alice made sure he took the model of the Avalanche with him as he stomped up the stairs to his room. Kathy went to the control panel and turned off the internet and cable for Sean's room. They both heard his protests, but then it got quiet.

"He's rather hurt," she whispered to Kathy as Emily went to get a board game called Stratego that they played occasionally. It was a game for two players and required deep concentration as they were warring with each other.

"He thought he got off scot-free, and I resent that," Kathy whispered back, handing Alice some ice water as she would be driving later, feeling it was better than any of the wines they would have normally indulged in.

"He learned different," Alice answered, taking a drink and hearing Emily return.

"He sure did," Kathy murmured in reply, her voice low enough that their daughter didn't hear. She took an unnecessary swipe at the counter to finish cleaning up before hanging the rag over the edge of the sink to dry out.

Alice played against Emily first, then Emily played Kathy before the two moms challenged each other. Emily went to bed. It took a long time for the competition to complete, but Alice won in the end. She smiled at Kathy as she took her wife's flag. Not one to gloat, she smiled and stretched, showing off her body against her shirt. Kathy turned away, feeling a sudden bolt of desire shoot through her as she began to clean up the game pieces.

They put away the game, and Alice readied herself to go out in the lashing rain.

"Damn, it's coming down. Let me get an umbrella," Kathy offered.

"It's cold too. You don't have to come out with me," Alice told her as she put on her coat. It *was* cold, and she could see that fog had rolled in a bit. Her breath condensed to steam as she stepped out onto the small porch and peered into the darkness.

"Nonsense," Kathy objected, pulling on her own jacket and holding up the umbrella she had grabbed. She walked Alice down to the expensive sports car. The rain was splashing onto the asphalt and concrete and bouncing up at her, wetting her jeans from the knees down as she held up the umbrella while Alice got in the low-slung vehicle. She wished Alice didn't have to go but stoically kept her silence.

"Thank you," Alice said, puzzled by the look she thought she saw in Kathy's eyes. It must be a trick of the lights. They had always called them the landing lights because they showed the walkway but were not too bright on the rain-swept path.

"Drive safely," Kathy said as Alice backed away. She was tempted to lean in for a kiss goodbye but knew it was inappropriate now and would only confuse the situation. "Thanks for coming!" she called as she waved. Alice waved back, closed the door, and started the car. Kathy hurried up the steps, aware that Alice watched her before turning the car around and driving down the long drive. The hum of the engine sounded more like the purr of a cat. *Appropriate for someone like Alice*, Kathy thought.

Alice almost felt sorry for the two sedans waiting for her. They couldn't help but see her headlights, which alerted them to the fact that she was leaving. She fishtailed slightly, showing off as she sped past them, the powerful engine easily eating up the paved road and roaring away from them. They both hurriedly started their engines and sped after their quarry. Their orders were to watch her and follow her, and since she now knew of their presence, they also tried to annoy her. They all judiciously ignored each other.

They did annoy Alice. That was probably why she chose to take the longer way home that night…it wasn't the fact that she wished she was going back to the house in Palos Verdes, and it wasn't the fact that she desperately wanted to be taking a hot bath with Kathy and later,

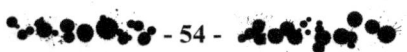

twining her limbs around her soon-to-be ex-wife. According to the paperwork, they would both be free by the new year. Driving onto the PCH, she was lost in thought as she expertly outdistanced her pursuers. The powerful engine continued to eat up the pavement as she applied a little more pressure to the gas pedal. Only the fact that the traffic lights slowed her gave them any hope of catching up. Occasionally, she slipped through a yellow light in time to lose them for a bit longer. She could have turned off, but they all knew she was headed to her other home.

Peering through the downpour, she slowed a bit. The puddles were becoming a bit deep for her almost brand-new car, and the ditches were running full. Anyone foolish enough to be out walking in this was sure to by swamped by any car passing them on the road. In fact, she saw more than one person enjoying the ditches and deliberately spraying water on the poor, wretched individuals who were unfortunate enough to be waiting at bus stops and huddling under the overhangs to avoid the downpour. She didn't find it funny, and in her mood, she was tempted to run one of them off the road. She constrained herself as her mood worsened.

As she was driving along with the headlights behind her rushing to catch up, she glanced behind her. The distinctive shape of one sedan's headlights told her he was catching up. She glanced forward just in time to hit the brake sharply as a boulder crashed down in front of her, bounced once, and rolled across the highway. She pulled around it just in time to get out of the way of a second boulder, but just when she thought she had passed the cliffs that were eroding from the rain, an entire chunk of hillside crashed down on the PCH. Alice wasn't as fortunate this time. One boulder bounced onto the hood of her car, spinning her, and the next one crashed over the roof and into the passenger side door. The window shattered, making a horrific sound, and she spun even farther. Alice was trying to control the car but was unable to turn out of the path of the oncoming mud, gravel, and boulders. Another one bounced over the car and hit the edge of the driver's side door, bending the frame. The open passenger window allowed rain-soaked dirt and gravel to spill onto the leather seat, rapidly filling that side of the car. The engine sputtered to a halt, trapping her and preventing her from moving out of the path of the oncoming deluge. She could hear the scrapes as the rocks, boulders, and gravel all hit her car.

Alice pushed against the driver's side door, watching in consternation as the passenger side of the vehicle continued to fill rapidly. She couldn't open her door; the bent frame was preventing that. The back windshield exploded from the force of the debris building up on top of the car. She tried to use her elbow to break the window but only hurt herself instead. Alice grabbed the headrest on the passenger side, trying to yank it out and failing. The dirt and rocks were too high, and they were still coming. She could hear the metal over her head beginning to groan in protest at the additional weight. She pulled at her own headrest, yanking and jerking and pushing the adjustment button that held it in place until it finally pulled free. She looked at the two metal prongs, then she pulled back and hit her driver's side window with them. They were designed to break the glass. The first blow didn't do anything but hurt her hand, and with her elbow already smarting, she didn't appreciate the added pain. She was desperate and trying not to panic. She kept hitting the window with the headrest, the soft leather protecting her hand from cuts, and the window finally splintered when one of the prongs penetrated it. She kept bashing at the window until she thought there was enough room for her to climb out. She dropped the headrest and tried to get out, but her seatbelt held her back. She heard the top of her car collapsing, the metal grinding even lower, and she saw her open window start to settle. The glass was no longer helping the metal support the roof and prevent it from caving in. She jabbed at her seatbelt release, finally feeling it give. As she pulled herself up again and tried to get through the window, she realized that the crushed engine had her right leg trapped below the dash. She tugged, but it wouldn't give. Her upper body was partly out the window, and the shards of glass were digging into her coat and ripping it to shreds as she struggled to pull her leg free. The rain was coming down, nearly drowning her. Then, she realized it wasn't rain. Dirt and debris were still coming down with the rockslide and pouring across the roof of her car. The ensuing mud was drowning her. The groaning of the metal was horrendous as her vehicle succumbed to the weight and slowly buckled.

Alice pulled and yanked at her leg; her back was being cut as it rubbed against the jagged edges of the broken window. As the hood settled once more under the weight of the onslaught, she realized she could no longer feel her leg, and she began to see spots through the mud and debris as she rapidly blinked it away through the rain. She could hear the pulse pounding in her ears, replacing the roar of the landslide and the scrape of stone against metal. Everything went black.

~The End~

❧ MALEVOLENT MALICE ☙

BOOK 27

Alice's accident puts an immense strain on the family dynamic that no one could have anticipated. Its far-reaching impact will alter their family in more ways than one.

"Mrs. Weaver?" a voice came to Kathy where she sat in the visitor's lounge waiting to hear the results of her wife's examination. When the police had shown up at their house in Palos Verdes, her heart had leapt into her throat. She remembered other times the police had shown up and did not like the reminder. It was quite late, and they pushed the button at the gate repeatedly until she got up and angrily demanded they cease, or she would call the police. When she learned it *was* the police at her gate, and they were there to tell her that Alice had been in a car crash on Pacific Coast Highway, Kathy had woken up. Any ideas of sleep she had thought to get after their family dinner together vanished. She looked up at the voice as both Sean and Emily hopped up from where they had been dozing in their chairs.

"Yes?" she said, her voice harsh, even to her own ears, from the tears she had shed. She cleared her throat as she stood up.

"You are Alice Weaver's wife?" the person verified, looking down at the paperwork on the chart.

"Yes. What…?" Kathy pleaded, anxious for information. They had been waiting here all night and well into the morning, and she hadn't slept much. Sean's snores on the couch had resulted in Emily shoving his feet to the floor and waking him, which started an argument between the teens and irritated Kathy, who snapped at them both. None of them were in very good moods.

"She's alive," the woman told her, seeing the immediate relief on Kathy's face. "Her leg is broken, and she's in pretty rough shape with plenty of contusions and abrasions. Was she ill recently?"

Kathy wasn't about to give out information about why Alice had been emaciated. There was no way they wanted there to be a record of that. She just shrugged and asked, "Is she conscious?"

"No, not yet," the woman stated, wondering at the lack of information in the system for their patient. All she had found was Alice's name and home address. "Do you have more medical information for your wife?"

Kathy shook her head, not about to give out information on her wife. She was just relieved that Alice was alive. She had worried that she would die when the police told her they'd had to cut Alice from the Ferrari, and she'd nearly been buried alive. A broken leg didn't sound like much based on what she had been told by the police who also informed her which hospital Alice had been taken to. Kathy was still suspicious about why the police had come to their house in person instead of simply calling. She was righteously suspicious of the authorities. "Can I see her?"

"They are still getting her cleaned up. That mud went everywhere, and we have to keep her wounds clean…" the woman began, glancing curiously at the brunette standing before her. "I'll let you know when she is in a room and you can see her." She looked at the two teenagers who were watching her, giving them a tremulous smile.

"How long do you think that will be?"

"Probably within an hour," she said and held out a bag containing Alice's personal effects including the dirty clothes they had cut from her body. Her cell phone had been in her pocket, and Kathy saw it as she sat back down. Staring at the dirty clothes, she wondered why they had bothered saving them.

"Mom, shouldn't you call someone?" Emily asked, trying to get her mom's attention.

"Shouldn't you eat something?" Sean said at the same time. He was always willing to eat, and he was hungry now.

Kathy smiled wanly, pointing at their cell phones. "You call Kit," she said to Sean. To Emily she said, "You call Andie." Holding up her cell phone, she pronounced, "I'm calling Portia."

At first, Emily and Sean were surprised to be given such responsibility, but both kids did as she asked. Sean awkwardly left a message on Kit's number explaining that Alice had been in an accident and had a broken leg, and she should call Mom. Emily did a little better. When Andie answered, she shared the news and advised they were waiting at the hospital.

"What do you need?" Portia asked after Kathy told her what had happened.

"Nothing. I'm just waiting to see her now," she said into the phone, hearing the awkward tone in Sean's voice as he left too much information on Kit's voicemail. She inwardly shook her head. That kid had a lot to learn. She was only vaguely aware that Emily was doing better with her call.

"You don't have to stay–" Portia began, then realized that Kathy would stay for the kids.

"I do have to stay, and I want to put a halt to the divorce proceedings until she's back on her feet and able to deal with everything."

"But Kathy, you're so close…" she started to say. It was only two weeks until the divorce would be processed, and the judge could sign off on it. She'd pulled a few strings to have it go through quickly and efficiently, so they could both start the new year free, and Alice hadn't seemed to object.

"*I'm* not in my right mind, and she's unconscious. Just put it on hold."

"If we leave it as is, it will–"

"And I'm instructing you to halt it! If I am required to make medical decisions for her, I need to be able to do that legally." She turned away from the kids, so they wouldn't hear her as they hung up from their own calls. "Who is going to do that for her, the kids?"

Portia had to admit she was right. She didn't know how bad Alice's condition was, and Kathy probably didn't have all the facts yet either. Alice might need extensive medical care. The terms of the divorce made it clear that Alice would keep insurance in place for the kids until they graduated college, but she knew the woman would have done that without having it spelled out for her. She was an honorable woman, and she'd been amenable to anything they'd asked. Even Nia Toyomoto, working with the attorneys in Los Angeles from her New York office, had been surprised by how much Alice had given in on the terms, giving Kathy more than the fifty percent she was legally entitled to. "Okay, I'll get that rolling and call her attorneys. What do *you* need?" she repeated. This time with emphasis, so Kathy would catch what she was asking.

"I'm fine," she answered automatically, but they both knew she wasn't. She was barely holding it together after realizing that Alice could have died in that landslide. The police had already informed her the car was totaled.

Portia called New York and spoke with Nia Toyomoto, then returned Andie's phone call. Afterward, she went to the hospital to support Kathy, but couldn't find her in the waiting room. They'd finally let the family go in to see Alice. Portia wasn't sure she should wait, and she certainly didn't want to see Alice. She had hoped her friend was finally free of the odd woman she had loved for nearly half her life. Theirs was a relationship Portia had never quite understood, and Alice had made her feel distinctly uncomfortable many times over the years. So many things she had done were illegal on so many levels, and Portia was positive that Alice was a killer. There was at least one guy she was almost certain Alice had done away with. She wanted her friend free of the entanglements, and she'd almost been free before this happened.

Alice fought the fog enveloping her mind that was brought on by the narcotics the doctors had prescribed to alleviate the pain they assumed she was in. She tried to make out where she was. For a heart-stopping moment, she thought she was back in prison. Then she became confused, thinking she was somewhere in Russia and trying to get home to California. As her thoughts began to straighten out, she felt her eyes smarting from the bright lights in her room, and she realized she was in a hospital. Unable to open her eyes, she mentally examined herself and found her body hurt as well. She was terribly dehydrated. Her mouth felt like cotton, and her lips were cracked. While attempting to move her right leg, she winced at the pain, alerting the male nurse entering the room that she was waking. The man left quickly to alert the doctor.

I do believe my leg is broken, she thought, moving other limbs and realizing she must be pretty scraped up based on all the things that were hurting. Her neck felt stiff too, and she had a terrific headache. Why the hell couldn't she open her eyes?

Alice was pretty beaten up. The rocks had battered her body as she lay half in and half out the window, and passing out had left her vulnerable to the mud, which had slowly been drowning her when some good Samaritans passing by had stopped to assist. Hers wasn't the only car under the landslide, but her spin had carried her to the edge where she and her car were slowly being crushed by the tremendous weight of the rocks and mud. The police and fire department got there in record time and relieved the people trying to clear the debris from the top of the smashed Ferrari. Efforts to remove the blonde woman from the sports car were unsuccessful as her leg was well and truly trapped under the dashboard. They'd had to use the jaws of life to release her from the wreckage, eating up precious time that might mean the difference between life and death.

When the woman was finally free, they quickly moved to get her on a gurney. The mud and rocks were rolling about her as they used a jack to keep the space open between the floor of the crushed vehicle and the engine to get her trapped leg out. They'd administered fluids despite the dirt, putting an I.V. in her arm as others used the jaws of life to free her. A tarp held up by several firefighters had enabled them to work despite the downpour and the constant threat of further landslides. It also kept the mud from drowning her, allowing them to keep her airway clear. By the time they freed her, a bulldozer had arrived to start clearing the highway.

The men who had been following Alice stood in the crowd of onlookers that gathered despite the rain, and they too breathed a sigh of relief to see Alice Weaver freed from the wreckage. They'd reported in and had been instructed by their respective employers to wait and see if she was freed. She wouldn't go anywhere if she were dead, and if she lived, she'd probably end up at the hospital.

As they pulled her clothes from her battered and bruised body at the hospital, they found her wallet containing her identification as well as her phone, which was locked. Her license indicated she had a home in Palos Verdes, and a sticker attached to it read: *In case of emergency contact my wife, Kathy Weaver*, and it provided her wife's phone number. The police had taken that information, and when they recognized the name, they decided to contact Kathy in person.

There were many lacerations on Alice's arms; one elbow was cracked from her attempts to break the window, and her back was treated for cuts from the broken glass. The leg break was serious. It started as a lateral fracture near the ankle, but the way the engine had trapped her leg had caused the bone to split up the leg. Many hours later, after six pins were inserted in her leg and the wound was cleaned and well wrapped, she was admitted to a room. It might take days to remove all the dirt from her body since they couldn't soak her in a tub. They were watching her for pneumonia, unsure how much muddy water she had inhaled.

"Alice?" Kathy's voice penetrated the fog. It sounded urgent.

Alice fought for consciousness, but it wasn't easy. The drugs resisted, wanting her to remain asleep. She was warm and tired, and she wanted to submit to the drugs' demands, but Kathy was calling, and she must answer. She *always* answered her wife, and she had fought so hard to get back to her. Her eyes fluttered, despite the light that was hurting them.

"She's awake," Kathy said unnecessarily. Her eyes were tearing up but only their children noticed.

"Mom?" Em asked in a little girl's voice. "You okay, Mom?"

"Of course, she isn't okay, dummy," Sean put in and then sniffed audibly. "You ruined the Ferrari," he added, and he saw the beginnings of a grin on Alice's face, which turned to a grimace as she also tried to chuckle.

"Not now, Sean," Kathy admonished, but she was smiling too.

"Ssss…sorrrry about the car," Alice got out as she fought the fog. The pain pierced her eyelids and every other part of her body she could feel. She groaned.

"Should I get a nurse?" Kathy fretted, watching the grimace on her wife's face and hearing her groan. She looked terrible. Everything was bruised, and Kathy could see there was a lot of tape covering the lacerations she had suffered. Alice was partially covered by one of those terribly unfashionable hospital gowns they made people wear. Kathy fought the urge to pull down the blankets and raise her wife's gown to see for herself how badly Alice was hurt. Her wife's leg was propped up on pillows, her arm in a sling. This didn't seem like a very professional setup in her opinion, but she hoped the staff knew what they were doing.

"Nnnnooo," Alice groaned as she finally pried her eyes open. What a beautiful sight! Kathy, Emily, and Sean were all there. For a moment, she'd thought she would never see them again. Everything came to her in an instant—Russia, the divorce, the CIA, the divorce. She frowned, wondering why Kathy was there, and then, Sean's attempt at humor and his comment about the car came back to her. Now, they made sense as she remembered the accident.

Kathy breathed a sigh of relief as Alice's eyes opened fully. Their odd color was still there along with the rich browns she had loved for so many years. The cat-like shape of her wife's eyes was beautiful to her, despite the lacerations on her cheeks from the rocks.

"Mom you look terrible," Emily said honestly, and Alice smiled. Her cut lip was throbbing and caused her to wince.

"Can I get you some water?" Kathy offered. Alice nodded. Her mouth was terribly dry, probably from something the doctors had given her. She glanced at the elevated leg and nearly groaned again.

"You really did it this time, Mom," Sean grinned, pleased to see her awake and unsure what to say. He wanted to hug her, but he didn't want to hurt her. Kit had told her family she was heading for the airport, and she would arrive anytime. She wanted to be there no matter what. If Alice didn't make it, she wanted to be there for Kathy.

"If…you're gonna do something…do…it…well," she said between the sips of water Kathy was gently plying her with.

They all chuckled, using humor as a distraction.

"Ms. Weaver I'm glad to see you are with us again." A woman in a lab coat walked in holding a chart. "I'm Doctor Bryant. I set your leg for you. You have six screws holding it together, and if you behave, you should be up and walking on it in about eight weeks."

Kathy looked on in surprise at the pretty, red-headed doctor. She didn't know what she had been expecting, but she thought she detected interest in Alice's eyes as she also took in the woman. Maybe she was imagining things?

"Hi. I'm Doctor Bryant. Are you Mrs. Weaver?" the doctor asked. holding out her hand to Kathy.

"Yes…yes, I am," she stuttered, suddenly feeling inept around this woman. She seemed so…confident. Seeing the children, her manners returned, and she introduced them too. "This is our son, Sean and our daughter, Emily."

"Wow! They look like both of you," the doctor remarked as she checked Alice's vitals. Turning back to her patient, she asked, "How are you feeling? Kinda crappy?"

Alice liked her immediately. She wasn't sure why. Perhaps because she'd been expecting a stuffy, old man doctor. She smiled slightly as she nodded. "Yeah, not feeling too great," she rasped out.

"Careful there. It's gonna feel like you have the worst sore throat *ever* for a few days. You must let your body heal, and we're gonna try to help by keeping you pretty drugged up. You inhaled a lot of mud, and we're gonna watch for pneumonia and infections as well. It took forever to remove all that glass from you, and some if it will probably work its way to the surface and cause you some discomfort. You've

cracked your elbow, but I see no reason why that won't heal," she pointed to the sling.

Alice liked that the doctor was giving her information without having to pry it from her.

"You were very lucky you didn't break more bones. One of the officers showed me pictures of your car, and I don't think you'll be driving for a while," she said with a little smile.

Alice nodded; her eyes fluttering shut again.

"Nope! We need you awake for this," the doctor told Alice as she continued her examination by shining a light in her eyes. "Has anyone ever told you that your eyes are shaped like a cat's?" she observed.

Alice chuckled, but that hurt and caused her to cough slightly.

"Easy there. Not too much coughing please, and no talking," the doctor warned, looking more closely at a couple of Alice's more noticeable wounds. "I'm going to have the nurse come in and give you something for the pain. You are going to be in and out of consciousness for days, but don't worry. We'll feed you with this," she tapped the I.V. and smiled at her patient. "You aren't going to feel like chewing and swallowing anyway," she added as she punched something on her pad's screen.

"Thank you," Alice rasped politely.

"I said no talking," she warned, shaking a finger at her patient and smiling. She patted Alice on her good arm in a spot that was bruised but not cut, then smiled at the woman's family and left them.

"Wow! You're a mess," Kathy teased, hoping that Alice was only being polite and wasn't interested in the doctor. Then, Kathy remembered they were still married. Even if she were interested, Alice wouldn't make any moves until the divorce was finalized. And besides, she was in no shape to make any moves on anyone. "You get better, and no talking," Kathy ordered, sniffing back some tears that were threatening.

Alice could sense something was up but couldn't quite put her finger on it; her mind was still a bit fuzzy. A nurse came in with a syringe and injected the contents into the I.V.

"You'll be asleep within a few minutes," she warned, glancing at the other woman and the children as she left.

"We should let you sleep," Kathy said, squeezing Alice's fingers.

"Yeah, get some sleep, Mom. You are gonna need it," Emily said, leaning over to kiss her carefully on the cheek.

"This is a heck of a way to get out of showing me the hiding places on Super Mario Bros.," Sean teased as he too leaned over and gave Alice a kiss.

Alice grinned at her son. He hadn't learned all the secrets yet, and she wasn't about to just show him. Instead, she'd been beating him by skipping levels because he didn't see or couldn't remember the shortcuts she used. Her mind was fading fast. Whatever they had given her felt warm in her arm. Her last conscious thought as she watched her family fade away was about how happy it made her that they were there.

"She looked awful," Emily stated as Kathy led them out into the hall.

"Shhh, she might hear you," Kathy admonished her daughter.

"She is out. They drugged her," Sean pointed out.

"Can we stay until she wakes up again?" Emily asked.

"No, we are going home and get some sleep ourselves. It will do us no good to neglect our own care. We'll come back at visiting time tomorrow…er, later today."

"We don't have to go to school?" Sean asked, brightening up. Christmas vacation started in a few days, and he didn't mind missing some more days.

"No, you will sleep until it's time for school and go in as usual," Kathy warned as they walked along the corridor. She was surprised to see Portia waiting in the lounge.

"Hey there. How is Alice?" Portia asked as she stood up. They hadn't let her in Alice's room to visit, citing the rule of family only, and she hadn't minded.

"She's drugged up," Emily announced, sounding almost happy about it.

"Yeah, she's kind of a zombie," Sean agreed, laughing.

"She's alive," Kathy answered, cuffing her kids affectionately to shush them. "I just want to get out of here. Thank you for coming, but you shouldn't have come out in this deluge," she nodded towards the downpour she could see outside. The rain hadn't let up.

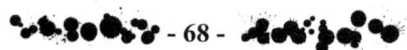

"I just wanted to be here for you guys," Portia admitted. She didn't know what was going to happen with Kathy and Alice now, but she really hoped her friend would quickly come to her senses. She'd put a stop to the divorce for now, but Nia Toyomoto had also been surprised by the development, saying she would have to consult with her client, Alice, before agreeing to the temporary halt. Neither lawyer saw any reason to put the brakes on their clients' divorce, but ultimately, that was their clients' decision.

"Thank you…really," Kathy responded, touched by her friend's compassion. She didn't think of Portia as simply her lawyer. They'd known each other since college, and while she knew very well her friend didn't trust her wife, she also knew Portia didn't understand or even know everything they'd been through together.

"Alice Weaver was in a near-fatal accident in Malibu," someone reported to Director Wolf.

"Does Madelyn know?" he asked, looking up.

"I don't know," he admitted.

"Don't you think you better tell her and her team then?" he asked. Damn! What if Madelyn thought he was circumventing her authority? He knew she'd be a formidable enemy, even if she worked under him. He'd given her carte blanche to pursue the information Alice Weaver had given them.

"Yes, sir," the man replied, backing away from the director.

Wolf watched as he hurried off. He considered where the investigation was going. Madelyn knew a lot more than she was letting on about this Alice Weaver chick. The redactions were bothering the hell out of him. The original reports couldn't possibly be taking this long to locate. Something was hinky about the protections this American citizen had been afforded.

"You can go home tomorrow," Doctor Bryant told Alice a couple days later after they'd had a chance to observe her and ensure the fluids

had had a chance to start their patient's healing process. Alice was permitted to talk now too, and her voice was sexy as hell as she was speaking very softly and still trying to be careful with it. The bruising around her neck from the rocks that pelted down on it had formed some interesting shapes. They'd already removed the sling, warning her to go easy on her arm as it healed.

"Really?" Alice rasped, her throat still feeling a little sore.

"Will your wife hire a nurse or take care of you herself?"

Alice blinked at that, surprised. She hadn't really thought about it, but she realized Kathy had been here every opportunity, fluffing her pillows and providing anything Alice needed. She was always sitting nearby and reading on her Kindle quietly as Alice dozed. "I guess I'll have to hire a nurse," she said, wondering who she should call.

Doctor Bryant wasn't surprised at that. Kathy, while seemingly very concerned about her wife's prognosis, didn't seem the most competent of women to care for her patient. Alice Weaver seemed a bit…intense. Alice was an active woman, from what she had gleaned, and she was underweight and would need nurturing and pampering while her leg healed. "Do you need some recommendations? I'm certain we have a list around here…somewhere."

"That would be good," Alice said, wondering if she should consult with Kathy on this decision. She recalled having an odd phone call with Nia Toyomoto about Kathy but couldn't remember the details. The discussion had puzzled her at the time, but she'd deal with that when she was home and off these damn pain meds. Her leg was causing her more pain than she had imagined and learning to walk with crutches was annoying but necessary, if she didn't want to use a bedpan. Her arm was stiff and the elbow was painful, but she needed both her arms to use the crutches.

Doctor Bryant had one of the nurses bring in a list of companies that supplied private nurses to clients. Remembering Sandi Pasternack, Alice suddenly had a premonition, and a shiver went down her spine. She remembered Sebastian's funeral and the odd expressions on everyone's faces. She had intended to do something about that at some point. She stared down at her wrapped leg. They hadn't put a cast on the leg yet but would do that before she left tomorrow. She knew she would be limited in what she could do. Thinking about what needed to be done to fulfill Sebastian's request to be avenged, she instinctively knew that Sandi Pasternack had had something to do with his demise.

That subject led Alice to other thoughts, and she remembered the interesting data she had found through her searches on the computers. She hadn't yet been able to replace all her old programs. In fact, some of them were illegal for individuals to own and were no longer available. In addition, some programs had been updated, and she had a huge learning curve to deal with. She'd been working on that and had planned to keep the momentum going when she'd had this accident. Her memory was sketchy, but she remembered someone had been following her. She wondered if they were somehow watching her hospital room now. She'd been on the trail of their employers, trying to see who had hired them. She was a bit frustrated because she wanted to know who was watching her and why. She speculated if one of the cars might belong to the Feds but realized Marilyn Korbel knew better than to do that. She also didn't think it was the CIA who had put the bugs in her house. It was frustrating to know that with her laid up her watchers could enter her home and replant their devices. She'd not had access to her phone, and she wondered where it was. She was anxious to look at the videos her own cameras would have taken in her absence.

Alice leaned back and sighed. There was only so much she could do from bed. When Kathy arrived for her customary visit, Alice casually asked, "Do you know where they put my phone?"

"Oh, it's with your personal effects," Kathy answered. "Your clothes were shredded from the accident and further destroyed when they cut them off you to reach your injuries. I threw the clothes out after emptying the pockets."

"And my phone?" she returned to the original question.

"I'll have to charge it and bring it in. Did you need something in particular?"

"Well, I have phone calls to make, and I thought it would be better to use my own phone. The nurses gave me a list of companies to call, so I could hire someone to take care of me, and I wanted to get on that."

"Oh," Kathy answered, sounding a little defeated.

"Oh?" Alice asked, wondering what her wife was thinking about.

"I thought you would be coming home to Palos Verdes. We could hire Sandi, if you need a nurse," she put in with a little smirk to show she was teasing.

"I do hope that is a joke," Alice asked to clarify.

"Of course. I don't want that woman—" she began just as Emily walked in.

"Hi, Mom. I brought you a candy bar," she offered as she came over and gave Alice a hug, a kiss, and a Hershey's chocolate bar with almonds.

"Thank you, honey," she answered, pleased to see her. She took the bar and ripped off the corner of the wrapper to eat some. "Why aren't you in school?"

"I had a checkup, and Mom picked me up early."

"Checkup?" Alice asked, looking at the two of them. "Everything okay?"

"She's doing well. Still underweight, but that is improving, and she's getting taller."

"Yeah, Sean can't call me shrimp for much longer," Emily added, aggrieved.

They all laughed. Sean could be a pain, but he didn't mean any harm. He had defended his sister to anyone who picked on the sickly girl. Emily had made great strides in improving not only her appearance but her health.

"So, when do you get out of this joint?" the teen asked, looking expectantly at Alice.

"Apparently, tomorrow," Alice answered.

"Oh, good! You can come home then!" she said excitedly.

"Hold on there..." Kathy put in, but the teen went on.

"You could probably stay in the basement. We could put your new computers in the office, and you could stay in Nan's old room until you're better." The teen had it all thought out.

Kathy and Alice exchanged a look.

Alice was gentle as she asked, "What about my house in Malibu?"

"Oh, no. You should be surrounded by those who care for you and can help you."

"Don't argue with her, Mom. She's got it all planned out," Kit said as she came in carrying a couple of salads, which she handed to Kathy and Alice. She frowned at the candy bar Alice was nibbling at.

"Hey there. You haven't visited much," Alice complained.

"I had to go back and finish some finals, but you didn't seem very with it the first visit anyway."

"All done for the semester?"

"Until January when I go back."

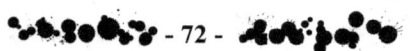

"I thought you were taking mid-term classes?"

"I decided that spending time with family was more important," she stated, digging into her salad to stop the conversation.

Alice let her off the hook, knowing those courses would have shortened her last term's load and hoping the young woman hadn't dropped them because of her but knowing she probably had.

"Oooh, yuck! They put some vinaigrette on this," Emily complained, wrinkling her nose.

"I think I gave you mine," Kit put in, exchanging the salads.

"I think they have you outvoted," Kathy murmured to Alice, who laughed in response. She was amiable to the idea of moving in with her family.

"You okay with this idea?" Kathy asked.

"It makes the most sense," Alice pointed out.

"What makes the most sense?" Emily asked, pointing with her fork.

"Me coming to stay in Palos Verdes. Do you think you kids can move my computers to the office there without breaking anything?"

"I'll drive over if you give me a key, and I can get Sean to help," Kit put in helpfully. She exchanged a look with Kathy, who nodded slightly. "I'll pick him up from practice and go down there tonight, okay?" She looked at Alice, who also nodded as she dug into the salad her daughter had brought her.

Kathy pushed the wheelchair with Alice's leg sticking out before her. It was propped on the leg lift and encased in a shiny, new cast. She was pleased that Alice was willing to come live with them for a time. Sean, Kit, and Emily had carefully loaded the many computers, along with their cords and monitors into the Rav4. Then, Sean guarded the cache of expensive electronics, something Kathy had insisted not be let out of their sight, while Kit and Emily went through Alice's closet and drawers to pack clothes and other necessities for their mom. Everything was waiting in the office and Nan's old room for her, so she wouldn't have to traverse the steps too often with her crutches. They'd done a nice job plugging everything back in, but Alice would have to start them up since none of the kids knew the passwords. Kathy found it comforting to see the office occupied again when she looked in on it.

It was odd to see Alice's clothes in Nan's room, but at least they were all under one roof again.

"Careful there. Slowly…" the nurse cautioned as Alice was transferred from the wheelchair to the Lexus passenger seat.

Alice, used to doing things on her own, had a hard time letting others help her. It was difficult to avoid hurting herself too; she had never been incapacitated in quite this way. She couldn't remember breaking a bone like this, although she suspected some of the ribs, fingers, and toes that had been taped up from time to time in her varied and active life had been broken.

She sighed mightily as they bundled her into the Lexus, hooked up the seat belt, and finally shut the door. Her crutches went up the side by the door and over her shoulder.

"All set?" Kathy asked perkily as she started the car.

"Yep," Alice said, but she didn't sound convincing.

"You okay? Need a pain pill?" Kathy asked, concerned at Alice's tone.

"Probably," she murmured. "I'm just glad to be out of there," she thumb-pointed back towards the hospital. "I have so much to do."

"What do you have to do?" Kathy asked, but she knew there were some things in Alice's life she didn't have the right to hear about anymore since she'd asked for the divorce.

"You know, I'd gotten the computers, and I'd just started looking into things…" she began.

Kathy wasn't sure she wanted to know what things, but she couldn't help asking, "What things?"

"You know how paranoid I can get. When was the last time we swept this car?" she asked, her hand gesturing to the entire Lexus.

Kathy got the hint. "Did you have the kids bring any of that equipment over?"

"I don't know. I'll have to see what's on my desk at the house. They might have thought it was computer equipment, but Sean helped me sweep the Malibu house, so he should recognize some of it."

"Yeah, that shook him. I don't want the kids involved in…" she began, then realized they'd be involved whether she wanted them to be or not. Look at Emily and how she had overheard a bit already. She knew the girl wanted to discuss it to have her curiosity appeased, but she'd shut her daughter down several times when she brought it up.

"How do we keep them out?" Alice's tone was a bit sardonic and bitter. She'd tried, and she'd succeeded on several levels, but the children had all experienced trauma at various times in their lives. That's what it was…just their lives.

Kathy sighed gustily through her nose as she turned on the windshield wipers when it began to rain. "I guess we just try and protect them as best we can."

"You know I'd never deliberately put them in harm's way."

Kathy glanced over, seeing the intense look and pain on Alice's face. She wasn't certain whether the pain was from her break or their conversation. "Of course, I know that." She went silent, just in case there was a bug in the car. She didn't want anything they said used against them in any way. They'd had enough of that. But there were questions she wanted answered now that she knew Alice had been looking into…things. She wondered if one of those things was the death of her former girlfriend, Linda. She hadn't had the nerve to ask again if Alice was investigating that for her.

Slowly, Alice hobbled up each step to the front door. The rain hadn't gotten too intense, but it was heavy enough that it made it hard for her to stay dry as Kathy attempted to help her up the stairs. It was very slow going.

Exasperated, she finally said, "I think I'd do better crawling," and got down on all fours to do just that. It had hurt trying to hop up each step, and now, she could use her knee, so her leg and ankle wouldn't be used.

Kathy nearly laughed aloud at the sight of Alice Weaver crawling up the steps to their house. She held the umbrella above her wife, but the ground and the bricks of the steps were already very wet.

Alice stopped crawling in the hallway once she was inside and out of the rain. She leaned against the wall, exhausted from her efforts. "That sucked!" she said succinctly.

"Mrs. Alice you need help?" Mrs. Fernandez entered the hallway looking concerned.

"No, thank you. We've got this. I'm just…tired," she said with a smile at the housekeeper.

Mrs. Fernandez was used to the odd behaviors of her employers over the years. She returned the smile and headed back to the kitchen where she had been cleaning when she heard them come in. She was pleased that Mrs. Alice was here. It always made Mrs. Kathy happier

to have her around. She didn't understand two women loving each other but had learned long ago to keep her mouth shut and mind her own business. They paid well, and it wasn't a difficult job. The children were nearly grown too.

"Ready to get up?" Kathy asked after a moment, waiting for the housekeeper to get out of hearing range. She was carrying Alice's crutches in one hand and gestured with them.

"Not really," Alice said, tired from her efforts. She took a deep breath and crawled again, the cast banging slightly on the tiles in the hallway and causing her to gasp at the pain that shot up her leg. She crawled to the couch to pull herself up. Her upper body strength wasn't what it once was, and she struggled as she attempted to pull herself up on the couch.

"Here, let's elevate that," Kathy said, putting the crutches within reach and grabbing pillows to prop up Alice's leg.

"Oh, gawd. I should probably go downstairs to the bedroom and–"

"You are not hiding away from the family down there!" Kathy asserted stoutly.

"The kids are at school, and you don't need me underfoot..." Alice objected.

"You are not underfoot. Look, the doctor said it was going to be six to eight weeks before you were walking on that," she gestured towards the foot Alice had just propped up. "So, you're stuck with us until then," she grinned at the phrasing knowing that Alice being here was not a burden. "Why don't you relax, maybe try to sleep?"

That sounded wonderful to Alice. She was exhausted from the effort of simply getting into the house. What the hell?

Kathy was in her element, taking care of Alice and having her wife at her mercy. She made lunch and attempted to feed her wife some soup until Alice pointed out that she hadn't broken her jaw or hands and could feed herself. They shared a laugh as they chatted over the vegetable soup and crackers. A full stomach, an overcast, rainy day, and her pain meds soon had Alice dozing off again. Kathy had to help her to the bathroom and stood outside worrying that Alice might fall until she finally emerged, clumping away, using the crutches, and nearly slipping on the tile floor.

"Careful there," Kathy cautioned, standing at the ready to catch her.

Alice was amused. She hadn't seen Kathy acting this protective since the kids were little. She was rarely ill herself, and Kathy hadn't needed caring like that in years, not since she'd returned from her own kidnapping, their sojourn on the island, and its aftermath. Alice tamped down those thoughts, feeling they were better left in the past. If Kathy wanted to take care of her, the least she could do was let her.

"Thank you," Alice said as Kathy brought her a TV tray and more soup. When she tried again to feed Alice, her wife took the bowl and spoon from her and dug in, amused.

"Do you want the TV on? Some music?" Kathy asked nervously.

"No, I like the quiet. The rain sounds wonderful," she admitted. They'd had a few dry days while she was in the hospital, and she heard that the PCH was open to traffic again. The county was clearing away the landslide in record time. "Why don't you get yourself a bowl and join me?" Alice indicated the TV tray, which held more crackers than she could hope to eat.

"That's a good idea," Kathy stated, realizing she was hovering. She returned with another tray and bowl of soup plus two glasses of water, which she shared with Alice.

"Thank you," Alice said. The soup was not providing enough hydration. She was parched, and the rain was making it worse. Unfortunately, the awkward silence continued, and when Alice finally finished and Kathy took away the trays, she maneuvered herself up to use the bathroom again.

"You okay in there?" Kathy called through the door, annoyed that Alice hadn't let her help her get to the bathroom.

"I'm fine," Alice answered, not willing to discuss the fact that the meds she was on had stopped her up. She was quite uncomfortable and in a little pain. Fortunately, the liquid was flowing from her well. She took a little longer than Kathy would have liked and another knock on the door had her sighing in exasperation.

"Everything okay?"

"Fine, just finishing up," she said, using the toilet paper and flushing for effect. She'd try again later. The crutches were annoying. She was forced to move slowly and carefully, and she was used to taking long strides. She hated how they hobbled her. Still, she knew

better than to let the cast touch the floor. That previous incident had proved it was extremely painful. Once back on the couch, she was exhausted. She fell asleep and never even felt when Kathy covered her with a blanket.

"Mom! You're home!" Emily nearly shouted when she saw Alice on the couch.

"She's sleeping, Em," Kathy cautioned at the same time, but it was too late. The teen had clumped in from the rain, seen Alice, and shouted, all at the same time. "Off my carpet, young lady!" she ordered, seeing Emily was dripping from the rain. "Hello, Carmen," she added belatedly, seeing Emily's friend and simultaneously tamping down her annoyance. Something about that kid annoyed them all, but Emily continued to loyally defend her friend if anyone even suggested she wasn't very nice.

"Hello, Mrs. Weaver," she turned to Alice, smiling her fake little smile and said, "Welcome home, Mrs. Weaver. I hope you're feeling okay?" Something about her voice was just as fake as her smile, but it was smooth as silk, and butter wouldn't melt in her mouth.

Alice responded in kind, her voice carefully controlled, so the teen would never suspect she didn't mean the insincere words she was spouting, "I'm better, Carmen. Thank you."

"I'm so glad you're home!" Emily said exuberantly, her shoes now off as she rushed towards Alice.

"Careful there...the leg," both Kathy and Alice cautioned as Emily nearly sat down close enough to bump it.

"New cast?" she asked, noticing the wraps she'd had in the hospital were gone.

"Yeah, they put it on this morning."

"Oh, we should sign it," Carmen said exuberantly, her own stocking-clad feet making indents in the plush area rug Kathy had decorated the living room with.

"No, I'd rather you didn't," Alice responded dryly, trying to figure out why she didn't like this teen. Was she just reacting to the opinions of others, or was she really seeing something that bothered her? "I'd like to keep it clean."

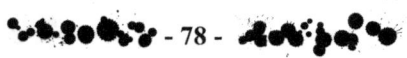

"Oh, c'mon, Mom. I want to sign it," Emily argued.

"Em, I find that tacky, and I'd rather keep it clean," she repeated, a little more firmly, and the teen subsided.

"C'mon, Emily. We have to get to work on that project," Carmen hinted, taking a step towards the stairs to the bedrooms.

"What proj–?" Emily started to ask before she looked up and caught on. "Oh, yeah." She looked back at Alice with a genuine smile. "I am glad you're home." She got up and hurried from the room. They could hear both girls tripping up the stairs and rushing to Emily's room.

"I'll bet you a hundred there is no project," Kathy said in a near whisper.

"You won't get any takers on that bet," Alice responded, wondering at the influence that teen had on her daughter. Still, it could be worse. At this age, Kit had been a target, and she'd dealt with a helluva lot more. "Where's Sean?"

"Probably at practice," Kathy murmured.

"Football is over, isn't it?"

"Basketball now," she corrected, getting up. "Do you need anything? More water?"

"Please," Alice stated, handing Kathy the glass she had been using.

Alice hobbled to the dinner table and took her customary seat at the end. She was pleased to see her whole family there, minus Kit, who would be flying back down for the holidays in a day or two. Mrs. Fernandez had made Hungarian goulash, and she served it with a type of bread akin to an Italian loaf. They could dip the bread in the sauce or put the goulash on a slice and eat it. Buttered and with garlic salt or powder, the bread was delicious and an excellent accompaniment to the goulash.

"We are going to float away if this keeps up," Mrs. Fernandez mentioned as she dished up food for the family.

"Everything okay at your house?" Kathy asked, concerned. She looked at Alice and mentioned, "Last year their house was flooded."

Alice nodded, wondering what else she had missed in the time she had been gone.

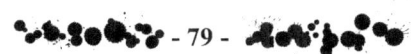

"All is good. The city put in some of those deep ditches next to the river, and it's draining well," the housekeeper answered. She went home nightly now, not even using the bedroom they had given her to use when she stayed over. The children didn't need her, and Nan was long gone. Alice would have the whole bottom floor to herself.

After dinner, Alice slowly made her way downstairs, and after homework, the children joined her and Kathy to watch some TV before heading to bed. It felt just like the old days. They had one more day of school before Christmas break, and Sean thought they wouldn't assign homework during vacation. He was wrong.

"Are you going to be okay down here?" Kathy fretted as she looked around the tiny room that had been Nan's. It was about the size of their master bathroom.

"I've stayed here before, remember?" Alice grinned as she sat on the edge of the bed. "But this time, I won't have to sleep in the closet."

Kathy laughed. Parts of the day had felt awkward, and she regretted that. Watching Alice sleep, it had hit her how close she had come to losing her wife. It was very real to her this time having seen Alice in the hospital all bruised and battered. She wondered, after all these months apart, if it was possible to fix their marriage?

Apparently, Alice was thinking the same thing as she asked, "You ever think about the fact that we are still married?"

"Yeah," Kathy admitted. She had thought of that…a lot.

"I know we are hard-headed people, but we've always been able to talk things through. We would take the time to think out our problems, discuss them, and work them out." She waited for Kathy to nod before continuing, "Do you think we were too quick to file for divorce?"

"Thanks for the we," Kathy responded with a small smile. "I know it was all me. I kicked you out when you got back, but I was so tired of the drama and worry."

"We shouldn't give up. We've invested a helluva lot in this marriage," Alice put in.

"Is that the only reason we shouldn't give up?"

Alice smiled at the challenging question. "No, maybe we shouldn't give up because we still love each other?"

"I do love you," Kathy admitted. "I feel as though I always have." She thought about everything Alice had seen her through and all they had been through, together and apart.

"Then why did you ask for a divorce?"

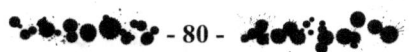

"Because I was tired of fighting the constant drama in our lives."

"You know I didn't cause all of it."

"Yes, I know that. Hell, it just seems to find you."

"Then what do you want from me?"

"An apology for starts."

"You know I would tell you I was sorry every day for years, if it would work. I can't prevent the things that happen to us."

"I suppose I need to apologize too. I need to say I'm sorry…but–"

"Kathy, if you are going to apologize and really mean it, it should never be followed by but…."

Kathy looked at her and realized the truth of the statement. Either she was truly sorry, or she was not. No qualifier was necessary. She nodded. "I am sorry. Period. The end."

Alice smiled sadly. They weren't healed, and they weren't going to just kiss and make up, but this was a start.

Kathy was surprised to find she was up earlier than Alice the next morning. She'd expected to find her wife hard at work at her computers, but instead, she found her still asleep in the servant's room. She looked tired, and that bothered Kathy, but she realized it could also be from the pain meds. Returning upstairs, she started breakfast, perhaps, stomping a little harder on the floor than was necessary. The kids appreciated a hot breakfast before they left for school. The rain had stopped, but it was cold outside, so they dressed warmly before catching rides with their friends. When Kathy went downstairs to wake Alice, she found her sitting on a desk chair with rollers, her broken leg propped on it as she used the chair to maneuver around the office.

"Are you hungry?" she asked, surprised that Alice was dressed in shorts and a sweatshirt. Then, she realized the pants they had ripped to accommodate her cast couldn't be worn all the time.

"Starving," Alice admitted as she plugged something in the back of her computer.

"They didn't set everything up correctly?" she guessed.

"Not even close," Alice laughed. "All they had to do was carry a couple things with the cords still attached. Still, they did a fairly good job," she stated and then scooted across to the other end of the desk to

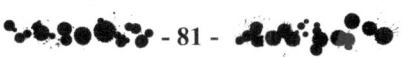

grab a zippered pouch, which she held up. "Sean remembered to bring this," she waved it towards Kathy, who came forward and opened it. "Here, you press this and this," she stated, demonstrating how to turn it on, "and this one will show you a prospect," she said meaningfully.

Kathy was confused for only a second before she realized a prospect meant a listening device or a bug, and she nodded. "Well, I'll do this after breakfast. Why don't I bring you a tray down here, so you can continue hooking your toys up and won't have to manage the stairs."

"I'd appreciate it," Alice replied with a grateful smile. It had taken her a bit to figure out how to use the office chair to accommodate the broken leg and maneuver around the room. It was going to hurt her crotch if she used it for too much longer, but fortunately, everything was almost set up. She did want to sweep the room for hidden devices. She'd gotten the last of her system connected, and the computers were firing up by the time Kathy returned with a tray, which held toast, still warm eggs, and bacon. "That smells delicious. I think you made all this to torture me," she teased.

"I forgot your orange juice!" Kathy said, placing the tray on the coffee table as Alice began to maneuver her chair over.

While lifting the dead weight of her leg off the chair, Alice nearly dropped it, which she knew would hurt. Then, she nearly fell when the weight of the cast unbalanced her. She plopped onto the couch and carefully lifted the leg onto the coffee table next to the tray before she tried to bend at the waist and reach for the tray.

"Hey, I've got that," Kathy warned her as she returned with two glasses, one containing orange juice and the other apple juice.

"I'm going to be peeing a lot," Alice stated, eying the two glasses her wife set down.

"One of these is for me," her wife admonished as she lifted the tray to put it across Alice's lap. "Eat," she ordered and then moved the orange juice within reach.

"Don't you have something to do?" Alice asked her wife as she dug into her eggs. They were light and fluffy and slightly runny, just the way she loved them, not too much salt either. She took a bite of the toast slathered with jelly, and she was pleased to discover it was cherry, one of her favorites. Kathy was spoiling her, and she loved it.

"Nope, I'm here to take care of you," she assured her, sipping at her juice.

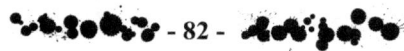

Alice was amused, wondering at that as well as the conversation they had last night. She wasn't ready to pick up where they had left off. There had been a definite rift between them, and she wasn't sure exactly how to heal it. They had a lot of talking to do, but they couldn't talk freely until they'd wiped the house once more. She wasn't certain that would wipe out all the bugs, but they could never be too careful. They'd made mistakes in the past and couldn't afford to make more in the future. The 'get out of jail card' she'd gotten wasn't permanent, and she knew someone was out there watching and waiting for her to make a mistake.

Alice watched, amused, as Kathy waved the transponder around the office, trying hard not to look awkward with her wife watching her. Normally, Alice would have done this job, but Kathy had determinedly taken the small machine and started the search for anything giving off a radio signal. This meter was very sensitive, and the computer's Bluetooth was producing false positives.

"You'll have to watch out for the router," Alice whispered, pointing to the one they kept in the corner. It had set off the meter. She nearly laughed when the bookshelf that held a new book containing a hidden backup of the computer's Bluetooth set off the meter.

Kathy nodded as she went through the two staff rooms and their bathrooms, but fortunately, the machine wasn't giving her any of the false positives it had signaled in the office. She'd seen the amusement on Alice's face, and she wasn't stupid. She knew there were probably things hidden by her wife in the office already.

Alice was hard at work on her computers when she heard Kathy heading upstairs after she finished wiping the wine cellar, the weight room, and the TV room. She'd laughed aloud when she heard the meter signal a problem with the book she had placed on those shelves too. She switched off the connection from her desk before Kathy could narrow in on it with the meter and find it. Alice heard her in the kitchen, the living room, and was able to guess where she was in the house as each door opened and shut. She had just found some information she was seeking on the computers when Kathy returned, three bugs in one hand and the meter in the other.

Alice cocked an eyebrow at them, then looked up at Kathy, who looked pale. She held out her hand, and Kathy placed them in her palm. She studied them and then crushed them with her other hand, rubbing them and smashing them with a stapler against the glass blotter on the desk. "Well, we were right to be cautious," she stated. "Where'd you find them?"

"One was in the living room, one in the kitchen, and one in Emily's room under her bed!"

"Emily's room?" she asked. They exchanged a look, both thinking about Carmen. "Do you think someone thinks Emily's the weak link?"

Kathy nodded, still pale. "I want to sweep the house again. I don't know if I got them all."

"I'm more than certain you did with that," she nodded to the meter. "That's top of the line. Did you do the cars and garage?"

"Yes, nothing."

"At least that's good."

"I got a couple of signals..." she began, looking at the shelf in the office and glancing towards the TV room.

"Yes, that's from the Bluetooth signals."

"Are you sure?"

"Yeah, I turned off the one in the TV room when I saw you were getting a signal." She indicated the computer and gestured towards the other room.

"So, you think I got them all?"

"Yes, but we should sweep once a week for a while. Maybe after Carmen visits?"

"You think that child would–?"

"You feel it too, don't you? She isn't a good friend for Emily. Even Kit mentioned it."

"Yeah," she agreed. Emily's friendship with Carmen was almost exclusive, and that wasn't good. She'd had so many other friends before that girl decided to fixate on her. "How's your work going?" Kathy gestured to the computer setups. She couldn't see the displays with the windows behind the angled desk, the glass tinted so Alice could see her screens.

"I think I might have found something, but I want to verify it before I proceed. I have some more work to do..." she hinted.

"I'm going to run this over the house once again for my peace of mind, and since it isn't raining, I'll walk around outside too."

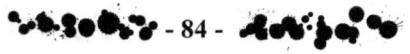

"Suit yourself," Alice told her. She knew that the meter would have already signaled if there were more. It was a powerful little gadget. It had found every single bug in the plaster of her house. She had to admit, that was a clever way to hide the bugs, and it had taken her all night to refill the holes with plaster. She wondered if her followers had been at the hospital and were here in Palos Verdes now. She recalled the electronics she'd found in the previous TVs she purchased as well as her son's reactions to her destroying the TVs. It hadn't been one of her better moments, and he'd been horrified.

About an hour later, Kathy came in with a tray loaded with sandwiches and drinks for them. "Someone in a sedan is parked on the road and watching the house," she stated as she sat down to each lunch with Alice.

"There might be a second one, so be careful," Alice warned her.

Sighing loudly, Kathy asked, "You knew?"

"Well, there were two of them when I was in Malibu."

"Two? My, aren't you important?"

Alice asked carefully, "You aren't angry?"

"No, more like resigned. It seems if you are in our lives there will always be something: some drama or someone wanting something."

"That's not true," she put in, but Kathy fixed her with a stare, and Alice started to grin. "Yeah, I guess. If I didn't have this," she indicated the cast, "I'd go confront them."

"Who do you think it is?"

"The sedan. Did you get the license plate?"

Kathy repeated it back to her. She'd read the plate while going to get the mail. Her wife had taught to be observant.

Alice nodded. Taking a bite of her ham sandwich and dipping her potato chip in ketchup, she acknowledged to herself that Kathy knew her likes. "That's the FBI," she informed her wife conversationally, gesturing with the chip.

"I thought you were off the hook?"

"I am, but who knows what they want now?"

"What do you think they want?"

"I don't know, but I am going to call Madelyn this afternoon and have her make it stop. Maybe I should call Nia too?"

"Nia Toyomoto?"

"Yeah, she does more than handle divorces from New York," Alice teased.

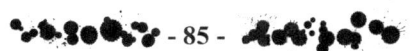

"You impressed the hell out of Portia when she learned Nia was representing you. Their firm in Los Angeles offered her a position."

"She take it?" Alice asked, surprised, then took a bite and washed it down with the water in her glass.

"No, she likes being independent. She's working out of her house."

Alice nodded, wishing their friend would take the job. But technically, she knew she couldn't since the Los Angeles office worked for Alice and was only indirectly supervised by Nia. It would be a clear conflict of interest.

Their conversations were more natural now that they knew they weren't being overheard, but who knew how long it would be before someone put some new bugs in their house?

"You said there was a second car?" Kathy asked as she finished her lunch and reached for Alice's plate.

"Yeah, it was sleeker, an Audi the last time I spotted it."

"When was the last time you spotted it?"

"The night I came over for dinner and drove home on the PCH."

Kathy got the drift right away. "Did they have anything to do with your accident?" she asked, concerned that this had become dangerous.

"I don't think an act of Mother Nature can be pinned on these guys. They could barely keep up to the Ferrari."

"Oh, Sean brought your mail over. We should have it diverted back here."

"Good idea. Where is it?"

"Top drawer," Kathy said as she took the plates upstairs to wash.

Alice made a phone call to Madelyn that afternoon.

"Alice Weaver for Madelyn Korbel please?" she said into the phone.

"Ms. Korbel is in a meeting. May I have someone else take your call?"

"No, you tell her I called, and if she doesn't want something bad to happen, she damn well better return my call soon."

"I beg your pardon?"

"You heard me, and if you didn't, you all can just play back your recording and listen." She hung up the phone, annoyed that Madelyn hadn't taken her call. How dare they set the FBI on her?

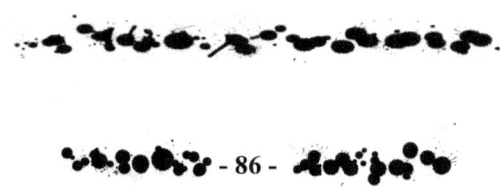

Madelyn was in one of her countless meetings, but this one was not about Alice Weaver or the many Russians they were investigating. There were other things on her desk these days, but the majority involved the piles of work that Alice's list had generated.

"Follow the money," she had told her team just that morning, and already, one of them had learned that there were too many banks involved to follow this trail. As well, some of the banks involved wouldn't share information that the agents needed, and legally, they didn't have to. Whoever had transferred the money from a couple of the dead men and women's accounts had known to never transfer similar amounts and never use the same method twice. That alone hid a lot as the money was split up.

Coming out of the meeting, she was handed her messages, and the last one had her hand shaking. The words 'something bad to happen' said a lot more than anyone else realized. Alice was probably getting pissed, and that was never a good thing. Madelyn knew she was out of the hospital and probably hard at work on the computers their people knew she had purchased.

"Hello?" Alice answered her cell, noting the unknown caller, which she normally wouldn't have answered.

"Alice, it's Madelyn. You called?" she asked, trying to sound casual. She worried that their time was up, but wasn't Alice laid up with a broken leg? *What could she do?* Then, she answered her own thought, *A lot.* Alice Weaver, with or without a working leg, could stir up a hornet's nest.

"Nice of you to return my call, Madelyn," Alice said sweetly. "You mind telling your FBI friends to stop watching my houses?"

"What? I ordered no tail," she began, lying instantly.

"Madelyn, you owe me. Let us both not forget that. That sedan is so obvious it's comical, but I'm fed up. They were chasing me on the PCH before my accident, and if I wanted to take that personally, we both know I'd be within my rights."

Madelyn swallowed. The carefully worded threat hadn't gone unnoticed. If anyone was tapping their cells, they might not pick up on that, but she was duly warned. "Noted," she acknowledged.

"I will give you a few more days to work on my information, but we both know I'm not a patient woman, and you've had plenty of time to come up with a name."

"I'll take care of it personally," she promised once again, knowing she had run out of time, and it was her own fault. Alice had certainly not given the CIA all the information she probably possessed, but the amount they had now was enough to embarrass the US government in ways that would undermine their credibility worldwide.

"Goodbye, Madelyn," Alice rang off.

"Goodbye," she returned and heard the phone cut off.

"You can't take a bath," Kathy argued as Alice inched her way up the steps, taking them one at a time.

"Look, I have to soak my pores. Those sponge baths, as much fun as they were, didn't remove all the dirt," she sounded sarcastic, but Kathy's thoughts instantly recalled the attractive doctor and subsided.

Kathy, looking at the fading bruises around Alice's neck and arms and the cast on her leg, let her go. In fact, when Alice was in their large tub with her casted leg hanging over the edge, she realized how humorous this situation was. Here was Alice, virtually helpless, and Kathy could take full advantage, if she wanted. She wanted.

"What are you doing?" Alice asked as the washcloth Kathy had been generously applying crept closer and closer between her legs.

"I think that should be obvious," Kathy answered, looking in Alice's slightly alarmed eyes. Her pupils were completely dilated, her arousal as obvious as Kathy's motions.

"Oh, yeah?" Alice challenged, then stiffened slightly as her wife dropped the cloth and her fingers began to play in the water. "You realize I'm helpless?" she asked, her voice becoming husky.

"Yes, that's where I want you."

Kathy squawked when Alice pulled her into the large tub on top of her fully clothed. In the struggle, Kathy accidentally hit the broken leg, and Alice stiffened again, this time in pain.

"Oh, God. I am sorry," Kathy said, trying to leverage herself off Alice.

"That's what we get for playing before I'm sufficiently healed," Alice said sarcastically. The huskiness in her voice was completely gone.

"Let's get your hair washed and get you out of this tub before we screw up that cast," Kathy said, getting up and climbing over the side while being careful not to touch the leg propped up on the side. Her own clothes and hair were dripping, and without another thought, she started stripping off.

"Oh, yes, let's," Alice said, amused and watching as Kathy took off her clothes.

Kathy looked up right after she had removed her panties and saw Alice's pupils were dilated again. She grinned slightly, finishing the process. While reaching for her robe, she made sure to bend at the waist and give Alice a view. She thought she heard a slight groan, but when she looked back as she tied on her robe, Alice was studying the rain that was pelting down and whipping against the bathroom windows. She moved over to wash Alice's hair, helping her get it thoroughly clean.

Getting Alice out of the tub involved a roll and a bit of a flop. They were trying to balance the casted leg without hurting her and failing. They finally got her in a robe and took a towel to her hair.

"This sucks," Alice stated, indicating her leg as she rubbed her hair almost dry. Using her fingers, she combed it, so it would stick up.

"It's life," Kathy responded, shrugging and pulling her robe tighter. She was blushing now at thoughts of her sheer audacity.

"I don't think Christmas could have been any better, but I hate that we had to take down the decorations," Kathy was lamenting a couple weeks later.

"Do you think Mrs. Fernandez minds that we cut her back to only three days a week?"

"Oh, heck no. She was talking about retirement last year, and I think this allows her to ease back slowly and still keep our house clean," Kathy laughed.

"Well, I will be glad to help a little when they let me have a walking cast," Alice complained, reaching into the cast where the hair on her leg had begun to grow, and she couldn't reach it with the damn razor. It itched horribly. The doctor said it was because the bones were knitting, but Alice wasn't so sure.

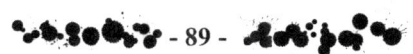

"You really gave that woman a hard time," Kathy pointed out, laughing. She had enjoyed taking Alice to the physical therapist the doctor had recommended. Alice was already asking about when she could get rid of this cast and get a walking cast.

"I want a walking cast. How is that giving her a hard time? Besides, I think she's a sadist with her stretch this and pull that bullshit. Does she realize how heavy this cast is?"

"That would be really funny if she was a sadist, and her job was to keep your muscles intact."

"No, it wouldn't! Did you see how much she liked having me try to raise my leg up above my body?"

Kathy laughed again. Alice had been working out on their equipment too and doing a lot of mumbling about getting back into shape. She'd liked seeing her wife's sweaty, glistening body, and she had worked out with Alice a couple times. They hadn't slept together yet. They just flirted outrageously and teased, but they both knew where they were headed and were enjoying the trip.

They both heard Emily come in and slam the door. She was crying, sobbing hysterically as she tried to rush by the living room and head for the stairs.

"Emily?" Kathy called, concerned.

"Honey?" Alice called at the same time.

"Just leave me alone!" she yelled dramatically as she stomped up the stairs.

The two moms exchanged looks of consternation. Kathy went to get up, but Alice grabbed her arm.

"Let me this time?" she asked as she reached for her crutches. She had gotten much better on them and easily raised herself up on her left leg, bent her right leg, and placed the crutches in her armpits.

Kathy watched as Alice made her way to the steps. She had used those steps a few times now, to get up to their luxurious bathtub, so she could soak her aching and sometimes sweaty limbs. Other times, a shower sufficed. One day, she'd hilariously slid down the steps on her butt, acquiring a rug burn in an inappropriate area and swore she'd stop that behavior evermore. This time, she grabbed onto the railing and

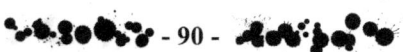

hopped her way up each step, using the crutches on one side to help her maintain her balance and keep her foot off the steps, so she didn't jar her bad leg. One by one, she hopped until she was up the stairs and could hobble on her crutches to Emily's room.

Knocking on the door, she called, "Em, could I come in?"

"I don't want to talk to anyone," the teen sobbed.

Alice's heart broke hearing her baby cry. "I just hopped up all those stairs to come see you," she guilt-tripped.

After a moment, the teen approached the door and opened it, letting Alice make her way in. Alice sat down on the end of her bed with a sigh. "There, that's better," she said, relieved. "Those steps are a challenge."

Emily looked at Alice warily. She rarely came to her room for anything good. She knew her dramatic entrance had precipitated this visit.

"Wanna tell me why I'll be replacing the hinges on the front door?" Alice opened the conversation.

Emily looked up and in Alice's cat-shaped eyes in horror, then saw the glimmer of humor and relaxed. Her own eyes were starting to curve at the corners as she grew into a young woman. She was looking more like Alice in that respect. "I had a fight," she said sulkily, looking at her quilt and starting to pick at imaginary threads.

"Anyone I know?"

Emily was agitated. She knew her moms didn't like Carmen and fighting with her best friend wasn't going to earn her any sympathy.

"Should I be oiling a shotgun?" Alice teased.

"What?" the teen looked up, alarmed.

"Well, I can't very well wrestle anyone," she indicated the cast she was wearing. This latest version the doctor had applied was an off-white color, but Alice hadn't told anyone it also had another property that was going to amuse her for the couple weeks she would be wearing it.

"No," the teen sighed loudly through her nose, exasperated at Alice's teasing. "It's not like that."

"Well, why don't you tell what it's like, so I can help?" Alice leaned forward to touch the teen's hand. "I do want to help," she said gently.

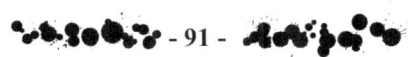

Emily heard the note of affection in her mom's voice. She knew Alice loved her just as much as Kathy did. "I had a fight with Carmen," she said, her voice still sulky.

"Was it serious?" Alice asked, and at the teen's anguished look, she corrected herself, "Of course, it was serious. I'm sorry." She sounded genuine. Alice couldn't help wondering if this would blow over with a good night's sleep. "Do you want to tell me what it was about?"

"Not really," she admitted.

"Okay," she said, surprising them both when she didn't pry. "Just know we're here if you want to talk about it." Alice reached for her crutches to leave.

Emily was shocked! She had been certain she was going to be forced to confess all. She didn't say a word as Alice hobbled out of the room. She heard her mom hobble down the hall and make her way down the steps.

"Anything?" Kathy asked. She was reading the news on her tablet and looked up as Alice made it down from the last step.

"Nope. She'll come to us when she's ready," Alice told her wife as she made her way towards the kitchen.

"Can I get you something?" Kathy called, getting up to follow her.

"I'm hungry. I don't want you to always be making us dinner, but I know I can't cook," she said, gesturing with her crutches.

"I have Mrs. Fernandez' leftover lasagna, if you're interested. There is enough for dinner tonight. All I have to do is heat it up."

"That sounds heavenly," Alice admitted, reaching for a glass and trying to open the fridge.

"Here, let me," Kathy told her affectionately, noting that Alice was getting more and more independent but still not quite up to the task...yet. She slipped by Alice and reached for the filtered pitcher they kept in the fridge to keep the water cold. She quickly filled the glass and handed it to Alice.

"I am always so thirsty; I wonder if I'm developing something."

"Like diabetes or something?"

"Yeah," Alice nodded, wondering how much she had screwed up her body with the starvation and other hardships she had endured in the past few years.

"The doctor gave you a thorough checkup when you broke your leg. Don't you remember?"

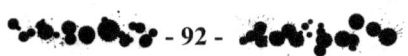

"That pretty doctor?" Alice teased and saw Kathy tense before narrowing her eyes at her wife.

"Yeah, the pretty one," Kathy said dangerously, and they shared a laugh.

Alice hobbled to the kitchen table and sat down while Kathy began to heat up dinner. They were both surprised to see Sean come home early.

"Didn't you have practice tonight?" Alice asked him, wondering if there would be enough lasagna for everyone with their son and his healthy appetite here.

"Is Emily here?" he asked, looking at his mothers and holding his gym bag over his shoulder.

"Yeah, why?" Kathy asked from where she had been checking the concoction in the oven over low heat. She hadn't wanted to use the microwave; this stuff splattered everywhere, if she wasn't careful. She'd slipped the last of the bread into the toaster, then flipped the other slices over, buttered them, and sprinkled them with a little garlic that would melt into the bread.

"Um, something happened at school today..." he began, then stopped when they all heard Emily stomping down the steps.

"Don't you tell them!" she shouted at her brother. "It isn't your place to say!"

"Emily!" Kathy said loudly over her shouting. "Lower your voice. You shouldn't talk to your brother that way."

"He's gonna tell, and it isn't his place to say," Emily asserted stoutly.

"Then maybe you should tell us," Alice said gently, watching her children closely. She could see that Sean was concerned and Emily was still upset.

"You said I could tell you in my own time," the teen responded, looking ashen.

"No, I believe what I said was that we were here to talk when you were ready. You said you had a fight with Carmen," she ignored the snort that emanated from her son, telling her that her words were correct but understated, "but you didn't mention there was an incident at school. I'd feel a lot better if you told us what happened in your own words."

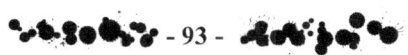

They waited a while, and finally, Emily's shoulders slumped, and she spoke in a little girl's voice that broke her mother's heart saying, "I can't."

"Of course, you can," Kathy encouraged her. "We're here for you."

Alice could see that Sean really wanted to tell them what he had heard, but she tilted her head as a sign for him to leave the room. She hoped his dirty, sweaty clothes were going in the washing machine and not remaining in that stinky bag. He reluctantly left the kitchen, and they heard him walking up the stairs. They weren't aware that he stopped on the top step and sat down, so he could listen to their conversation.

Emily could see she wasn't going to escape her mothers' looks. They were both there, expectantly waiting for her to begin. How could she tell them? It was all so humiliating. "Remember when I stayed over at Carmen's last weekend?" she began.

She looked up in time to see them both nod. Kathy had turned the oven down to a low heat and left it, so she could sit next to Alice. She had a feeling she should be sitting down for this, whatever it was.

Emily quickly looked down again. "Well, there were a couple other girls there with us, and we got to playing truth or dare."

This didn't sound good. That could be a very dangerous game. Both mothers stiffened marginally.

"Well, Carmen asked if I had ever kissed anyone, and I didn't want to admit I hadn't, so I took the dare. She made me drink this horrible alcohol she had stolen from her parents' liquor cabinet."

Alice and Kathy exchanged a look, a little relieved.

Then, Emily went on. "I didn't think anything of it as I took the shot."

"How big a shot are we talking?" Alice asked softly, wondering where this was going.

"Oh, it wasn't that big, not the whole glass," she said, indicating the glass of water Alice was drinking.

"So, say this big?" Alice indicated halfway on the full-sized glass with her finger.

"Yeah, that's it," the teen naively agreed.

Alice glanced at her wife for a second before looking back at the teen. "Did you have to take more than one shot during the course of the game?"

"Yeah, but only because I wouldn't answer the questions she was asking about you and mom."

"Like what?" Kathy asked, growing angry to hear the little twit was being so nosey.

"She just wanted to know if you two are getting back together, if the divorce is off, and how you got out of the bankruptcy." She saw her parents exchange a longer look. "Don't worry. I didn't tell her anything!"

"So, what happened at this party, Emily?" Alice asked, her voice calm, and to Kathy's ears, dangerous.

"Nothing…or so I thought. We just went to bed after a while. Then today, I saw some pictures they took of me after I went to sleep."

Kathy laughed, relieved. This wasn't so bad. "Did they draw a moustache on you with permanent ink?" she asked before she realized it would still be on Emily's skin if they had done that.

Emily shook her head.

Alice leaned across the table and reached for the teen's hand. "Emily, honey what did they do to you?"

The teen started to cry. "They took my clothes off and took pictures of me *naked*," she admitted. "I've been laughed at because I have a bush," she sobbed, gesturing towards her crotch.

Alice pulled her daughter into her arms and held her as she cried, looking over the young girl's head at Kathy, who looked on tenderly. "It's all right, baby. It's all right," she crooned, ignoring the pain when the teen accidentally jostled her broken leg. She had flinched slightly. The teen didn't notice, but Kathy saw the grimace.

"No, it's not. They shared them all over school, and now, everyone knows I have a dark bush," the teen cried, the sobs becoming more intense.

They had to wait a while for her to get out all her tears. Kathy took a turn holding the distraught teen. "You know, a lot of women still grow a bush," she tried to tell her, but she knew it was too soon. The teen thought her life was over. "It's natural, and there is nothing wrong with it."

"Who was at this party?" Alice asked, innocently, as the teen gathered her wits.

"I thought they were my friends, but they were laughing at me too, and they shared the pictures on their phones!"

"Was your face in the pictures?"

"Only on one, and when he saw that one, Josh Maclamay said I had apple titties. Oh, God! I can't go back to school!" She started crying again, tugging at both her mothers' heartstrings. She started hyperventilating, and Kathy sat her down next to Alice while she fetched a brown paper bag for the teen to breathe into. Alice held her daughter tightly in her welcoming arms. Once she had calmed again, Alice got her to give up the names of the other two girls with Carmen. She was too upset to eat, so Kathy helped her upstairs. Sean hid in his room until he heard them in Emily's room. Then, he snuck downstairs to find Alice hobbling in front of the stove.

"Here, I'll do that," he offered, seeing her trying to pull the lasagna out of the oven and hold herself up at the same time.

"Don't eat it all until everyone has had a chance to taste it," Alice teased as she went to sit back down. Once she was settled, she asked quietly, "You heard?"

He turned slightly and nodded. "I also saw a couple of the pictures. It's bad, Mom. It's really bad. Only one has her face and tits in it, but–"

Alice held her hand up. "Breasts, please," she corrected him. Slowly, she got his version of the story. The story that was circulating was that Emily willingly drank the Ukrainian or Russian vodka and had showed off for the girls. They said she was trying to entice them into kissing her and sleeping with her, just like her mothers. At least, that's what he heard was going around.

"I saw the pictures. She was laying down, and they could have placed her any way they wanted for the pictures," he told his mom sadly. "She was completely passed out, and they took advantage of her. I don't think she was showing off or asking them to kiss her. It's that Carmen bitch who is probably spreading the story along with the others."

"You looked at pictures of your sister?" Alice asked, suddenly wondering if they had more of a problem than just Emily's.

"I didn't know they were her. I haven't seen her naked since we were about six," he said indignantly. "One of the guys showed me the pictures, and after I saw them, they told me it was my sister. Then, they showed me the one with her face and tit…um breasts in it. I decked him, and they want to see you at school tomorrow," he informed her.

"I'll just bet they do," Alice murmured, wondering what the hell that meeting was going to be like.

Dinner that night with Kathy and Sean was quiet as they were all lost in their own thoughts. After Sean went up to bed, his gym clothes and bag placed in the washing machine, his mothers began to talk.

"Call Portia. Several crimes have been committed here, and I want her to look into them."

"You want me to call Portia?" Kathy asked, alarmed. She knew Portia only wanted to talk about the divorce.

"Well, she isn't going to like me asking for her advice on this. Feeding alcohol to a minor, no parental supervision, child porn, the school, whatever? We need legal advice on this," Alice warned.

Kathy finally agreed and called her friend after glancing at the clock and realizing it wasn't too late.

Portia was shocked to hear why they were calling, and she agreed to meet them in the morning before the school meeting. Neither of the kids were going to school the next day, and Alice wanted the adults to all go in together.

It was a small group waiting in the principal's office the next day. The chairs were deliberately uncomfortable as they were meant for students who waited on the principal's pleasure. Today, two parents and a lawyer waited patiently. Well, at least two of the three women appeared to wait patiently. The other one kept tapping her crutch on the floor and annoying her wife, who finally took it away. Alice continued her tapping with the second crutch, and Kathy had to take that one too.

"Really?" Kathy asked as she took the second crutch from an agitated Alice. She'd had all night to think about this and what it meant for their daughter.

Portia had come over for breakfast. She saw that Kathy and Alice were presenting a united front on this outrage for their daughter, even though Kathy told her that she and Alice weren't together. She was outraged on their behalf. Poor Emily was one of her favorite kids, and she had spent half the night looking up legal statutes about this.

"Mrs....s Weavers?" the principal stuttered, not sure how to address the two women, and looking on curiously at the woman that accompanied them. He gestured to his office and grabbed a third chair because it was apparent that all three women were coming into his office.

"Thank you, Mr. Engle," Kathy said politely. Alice hobbled by, not saying a word, but her eyes glared at the man and made him slightly uncomfortable. Portia nodded cordially but didn't say anything as he closed the door behind them.

"I'll get right to the point," the man began, trying to take control of the meeting. "Sean will be suspended for–" but he stopped abruptly as the blonde Mrs. Weaver held up her hand.

"That's bullshit! And before you continue, I want to know what is going to happen to the student who provoked him?"

"We have a zero-tolerance policy on fighting, and Sean clearly started the fight–"

"You obviously didn't investigate this matter thoroughly enough to discover the reason Sean felt he had to defend his sister. I want to know how the other students involved are going to be punished. What are you going to do about it?"

"I see no reason–"

Alice cut him off again. "Then, I think you should see a reason," she said ominously, "before I call the police."

"I don't understand. Was Sean hurt? The police? This is a school matter..." he left off as he saw her eyes were changing to an ominous yellow-orange. Surely, he was seeing things?

"Mr. Engle, is it?" Portia put in. She could sense Alice was about to let the man have it, and she didn't want Alice to ruin her opportunity.

"Yes, and you are?"

"I am the Weavers' attorney," she interjected before anyone could say anything. She sensed both Kathy and Alice were warming up. "Perhaps, you are unaware of the crimes that were committed on your school grounds yesterday."

"A school fight is hardly a crime–"

"No, but child pornography is," she interrupted him calmly and watched as he looked at her with genuine surprise.

Alice and Kathy also noted it and calmed marginally; he hadn't known.

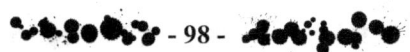

"It's obvious you didn't investigate the fight fully, and you never asked Sean why he struck the first blow. If you had, you'd know the boy in question showed him pictures of a *naked* girl. It turns out the boy identified the girl in the pictures as Emily Weaver. The pictures were taken without her consent by some girls from your school after they plied her with vodka at a social engagement in one of their homes. They admitted it."

By the time Portia finished with that recitation, Mr. Engle's jaw had dropped.

"I am asking you what you intend to do about this before we go to the police and file charges against everyone involved? You will, of course, be cited based on your actions, or should I say your inaction."

"I believe I am going to have to consult with the school board and our attorney before I say another thing," Mr. Engle stammered.

Alice made a move to get up, but Portia put her hand on her arm and squeezed.

"That is probably wise, but please be aware that you will be named in our lawsuit against the school, the girls' parents, and the boy showing the pictures since you didn't investigate this properly in the beginning. California Penal Code 311.1(a) states that anyone in possession of child pornography can be pursued criminally. Emily Weaver is underage, and as such a minor, and this constitutes child pornography. If those images were shared beyond the state of California that is a federal crime. I intend to pursue this to the fullest extent of the law."

"Now see here–" he began huffily, trying to take control of the meeting again, but Portia was ready for him.

"I suggest we call the police now and have them question the students involved. We will see what actions are necessary from a legal standpoint from there."

"I can't have the police question these students without their parents' cooperation. There are some very important–"

"I assure you, Mr. Engle, there is no one more important than my clients," her hands spread out to encompass both Kathy and Alice. Alice was glaring at the principal at this point and making him sweat. There was something about those eyes.

Alice added, "I have enough money, sir, to make sure this is pursued by every friggin' lawyer in Los Angeles, if need be."

He swallowed and grabbed his phone. "Mrs. Carlson would you please call the police and ask them to send a couple officers to the school? Never mind why! We have a crime to investigate!" He hung up the phone and sat back in his chair, feeling more helpless before these parents than he'd ever felt. Alice Weaver was making him decidedly uncomfortable. For some reason, her threat carried more weight than the lawyer's. He didn't understand why, but the lawyer seemed much less…intimidating.

The police interviewed Alice and Kathy both together and separately. Each time, Portia insisted on sitting in on the interviews. Several detectives were brought in, and they reviewed the notes and asked questions of their own. Kathy finally drove home to get their children, so they could tell their own versions of what happened. Emily pleaded with her not to force her to tell strangers what happened, but Kathy gently explained that sharing her story would protect other people like her and maybe prevent them from experiencing something similar. What Carmen and her friends had done was a crime, and the police needed to investigate it fully before it happened again and spread. The child was horrified to realize how many people out there might have naked pictures of her!

Parents of the girls accused were called. A couple showed up with their own attorneys in tow and some showed up alone.

"You may certainly talk to my daughter," one of the parents stated, "and confiscate that damn cell phone!"

Another refused because they were unsure of their child's rights without the guidance of an attorney.

With police on campus, the principal's office being used, and kids seeing parents in there, word soon spread as students speculated about what was going on. Amazingly, the kids had a lot of it right.

Sandi and Richard Pasternack refused to allow their daughter or her phone to be brought in. They also brought an attorney to the school with them. They glared at Kathy and Alice Weaver, but Alice stared insolently at them, which made them decidedly unhappy. When Carmen was brought in to her parents, she immediately went to her mother and started crying. No one had told her why she was being taken out of class, but seeing Emily and her family there, she could guess. What had started as a harmless little prank had been blown all out of proportion. She'd only shared the pictures with a few friends. She hadn't expected them to share the pictures too.

Portia had warned Alice not to say anything about the underage drinking, but the police had talked to the Pasternacks and confirmed that all four girls had spent the night at their house over the weekend and had been unsupervised for a time.

"What a mess," Alice sighed as Kathy drove them home in her car. The kids were very quiet in the back seat.

"Can we ever go back to school?" Sean asked. He still had basketball, and he'd like to finish it, but he knew he couldn't say that because it would make him sound selfish.

"We don't know yet," Kathy put in, glancing at Alice.

"It's all my fault," Emily put in, covering her face with her hands and starting to cry.

"How is it your fault?" Sean scoffed at her, annoyed with her crying. "You didn't take the pictures, those idiot friends of yours did."

"They aren't my friends," she said through her tears.

When Alice turned to try and comfort her daughter, she banged her leg on the car and winced. "Your brother is right. They shouldn't have given you the vodka or taken the pictures. This isn't your fault."

"I can never go back to school again!" she said with a hiccup through her hands.

Alice reached out and tried to hold her daughter's hand, but the angle was wrong, and she couldn't reach her when she pulled back and began to weep forlornly. She glanced at Sean, and with a roll of his eyes, he reached out and pulled his sister to him. She stiffened but then gratefully held on to him for all she was worth as she cried out her angst. The sobs were breaking her mothers' hearts.

"Technology allows crimes that are committed via social media to be prosecuted by applying existing statutes. I'm contacting the Feds since I'm certain someone from that high school has already sent it to someone out of state. It's just a matter of time before we get someone to admit it," Portia said, discussing the case with them. They had spent most of the day at the school dealing with the police and the other parents involved. One girl still had the pictures on her phone, and her father, disgusted, had voluntarily given the evidence to the police. He'd also let his daughter give a statement without having a lawyer present. The evidence was very damning to the three girls involved. "Under federal law…" Portia droned on, informing her clients how she was going to pursue their case. They were going to sue the school, the three minors involved, their parents, and most especially, the Pasternacks. They would sue not only for the porn but also for the liquor and the lack of supervision. The police would have to sort out a lot of it, but then, there would be the civil cases. Alice was furious.

"What about me?" Emily moaned repeatedly after Portia had left. She didn't want to go back to that school…ever. Everyone knew about the pictures or had seen them in some shape or form. It was humiliating.

"What about you?" Alice finally asked. "What would you like to do?"

"I want to die," the teen said dramatically.

"Well, that option is out. Why don't we plan on sending you to another school? Think about that for a while?"

"They'll know though!"

"We could send you out of state or even out of the country, if you wanted," Kathy said softly, but her heart was aching for her daughter. She'd been through so much. Those girls she had once called 'mean girls' had set her up…and for what? They were going to be prosecuted since they were all older than Emily, who was most definitely under eighteen and a minor.

"You'd send me away?" she asked, horrified.

"Nope, not if we can find some other way for you to finish high school…just not there!" Alice put in forcefully.

"Can't you do something to them?" Emily asked naively.

"What do you mean?" Alice asked, but she knew what the teen was implying. She glanced at Sean but didn't think he had picked up on anything beyond suing the parents.

Emily started to ask Alice to do something again, and then, she saw the intensity in her mother's eyes and decided not to. Glancing at Kathy, who had also gleaned what the teen was about to ask, she turned away, ashamed.

"I want to go back," Sean put in, completely uncomprehending the byplay between his parents and sister.

"Why?" Kathy asked before Alice could. She thought Alice would have come across as hostile, and she wanted to avoid that conflict.

"I'm not afraid of those assholes–" the teen began.

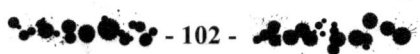

"Language," both his mothers said, looking at each other and trying not to laugh.

Sean grinned, realizing they had said the same thing at the same time. "Sorry," he apologized. "I just don't want them to think I wouldn't stick up for my sister," he put in. He'd heard about the fact that he could have been charged for assault. The parents of the boy he punched were already griping, but Portia had put an end to that nonsense by pointing out that their son had shared child pornography, and they would be lucky if the police didn't charge him.

Sean looked at Emily. She'd always been so sickly and small, and he'd really felt bad for her when she was so sick, especially when he couldn't do anything to help her because his blood wasn't even compatible. Now, this. He felt worse for her now. That damn Carmen! She had hit on him so many times. She had even asked if she could touch him. He'd been tempted but knew he couldn't do that with his sister's friend, so he refused her. It had been a near thing a few times. He'd had to lock his bedroom door when she slept over. His hormones were all over the place, and his friends were no help. They'd encouraged him to screw the girl. He was glad now that he had never touched her.

"I mean nothing against you," he said apologetically to Emily. "I think you shouldn't have to go back if you don't want to, but I'm going to show them that I have nothing to be ashamed of. You were a victim of some really mean girls, and I hope they are all expelled."

They all hoped that, but the principal was taking that under advisement. He was talking to the board and their attorneys. Alice Weaver's wealth and her threat of impending lawsuits were nothing to sneeze at. They needed to appease her quickly.

All three girls were expelled. Several other students involved had shared the pictures, and they were given suspensions—some in school and some out of school—but everyone was warned to delete any remaining pictures and not to share them further by any means. It was too late though; the damage was already done. Emily Weaver would not be returning to school, and people steered wide of Sean. As a jock, he was much more visible than his sister, and a lot of people cut guys like that some slack. As rumors spread about him beating up someone for sharing pictures of his sister, his reputation grew, and despite conversations with his mothers, his ego took a boost.

"We can't send her to a convent," Kathy hissed as they discussed where to send Emily. She had made it clear she didn't want to go back to school…ever. That wouldn't be allowed. Alice had offered to hire a private tutor, so they could home school her, but they both agreed that was not in their daughter's best interests.

"I don't ever want to send her away. I've already missed so much of her life." Alice lamented the loss of time with her daughter, and she was hurting over the whole incident. Portia had contacted the Feds and was working with them to determine which crimes to prosecute and how to proceed. The police were charging the girls and their parents and so were the Feds. It was a legal nightmare for all of them.

"I don't want to go away either," Emily put in, her eyes blood red from so much crying as they tried to sort out this situation. As she came downstairs where they were talking, she'd overheard Alice and felt bad that she was upsetting her parents.

"C'mere, honey," Alice said, gesturing to her daughter and making room next to her on the couch where she spent most of her time. She'd not been able to check her programs and do the work she had set for herself with this latest melodrama, and that was frustrating her too.

Alice had not used her cell in days, and Madelyn was growing frightened about what that might mean until her contacts in Los Angeles had informed her of the scandal involving Emily Weaver. She had stopped calling. Alice would call her when she was ready. Until then, Madelyn had a lot of work to do, so she would have answers for Alice when she called back.

"There's this school, and from everything I've seen and the people I talked to, the school seems very good. It's still here in Palos Verdes, and it's called Peninsula."

"I've heard of them. They're snobs, and the school is so small!" the teen said, outraged.

"It's close, so you wouldn't have to commute far," Kathy put in, hoping to alleviate the teen's concerns. "It is small, and they do K through twelve."

"Then everyone has known everyone for life," the teen said sadly. "I'll be an outsider, and they probably have heard about me or seen the pictures," she added miserably, hanging her head in shame.

"I've gone to the school," Kathy put in. "They are willing to take you because of your grades. They didn't mention the scandal, which will die down eventually."

"Not with you suing everyone," the teen asserted, looking up.

"How do you know that?" Alice asked.

"It's all online," she waved downstairs towards where Alice had her computers set up. "It's all there for anyone to read. Some even have accompanying pictures, if you want."

Alice looked up at Kathy. They should have anticipated that. She made a mental note to call Nia and Portia to discuss the option of shutting down those sites or going after whoever was posting that smut, but she realized they wouldn't be able to get rid of everything.

"Well, ignore it for now. You're braver than that, and we don't want you to go far away. We want you to live here at home and go to school, so we have you to ourselves for a few more years." Alice cuddled her daughter closer under her arm.

"Are you staying here then? Are you two back together?" she asked, looking up at both parents.

"We have been trying to work things out," Kathy began and looked at Alice, silently asking her to continue.

"You know we've always loved each other. We just need to figure out some things."

"Gosh, kiss and make up already," the teen said, and they all laughed.

"So, will you give Peninsula a chance?" Alice asked. She carefully schooled her face, so Emily could make the decision herself.

The teen sighed loudly and gustily. "I guess I have to go somewhere."

Her parents smiled over her bent head. That was one problem solved.

"The Pasternacks want to settle with you; they don't want to go to court," Portia told them during their umpteenth meeting to discuss the case a few weeks later. There were police lawsuits, lawsuits by the Feds, and now, civil lawsuits by the Weavers against all the people involved. The countersuit filed by one girl's parents against Alice and

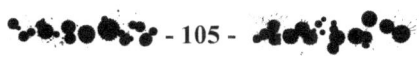

Kathy would soon be dismissed since their daughter had admitted online to her friends that she had done what she was being accused of. They'd taken screen shot evidence of her confession to Portia. They were also pursuing the sites that had posted pictures of Emily online as well as the kids who had posted them. Already, one child predator had had his parole revoked over possessing them. He claimed he had been set up, but the judge didn't buy it.

"Well, at least Emily seems to like her new high school, even if she hates the uniform," Kit told her moms as she watched Alice hobbling around on her crutches. She'd been horrified when her sister described everything that had happened. She had gone into much greater detail with her sister than she had shared with her mothers and was still confiding in her. Still, a lot had come out, and it turned out Carmen had been manipulating Emily for a while, making her do things she shouldn't have been doing. Theirs was a passive-aggressive type of relationship. Alice was horrified when Kit pulled them both aside and told them. Kathy would have gone to Emily immediately if Alice hadn't stopped her.

"She won't confide in Kit again if she knows she told us," she pointed out.

"But she did tell us and—"

"And you'll keep it to yourself. I hope that someday she feels confident enough in us to trust us with the worst of it."

Kathy sighed. Alice was right. She was usually right, and that was irksome. Things had been so dramatic for weeks and months now. Alice was still in her cast, still staying with her family, and still using her crutches. The fracture was taking forever to mend, and Alice was growing very restless.

"John asked me to meet his parents at Easter," Kit continued.

"Is it that serious?" Alice asked.

"No. I turned him down as I am not ready to do serious. I told him he could bring them by for lunch sometime on campus in a casual atmosphere, but there was no way I was going to their place for Easter."

Atta girl, Alice thought and then smiled at her daughter. "You're pretty adamant about that?"

"I have school to finish, and I don't want distractions."

Kathy shared a look with Alice. Their daughter wanted to be an adult so badly.

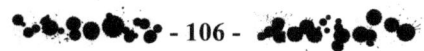

"You and Mom gonna make up and live together?" Kit asked as Kathy drove her to the airport that Sunday.

Kathy sighed again. She'd just been wondering that herself. "I don't know. We were starting to work on that when all this happened, and really, we've had no time for us through it all."

"Are you going to settle with the Pasternacks?" she asked next. She didn't know them as Emily had because they'd moved in after she left for school.

"I don't know. Portia told us to think about it. We have a pretty strong case, and they could lose a lot, but I don't want your sister to have to testify if we can prevent it."

"Wow! This is a heck of a mess, isn't it?"

"It sure is, honey. It sure is," she agreed. She was relieved when the conversation turned back to school and they could discuss the courses she was taking this final semester. As Kathy dropped her daughter off at the airport, a common occurrence now, she thanked her lucky stars that Kit didn't seem to have any drama in her life now. Kit needed normal, and Kathy hoped she had it.

Alice was back at work on her computers. She'd set up red flags for anything posted online involving Emily Weaver. Her programs did a lot more than the search engines. While engaging several search engines to look for the key words she set up, she also incorporated picture recognition software to hunt for photos of Emily. She didn't appreciate the young girl and child porn she was receiving in response to her inquiries, and she was deleting it as soon it landed in the folder she set up. It disgusted her. At another point in her life, she would probably have gone after the perpetuators of this sort of thing, but that was someone else's job. She was only concerned only with the pictures that contained Emily's nude body, and she'd seen so many. Some had been altered but were clearly still their daughter's boyishly slim body. Emily did have apple-shaped breasts forming, but in time, that would all change. Alice had attached several viruses to these photos, and she knew it was causing havoc for the perverts sharing that crap.

She'd noted that the sedan following her was now gone, but the Audi remained, and it was replaced occasionally by a Mercedes Benz that she'd traced to a shell company here in Los Angeles. She'd had Google Maps look it up, and she'd gotten a view of the place, but it would require a personal visit because they had no computer lines she could tap into. Alice looked at her broken leg, dismayed that the complications thus far had stretched out the original eight-week prognosis. She was sick of using the crutches, and it was making her decidedly touchy.

Iggy thought back to the recent conversation with his boss. "You aren't producing as well as some of my other men. You need to step it up," Artum had told Iggy conversationally. There was a hidden menace in the warning, and they both knew it. Either he brought in more, or he would be terminated.

"I will," he had promised, wondering what he could do to satisfy his boss. Things had gotten lax since Sebastian had fallen ill, and now, they were all chaffing under the tightening knot around their necks. They had sworn loyalty to this man after Sebastian realized he was failing.

Gathering his crew, Iggy outlined what he wanted them to do but told none of them who owned the house they were going to hit. There were four in the crew including Iggy. They all wore black as they crept up on the house. The electricity was cut, but they didn't know there was external, uninterruptable power sources within the house, which backed up the computer, the security, and many other functions throughout the home. As they approached, they were observed and photographed. They had been anticipated.

With Kathy's help, Alice had set up some new perimeter video monitors on the property. It was difficult because Alice couldn't move, and Kathy didn't understand about line of sight and other installation factors, but they managed to install the new cameras on the property. It was these motion-sensitive cameras that alerted Alice and Kathy to the presence of intruders that night. As the men advanced on their home, both their phones and Alice's computers began recording and sending pictures to the cloud. Because the electricity had been cut, they couldn't press their panic button to alert the alarm company. Also, because the electricity had been cut, the alarm company had already been notified of an outage and were on their way to investigate.

The men were bold, Alice had to give them that as she watched the videos after the fact. She sat on the couch across from Kathy in a chair, and both were riveted watching the action picked up by the cameras. The intruders came right up to the front door and used a post driver to splinter the expensive and formerly beautiful front door. As a home invasion, the element of surprise had failed because of their cameras.

The men started shouting, and Alice wondered if they realized they were shouting in Russian. Kathy's eyes nearly bugged out of her head as she stared at the intruders who easily woke the children. Sean and Emily came running down the stairs, and the men shoved them towards their parents.

"You! Stay!" the tallest and broadest man ordered in English.

Emily ran to Alice who held her close while watching the men and wishing she could get up.

"No!" Kathy grabbed Sean's arm when he would have lunged at the man. She could see his gun even if the boy could not.

"Don't move," one of the men said as he advanced on the teen, and without any warning, he smacked the boy upside the head. Sean's head flew to the side, and he hit the ground. The butt of the gun inflicted a laceration about two inches long that immediately started to bleed.

"No!" Kathy screamed, anguished to see her son struck down. He got up almost immediately, but at a gesture from Alice, he sat back down. He was seething with anger as he wiped at his throbbing wound.

Two of the men were shining flashlights around and began to grab trinkets and anything of value they could put into bags.

"Where's your money? Where's your safe?" one of the men asked Kathy in a thickly accented voice. They laughed when they saw Alice was laid up and looked helpless. Her leg was propped up on cushions as she held Emily in her arms, and her glow-in-the-dark cast, which had provided her with much amusement the past couple weeks, emitted an odd hue in this light and made her appear even more vulnerable.

Kathy exchanged a look with Alice, and she nodded slightly. They hadn't armed the bear trap in the safe this time, and perhaps, they should have. Still, if they cooperated, maybe the men would leave quietly. Kathy made to get up, and one of the men said something derogatory in Russian as he shoved her.

The two who were filling their sacks went upstairs. They shone their flashlights in the rooms one by one as they searched for valuables. They tossed all the rooms, even Kit's, which was obviously not in use.

"M…m…mom?" Emily stuttered.

"It's all right, honey. We are going to be okay," Alice assured her, rubbing her back as she stared at the man who was guarding the three of them. She might not be able to see the full face beneath the mask, but she would recognize his build and his eyes. There were other telltale signs he was giving off, but only someone with Alice's unique powers of observation would realize that.

Two of the men returned before Kathy and the other man, and Alice worried about what they were doing in the other room. Had he done something to her wife?

"What is up with her?" One of the men gestured towards Emily, who was shaking and in shock. She was rubbing her arms and starting to rock in her mother's arms.

"Not much meat on that one's bones," the other one joked.

"Still, they all look alike in the dark," the first one quipped, and they laughed.

They were speaking Russian again, but Alice never flinched or blinked as she stared at the three of them, memorizing body size, stance, and gestures. She would recognize these men if she saw them again. She *had* to recognize them.

"We should take these women and sell them. There wasn't much here to steal," one of the men said to the guard.

"Those two women are too old, and that young one is too skinny!" he replied.

"We could fatten her up, eh? She might be a good whore, and I know someone who would pay big money for one as young as this."

They laughed again as they commented more and more about Emily, laughing about what they would do to a girl as young as she in such a place. Alice's eyes turned from yellow to orange and back again as she contemplated their deaths.

Kathy returned, and the man showed the others the cash, which he stuffed in one of their sacks. The three of them hefted the sacks they had collected and were getting ready to leave.

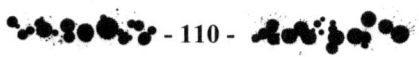

"You will do nothing, and you will tell no one," the big burly man told them. He was obviously in charge, and he ordered the men about in Russian. Alice narrowed in on the black track suit he was wearing. He produced a roll of duct tape and started with Sean, taping him to the chair he was sitting in and putting tape over his mouth. Next was Kathy, and he forced her down in a chair. He gestured to Emily, who shook her head. She wasn't leaving the protective arms of her mother.

"You! Come here now!" he ordered the young teen, and she shook her head again. He took three strides and ripped her from Alice's arms, grabbing her arm and pulling her up forcefully. She screamed as he began to frisk her, unnecessarily feeling her up as he held her to him and laughed. He was making crude remarks to the other men who were laughing and enjoying this display. He made sure the teen struggled against his much larger body, enjoying the scuffle. He taped Emily to a chair, easily overpowering the young woman, and then, he contemplated Alice. The glow-in-the-dark cast she was wearing amused him.

As he was walking by her on the couch, she casually leaned down and rapidly brought her crutch up. In mid-stride, it struck him squarely between his legs, and he went down like a sack, clutching his crotch. Alice had waited for this moment, and she quickly reversed her crutch to come down on his neck. She leaned her weight on it, and he started gasping for air and grabbing at the aluminum supports. "You may have won this round, *comrade*," she said in clearly enunciated English, "but you have not won the war."

Two of his men dropped the sacks they had hefted, the glass items in them breaking when they hit the floor, and they leapt to help. They pushed Alice back on the couch, and her broken leg came down on the coffee table edge, causing her excruciating pain. She gasped at the sharpness of the pain, hearing Emily's sobs and Sean's frustrated breathing. She exchanged a look with Kathy before the blow to her cheekbone caused her to black out. She knew nothing until she heard sirens faintly in the background and woke to find security officers in the living room. There was no sign of the men who had invaded their home.

The police arrived, closely followed by an ambulance for Alice. Alice refused to leave even though her cheekbone was bleeding and her leg cast was splintered. A statement was given, and their house was completely searched and processed. Kathy promised to follow with the

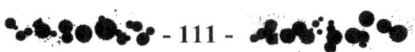

kids if only Alice would go to the hospital. Alice's family followed the ambulance in the Lexus after they had locked up, such as they could with the splintered front door. Two officers had to be stationed outside the front door since it was now useless. The men had left the post driver by the door, but unfortunately, they had been smart enough to wear gloves and there would be no fingerprints. Alice gladly turned over the security tapes they had captured in the home security system, not mentioning the cloud recordings they could access from their phones. The police discounted Alice's assertions that the intruders were Russian nationals as Alice didn't tell them she had understood what they said, and the other three victims' accounts didn't clearly identify the intruders either.

Alice was released from hospital the next morning. She had tape on her cheekbone that matched the tape on Sean's head. He had refused to let the doctors stitch his wound as he didn't want a scar, and Alice had laughed at him although she did the same on her own cheekbone. They both looked a mess as the bruises began forming, and Alice's new cast fit in well with its brilliant and obnoxious purple color.

"Okay, you guys. No more hospitals," Kathy ordered as they surveyed the damage to their persons. Later, they also gauged the damage at the house.

The insurance company was called, and a master craftsman came to assess the front door. In the meantime, they placed heavy plastic against the door to keep out the rain and wind drafts, and they nailed some plywood over the space while he made them a new door.

"Mom can I talk to you both?" Emily approached them where they sat in the living room going over the list of stolen items a week later. The insurance company had disputed their first list, but fortunately, Alice had pictures on her computer of the valuables that needed to be replaced. There were things like Waterford crystal, an original Van Gogh painting, and various sentimental items.

"Sure, honey. What is it?" Kathy asked, looking worried. They both knew that Emily had gone through a lot in a very short time.

"I want to talk about the other night," she began, a quiver of nervousness in her voice. "I've never felt so helpless before in my entire life," she finally admitted, wringing her hands. "That stuff that Carmen and the others pulled made me feel vulnerable. They took advantage of me when I was helpless, but they didn't touch me like *he* did. They touched me here," she pointed to her head.

Kathy made a move to go to Emily, but Alice waved her back. She wanted to hear what their daughter had to say, and she could see the kid had worked herself up in order to talk to them.

"I don't ever want to feel like that again. *Never!*" she said fiercely.

"Do you want therapy?" Alice asked, carefully.

"No, I want you to train me. I know you used to work out, and you know karate or something, don't you?" Emily looked straight in Alice's eyes. The color of their eyes didn't match, but the shape was becoming similar.

"Or something," Alice admitted, glancing at Kathy, who looked horror-struck. "Just because I know martial arts doesn't mean I could have done anything." Alice gestured to her latest cast, something the doctor had said might set her recovery back by weeks or maybe months. She wasn't thrilled with that prognosis.

"But you have confidence, which is something I'm lacking. I was so scared, Mom. I wanted to pee myself. I don't want to be scared anymore," she admitted, sounding like a small child instead of a teen on the cusp of womanhood.

"I don't know, honey. That was a long time ago and–"

"No, Mom. If you won't train me, then I want to take classes. Someone will train me," she said fiercely. "I want to learn."

"But a martial art isn't going to prevent people like Carmen taking advantage of you," Alice pointed out.

Emily looked hurt for a moment, and Alice would have taken it back if she could have. Instead, Emily surprised her with her response. "I might not have even taken that drink, knowing what I know now. You don't drink often, and you never let yourself lose control," she pointed out.

Alice glanced at Kathy, who looked as surprised as Alice felt. Their little girl had done a lot of growing up. They had both heard the screams as their little girl combatted her nightmares. Kathy had gone to her, woken her, and held and rocked her like a little girl several times since the home invasion. She would have done anything to give her daughter back her innocence.

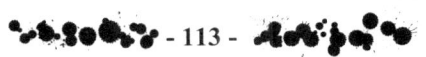

"Well, I can't do anything in this condition," Alice said, spreading her hands and indicating her broken leg. It was taking a long time to heal.

"Okay, but can you tell me how to start?"

"You start with your mind. Learn everything you can…" Alice began, hoping to dissuade her daughter from the physical side of her plan.

"I'm already an A student," Emily pointed out.

"Then take languages and learn what you can from other cultures."

"How will that help me defend myself?" the astute teen asked.

"Knowledge is power." Alice held up her hands in surrender at the teen's suspicious look. "Seriously, as cliché as that sounds, it's true. I understood exactly what those men were saying tonight. I didn't let on, so they continued speaking in their language, and that will give me clues to help figure out who they are."

"Why didn't you tell the police?" she asked.

"Because, they would have gone after some very dangerous men, and I want to be the one to find them and deal with them," she thought. She wanted to tell her daughter but refrained. "Because I'm not certain of everything I heard, and the police would have wanted to know how I learned the language," she told her instead.

"Is it because of the time you spent in Russia?" Emily asked, referring to the things she had overheard and directly addressing information she had been prevented from asking about before by her mothers.

"Yes," Alice admitted but wouldn't tell her more. She could see Kathy was looking stricken, ashamed that their daughter knew too much, and she didn't want to upset Kathy further. "So, back to what I was saying. Take languages, take computer, math, and the sciences…learn. You must be able to outthink an enemy."

"How did that help you tonight?" the teen asked flippantly, then realized how saucy she sounded. "Sorry."

"No, you have a valid point. I couldn't do much with this," she indicated her leg. "But maybe, someday, I will be able to do something. Until then, my brain is going to work." She gestured towards the office downstairs, then drawing her crutches to her, she got up, indicating the conversation was over.

"Did I upset her?" Emily asked Kathy, who had gone back to working on the paperwork the insurance company required.

 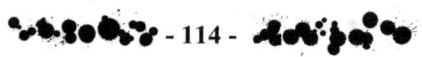

"A little," Kathy admitted, looking up. She would bet she was a lot more upset than Alice was. "She was frustrated that she couldn't defend you against men like that." She'd seen the look on Alice's face and how Emily had fought against her attacker. She had been completely defenseless against his strength and his desire. Even Sean had wanted to attack in defense of his mothers and sister. Kathy had been thinking about this intrusion a lot. A home invasion violated more than the home; her mind was a whirl. For the first time in a while, her home was not safe; it was not impregnable. Those men had busted in and touched her children. She leaned back away from the insurance paperwork. She didn't care about the things they had stolen.

"I didn't like it either, but why won't she train me?"

"Because, like me, she probably doesn't want you to have to learn those things."

"You don't?"

Kathy shook her head. "I don't want you to know that there are men like that in the world and there are women like Carmen in the world. I'm sorry. I feel like I have failed you."

"But don't you see, Mom? We had no way to know those people would come into our lives or what they were really like. I want to be ready if that should ever happen again."

"We'll see," Kathy said, non-committally, and the teen had to be happy with that semi-promise.

Kathy waited until she heard Emily go back up to her room before she made her way into the kitchen. Mrs. Fernandez had helped them inventory some of the losses and clean up the mess the men had made. They had broken some things just because they could. These items were not of any real value and they had simply broken them because they wanted to be vicious. She had lost things, but her most valuable possessions—her family—were still alive. After taking a quick look around and obsessively checking the doors leading to the balcony, she made her way downstairs to where Alice was typing away on her computer.

"Hi there. Emily get to bed?"

"Yep, I think so. I also think she's making friends at the new high school."

"I hope so," Alice said. The weeks had started to blend, and she had worried excessively over sending her to a new school. Sean had confided that Emily's name was a touchy subject at his high school, but his friends had banded together, and anyone who dared disparage her or the Weaver family had to answer to them.

"Whatcha working on?" Kathy asked playfully, wishing they could get back to the seduction she had planned before everything went to hell.

Alice smiled a little, hearing that special note in Kathy's voice. "Something I was looking at before Carmen disrupted our lives."

"That thing you called Madelyn about?"

"Well, that too. You noticed the sedan is gone?" she pointed out again unnecessarily. Of course, she had noticed.

"Yeah, but between that Mercedes and Audi, we still have someone watching you," Kathy pointed out in return.

"I may have an answer, but I'm going to leave this program running tonight and see if I can find…" she began musingly as she typed a little more and then looked back up. "I'm beat. Want to go to bed?"

Kathy raised her eyebrow. "My bed or yours?"

"Really? Are you ready for that?"

"No, but I could use a damn good cuddle, and if I remember right, you're a good cuddler."

Alice smiled. It was baby steps like this that meant the world to them. She got up on her crutches, turned out the lights, and left her computer running on the program she hoped would give her some vital information tomorrow. Alice and Kathy went together into the servant's bedroom and cuddled the heck out of each other.

Alice knew Kathy was gone the moment she woke up. The other side of the bed was long cold, and it disappointed her. They'd kissed, only for a moment, and they had fallen asleep just cuddling. It had been pleasant, and she thought they were both happy with how the evening had gone. She rolled over, the heavy cast on her leg hitting her other leg painfully with its weight. Then, she realized it was much later than she had originally thought when she gazed upon the clock. No wonder Kathy was long gone. She'd have had to drive Emily to school, and if Sean hadn't caught a ride with a friend, she would have taken him to the public school afterward. They made sure not to add to Emily's stress by taking her anywhere near the old high school.

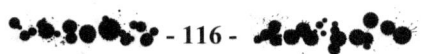

Alice slowly rose, reaching for her crutches and making her way into the bathroom. As she was sitting there making her stream, she remembered the program she had left running overnight. She hurried through her morning absolutions, not bothering to take off her pajamas, and made her way to the office.

She went through everything the program had found, carefully cross-referencing the information, and the blood drained from her face when she had verified the data. She reached for her cell phone and returned one of Madelyn's many phone calls. She was pleased when the woman picked up on the second ring since it was four hours later in Virginia.

"Alice, I'm so glad you called. I have that information I promised you."

"Senator–" was all Alice managed to get out before the line made a horrible squawking noise in her ear, and she knew that Madelyn could no longer hear her.

~The End~

❖ MILITARIAL MALICE ❖

BOOK 28

Alice's unfinished business has caused her and her family a lot of unforeseen aggravation, and Alice seeks to make amends. But it seems life isn't finished with her yet. Just when Alice thinks they're about to be happy again, life throws her one more curve, and this one is a doozy!

"Madelyn, can you hear me?" Alice called into the phone, only to hear it squawking horribly again. She knew that sound, so she hung up and immediately started typing on her computer. She was quickly firing up another computer to send a cross connection and scramble the signals in the house.

"Alice, what's wrong with my cell phone?" Kathy asked as she brought down a tray with Alice's breakfast. She had the tray in one hand and was holding up her phone with the other, a questioning look on her face.

"Someone is *deliberately* scrambling our signal," she said as she typed rapidly. "Try using it now," she said as Kathy set the tray down on the edge of desk. "Never mind," she said when her own phone started ringing.

"Alice? Did you hang up on me?" Madelyn asked worriedly from across the miles.

"No, someone was listening and scrambled my signal here. I was asking you if it was Senator Ken Edwards' name you found in your information?"

Kathy's head snapped up from where she had been looking at her phone. She knew that name, but she had only heard it in passing, and it had been before she and Alice got together.

"Yes, but how did you–?" Madelyn asked and then stopped herself as she realized who she was talking to.

"Thank you, Madelyn. Your debt is paid." She went to hang up, but the CIA operative stopped her.

"Wait, Alice. I need more…" the woman began, and when Alice heard her, she stopped her finger from disconnecting the call.

"No, Madelyn. We're even. You took too long, and I discovered the information for myself. If anything, I would say you still owe me," Alice pointed out, wanting to bank future points in case she needed a favor. She never knew when that might be necessary.

"I tried–" she began, but Alice interrupted her.

"You failed." They both knew Alice was right.

"Do you want my help with the school–?"

"Already too late on that."

"How about the home invasion?"

Alice knew she was being monitored since the agent had that tidbit of information too. "Again, *too late*."

Madelyn sighed. That tone of voice could mean many things. She knew Alice had more material, and Wolfe was not going to be happy if she didn't get it from her. A lot of Madelyn's job was playing a waiting game, and all she could do was offer help in exchange for information. "Well, you know I'm here if you need–?"

"Yes, I have *your number*," Alice interjected, smiling at the double entendre and hanging up the call.

"Senator?" Kathy asked as soon as Alice was free.

"Well, senator no more," she pointed out.

"But…?"

"Remember the husband and wife team that were involved with Connie?" Alice asked her wife, watching her reaction to the question.

Connie had been one of the four amigos back in college. There had been Kathy, Portia, Andie, and Connie Weaver, Alice's twin sister. They'd all attended college together at Stanford while Alice went to Harvard back east. The name of Alice's sister invoked a lot of pleasant memories for the now much older woman. Their oldest daughter, Kit, was attending the same college Kathy had attended, and she was having some of the same experiences. "But after all these years?"

"I'm betting that Audi," Alice nodded her head to indicate the car that was parked regularly on the street, "has a triangulation gadget and is scrambling our phones if we mention his name, which just happened. Where's the meter?"

"Will that…?" Kathy started to ask as she went to the bookcase to retrieve the meter.

"No, but I want to sweep the house again. We had a lot of people through here with the home invasion."

Kathy agreed, and with Alice watching, she swept the office. "Wasn't the senator in prison?" she asked as she worked. Alice turned off the router, so it wouldn't send out false signals.

"He might be out," she answered, realizing she hadn't kept up on that situation.

She could see Kathy had finished scanning the TV room and was heading for the exercise room. Alice had spent a lot of time in that room recently, working out and bringing her body back to a level of fitness she had missed. With her weight gain and enforced inactivity, she felt she had been losing muscle mass for a long time. She intended, especially once her leg was healed, to get back into shape and was working daily towards achieving her goal. Her physical therapist had noted the tightening of Alice's muscles all around the leg and worried that she was working the healing limb. Alice assured her she wasn't, and that was the truth. She *had* tried, but it hurt too much.

Kathy returned half an hour later after sweeping the entire house and even taking a walk around the perimeter. The meter hadn't measured any listening devices other than the small night vision cameras they had installed themselves.

"Okay, we can talk," Kathy announced as she placed the device back on its shelf.

Alice looked up from her computer. "Apparently, Ken Edwards got out of jail a few years ago and wants revenge. At least, I think he wants revenge since he seems to be behind the bozos who scrambled our phones when his name was mentioned this morning." She indicated the cell phone and her computers where she had gotten the information that Madelyn just confirmed. "That means they are listening to our phone calls for any sign that we know his name, and *now*, he knows."

"What does that mean?" Kathy asked, but in her heart, which was sinking at the news, she already knew the answer.

"He is going to assume that I am coming for him."

"And are you?"

"I have some research to do first." Alice indicated her computers, then she also pointed at the cast on her leg. It felt like her leg was taking forever to heal, and it was annoying the heck out of her. They hadn't given her a walking cast yet, and she was still forced to hobble around on crutches.

"I wouldn't have thought he'd ever get out of prison," Kathy mused, remembering what little information Alice had mentioned about him over the years. She knew they had all been saddened by the loss of Constance, Connie as she was known to her loved ones. Kathy had often wondered about her friend but never asked Alice about Connie's habit of attracting rich men into her life. Connie's dead body had been dumped in her house, if Kathy recalled correctly. Alice had found her sister, and her subsequent investigation had led to the senator and his wife, also a senator. Apparently, Ken had killed his wife plus Connie and several other women. Kathy wasn't about to bring up that painful memory with Alice, even if she was a bit sketchy on some of the details.

"Well, with *good* behavior, he must have come up for parole," Alice murmured as she thought about the fact that she had missed this detail and allowed the senator live, even if it was in prison. It had been so many years, and she never suspected the man might look her up and cause the disruption in her life she now suspected he was behind. All their problems with the IRS and the police might have been instigated by tips from this man and his friends. She was certain he had influenced all the right people, many who might believe his story that he had been unfairly convicted. Still, he had been a powerful man, and he would have maintained his contacts. Her eyes narrowed as she contemplated what she already knew and what she still had to investigate.

"You think he was involved in the home invasion?"

"No, that wasn't him," Alice said with absolute confidence.

"No? How do you know?"

"Do you *really* want to know?" Alice asked, raising a brow and wondering if this was going to be the straw that broke the camel's back for her wife. They had been working on repairing their marriage, and they had to do something about the divorce, or the courts would dissolve the paperwork, and they'd be back at square one if they wanted to proceed after all.

Kathy thought about the question and nodded. It was important that she know what was coming that might affect their family. She should prepare herself for it, so she could do what she needed to protect them. Alice was good at solving this sort of thing. She'd take the battle to them and their enemies.

"Remember Sebastian?" Alice asked conversationally, leaning back in her chair with her leg propped on a footstool. Her leg was itching again, which supposedly meant it was healing. She was certain the itching was caused by the dark hairs she could see growing in the cast as well as all the castoff skin that was building up from the daily shedding her leg was doing as it healed. She'd seen what her foot looked like the last few times they'd changed the cast; it was gross with the buildup of dead skin at the bottom.

"Isn't he dead?" Kathy asked, thinking she'd heard Alice mention that.

Alice nodded as she remembered the funeral she had attended before her accident. "He left an heir, and I believe his heir may have had his people pay us a visit. I'll be looking into that when this is better," her hand swept across her leg indicating the cast and the underlying break.

Kathy nodded. That home invasion had been terrifying, not knowing if the men were going to physically hurt them or the children. Fortunately, the ten thousand dollars in their safe had seemed to satisfy the men. What she really hated was how their assault had affected Emily, who was now obsessed with defending herself and never allowing herself to become a victim again. Kathy knew Emily was reacting more to the betrayal of Carmen and her other friends than the home invasion, but having that man touch her had really frightened the young teen.

Had Kathy known what the men were saying about their daughter, she'd have been even more furious. Alice had understood their Russian comments and knew Kathy would have been just as murderous in her thoughts as Alice was when she heard them.

Alice had a lot of planning to do, and her leg was hampering her physically and mentally. In her mind, these people were already dead. It was just a matter of how and when Alice would bring about their deaths. She turned back to her 'research' on the computers.

It had been months since Alice broke her leg in the landslide on Malibu's Pacific Coast Highway. As Kathy drove her to check on her house, Alice looked over where the hillside had come down. She saw very few signs of the mud and rocks that had rained down and enveloped her Ferrari that night. The insurance had paid for the expensive sports car but only time would heal the injuries. There were no signs left on her skin of the bruising the rocks had caused, and the abrasions had long ago healed, so the cast on her leg was the only remaining evidence of the long-ago near tragedy.

"Penny for your thoughts?" Kathy asked, seeing Alice so still. She wasn't agitated, which would have been a better sign.

"I'm thinking that California does a good job of erasing things," she admitted cryptically.

Kathy gulped. Although she knew Alice had justified the many killings she had committed over the years—hell, Kathy had participated in several of them—she still couldn't get past the fact that her wife was

a serial killer. She wasn't your *average* serial killer with a pattern or a compulsion to kill. It was more like her justification to right the wrongs of her world. Now, according to what Kathy knew, there were a couple more people in Alice's crosshairs, and it was only her broken leg that was preventing her from carrying out even more killings. Kathy always worried that Alice would screw up and get caught, and then, she would have to watch as her wife was given the electric chair or a lethal injection for her crimes. Alice wasn't perfect. She had complained about getting older, but so far, they had been very, *very* lucky that she hadn't been caught.

The house in Malibu was in order. It was a bit musty from the windows being closed and locked, but nothing seemed out of the ordinary. They opened the windows while they were there to catch a cross breeze. They'd brought the meter to test the house for bugs and found nothing. Apparently, since Alice's main residence had moved back to Palos Verdes, so had her followers. Madelyn had gotten the FBI to stop tailing her, but she could do nothing about Ken Edwards' flunkies. If Alice had asked her for that favor, she would have used her position in the CIA to make it stop, but Alice wouldn't ask. They both knew Alice would handle it herself in her own unique way. Already, Madelyn had people watching the ex-senator, who was now some sort of motivational speaker earning a pittance compared to the hundreds of thousands, maybe even millions, he had earned back in his days as a senator alongside his wife. They had been the golden couple and were compared to the likes of the Kennedys. Their deviant lifestyle had been the death of them after they killed Alice Weaver's sister, Constance.

"Why don't you put this place on the market?" Kathy asked as Alice clumped around checking the less obvious locks she had installed versus the locks that were blatantly obvious to the casual observer. She shut the windows again and made sure their locks were in good shape.

Alice stood up, balancing on her crutches as she looked at her wife "in name only." They had yet to become physically intimate again since Kathy had asked her for a divorce so many months ago. "I don't think we're there yet, are we?"

Kathy flushed. So much had gone on in their lives since Alice's accident, and they hadn't yet moved beyond the point of being anything other than housemates, although the children were happier they were all under the same roof. Even Kit had commented on it when she came home for visits, but they weren't yet wives in every sense of the word.

"No, not yet. I guess not," she admitted ruefully and let the subject drop.

Alice climbed the much steeper stairs of her house, one awkward step at a time, and she checked all the rooms on the second floor. Glancing at the unused gaming set-up gave her an idea, and she fired it up as she continued looking around the other rooms. She was checking for something...anything out of place. When she returned to the gaming room, she also started up a game she had enjoyed with her son, one that allowed instant messaging between the players. She left a cryptic message for someone on the game, which would set something in motion and would be waiting for her when she chose to return and receive her own messages. It was something she had set up previously as a safeguard to avoid being watched. Many people were watching her, but they were looking at the more obvious computers, which Alice Weaver and her investments were known for. After shutting down the game and the gaming computers, she made sure everything else was off in her son's room before she carefully descended the stairs and found her wife looking out at the gorgeous Malibu beach. It was a cold, brisk spring day, but the sky was clear and sunny with no signs of rain. The wind had blown away the storm clouds and people were taking advantage of this break in the weather to walk the beach.

"This is such a pretty view," Kathy commented as she heard Alice and her crutches clumping up behind her.

"Yes, it is," Alice admitted, looking out.

They didn't need to say more. They'd been married a long time and understood what the other was thinking without spoken words. It was a comfortable silence each had missed in her own way, not realizing until that moment they hadn't had it for a while. Being together like this and enjoying the beauty together was enough...for now.

As they drove home with the ever-present Audi behind them, Kathy got mad and sped up.

"Careful there, Mario," Alice teased, wishing she was behind the wheel.

"Why can't they just leave us alone?" Kathy lamented angrily. She passed several people only to find herself stuck at the back of a long line of cars. The Audi effortlessly kept up with them, allowing just enough distance between the cars that it would not be obvious to the casual observer. Alice was not a casual observer and Kathy was aware of them now too.

Alice waited to confirm that the Audi was passing some of the same cars Kathy had passed. "Pull onto this road *NOW!*" she told Kathy suddenly.

Surprised, Kathy instinctively listened to her wife and spun the wheel, nearly cutting someone off and causing a pedestrian that had been about to cross the street that intersected with PCH to pull back in alarm.

"Go down there and quickly back into the first driveway," Alice pointed. She looked back to see if the Audi had seen where they turned.

Kathy was busy doing what Alice had commanded. She was amused at this game of cat and mouse. She too wished Alice was driving, but she had really enjoyed that Alice relied on her to cart her around to appointments and such. She only regretted that Alice wasn't yet in good enough shape to stop the people who had been following her for so long. She remembered how impressed she was when Alice broke the undercover officers' window with a rock when they were watching the women's house.

They both sat in the car and listened to the engine humming quietly as they waited…and waited. Eventually, the Audi sped past them on its way down the road. "Wait…" Alice cautioned, putting her hand on Kathy's arm when she seemed about to put the car in gear. She waited two minutes before she let go of Kathy's arm and nodded. Kathy inched out of the drive she had backed into and looked both ways, but she saw no sign of the Audi.

"You know, they'll just go to the house in Palos Verdes and wait for us?" she asked dryly.

"Yeah, but it will unnerve them that we got away so easily," Alice pointed out with a laugh. "It's a head game, which I think is overdue. Why don't we stay away for a while? Is Mrs. Fernandez at the house today?" At Kathy's nod, Alice asked, "Why don't we go out for dinner? I'm sure the kids will be okay if they come home and we're not there."

Kathy was thrilled with the idea. It had been a very long time since she had been on a date with Alice. They were both dressed casually. Alice wore her ripped pants that fit over her cast and a jean-jacket with a t-shirt underneath, and Kathy had on casual jeans and a quilted jacket over a button-down shirt. "Where should we go?"

"How about a drive-in?"

"Theater?" Kathy asked, confused.

"No, something like Sonic or another fast-food place, if you prefer. Surely, Los Angeles has plenty of drive-ins like that around."

They ended up going to the drive-in chain, Sonic, where they both had bright, colorful drinks, hamburgers, and fries. They talked like they had in the olden days. It had been a long time since they treated themselves to a date, and they both thoroughly enjoyed it. It was quite late when they arrived home, and the familiar Mercedes was waiting at the side of the road in place of the Audi. The two occupants tried to duck and avoid the headlights of the Lexus and failed. Alice laughed at her watchers as she and Kathy drove by, the gates of the Palos Verdes estate closing firmly behind the sporty Lexus.

Director Wolf was not a happy man. They had invested months of investigation using teams of people in cooperation with the FBI, and they hadn't gotten much on the people that Alice Weaver had brought them. Yes, they had reams of paperwork on these families and extensive biographies, but the only thing these people had in common was they were all wealthy, linked to the mob, and dead. Try as they might, they had found no proof that Alice Weaver or Sasha Brenhov were connected to those deaths. Some of the properties these people had previously owned were now owned by the Brenhov holdings, but that was inconclusive. Some of the properties had been owned before, so there could have been a sale and a resale. The agency simply didn't know. None of the evidence they had tied any of it to Alice Weaver except superficially. She was thought to have been in the company of the Russian woman, but that didn't prove anything. There were no signs of the enormous wealth that Brenhov had. Alice Weaver was back with her wife, so their combined wealth was reasonable and now in line with the IRS after the deal they had cut. It was all provable wealth. He hated that! He was certain she was dirty! Madelyn Korbel was no help either. He suspected she somewhat admired the woman who had blackmailed the CIA and by association, the United States government.

"Did you give this information to Alice Weaver?" he indicated the file containing the name of a former senator. Ken Edwards was a widower, who supported himself with speaking engagements these days. He had gone to prison for the death of his wife and Constance Weaver, the sister of Alice Weaver. That fact alone raised eyebrows in their investigation. It was too much of a coincidence to believe there wasn't tit for tat going on here. Someone wanted revenge.

"No, sir," she admitted to him.

"You didn't? Didn't you promise her–?" he asked, pleased that maybe she was finally on board and ready to help thwart this mysterious woman.

"No, sir. Alice *gave me* the senator's name, and I confirmed it," she clarified.

"What do you mean she gave it to you?!"

"Somehow, she had already uncovered that information, and she wasn't going to wait for us to give her the name of who had had her investigated." Madelyn waited for him to blow his top. If he really thought about it, this meant they still owed Alice. It had taken them months to ferret out information that Alice had probably gotten in weeks. Whatever her sources of information were, they shouldn't be superior to that of the Central Intelligence Agency or the Federal Bureau of Investigation.

"What's this I hear about her kid being involved in child pornography?" Wolf asked, changing the subject and dismissing some key evidence he had overlooked.

"Emily was the victim, not the perpetrator," she told him. "It's in this report here that Givens had sorted. The feds are looking into the situation because it crossed state lines."

He sighed. This was just one more thing about this Weaver woman that was hinky. "She didn't divorce her wife?"

Madelyn shook her head. "Apparently not, sir. Since the accident where she broke her leg, she's been living back in the Palos Verdes home." This information proved they were still keeping tabs on Alice, but then, he had ordered it. While the FBI had been pulled off the surveillance, there were other means for watching a subject.

"What about the Malibu house?"

"Empty, sir."

"Must be nice to be able to afford that kind of waste," he mumbled, pretending to look at one of his reports. Madelyn knew he was faking it because the report was upside down.

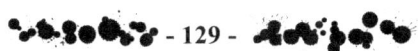

"Was there anything else?" she asked, wanting to get back to work. She had dozens of cases besides Alice Weaver's on her desk.

"Yeah, sure. Dismissed," he waved her off and sat down, thinking about these developments and wondering what Alice Weaver would do with the information. Trying to bypass Madelyn, he discovered she was already ahead of him and had the former senator under surveillance. He smiled. She was good...she was *very* good.

"Okay, Alice. This is the day you've been waiting for. Now, this walking cast is just for *walking*. You are not to be run in it, which would crush it. Walk only! And you still can't get it wet. I know you've been walking on this," she indicated the cast they had just sawed off, "because the bottom is filthy." It was obvious Alice had turned it into a walking cast. "Please try to be careful and restrain yourself in this new cast. Also, no lifting weights with this leg *yet*," Doctor Bryant warned her. The doctor knew that Alice had tried to be patient about the delays, but there had been so many complications. The pins and the breaks had been complex, and it had taken an extraordinary amount of time for them to heal.

Alice tried out the walking cast, using the wall, the counter, and her wife to maintain her balance. "Should I keep the crutches?" Alice asked the doctor, feeling not too thrilled at how unsteady she was; she had thought the new cast would act like a brace.

"No, let's try this cane," the doctor offered one to her. "This should help with your balance."

Alice liked how the cane looked, and it did help her keep her balance and avoid falling flat on her face. She had to go slow, but she could keep going. She nodded. "How long will I have to wear this?" she asked, indicating the new cast.

"As long as it takes," Doctor Bryant answered cryptically with a smile. She knew how impatient Alice was. She wanted to be running, but her leg simply wasn't up to it yet. Alice had asked the physical therapist about getting her leg back in shape and eventually jogging or running, and the therapist has reported that conversation to the doctor. They had all noticed the increased muscle tone throughout the rest of her body.

Alice had even gone so far as submerging her last cast in the bathtub deliberately, so they were forced to put on a new one. The wetness had soaked into the cotton and remained against her leg and foot until they could fit her in for a last-minute appointment. They'd had to peel off all the dead skin, leaving the foot cold, vulnerable, and itchy as it dried out in the exposed air. Fortunately, the leg was healing well, if a bit slow. "Look at that!" Alice exclaimed, pointing to the long, dark hairs. "I'm blonde, and my hairs shouldn't look like that!"

"Well, as you get older–" the doctor tried to tell her, but Alice wasn't having any of that.

"I had all that hair removed with a laser years ago. Why is it reappearing now?"

"It's not as thick as you think it is. It's just noticeable because you aren't used to seeing it, and your skin is white without your summer tan."

Alice was annoyed. She couldn't shave it, and she certainly couldn't pluck that many hairs. "I tell you, when this cast comes off, I'm making an appointment with the laser hair removal people. They better remove this hair once and for all, or they're going to refund me for the expensive treatments I paid for all those years ago!"

"Your body has changed as you have aged," Doctor Bryant told her. "You must have noticed some changes?"

Alice had to admit the doctor was right but excess body hair was not something she wanted to deal with. She'd have it zapped at the first opportunity.

Kathy thought it was hilarious. Alice was always so fastidious, and she had carefully groomed her body over the years. In fact, when they met, Alice had helped Kathy change her style of clothing, get rid of unattractive outfits, and learn how to keep herself impeccably. As a result of Alice's teachings, she felt better and was more confident.

Using her new cane, Alice and Kathy, accompanied by Nia Toyomota and Portia, entered an office in downtown Los Angeles for a meeting with the Pasternacks and their lawyer. They had come to sign a settlement and avoid dragging their case through the courts. The Pasternacks' homeowner insurance was paying most of the settlement amount, and Alice had to wonder how much was actually coming out of these people's pockets. Emily had let slip that Carmen was using her mother's being out of work as an excuse for why she had been acting up, but they weren't buying it.

"Well, if you'll sign here and here and here," the Pasternacks' attorney stated, but Nia held up her hand and quickly reviewed the paperwork. When she was done, she showed the paperwork to Portia, who also quickly glanced over the papers they had prepared before nodding and allowing Alice and Kathy to sign. A cashier's check was then passed across the wide table and everyone rose.

"I am sorry for everything that happened," Sandi stated, holding out her hand to Kathy. Richard held out his hand to Alice, who took it begrudgingly.

"Ouch!" Kathy exclaimed, pulling her hand back quickly.

"Oh, I'm sorry. It's this old ring of mine. It catches on things sometimes," Sandi said, but her apology sounded insincere to Alice's ears. When Sandi held her hand out to Alice, she refused. Alice held her hands up high and gave a slight laugh, and Sandi realized Alice wasn't going to shake her hand. Her eyes narrowed fractionally, but she laughed it off with good grace while exchanging a look with her husband.

They all left the building, Nia and Portia with their clients in one elevator, and the others using a second elevator in the highrise. "Well, that's that, and I'll head over to our offices to file these," Nia stated, patting her briefcase where she had placed the signed documents. The Pasternacks' attorney also had duplicate copies for their records. "Hopefully, I won't hear from *them* again," she indicated the defendants, who had arrived in the lobby more quickly than they had.

"And the other lawsuits?" Alice joked. They all knew those other suits might take years since not everyone was willing to settle. Still, it kept the lawyers busy, and Alice didn't mind. Nia had enjoyed the trip out to California, and she was considering an offer to run the office out here but before she made a decision, she had to discuss it with her wife.

"Mom, you're walking!" Emily greeted them when they arrived at the house. She was coming up from downstairs, where it looked like she had been working out. She was wearing sweats, a tank top, a sports bra, and looked a little sweaty.

"Yep, I'm crutch-free, for now," she answered with a smile although Kathy was carrying the crutches just in case. They'd paid for them in full, so they might as well keep them.

"I'm putting these in here," Kathy indicated the hall closet.

"Hopefully, I will never need them again," Alice put in as she slowly headed for the kitchen, where she found Sean and one of his friends wolfing down a tremendous amount of food. "Hi, there," she said by way of greeting.

"Oh, hi, Mom. This is Greg, and we're just catching a snack," Sean told her.

"A snack?" she laughed as Kathy came up behind her. Their snack looked like it was enough to feed a small nation.

"Yeah, we needed sustenance while we studied. You know, finals," he told her as he shoved half a Twinkie in his mouth and washed it down with half a glass of milk.

"Manners," Kathy cautioned him, not liking how he was shoving the food into his mouth. That would have given her heartburn or choked her.

"Which test are you studying for?" Alice asked, amused by her son. He was growing so big and strong, and it amazed her that he had her genes and had come out of Kathy.

"Calculus," both boys mumbled, their mouths filled with food.

"Oooh, gross," Emily said as she came into the kitchen. No one was sure if she was grossed out by the food they had in their mouths or the subject matter.

"C'mon, guys. Manners?" Alice put in, seeing them through the eyes of a parent.

Both boys grabbed napkins and hid behind them as they chewed with their mouths open until they could finally close them and finish chewing. Alice rolled her eyes and turned away, trying to hide a smile from Kathy.

"Alice, I think you should come upstairs," Kathy began hesitantly.

"Did I forget something?" she asked, looking up from the computer information she was examining, trying to gather as much material as she could. There were some things that weren't going to be public knowledge, such as motives and manipulations, but there were other ways she could get the data she needed. She wanted a complete dossier on all the people she was investigating.

Kathy nearly laughed. With a twinkle in her eye, she said, "If we are ever going to make this a proper marriage again," she started, referring to their interrupted conversation earlier that week, "I think we should start sleeping together. Don't you agree?"

Alice tilted her head. "Are you ready for everything that entails? Do you understand what that means? I haven't changed. Circumstances may have changed," her hands encompassed her casted leg, the new computers, and the problems she was working on, "but it's the same shit with different players."

Kathy sighed. She hated being reminded that their life was in a constant state of drama. "I know, but I want to somehow move past all this shit," she spread her hands this time to gesture towards the computers Alice was so diligently working at, "and have a life of our own."

"Do you realize what I'm going to do to these people?" Alice asked, pointing out the obvious.

"I thought you were going to wait until–" she started to say and stopped herself abruptly when Emily walked out of the exercise room.

"What are you two talking about?" she asked, her chest heaving.

Alice was used to hearing her daughter working out in there, using the machines and watching YouTube videos to learn karate. Alice had seen on the video feed from the house that Emily was getting the basic moves, but there were little nuances that were missing, and only a good teacher could impart those things to her. Remembering her own teachers, Alice inwardly shuddered. "Were you eavesdropping?" she asked, sounding amused.

"Not deliberately," she responded, suddenly worried. She knew a few things she shouldn't, and she would have liked to talk to her moms about it, but Kathy always stopped her. And when she approached her, Alice just referred her back to Kathy.

The moms exchanged a look; Kathy looked worried.

"I'm just doing research," Alice told her daughter. She wasn't lying. She stared her down, waiting to see if she would challenge her.

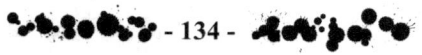

"Mom, I think we both know that's beyond mere research," she said exasperatedly.

Alice didn't answer. She merely stared at her daughter and waited.

"Have you been working out, honey?" Kathy asked into the silence, trying to distract the teen.

"Mom, don't do that. I know you don't think I'm an adult yet, but I'm not stupid," she added. "I know you're planning something," she gestured towards Alice and her computers. "I wish you'd train me to defend myself, so I could help."

"Absolutely not!" both women said at the same time, then looked at each other and laughed.

Em rolled her eyes and shook her head. She couldn't fight both her mothers. She knew it was Kathy's decision and Alice would follow her lead. She also suspected Alice might teach her to defend herself, if the decision was left up to her. Then again, seeing Alice's laser-focused eyes watching her, maybe not, despite the laughter. "C'mon, Mom. Can't I at least take lessons at a dojo?"

Alice looked at Kathy, waiting for her to make the decision. She wouldn't interfere on this one. She knew the kid was desperate for direction because she had heard her crying a couple times when she didn't think anyone could hear her. If she could have, Alice would have gone to the girl and comforted her. Listening to her daughter cry only made her more determined to even the score with the people who caused her pain. Since Alice wasn't yet physically ready to exact revenge, she was taking the time to plan her future moves with military precision. She had maps of Sebastian's properties, those now controlled by others and those owned by Artum and his associates. From what she could glean, Artum was acquiring more properties, not very discreetly either. His holding company was almost too obvious, even though he had layered it in several trusts and other poorly named companies.

"Honey, you're doing fine on your own," Kathy answered, moving over to put her arm around her daughter and ruffle her hair.

"Mom!" Em said, twisting out of her mother's grasp and standing at arm's length. "That's just it. I don't know what I'm doing! YouTube isn't enough." She turned back to Alice. She had seen her stretch and work out, maybe not to the full extent of her abilities, but the little she had seen over the years told her Alice knew what she was doing. Em reached out to her. "You know stuff. Why can't you teach me?"

Alice glanced at Kathy, who looked hurt by the question and by the fact that her little girl didn't want to be held by her. "I don't know if this is the right time," Alice began, earning a glare from Kathy. "I'm laid up, and you're–"

"Too young?! Is that what you were going to say? What if those men come back? I heard that sometimes they wait until the insurance company pays for the damages and replaces the things they stole, and then they come back to steal from you again."

"Who told you that?" Kathy asked, shocked.

Alice watched the exchange between her wife and youngest daughter. She was worried about that too, and the fact that her leg had taken so long to heal hadn't helped her impatience.

"My friends?" she began, but there was a hint of doubt in her voice, and Alice zeroed in on that.

"Which friends?" Alice asked. "You haven't mentioned making any new friends at your new school," she offered, giving the teen an out. She could tell the question had unnerved the teen.

Em started to squirm, wishing she hadn't pushed things. Now, they would know.

"Which friends?" Kathy asked in a kinder tone, watching her switch from leg to leg in her desire to get away. It was obvious the teen was uncomfortable.

Em looked away from her moms, looking everywhere in the room but towards them. Finally, her eyes settled on the floor, and she mumbled something.

"What was that?" Alice asked, waiting for the answer she already knew was coming. She'd begun watching the kid's activities again and had been waiting for something like this. Em had complained about lagging computer speed a few times, but in fact, it was Alice deleting some things she shouldn't be saying to her friends, especially on the internet. Alice was fast, but she wasn't that fast. She also wasn't always on her computer, and the logs she saw annoyed her when she realized that her daughter was still friends with undesirable people.

"Carmen," she said in a soft voice.

"You're still in contact with her?" Kathy asked, alarmed. She glanced up at Alice.

"She said she was sorry," Em answered defensively.

"Are you aware that those pictures of you are out there forever? No matter if the feds investigate the people that download those pictures of

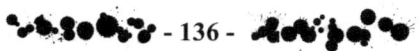

you, they will have pictures of your body and your face forever." Alice pointed out, watching as her wife flinched, and the girl cringed. "That is the friend who heedlessly shared your pictures around school...the school you can no longer attend because of your humiliation."

"She didn't think, and her mom was stressed, and she was upset–"

"That doesn't matter! She did that to her *best* friend," Kathy pointed out, angry at the teen for being so foolish.

"Are you aware that your so-called friend has been encouraging others to share the pictures?" Alice asked. She would have stood up, but her leg was pulsing as her anger with the teen caused her blood to boil. She was holding herself steady, showing no sign of her agitation as she sat behind the desk.

"How do you know that?" Em asked, aghast and willing to defend her friend to her parents.

"Because the twit puts things up in a public forum where anyone can see it," Alice lied cheerfully. She didn't tell her daughter that she'd sent the little bitch a song purportedly from Emily, which contained a backdoor virus. Now, she had a keylogger as well other software she could use to spy on Carmen, and she had seen what the girl was up to. It had taken a lot of hours to find out what the foolish girl was up to because she was a social butterfly, but Alice felt it was worth every minute. She reached into a drawer and pulled out a disk, flinging it across the room at her daughter like a Frisbee. "Here, look at what your *friend* has been posting about you. She's using you in order to get more information, so she can laugh at you and disparage you further."

"Alice," Kathy said warningly, but neither of them heard her. Similar eyes were staring at each other: one giving off hurt, the other, lightening sharp anger.

"She wouldn't..." Emily began, but her words lacked conviction. Yes, Carmen had been nasty to others, even occasionally, to her friends. Now, Em fingered the crystal disk case thoughtfully. "Where'd you get this?"

"I told you, she's a twit and posts things publicly. You are being duped, and I know you are smarter than that. Wake up, Emily! That girl hurt you." Her hands spread in a gesture encompassing their house. "She hurt your whole family, and she isn't stopping. Some people just can't resist hurting others. They are so self-absorbed they think they must strike first before someone, anyone, does it to them."

"I wouldn't–" she began, aghast at what Alice was telling her.

"Look at that," Alice gestured to the disk her daughter was holding. *"She* would. No, you wouldn't do that because your mother and I brought you up with values and ideals, but there are people out there that don't have any, at least, not the same values and ideals you were taught." She didn't tell the teen that she'd been investigating the Pasternacks and learned Richard was involved with dirty money, but she'd suspected that would be the case since he was involved with Sebastian and Artum. Sandi wasn't much better. Twelve of her last fifteen patients had died sooner rather than later, and the other three...well, those cases had ended up in the hospital, and they had also eventually died. Being involved in end-of-life care and hospice meant that someone like Sandi could operate with impunity, if she was careful. Remembering how Sebastian had looked and what he had told her, as well as her own observations from meeting the woman, Alice was convinced that Sandi was a killer.

Emily didn't want to believe her mother, but she knew Alice wouldn't lie to her, although she suspected she often bent the truth. Now, she just wanted to escape their scrutiny, so with a huff, she took the disk and headed for the steps.

Kathy waited until she heard the teen slam her door upstairs before asking, "Did you have to tell her that way?"

"Yes, I did. We must stop molly-coddling her. She deserves the truth. She's already hurt and angry. If I could, I would teach her the basics of karate. That twit went so far as suggesting that someone should *do something* about Emily Weaver, implying they should attack her physically. Why? All because Emily didn't like her naked body being plastered all over the internet and all over her high school. Did Emily deserve that?" She waited for Kathy to answer, and when she didn't, she went on. "Our daughter has been irreparably hurt. All we can do is try to make it slightly better. We sent her to another high school because she didn't want to face those people, but she has seen them. She's reached out to them," she gestured to her computers. "They aren't going to leave her alone either."

"So, what do you suggest? We turn her into...you?" Kathy asked angrily.

"No, I don't want that. I just want her to be able to defend herself, only if it becomes physical, of course. She's doing okay, but she lacks finesse and certain techniques...."

"You've been watching her?"

"Of course, I've been watching her. I have nothing else to occupy my time," her hands gestured to the computers again as she answered the last question sarcastically. "I love our children as much as you do, and I'm trying to protect them. That's what I do best."

"Are you saying I don't or wouldn't protect our children?" Kathy asked angrily. So much for inviting Alice back to her bed. This had gone from bad to worse quickly.

"You absolutely would," Alice assured her angry, prickly wife. "You are also the one that nurtured them and taught me how to do that too."

Surprised, Kathy blinked at the back-handed compliment. She calmed a little. "What are we to do?"

"You know what we are going to have to do…eventually."

Kathy turned white. She whispered furiously, "You aren't talking about killing a teenage girl, are you?"

Alice was surprised, and her eyes flared as she pulled back slightly, almost as though she had been hit. "No! Not at all!" she assured her wife. "I'm saying we teach Em to defend herself both physically and mentally. She needs some toughening up, and that's why I gave her the disk. It contains carefully selected items to prove that her *friend* is setting her up yet again and will continue to do so, if she continues that unfortunate friendship. I wish to God she had never become Carmen's friend."

Kathy was relieved. "I'm not ready for you to teach her. The little you told me of your teachers…."

"I would never use those techniques on *our* daughter," Alice assured her, not wishing to discuss her own instructors or the fear she had lived in for a long time until she became good enough to fight back. She wouldn't do that to Emily…ever.

Kathy was further relieved and relaxed a little. "How bad–?" she began to ask, wondering about the disk, when she heard Emily's bedroom door open. She must have flung it open. The sound of the door hitting the wall was loud, and the teen came running down two sets of stairs into the office.

"Is that all really true?" the anguished teen asked, pointing towards her bedroom where her computer contained the files Alice had put on the disk.

"You couldn't possibly have read all that," Alice commented dryly, knowing exactly what was on it.

"No, but the little I did read was horrible!" She started to cry. "She's awful!"

Alice nodded, wishing she could get up quickly to comfort her daughter, but Kathy was there and pulled the unresisting teen into her arms. Alice rose and grabbed her cane to hobble over. Emily was surprised and pleased to feel both her mothers embracing her as she sobbed out her hurt.

"I want to die," she said through her tears, her body shaking as she experienced another shock.

Kathy exchanged a look with Alice, wishing she could take away the hurt.

"I want *her* to die," she said, and Alice looked meaningfully at Kathy, shaking her head. She would never kill a child, no matter how evil she was.

Kathy wished she could wake up. Getting the kids off to school was exhausting her. She was glad it was nearly the end of the school year. Taking Emily to her school and then doubling back to drop Sean at his school when he couldn't catch a ride with a friend, was becoming too much. They had a lot of activities planned for summer, one of which was a surprise trip Alice had planned for the family that included Kit. The trip encompassed two weeks of camping in Sequoia National Park and then on to Yosemite, necessitating the rental of an RV and lots of secret plans. Kit had loved every moment of the planning. Sean would graduate next year and go on to college. He was already being scouted and might get a scholarship for football or basketball. They were all justifiably proud.

"Finally, this damn thing is off!" Alice said as she put on the boot the doctor had given her. It was her first time not wearing a cast in months. What had begun as a need for eight weeks of wearing the infernal walking cast had turned into eighteen weeks. She was finally done with the cast but had to continue physical therapy to regain the strength in her leg. She also had an appointment with the laser surgery place she had used long ago to remove her regrowth of leg hair. Apparently, as she became perimenopausal, the hairs were growing back, nowhere else so splendidly as on her leg where the break had occurred.

"I thought laser surgery killed the follicles and the roots, so I wouldn't ever have hair growing here again?" she had asked when she called for the appointment.

"The human body is a wonderous thing and heals itself marvelously. It's been more than seven years and your body does regenerate itself," the staff member pointed out. Alice had been annoyed but made the appointment to have the hair removed once again. She knew it might take several sessions, and they would charge her accordingly.

"Are you going to buy a car?" Kathy asked, still loving the fact that Alice was depending on her to be driven everywhere. It gave them an opportunity to talk privately without the children. They had started sleeping together again, but it wasn't very good sex. It was almost like Alice wasn't trying. The passion they had both enjoyed in the past wasn't as intense. The doctor said the things Alice's body had been through—the starvation and other extremes she wouldn't elaborate on—were causing her to go through early menopause, and that was causing all sorts of changes to her body. Kathy wasn't surprised to learn that reduced sex drive was just one of many symptoms of perimenopause.

"You don't want to drive me around in this?" Alice asked, caressing the dash of the lovely Lexus. It really was an attractive car, and now that summer was approaching, they could ride with the top down. Alice liked the car, but she realized she really did need one of her own.

Kathy preened, knowing she had bought a nice, luxurious car they both enjoyed. It wasn't as fancy or expensive as the Porsches that Alice had owned in the past, and it certainly wasn't in the same class as the Ferrari Alice had owned for a short a time, but it was a beautiful car. "C'mon, there are things you are gonna want to do with your own car," Kathy pointed out in a laugh.

Alice agreed. "What kind of car do you think I should get?" she asked, pleased that Kathy wasn't offended.

They discussed various cars they had owned over the years and then, Kathy blurted out, "Not another Ferrari!"

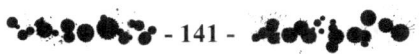

Alice laughed. No, that car had been totally impractical for her.

"What about an SUV?" Kathy asked, remembering the Nissan and the Jeeps Alice had previously owned and wondering about the storage units. She speculated that Alice had begun hiding those sorts of things from her again since she had taken over the finances. Kathy was pretty sure though, that Alice hadn't returned to the house in the valley for a long time.

"Well, it would certainly be more practical than a sports car," Alice mused, thinking about the sports cars she had owned and what she would need now. She'd loved the feel of her Porsche over the years, especially their power, but they were too distinctive. She really could have both a Porsche and SUV, if she was so inclined. She wasn't.

Alice ended up buying a Land Rover Sport based on her son's research. It was almost as though he was trying to make up for past behaviors. He'd surprised her when she'd indicated she was in the market for an SUV. He'd suggested Porsche, Maserati, and a few other vehicle manufacturers. She hadn't even known they made SUVs. She test-drove the different Land Rovers, but she hadn't liked the older, boxy-looking ones. When Sean brought her the specs on the Sport, he had apologized for its $68,000 price tag. But by the time Alice had added several upgrades, it was even more expensive. She'd refused the red color that looked sexy hot, wanting a more nondescript vehicle for what she knew she would be doing in the coming months.

"I like this," Kathy said, settling back into the new SUV's upholstery and looking over all the gadgets on the dash.

"It's nice, isn't it?" Alice agreed.

"Can I drive it?" Emily asked from the back seat as they headed out on a pleasure drive.

"Not for another year," Alice warned her, laughing at her daughter, her eyes twinkling in the rear-view mirror.

"Half a year," her daughter corrected her, feeling pouty at the reference to her age. She had, after all, driven the RAV for her mother once.

"What about me?" Sean asked, sounding a little defensive. After all, he had gotten his driver's permit.

"I think you can use the RAV, now and again," Kathy put in before an argument started. "Let your mom enjoy her new car. She still has to get used to its power," Kathy teased. The new vehicle had power, but it was nothing like the over-priced sports cars she had previously owned.

"I think this will suit me fine," Alice stated, glancing in the rear-view mirror at the car following them and sighing.

The family went out for dinner, the four of them pretending it was like old times and succeeding at the farse. Both moms knew it wasn't as good as the old times. They were aware they were being observed, but for the kid's sakes, they weren't about to spoil their time together.

"What are you doing?" Emily asked as she came up behind Alice quietly. She'd been practicing in the exercise room and was pleased when Alice flinched in surprise.

"Snuck up on me, didn't you?" Alice asked, unable to hide the weapons she was working with. She froze instead, wishing her daughter would just turn and walk away.

"Is that a bow and arrow?" Em asked, surprised when she realized she wasn't quite right. "That's a crossbow," she corrected herself as she walked farther into the office where Alice was working. "Can I try it?" she asked as she reached for one of the shortened arrows, and Alice pulled them out of her reach.

"No, I don't think your mo–" she began just as Kathy entered the office. She sighed. She was so busted.

"Alice, is that a crossbow? What the heck!" Kathy asked, looking between her wife and daughter.

"I just hauled it out to–" she began, but Emily interrupted her.

"You already had this? I never saw it before."

"That's because you've been a little kid for a long time, and Mom asked that I keep my toys out of sight from nosy buggers like you," Alice told her, trying to alleviate the tense moment she found herself in.

"But why are you working on it?" Emily asked. The rag and the oil were obviously used to shine it up.

"I was just looking at it," Alice fibbed, glancing at Kathy, who didn't buy it either, but Kathy realized they needed to divert the teen's attention. "You have to take care of your things."

"Speaking of which, did you make your bed? Didn't you say there was an end-of-year pep rally you wanted Sean to take you to?" Kathy put in.

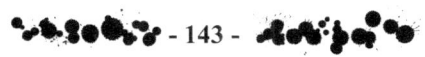

"Oh, yeah," the teen said, sounding suddenly excited. As she left the office, Em looked over her shoulder, her long hair swinging. and said, "I want to try that thing!"

Both moms waited until they heard her bedroom door close before Kathy turned on her wife. "Are you insane?!"

"I thought she had already left for the pep rally. I thought it was safe to start working on it." Alice raised her hands in mock defense against her wife's attack.

"Where in the world did you have that hidden?"

Alice just raised an eyebrow. "I think it's time we took the battle to them, don't you?" she asked instead.

"Were you at the house in the valley?" Kathy asked, wondering when she would have gone there. She'd only just brought the Land Rover home and hadn't gone anywhere except to dinner with the family.

"No, I haven't been there in a long time. Although, I should probably..." she mused, thinking of her previous uses for that house.

"Sell it," Kathy finished for her.

"What?"

"Yeah, I think it's time you sold that place as well as the Malibu house."

"Well, the Malibu place, sure. But the house in the valley? Where would I train?"

"How about here?" her wife gestured towards the exercise room their daughter used just as much as their muscle-bound son.

"Oh, and where do I hide the knives when I'm not using them?" Alice asked, sounding a little sarcastic.

"Well, I—" Kathy began and realized it was futile. She knew about the house and the reason for it. It wouldn't do to bring those types of things into this house.

"Look, I haven't been there in a long time. I haven't worked out like that in just as long," she gestured to her booted foot. She had the cane nearby in case she needed it for balance, but she liked that she could still drive her new Land Rover without worrying about the boot. She needed to get out. She had *things* to do.

"So, what is this?" Kathy asked, getting back to the crossbow.

"I thought I'd use that sedan for target practice," she said with a small grin twitching at her lips.

Kathy laughed. She didn't object. She was sick of that car sitting outside their gates too. "Can I come?"

Alice was surprised. She had planned to hobble out to the cliffs and come at the car from a different angle, so they wouldn't know the attack was coming from the Weaver estate. "I only have the one crossbow," she pointed out, picking it up and giving it a rub with the rag.

"Show me how it works. I want some payback after all we've endured."

Alice gladly showed Kathy how it worked. This reminded her of when she helped Kathy get over her hurt all those years ago. Teaching her how to work with knives and how to physically defend herself had given her self-confidence. They went out into the backyard, far from the eyes of their intended victims and away from the children.

"I like this," Kathy admitted as Alice showed her how to put her foot in the cocking stirrup. The crossbow was planted firmly on the ground, so she could pull the string back. Alice had to use her left foot since her right foot was booted, but the challenge was something she was clearly up to.

"These are cocking ropes. They make it easier for women to cock a crossbow since they don't always have as much upper body strength as guys," Alice said, showing her the correct way to use it. She put the middle of the cocking rope in the groove. It tightened the rope as she pulled on it. "You put the bowstring on the groove, and that creates the tension that pulls the bowstring back." She demonstrated. "Some people mark the spot with a marker, so they put the hooks in the same spot every time. You want the hooks oriented correctly." She showed her wife that the open side of the hook was facing outward.

"Jeez, I thought you just pulled it back, put the arrow in, and let it fly," Kathy murmured, trying to remember everything Alice was showing her. Neither of them noticed that Emily was watching from one of the upstairs' windows. With the window ajar, she was listening unashamedly as Alice instructed her mother.

"You want to adjust the ropes slightly, so the handles are aligned with each other and you have even tension on both sides. That way, you are pulling them at the same time. You don't want to be inconsistent here as it will affect your accuracy and make it harder to pull the bowstring back."

It was obvious Alice had done this before, and Kathy watched as her wife effortlessly pulled the string back in one forceful, fluid motion. They both heard three clicks. "Now, it's cocked and in the ready position," Alice showed her. "Keep your finger off the trigger and the safety on." She demonstrated the process for Kathy, then had her repeat it.

"Now, the arrows?" Kathy asked, getting a little excited by the instruction and Alice's proximity. Her breathing was coming a little faster.

"They are called bolts since they are shorter. Only put one bolt in the groove. See the colored fletching or "wings" at the end? You want to make sure that is placed in the barrel groove. You could damage the bow if the bolt isn't placed correctly. You also have to ensure the nock at the very end of the bolt is positioned against the bowstring correctly." Alice demonstrated, keeping her hand behind the safety line, which she pointed out to Kathy, and sliding the bolt into the barrel until it was firmly seated. "This bow has a clip," she pointed, "that keeps the bolt from sliding around."

"Now, are we ready to fire?" Kathy asked excitedly.

Alice nodded and looked around for a target. They had elephant palms in the gardens, and the leaves would be perfect.

Kathy's first shot totally missed, and the bolt sailed above the concrete of the pool and landed in the water.

"Take a more athletic stance. Since we don't want to be seen, aim down the scope, or these sights here," she showed her wife the notched V in the stock.

"Why'd I miss? That's a pretty big palm."

"You jerked the trigger when you fired and that decreased the accuracy. Keep the crossbow aimed at your intended target."

"Are you going to kill those men with this?" she asked, only slightly horrified at the thought as she lowered her voice.

"No, but their tires and their pretty paint job may suffer some damage," Alice answered, outraged. Besides, with the boot on her foot, there was only so much she *could* do.

They practiced a while, losing bolt after bolt in the pool, but Alice didn't mind. She could retrieve those. After a few more shots, she put bowstring wax on the crossbow strings. "That will keep the strings from breaking," she informed her fascinated wife.

"Can't we practice without the arrow?"

"No, you should never fire a crossbow without a bolt in the latch. That could ruin your weapon. The vibrations, also known as the kinetic energy, is absorbed by the bow. You can also be hurt by that," she explained patiently to Kathy.

The elephant palms weren't thick enough for the bolt and wouldn't absorb the blow, so Alice hadn't planned on practicing. "Okay, get the kids going, and when they've left, we can use this for real," she promised as she put the crossbow down by the pool and began to take off her boot.

"What are you doing?" Kathy asked, confused.

"I'm going to retrieve those," she gestured to the bolts lying at the bottom of their pool, "and put different points on the tips. I don't want them traceable to us."

Kathy smiled as she left to get the kids ready. By the time she returned, Alice was nowhere to be found, and she was disappointed, thinking her wife might have gone without her. Finally, she found her in their bedroom. She was laying out clothes for Kathy to wear. Alice had already changed and slicked her hair back, and she was wearing a black knit cap.

"These look like jogging clothes," she commented as she started to change. God, she was already tired, and she had merely practiced for a short time with the bow.

"Yes, they are," Alice agreed as she finished dressing. "That way, if anyone sees us, they will think we are out for a jog. Although," she gestured to her boot, "they won't buy that I'm doing anything more than a fast walk," she chuckled.

Kathy was always impressed by how carefully Alice thought things out. She knew her wife probably wasn't overjoyed to have her along, but Kathy had hated how she always felt excluded. She heard the Velcro tightening on the boot as Alice stood up. "Do you need your cane?" she gestured to the walking boot she was wearing.

"Probably, but I'm going to wing it," Alice responded.

They walked to their back gate. Kathy had the gate key firmly in hand, and they went through to the path that ran along the tops of these bluffs down to the beach below. Instead of taking that path, they continued past their own property towards some of their neighbors'. Walking briskly, Alice held the crossbow down at her side, so it was less visible. Kathy was carrying a dozen bolts in her gloved hand.

Alice had been sure to rub them down, so no fingerprints could be used to identify them.

They approached the sitting car, the two men inside reading the news on their phones. Alice knew the light from the phones would temporarily blind them in the night, but she also knew the darkness of the night would make accuracy with the crossbow more difficult. She didn't think Kathy would hit anything but gave her the first shot. She watched as her wife confidently used the instructions she had just received to pull the bowstring back and insert a bolt. She aimed carefully at the tire they intended to flatten, instead hitting the rear quarter panel squarely. Both men sat up, wondering about the noise, but before they could move to inspect, Alice had another bolt in the crossbow and was aiming. This one didn't land where she wanted it either. She was out of practice, but she did manage to hit the tire, although it landed on the opposite side of the car from where she had planned. At least it hadn't hit the metal cover. The tire air blew out as soon as the sharp point of the bolt pierced it.

"More?" Kathy asked, excited and exhilarated at this unexpected caper.

"I don't know if we have the time," Alice said as Kathy prepared to put another bolt in the bow. Alice was watching the men, and she was shocked when one got out of the car just as Kathy fired again. This bolt hit the steering wheel column.

"Jeezus!" they both heard the man yell as he dove for the asphalt.

"I think we should be going now," Alice whispered, trying not to laugh at her exuberant wife. She'd enjoyed this far too much.

They backed away, the dark clothes making it easy to fade into the night as they headed for the path behind their house. It was much more dangerous traveling at this time of night, and they stayed near the fences, so they didn't get too close to the bluff's edge.

"Think they will leave?" Kathy asked as she unlocked their gate and they passed through.

"No, but I'm sure they'll think twice before screwing with us anymore," Alice answered. She hadn't intended to hit them, but damn, Kathy had come close with that third shot.

Alice hid the crossbow under her desk, using clips to keep it where no one would find it. She dropped the extra bolts into the bottom drawer, forgetting about the incident in the rush of data she had to analyze. Kathy watched as her wife became engrossed in the various drawings of buildings and structures, wondering which properties those were. Kathy busied herself reading the information Alice had given her about Carmen, and she was growing increasingly angry with the girl as she realized how manipulative she had been with their daughter.

The excitement of the evening didn't end immediately. Kathy was still worked up hours later when they finally went to bed after the kids got home. She shared a tub with Alice, who was enjoying the freedom of taking a bath without her boot. This led to a pleasant moment in the tub, each achieving a satisfactory outcome of the lovemaking that ensued, but that wasn't enough for Kathy this time! As Alice dried off, put her boot back on, and grabbed her robe, Kathy vigorously pushed her against the wall of the bedroom.

"Wha–?" she began, but Kathy was kissing her hard.

"That was so exciting…" Kathy murmured between the hot kisses she was pressing on her surprised wife.

Alice wasn't used to Kathy being this forceful. Their love life had kind of sucked in the past few months, but this was exciting! She went to push back, but Kathy wasn't having any of it.

The brunette pushed against her wife, holding her firmly in place as she kissed her deeply, her hands running along Alice's bath-warmed body. The heat between them was no longer caused by the hot bathwater but from the blood running below the surface as Kathy began kissing along her neck. She was sucking the skin into her mouth and tonguing her. Slowly, she kissed her way down to Alice's breasts, kissing intensely on each tip.

Alice gasped. Her breasts used to be so pert but now hung down. It also didn't help that there was excess flesh on them, but Kathy didn't mind, and the sensations still pulsed through her wife's body as she tongued the nipples, sucking on them and causing Alice to gasp again. Alice plunged her hands into Kathy's hair, urgently pressing her wife's mouth against her bosom.

Kathy's hand moved between Alice's legs, searching for and finding the erect little nub she knew would be waiting for her. At first, she wasn't sure if Alice was still wet from the tub or from her own juices, but she debated that only momentary when Alice responded to her attack. Kathy kissed her way across Alice's stomach and down until she could toy with the nub using her tongue and lips.

Alice looked down at her wife kneeling between her legs. The sight of her wife's mouth busily engaged on her clit caused Alice to throw her head back and bang it against the wall. She didn't mind the pain. Her brain was short circuiting as she came quickly against Kathy's mouth. The orgasm in the tub was adequate but *this* was primal and all-encompassing. She felt marvelous as she bucked against Kathy's mouth.

Kathy smiled, thrilled that she could still cause this response in Alice after all their years together. The heel of her hand rubbed against the flesh causing pleasure-pain that she knew her wife enjoyed. She began to rise and kiss her way up her wife's body again, reaching around to squeeze Alice's firm buttocks.

Alice, completely aroused and satisfied with her own orgasm, grabbed her wife's robe and spun them, nearly falling over the boot on her leg as she attempted to take control of the situation and give her wife the same treatment she had received. It took longer as Alice didn't have the agility she'd once had, but Kathy was biting down on the back of her fist to hide the cries of her own orgasm as Alice slowly stood up and continued to play with her heated body. As she played once again with Kathy's breasts, a frown appeared on her face.

"What? You don't like them anymore?" Kathy teased as her eyes started to focus. She was enjoying the aftermath of the passionate lovemaking with her wife.

"No, that's not it. You have a lump," Alice said as she tenderly felt it.

"Oh, that. It's nothing. I have another one over here," she said, pointing to her other breast. "It's just a fatty lump."

"When is the last time you had a mammogram?" Alice asked.

"C'mon, don't ruin the moment with–."

"I'm serious. When is the last time you went for a checkup? Between the kids and me, when have you taken time to care for you?"

Kathy stood transfixed. What a helluva comedown after a thoroughly enjoyable lovemaking session with her wife. She fixed her robe, pulling it closed to her wife's gaze as she shrugged her shoulder. "I don't really remember," she admitted.

"Will you make an appointment…Please?" Alice added gently.

"Okay, okay. I'll go. Jeez," she said begrudgingly.

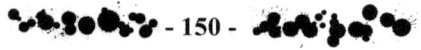

"Thank you," Alice replied, attacking Kathy again with her lips. She wasn't finished. Their time together had been too pleasurable to allow it to end on a discussion about healthcare. With Kathy's legs wrapped around Alice's waist, the women soon forgot about the lumps and enjoyed each other in a healthier way.

"Can I come with you?" Kathy asked a few nights later.

"Come with me where?" Alice hedged, not used to talking about these things.

"Alice, does that belong to the guy that caused our IRS problems or one of the guys that robbed us?" she gestured to the diagrams of the properties.

"Jeez, is it that obvious what I'm doing?" Alice asked aloud, wondering if the children had noticed too.

"No, but I know you, and I also know *that* is going to slow you down," she pointed to the boot on Alice's leg and foot. "I want to help. What he did affected my family too," she said earnestly.

Alice didn't have the heart to turn her down. They had to be careful though. Emily was getting too good about sneaking around and overhearing things. They planned their strategy carefully.

"Want to go hear a motivational speaker?" Alice asked a few days later, holding up a paper she had just printed out.

"Why would I want to hear a motivational speaker?" Kathy asked, wondering if that was simply a rhetorical question. As she looked at the paperwork, she realized Alice was talking about going to see the former Senator Ken Edwards. "Are you going to kill him?" she asked, lowering her voice.

Alice laughed. "No, but he is going to wish he was dead. That's who is watching our house," she gestured to the car outside. The car they shot up had been replaced with another car, and she smiled thinking about using it for target practice again.

"What are you smiling about?" Kathy asked, her own lips parting as she returned the smile.

"Wanna go target practicin' tonight?" Alice asked, reaching to unlock the desk and check on the bolts she'd hidden there. Her smile faded when she realized they were gone. "What the hell?!"

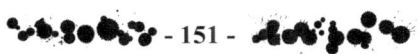

"What's the matter, babe?"

"Look! That's where I put them," she indicated the empty drawer. "Or did I?" she mused as she began to open the other drawers one by one. None of them contained the missing bolts. Next, she got down on her hands and knees to check for the bow, and it was missing too. "What the hell?!" she repeated as she started to rise and hit her head on the desk. "Christ!" she swore as she rubbed her head and pulled it out from under.

"Are you okay?" Kathy asked worriedly. She had heard the head hitting the wood, and it sounded painful. Alice rarely swore, but she knew it was probably justified by that hit.

"The bow is missing," she informed her wife.

"What? Who...?" she asked, and they both spoke in unison, "Emily!" Kathy looked angry as she walked to the doorway of the office and called up the stairs, "Emily, will you come down here please?"

Alice finished pulling herself out from under the desk and sat on the chair, still rubbing her head as she listened to their daughter galumphing down the stairs. "Yes, Mom?" she called before she came down the second set of stairs.

"Could you come down here please?" Kathy asked, revealing nothing in her tone.

Alice had to hand it to her wife. She would have gone up to the kid's room and confronted her, but this was a much better to way to handle things. She was still rubbing her head when the teen walked into the office, looking curiously at her parents.

"Did you take something from this office?" Kathy asked carefully, looking at her daughter. She was as tall as Kathy now.

"Take something?" she asked, trying to sound innocent.

"Did you take the crossbow from under the desk and the bolts from the drawer?" Alice asked more directly, looking angrily at the teen. Damn, her head hurt! She stopped rubbing it to glare at her daughter.

"I just wanted to try it...and then..." she began, shifting uncomfortably as both her mothers looked at her. Now, she looked decidedly guilty.

"And then?" Alice prompted. She wasn't feeling very patient at that moment.

"I...ah...used it."

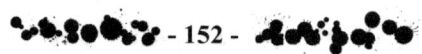

"Oh, my gawd! Emily, did you kill someone?" Kathy gasped, and both Emily and Alice looked at her in horror.

"NO!" Em nearly shouted. "I just used all the arrows up."

"Bolts," Alice corrected automatically. "Were you target practicing?" she asked, relieved Emily hadn't killed anyone. That hadn't been *her* first thought, and she wondered at where Kathy's mind had gone for that one.

"Sorta," the teen said uncomfortably. She was squirming. "I just wanted to teach them a lesson."

"Teach *who* a lesson?" Kathy asked, her tone angry. She wanted to get to the bottom of this *right now*.

Emily looked up, first glancing at Alice then at Kathy. She had meant to have the bow back under the desk before they found out. She couldn't retrieve the arrows, and she had thought maybe they wouldn't notice. Apparently, she was wrong.

"What aren't you telling us?" Alice put in.

"Do I have to–?"

"Every word," Alice commanded, waiting. She knew she wasn't going to like her daughter's answer, and she could see Kathy was becoming impatient.

"I shot out the Pasternacks' windows," she said, looking down at her shoes and mumbling.

"You did *WHAT*?!" Kathy asked, practically shouting. She hoped she hadn't heard correctly.

"I shot out the Pasternacks' windows," she repeated, a little louder.

Alice nearly laughed. Instead, she asked, "Did you break all nine of their windows?"

The teen looked up, and Kathy looked at Alice with a frown. "There were nine bolts left," she reminded her wife.

Emily shook her head. "No, I didn't hit all the windows at first, but eventually, I did."

"Eventually?"

"Well, I retrieved the arrows that hit the stucco," she explained.

Alice restrained the laugh that wanted to spill out. "Were they home?"

Emily shook her head again.

"Where's the bow?" Kathy asked at the same moment Alice asked. "They are going to find your fingerprints, you know?"

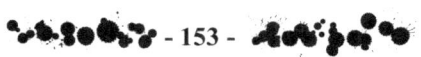

"No, they aren't. I wore gloves," Emily explained, then looking at Kathy, she said, "The crossbow is in the garage. I was waiting until you were gone, so I could put it back," she gestured at the desk.

"How did you know to wear gloves?" Alice asked, turning the teen's attention back on her.

"I watched when you were showing Mom," she gestured to Kathy. "I listened to everything you told her."

Alice sighed, wiping her hands across her face. "You realize–" she began, then changed her mind as another thought occurred to her. "When did you do this?"

"Earlier tonight," the teen replied in a small voice as she fidgeted, wondering how much trouble she was in.

"You could have been caught!" Kathy gasped.

"They weren't home. I saw through a fake account that they were going out to dinner. I already had the bow, and I practiced like you did," she told Kathy. "I went over there and started firing at the windows. I missed several times but retrieved the arrows, so I could try again."

"Don't they have a security system?" Alice asked, thinking this through and wondering if they were going to have to hire Portia to defend their daughter. This was serious.

She nodded but added, "I turned it off."

"Turned it off how?" Kathy asked, sounding incredulous at their daughter's story.

"I knew the code. They hadn't changed it, so I turned it off and shot the windows. That took a while since I had to keep retrieving the arrows until I could hit the windows. Then, I turned it back on with a delay and left."

"No one saw you?" Alice asked.

The teen shook her head.

"Do you know how dangerous that was?" Kathy asked angrily. "You could have been caught!"

"I know, but they need to pay for–"

"Emily, you know it was wrong. That bow is not a toy, and you were told not to touch it," Alice told her.

"But I–"

"Nothing you say right now is going to justify using that crossbow to get even with the Pasternack family," Alice interrupted.

Emily hung her head and then, they all heard the gate buzzer. Alice looked up at her computer and switched it to their security system. She saw a sheriff's car at the gate. She glanced at Kathy, who was frowning at her. Alice nodded her head towards the screen, and Kathy walked across the room to look at the camera shots. Emily followed and gasped, "They know!"

"No, you don't know that. You are to stay down here," Alice said, rising, then with one quick swipe on the keyboard, she cleared the screens. She used her cane to move over to the panel on the wall where another camera showed her the face of the person who had buzzed. "Yes?" she called into the speaker as she pressed a button.

"Hello. We are doing a routine patrol and would like to ask you some questions, if we may?" the officer said, looking earnestly into the camera.

Alice pressed another button, opening the gate to the patrol car. Looking at her daughter, she repeated, "You stay down here and don't move." She limped out of the office and Kathy hurried to catch up with her. By the time the sheriffs got to the door, Alice had made it up the steps and was opening it. "Hello. Can I help you?" she asked innocently. "Hi there, ma'am," he said, removing his hat and looking curiously from Alice to Kathy.

Alice could tell this officer didn't know the problems they had experienced last year; he didn't know them. "Good evening. Would you like to come in?"

"No, ma'am, that won't be necessary. Do you know your neighbors?" he asked, gesturing to the estates on either side of their own.

"Mmm, a little but only in passing really," she admitted. "What is this about?"

"One of your neighbors was vandalized and we," he indicated the other officer down a few feet on the steps, who was watching them and looking about, "are inquiring if any of their neighbors saw anything."

"Vandalized? What happened?" Alice asked, sounding as if butter wouldn't melt in her mouth.

"Oh, a few windows broken. Have you had any problems like that?"

Alice shook her head and glanced at Kathy, who repeated the gesture. "We had a break-in last December but nothing since," she told him and saw the other officer nod. So, he had known about that. "Don't they have cameras or a security system?"

"Apparently, none of that was working at the time," he admitted. "Well, ma'am, if you see anything, please give us a call."

"We'll do that," Alice assured him, and as he went to leave, she asked, "Um, which neighbors were vandalized?"

"Oh, the Pasternacks over there," he said, pointing to the house across the acres.

Alice nodded and watched as they went down the stairs. She waited until they were through the gate and in their car before she shut the front door and leaned against it. She looked at Kathy and rolled her eyes. They both headed towards the stairs.

"Why did you ask who it was?" Emily asked, proving she had been listening.

Alice waited until they were all sitting on the couch before she said, "Because most people would be curious who it was, and if I hadn't asked it might have raised their suspicions."

Emily swallowed this bit of news.

"Now, young lady, we need to talk about this," Kathy put in.

"They are going to get away with–" the teen began defensively, but Alice cut her off.

"No, we got a huge settlement out of them."

"That's nothing. They won't even miss the money, and money won't get back my…" she trailed off.

"No, it won't, but I'm dealing with it, and you have to trust me on that." Alice warned her, "No more of this, Emily. I won't countenance you destroying property like that. You might have been caught, and you can bet they are going to be suspicious of you. We live far too close for them not to think of you or your brother for this act. Do you want Sean to get in trouble for something he had nothing to do with?"

Emily shook her head, suddenly scared that her big brother was going to get into trouble because of her. He'd already been threatened with suspension from school for fighting. She hadn't meant for that to happen, and she didn't want to get him in trouble; she just wanted to scare them a little. She thought the cute little arrows would work perfectly for that.

"Go get me the bow, and your mother and I will discuss your punishment," Alice said sternly.

Emily got up from the couch and dejectedly went to fetch the bow where she had hidden it in the garage.

"What are we going to do?" Kathy asked in a whisper.

"I have no idea. What's the usual punishment for using a crossbow on someone's windows?"

"Don't make me laugh," Kathy said, putting her hand up to her mouth to hide her smile. She could see Alice was having trouble keeping a straight face as well.

Emily came in holding the bow and handed it to Alice. She looked dejected. Alice hobbled over to the desk to place the bow on it.

"Look, honey, we just want to keep you safe. Trust me. These people will pay for their crimes–" Alice began.

"They wrote a check, that's it! And Carmen isn't paying," she argued passionately.

"No, but in the long run, what do you want to see happen to her? Do you want her dead?"

"Nooo," Emily moaned, horrified at the thought as she sat on the couch, "but I want her to pay for what she did."

"She will, honey, but it is going to take time. I want you to promise you won't do anything again without discussing it with me first," Alice directed, and when Emily looked like she would argue further, Alice put up her hand. "No! Promise me."

"I promise," the teen mumbled, hanging her head.

"Now, your mother and I haven't agreed on a punishment yet. I don't want you to tell anyone about this. I mean no one, *ever*! You never know who might be listening, and you certainly cannot ever tell anyone in an instant message, text, or any form of written word. No bragging and no confiding in even your dearest friends...Okay?"

Emily looked up, troubled.

"You haven't already told anyone, have you?" Alice asked, concerned.

She shook her head solemnly, and her mothers believed her.

"She will suffer. One day, she will suffer. I promise you!"

"Will I get to see her suffer?"

"You want revenge that bad?" Alice asked kindly.

"What she did–"

"Was horrible," Alice finished for her. "But do you want revenge so bad that you are willing to see her hurt?"

Emily had to admit that she didn't want revenge that badly.

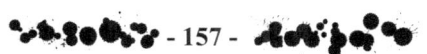

"What *do* you want?" Kathy asked kindly, feeling badly for her daughter and everything she had gone through.

"I don't know," the teen said, despondent and starting to tear up. Kathy put her arm around her daughter's shoulders, turning her head aside to cough into her sleeve.

Alice looked at Kathy and wondered about the cough. She hadn't sounded congested earlier. "What would you like me to do?" she asked the teen sadly.

"I don't know, Mom. I just feel so helpless. They got away with everything, and Carmen is still able to move about freely, doing whatever she wants, whenever she wants, without any repercussions."

"She couldn't go back to your old school. She and the others were expelled," Kathy reminded her.

"Yeah, but she talks about how great her new school is, and—"

"Don't listen to her. I bet if you stopped checking up on her and making fake accounts to see what she is up to, you wouldn't feel like this," Alice pointed out. "She also didn't get into any schools here on the peninsula. Not even the private schools would take her or the others, and her parents have to drive her into LA to go to school."

"How do you know?" Emily asked, looking up, her eyes filled with tears. Kathy looked up too, wondering.

"Let's just say I made sure of that," Alice told them with a small eye roll to express her fake innocence. That gesture had them all smiling slightly. "I didn't do anything any other concerned parent wouldn't have done. Who wants deviants in their local school system?" she asked in her most prissy voice. They all laughed out loud at that.

"That's funny," Emily admitted, wondering how Alice had accomplished that. "But they still haven't paid for what they did—"

"No, and they may never pay for it," Alice admitted ruefully. "All we can do is move on and live well. People like that eventually get theirs. You have to believe in fate."

Long after their daughter had gone to bed, Alice and Kathy lay in bed talking about the events of that night. Emily knew she was going to be punished for her actions, just not that night. "You know, you can make sure those people pay for what they did," Kathy pointed out.

"Yes," Alice nodded as she agreed with her wife. "And, they will. In time, they will."

"What do you have planned?"

"Nothing yet," she admitted. "Again, everything in time."

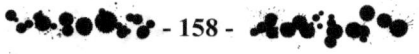

"We are watching the former senator. Ken Edwards is a natural target, and if Alice Weaver goes for him, we've got her," one of the FBI agents reported to Director Wolf.

"It isn't going to work," Madelyn told her boss. "She is smarter than that."

"We'll see," he replied. "She's bought tickets to his latest session for her and her wife."

"A session?" Madelyn asked, raising an eyebrow as the agent left the room after giving them a report on his latest findings.

"Yes, one of those motivational talks he gives where he sells the books and other paraphernalia that earn him a good living. He," his chin indicated the agent who had just left, "told me that Alice bought two tickets to the next event."

"How closely are you watching this Ken Edwards?"

"Well, he is out of prison, so we can have others watch him for us," he admitted, not giving her a complete answer.

Madelyn understood they wouldn't tell her everything, but she felt that setting up Alice Weaver was a bad idea. They still didn't have the information they needed from her. She sighed. They weren't going to listen to her. What did she know?

Ken Edwards' voice tapered off as the spotlight moved, and he was finally able to see his audience. He swore he was seeing a ghost from his past. He realized he was seeing an older version of Constance Weaver in the form of her twin sister, Alice. Sitting next to Alice was a pretty brunette. He recognized her as the wife from the surveillance photos. What a perversion! During the time he had been in prison, they had passed laws allowing LGBT people to marry. As a senator, he would have completely opposed such legislation, even if he had participated in such perversions in prison. He justified his behavior in many ways, not the least rehabilitated from his crimes. Had anyone explained to the asshole that these were not perversions but his own sanctimonious beliefs, he would not have understood.

Returning to his well-prepared speech, he continued to inspire those that were new in his audience as well as those who already believed in him. He still had his good looks, if slightly aged, and people were drawn to that as well as his charismatic charm, which would have won him the White House had he been able to continue in politics with his wife at his side. They had been presented as the perfect couple. Unfortunately, they had participated in auto-erotic asphyxiation and had killed too many people. Constance Weaver was one of their victims. Connie, as she was known to Alice, had been a bit of a wild woman. As time went on, her husbands had increased her wealth, each leaving her marginally richer than the last. But when Connie had happened upon the Edwards, she had, unfortunately, met her match. After Ken had filmed the accidental killing of his own wife, that film and many others had found their way into the hands of multiple TV stations across the country. Time and the public's short attention span made the Edwards' story old news. People had forgotten his many crimes.

"Alice, it's a pleasure to see you again," was his phony comment when he saw her at the meet and greet afterwards. He had been signing books when he saw the two women walking by and got up to greet them.

Alice would have been content had they simply not run into the man. She had seen him falter when he first saw her in the audience and that was enough for her...for now. She knew she unnerved him. She didn't say a word, just stared at him with her odd cat-like eyes.

"And this must be Kathy. How do you do?" he asked, offering her his hand.

Kathy ignored it, looking him up and down and wondering what rock he had crawled out from under. His good looks had faded, and she could see his blonde hair was thinning. She turned to cough into her arm, and it turned into a spasm, which she hadn't anticipated. Alice looked at her, deeply worried.

The former senator also looked at the woman in alarm and hurried on, pretending they hadn't noticed him or his attempts at a greeting.

"Are you okay?" Alice asked her.

"Water," she gasped, and they headed for a drinking fountain where she calmed her cough. "That was so weird," she stated.

"Kathy, have you made that appointment for a checkup yet?" Alice asked, taking her arm and leading her out of the conference room. Not surprisingly, Edwards had not been very motivational to either of the women. Truthfully, they found him quite boring.

"No, but I will," she promised as they stepped outside into the southern California sunshine. Both reached for their sunglasses.

"Mrs. Weaver?" a voice stopped them as they began to descend the steps of the hotel.

"Yes?" they both answered, looked at each other, and laughed.

"Mr. Edwards would like to talk to you," the man gestured. Judging by the dark glasses and earpiece he was wearing, he was obviously security.

"Well, we don't wish to talk to *him*," Alice emphasized, dismissing the man and attempting to walk past him, her hand on Kathy's arm.

"I don't think you understand," began the man, grabbing Alice's arm.

Alice had anticipated the move and swung her outstretched arm around his quickly, twisting it behind him and using her booted leg to step down on his insole and then kick him in the shin. "You let me go!" she said loudly and distinctly, so that passersby saw her as he went down. "How dare you touch me! Are you aware that Edwards man is a killer? He killed my sister!" Her voice got louder and louder, and people were obviously listening since they were staring at the man she had downed. A crowd began to gather.

"Alice," Kathy gasped, pulling her away. She wasn't sure if Alice was playing with the man or had lost her cool. They walked in silence. Alice limped on her booted leg, using Kathy as the crutch she hadn't thought to bring. Her cane was in the SUV. Once they were in the Land Rover, Kathy asked, "Are you okay?"

"Oh, yes. My public display is going to bother him," she said cheerfully, pointing behind them with her thumb as she started up the SUV and put on her seat belt. "Want to unnerve someone else today?" she asked.

"What in the world?" Kathy asked, grinning at the cheerful tone in Alice's response. "What do you have in mind?"

"Let's strike a blow for us and for Emily," she said mysteriously as she headed for Beverly Hills. The Land Rover was gobbling up the miles effortlessly as she drove. They talked about everything but where they were going and what they would do. Kathy was enjoying

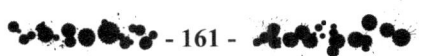

the time with her wife, and she loved the mischievous tone of Alice's antics.

Kathy looked on curiously at the beautiful homes they passed. They had looked at some of these very estates when they were in the market for a home because Alice had wanted something near the ocean. She'd been very certain what she wanted, and she hadn't like it when they moved from the marina because they'd outgrown that condo.

Alice stopped at a large gate and pushed the button, waiting for the tinny voice to ask her, "How can I help you?"

"Alice Weaver to see Artum," she said and waited.

"See *who?*" the voice came back almost immediately, responding too quickly to feign innocence.

"Tell Artum I know he is living here. This was Sebastian's house, and I know he took it over. If he doesn't see me now, he will regret it."

Kathy recognized the name Sebastian; she had met him at Alice's memorial service. He had been a big, bluff man, a Russian, and she looked curiously through the iron gate which opened shortly after Alice's statement. She glanced at Alice and saw she was grinning as she drove onto the estate. The circular drive ended in front of the big mansion. Kathy was alarmed to see men with automatic weapons walking about. As Alice parked the Rover, one of them came towards the SUV and opened the door for Kathy. Another jerked Alice's door open, and she was amused when they indicated she should get out, then immediately began to pat her down.

"I suggest you take your hand off my boob before I break your arm," Alice said conversationally, prompting sounds of outrage from Kathy. In two seconds flat, the man in front of Alice went down, his gun in her hand and held against his cheekbone. Dropping the gun, Alice sprinted as fast as she could move with her brace, heading around the front of the vehicle to see Kathy protesting violently about being patted down by another guy. "Hey! That's my wife you're manhandling," she protested. The man turned to her, his gun crossing in front of his body. Alice grabbed it and heaved it upwards where it hit his chin, and the man went down, surprising them both.

"Easy there," a voice called with amusement as Artum came out onto the porch of the mansion. The scene before him reminded him of a conversation he'd had with Sebastian on this very porch:

"Don't touch Alice Weaver," Sebastian rasped, reaching *imploringly towards Artum. They were sitting in the evening air and*

Sebastian, who was on oxygen, had a tube fitted around his face, so it could go up his nose.

"Who is this Alice Weaver?" Artum asked, wondering how she had the impunity to come and go despite all their security precautions.

In his mind, Sebastian thought about Alice, going over the many years he had known the woman. Artum thought he had fallen asleep when he finally opened his mouth to speak. Breathing heavily, he had difficulty getting the words out. "I...do...not...know...really." Over the next hour, he slowly and methodically explained what he did know about the mysterious woman. He spoke of how she had bested him time and again, and he had learned not to cross her. He reminisced about how he had lusted after her and had been unequivocally rejected. Before exhaustion took him, he grabbed Artum's arm and implored him one more time, "Don't touch Alice Weaver. She...will...kill...you...all."

Artum wasn't alarmed by the warning, but he took it to heart. There were many people in their organization throughout the world who were not to be touched. Their immunity allowed them to enrich all without restriction, but this was unprecedented since Alice wasn't part of their organization, at least not from what he could tell. He nodded in agreement as Sebastian fell asleep. Alice Weaver would not be touched.

Now, remembering that long-ago day when his uncle had warned him about Alice, he still could not see why Sebastian felt the warning was necessary. He glanced curiously at his man, who was slowly rising and saw the mayhem on his face caused by the blow that had downed him. As he brought his gun to bear, Artum called, "I wouldn't," in Russian.

Alice looked up at the two men on the porch and recognized Artum. She straightened her clothing and looked to make sure Kathy was okay. She nodded curtly after seeing the look on her wife's face and straightened her own clothes that had been mussed by the man putting his hands on her.

"Artum," Alice said coldly. "I come to pay a visit, and this is how you greet me?"

"You should have called first," he said with a grin. She didn't seem that formidable an enemy, and yet, even from fifteen feet away, those eyes were making him uncomfortable. She was wearing a boot that he'd seen on people after they broke their leg, and she was limping.

She was a petite woman with spikey, blonde hair. What was it about this woman that had so unnerved his uncle? "Would you like to come in?" he invited, his hands gesturing towards the mansion.

"We would," she stated, taking Kathy's arm at the elbow with her fingertips. "Let me introduce my wife, Kathy."

"How do you do, Mrs. Weaver?" he asked charmingly, taking her hand when she was close enough and kissing the back of it while he bowed at the waist. He stood again and released her hand, a twinkle in his eye as he looked at her. "This way please," he gestured towards the house again where the door was being held open by yet another man. He noticed his other guard had gotten up from the ground on the other side of the Rover, and he glared at them both, earning a slammed door on each side of the Rover. *These guards of mine!* he thought.

"May I offer you a drink?" he asked as he welcomed them into his living room and made his way to a bar in the corner. The room was excellently appointed with couches, rich woods surrounding the windows, beautiful display cabinets, and a large mantle over the fireplace. "Would you like to sit down?"

It was the mantle that drew Kathy's attention, and she stopped to look at something, drawing Alice's attention to it with her eyes. After this exchange, they went to sit down.

"Thank you, but a drink isn't necessary," Alice answered for them both, making sure that Kathy was comfortable and exchanging another look with her. "I've come to you because I have a problem you can help with me with."

"Oh?" he asked, pouring himself two fingers of whiskey in a glass. "What could I possibly do for you?"

"You can tell me where I might find a man who works for you. His name is Iggy?"

"Iggy?" he asked, as though he had never heard the name.

"Come now, Artum. Let's not play games. Ignat Koslov works for you, and I would like to speak with him about a situation he and his men caused my wife and me." She sat back on the couch, seemingly unconcerned. Kathy looked on curiously, realizing there were meanings within meanings in what Alice was saying. She never noticed Alice's sleight of hand as she dropped something into the couch.

"A situation?" he asked, sounding intrigued as he came to sit across from the two women on the couch.

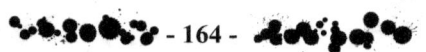

"Oh, yes. He has caused you a bit of embarrassment, I believe?" she asked, sounding cordial as she leaned forward slightly, her fingertips touching the edge of the coffee table briefly before she leaned back again. Kathy looked from Alice to the man sitting across from them. He was tall and handsome, and he looked dangerous. His beard was trimmed immaculately and sculpted along his jaw. His jaw was twitching. Alice could see she had hit home with the word 'embarrassment.'

"What kind of embarrassment are we talking here?" he hedged, hoping it hadn't become public knowledge. His tone of voice had changed slightly.

"I think you may not be aware of this particular embarrassment?" she put in, a smirk on her face.

"How would I know what you are talking about?" he inquired, becoming impatient with her cryptic statements.

"If you knew what he had done, you wouldn't have my Fabergé egg displayed on your mantel over there," she said, nodding towards the beautiful cobalt blue and gold specimen. "I would like to talk with Iggy *personally*," she emphasized.

"I'm sorry, I don't know what you mean..." he began, but he was afraid he did know. Iggy had given him the egg as a sign of respect, apologizing for taking so long to pay his dues. He had thought the man had finally realized he owed great homage to the new leader.

"I see. You are going to protect him then?" she asked conversationally, studying her fingernails as she looked up suddenly, peering across them and right in Artum's dark eyes.

"No, I'm not protecting him. I simply don't know what or who you are talking about. I don't know anyone by that name."

"You, sir, are a very bad liar. Ignat Koslov violated my home. He came onto my property, broke down my front door, and stole that item," she nodded towards the egg, "as well as many other valuable items. I can get you a list," she said sarcastically. She continued when he would have interrupted, "However, I can see there is no honor in this house anymore. He touched my daughter, and he and his men threatened to put her in a whorehouse, discussing quite intimately how she would be used," she told him, watching Kathy from the corner of her eye.

Kathy sat up straighter. She was outraged that Alice hadn't told her that!

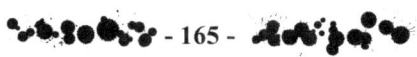

"As I see you will defend your employee, I must warn you now…Turn him over to me and return my things, if you want this to all be over."

"I'm sorry, I don't know what you are talking about," he said, but he was disturbed to realize he believed her. How dare she come into his home and threaten him…It was a threat, wasn't it? She'd stated her conditions but not really in a threatening manner.

"I'm sorry too," she said and looked at a horrified Kathy. "Shall we go?"

Kathy nodded numbly as Alice helped her to her feet. Artum immediately rose, showing he had some manners.

"I am sorry for any misunderstanding between us–" he began diplomatically, but Alice interrupted him, raising her hand to halt his insincere apology.

"There is no misunderstanding," she clarified as she escorted her wife from the room with the taller man following. Alice made sure Kathy was tucked in the Rover. "Say nothing now," she warned her quietly. Alice limped around the SUV, smiling—smirking really—at the two men she had downed. One was going to have a black eye and the other still had blood on his lip. She got behind the wheel of the Rover and started it up, driving slowly down the circular drive and waiting a heart-stopping moment for the gate to open, fearing it might not and ready to ram it if necessary. Slowly, it opened, and she glanced in the rear-view mirror to see Artum staring thoughtfully after them from the porch.

"Why didn't you tell me what those men had said about Emily? How did you know–?" Kathy started up as soon as they turned down the road from the driveway.

"Because I didn't want you getting angry about it and chewing on it until I could do something," she told her wife honestly, glancing over as she pulled her seatbelt tighter. "We are going to do something," she continued, "I promise." "Right now, let's go meet with Charlotte and get that house on the market."

Kathy blinked at the abrupt change of subject. She'd been horrified and angry, and now, she was confused. "Which house?"

"The one in Malibu. Have you changed your mind?" she teased.

"How can you do that?" Kathy marveled, calming down.

"What? Sell a house?"

"No, how can you make a complete about-face during a conversation?"

"About-face about what?"

"Stop playing games with me, Alice."

Alice chuckled. "I'm already over being mad. You just found out what they said, so you can be angry. You will deal with the anger in your own time. Meanwhile, I wanted to get a lot accomplished today and tonight, and I know you have been wanting me to put the Malibu house on the market for a while. I want you to go to the doctor…so it's a tradeoff. Okay?" Alice reasoned.

Kathy shook her head, sighed loudly, and said, "Okay, deal."

Alice chuckled again as she drove to Charlotte's office. She was surprised and pleased to find the realtor was in. The woman was ecstatic to take that listing again. She didn't promise anything, but Alice gladly gave her the keys to the place, signed the paperwork, and agreed to have professional pictures taken. She didn't understand why they couldn't use the previous pictures since the place had been off the market for less than a year. It wasn't like it had changed a lot.

"We should have Sean go over and get the computer games," Alice mentioned to Kathy as she drove back towards Palos Verdes and home.

"I'm surprised he hasn't mentioned those games," Kathy put in. She was so tired. They'd done so much today and that news about what the men had said about her daughter was preying on her mind. She was glad Emily hadn't realized what those men were saying. She was already frightened enough.

"Well, most of the games are duplicates," Alice reminded her, keeping an eye on the traffic and noticing the car that had just started following them again. She hadn't seen the tail while she was in Beverly Hills, but it had followed them to the hotel where Ken Edwards had given his pretty, little motivational speech.

"Tell me, Alice. What was the point of today's visit to Artum?" Kathy asked.

"You have to ask?" Alice was amused. It had been quite a full day, and she'd like to go out tonight but didn't know if Kathy was up to it. She looked tired and worn out.

"Why don't you give me a recap?" Kathy requested. "I'd like to know what you are thinking."

"Well, we unnerved Ken Edwards. His people are going to be given a chewing out. He doesn't suffer fools gladly and thinks of those who work for him as minions and peons. They are paid to do a job, they are not paid to think. So, if they don't do the job, they will earn his ire. I'm betting he's having a royal hissy fit at someone today because no one warned him we would be coming. He would have expected someone to give him a heads-up that we would be in his audience.

"Just now, I wanted to serve warning to Artum. I'm sorry I didn't tell you some of it beforehand, but I wanted him to see your honest reaction. I didn't want anything to look feigned about you playing the outraged mama. I believe your shocked reaction worked in our favor, and when we go after his assets, he is going to want to give me Iggy on a silver platter." She paused to grin at Kathy, "Believe me, we are going to destroy a lot of his assets in retribution."

"And the house in Malibu?"

"Well, that was to make up for not telling you what those men said about our daughter. It's a peace offering. I checked the other day, and the prices in Malibu are sky high right now. Maybe it's because summer is almost here, but in any event, I don't expect the house to be on the market for very long. It was a good investment, and since the government will be looking at our tax returns pretty closely for the rest of our lives, this should look good."

"What about your girlfriend?" Kathy asked suddenly. She had been meaning to ask her about the other woman for a while. It was one of those things that she wanted to bring up but wasn't sure she wanted to know the answer since Alice was once again in her bed.

"Girlfriend?" Alice asked, genuinely confused.

"I saw the nightgown on your bedroom floor when you showed me the house."

Alice started to laugh. then seeing Kathy's outraged face, she sobered up before saying, "That was a plant."

"A plant?"

"For whoever was watching the house. I wanted them to think I had someone there. I wanted them to worry a little if they checked the house and found it there, wondering how she had gotten in there without them seeing. I left that lying there for days. I cannot tell you how hard it was for me to not clean it up," she admitted.

Kathy started to laugh. She knew how fastidious Alice was, and yes, it would have been extremely hard for her to leave a piece of clothing lying on the floor.

"It was just a bonus that you came over when you did and saw it."

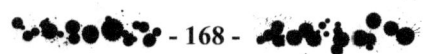

Remembering the reason for that visit, Kathy sobered. "Did you ever look into Linda's death?"

Alice glanced over and saw the sadness on her wife's face. "Did you love her that much?"

Kathy immediately shook her head. "No. I did think of having a future with her at one time, and I'm just sad that she is dead."

Alice was relieved. She hadn't wanted to tell Kathy, but she decided there was no time like the present. "I think Ken Edwards had Linda killed."

"What?"

Alice nodded. "I think he was hoping to pin it on me along with the IRS cloud and the other investigations. He never thought I'd go to the CIA and get a letter exonerating me from prosecution. I am betting he doesn't know why all investigations stopped and he's still wondering why we aren't destitute and homeless."

"How are you going to pay him back? Are you going to kill him?" Kathy might understand Alice's reasoning if she wanted to kill him. The man certainly deserved to die if he had ordered Linda's death, not to mention everything he had put them through. Still, she didn't have to like it.

"Oh, no. I'm thinking we should let him live," Alice told her as she turned onto their street.

"What? Why? What do you have up your sleeve?"

"I think allowing him to live will be more of a punishment than simply killing him. Killing him would end his suffering too quickly. I honestly haven't thought about him in years, which is why it took me so long to figure this out. Now that I know who's behind this, more pieces of the puzzle are starting to fit together. He isn't alone in this. I believe he's called in some old favors, and I'm just trying to figure out exactly how many people are involved. I want to see who the players are in this mess he has made."

Alice's eyes narrowed as she approached their driveway. The gate was open, and a car was parked at the bottom of the walkway. She didn't hit the garage door opener as she approached like usual. Instead, she parked in front of one of the garages. They both got out of their car and looked at the man, who had gotten out of his car when they drove up.

"Can I help you?" Alice asked, walking around to the passenger side of their car and standing next to Kathy.

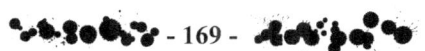

"Are you Alice and Kathy Weaver?" he asked.

Feeling a premonition of imminent disaster, Alice took one step forward, putting Kathy behind her and putting herself in a position to protect her wife. She said, "Yes, we are. Can I help you?"

"You can drop the fucking lawsuit against my daughter!" he told her, walking forward belligerently.

"Careful, Mom. That's Angelica's father," Emily called from the top of the stairs where she had just come out with Sean.

Angelica. That was one of the three girls who had shared Emily's pictures online. Alice remembered seeing this man at the school. He had been the one who refused to cooperate. The parents of the third girl had willingly turned their daughter's phone over to the police, and it proved she not only took the pictures but was sharing them.

"You don't know who the fuck you're dealing with," he got right up in Alice's face, looming over her petite frame.

"You don't know who you are dealing with either," she answered, a tight little grin forming on her face.

He almost took an involuntary step back when he noticed her odd-colored eyes. It angered him that she had caused him to show this sign of weakness, almost as though she could scare him.

"I suggest you leave. You are trespassing." She cocked her head sideways slightly, daring him to touch her or assault her.

"I thought you could be reasoned with..." he began belligerently.

"You thought wrong. That's what lawyers are for."

"You're going to beggar me with—"

"Considering what your daughter did, maybe you should be beggars," she taunted, waiting to see what he would do. Her stance made her appear ready to take him on, despite the brace on her leg. Kathy knew it, and Emily recognized it from her videos, but the man had no clue. Sean was worried about his mothers. He had pressed the panic button when the man slipped through their gate and had come banging on their front door, so he knew security was on the way. Neither of the kids was going to open the door to that.

"Why don't you just leave?" Sean asked from where he stood above them on the steps. "Security and police are already on their way."

"That's it! You rich folks just hide behind your fences and the law," he spat out, looking at the young man, then down at Alice again. He was trying to intimidate her with his size. As he looked at Kathy, Alice stiffened. She heard Kathy discreetly coughing behind her.

"Yeah, that's us, hiding in plain sight," she said mockingly. "Why don't you take my son's advice and leave before you find yourself in a whole heap of *more* trouble." The man's back was to the security vehicle she could see coming down the road. Its lights were flashing, and it was followed closely by a sheriff's vehicle. "Breeding shows. Your daughter probably did what she did because she has a father like you."

Kathy gasped from behind Alice at her taunt. Emily's eyes opened wider, and Sean was certain he was going to have to leap to his mother's defense. He took a couple involuntary steps down the stairs to get within range, just in case. If anything, at least he could tackle the big guy.

"Who the fuck do you think you are–?!" he began, but Alice cut him off.

"I'm the homeowner, and you're trespassing," she said loudly as the security car pulled up with its windows open. "You weren't invited here, and you're threatening me."

"Mrs. Weaver, is everything okay?" one of the officers called as the security guards exited their vehicle.

"No, I'm not okay. This asshole has been threatening me, and he is trespassing on private property. I've asked him to leave a couple times."

"Sir, you are going to have to leave, or we will arrest you for trespassing," one of the officers began.

"No, you arrest him for trespassing *now!*" Alice directed them, seeing the sheriff getting out of his patrol car. The way the sheriff and security vehicles were parked, this guy wasn't going anywhere.

It took an hour before they finally took Angelica's father away in handcuffs. Despite his arguments, they towed his truck and charges would be filed. Alice got her way. She agreed to stop at the sheriff's substation to sign the paperwork for her complaint in the morning. No matter who the guy was, he would be spending the night in jail.

"Jeez, Mom. I thought that guy was going to take a swing at you," Sean said after they had all gone.

"How the hell did he get in?" Alice asked, glancing at Kathy as they all started walking up the stairs to the front door.

"I'd just gotten here with the RAV, and when I went inside the doorbell rang. I thought that was odd since I hadn't heard anyone at the

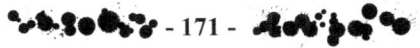

gate. He must have driven in right behind me, and as I walked through the garage, I didn't see him."

"Aren't you supposed to ask before you use the RAV?"

"I did ask. Mom said I could use it," he gestured to Kathy, who nodded.

Alice shook her head. Just what she needed, another situation. Later, she commented to Kathy, "See, I don't go looking for these things, they find me."

"I know," she answered, coughing again. "You are a drama magnet."

"Are you calling the doctor tomorrow for an appointment?" Alice fretted.

"Yes, I promise. Weren't we going out tonight?" Kathy inquired. "Didn't you have something planned?"

"Damn! I forgot, and with all this drama, we might be too late," she answered, looking at the time on her phone. "Think the kids will miss us if we have a date night?"

"A date night?"

Alice nodded. "That's what we are telling them. Make sure you change into your black jogging outfit while I go pack the SUV. Could you bring my clothes with you?"

Artum learned of the fire from the Los Angeles Fire Department the next day. They showed up at his gate accompanied by the police and informed him that a warehouse he owned had gone up in flames the night before. Apparently, it was a six-alarm fire and had burned so hot there was nothing left. The police wanted to know if he had any enemies since it looked like the arsonists had used some type of accelerant. Artum cursed after they filled him in on all the details. He had lapsed his insurance on that warehouse thinking no one knew he owned it, so it was an unnecessary expense. After Alice and Kathy Weaver's visit the previous day, he hadn't been very pleased, and he was certain now, he should have heeded Sebastian's warning. Over the following nights, he lost two more warehouses and a house that no one even knew he owned. Two of Iggy's subordinates were missing as well. At first, he questioned if Alice Weaver might be behind his losses, but he sincerely doubted it after meeting her and seeing her physical stature. Somewhere, he must have created an enemy, and it was costing him a lot! "Where is Iggy?" he asked after learning about the fourth fire.

Kathy hadn't been this excited or scared in a long time. They'd gone to the house in the valley and taken their time to lose the tail. Alice had gone to a panel in the 1970s wall, which Kathy had never noticed before. She lifted the wood paneling, and behind it were standard wall braces with multiple shelves of supplies between them. Kathy watched, amazed, as Alice picked and chose from the array at her fingertips. Once her arms were full, Kathy helped her pack everything in the SUV. Later, they hauled everything into that first warehouse but not before they stopped to fill a couple gas cans and pick up some throw-away cell phones. Alice had expertly picked the lock of the warehouse, and the two women hauled in the gasoline, spilling it along the aisles from one shelving unit to another. When they were ready, Alice showed Kathy how to wire a cell phone to a primer cord.

"When I call this phone," Alice indicated one of the throw-away phones she had purchased, "it will send a spark to this," she pointed at the cord, "and the spark will trigger that," her arm gestured towards the gasoline that ran deep into the old warehouse.

"Why are there no guards?" Kathy wondered, rubbing her gloved hand across her nose and noticing the smell of gasoline on it.

"Artum must not think it is necessary, and it's probably cheaper," she reasoned as she rigged the set-up, left the phone on the desk, and rose. "Let's get out of here," she said as she glanced around for cameras one more time before they left the warehouse.

As they were driving away, Kathy asked, "When will you trigger it?"

"Let's get a couple more miles away and then call," she said, reaching into her pocket for the paper where she had jotted down the number of the phone left on the desk. "Would you like to do the honors?"

Kathy eagerly reached for the phone and after turning on the overhead light, she keyed the number into the phone. "When do I hit send?" she asked eagerly.

"Are you that eager to commit a felony?" Alice asked, amused as Kathy turned out the light.

Kathy coughed to hide her laugh. "No, but I do want to meet this Iggy guy and have a few words with him on our daughter's behalf."

Alice nodded. She was quiet as she drove a while longer, then she said, "Call the number."

Kathy eagerly pushed the send button. She heard the phone ring once, then a second ring, and finally, it made an unusually fast beeping sound. "That's it?" she asked, disappointed as she closed the cheap flip phone.

Alice nodded. "We don't want to be anywhere near that warehouse when it goes up in flames. Watch the news for the video."

"That's anticlimactic," Kathy said, her voice sounding a bit down.

"I have a police scanner, if you want to listen to that," Alice pointed out.

They went out several nights in a row and were enjoying the excitement of hitting what seemed like random places, first some warehouses and then, a good-looking, empty home. One night while they were at one of the businesses, they ran into two of Iggy's friends. They recognized them as two of the men who raided their home, despite the disguises they had worn. Alice's research had produced photos of the men, and once she verified their identity, Alice let Kathy have a few words with them.

"We did nothing, missus," one of them denied, his thick accent revealing his fear. Alice had tied the men up with wire, and it was now digging into his wrists. If either of them struggled too much, the wire was positioned to cut into their veins.

"Ty izhesh," Alice said in Russian, repeating it in English for Kathy's sake, "You lie."

He looked surprised by the petite blonde with the slicked back hair. Her accent was rough, but he understood her clearly, even before she repeated it in English.

Kathy looked surprised. She hadn't heard Alice speak Russian before. It was obvious both men understood her, judging by their shocked expressions.

Kathy told them in no uncertain terms what she thought of them and their comments about their intended plans for her daughter.

Alice asked a couple pertinent questions, but it was obvious they were reluctant to answer. She pulled a knife from her metal belt to help convince them, and after she began to slice along the neck of one man, he began to spill the information she required. The other man needed no further encouragement, and he too began giving her relevant information. They didn't tell her anything she hadn't already learned on her own, but they confirmed and verified things for her.

"Now, what do we do with them?" Kathy asked in a whisper as Alice covered their mouths with duct tape, wrapping it completely around their heads. Alice had explained if they only wrapped their mouths, the duct tape might come off when it got wet from the saliva. Kathy appreciated the new knowledge. She would have laughed at the trivia, if they weren't in such a dire situation.

"What do you want me to do with them?" Alice asked. She kept her voice equally low where they stood across the room, her eyes glittering in anticipation.

"What do you mean, what do I want *you* to do with them? I'm in on this too, aren't I?"

"Okay. It was *our* daughter they talked about," and Alice went on to remind Kathy exactly what the men had talked about doing to Emily. Kathy's ire rose even higher.

"I'll kill them!" she vowed.

"Killing them won't make them suffer," Alice pointed out.

"If we let them go–"

"They will warn the others," Alice finished for her.

"Then, what?"

"If there are no bodies, the police can't investigate. If no one ever finds them, they will always wonder what happened to them," she pointed out. "If we don't kill them, we won't have their deaths on our conscience…but they will die, and they will suffer," she added.

"So…what? We leave them here?" But Kathy realized if they burned this place down, there would be bodies. "No, not here," she shook her head. "Then where?"

Kathy helped Alice put the tied and taped men in the back of her SUV on top of some plastic she had draped there. She tied their legs together and warned them, "Ne dvigaysya." They would have fought, but she'd knocked them down, stunned them, and the wire on their wrists hurt. Her admonishment, "Don't move," would be obeyed...for now.

As Alice drove to Long Beach, Kathy sat in silence. Her heart was pounding, and as badly as she wanted to discuss their plan, she would obey Alice, who had touched a finger to her mouth to shush her. The radio muffled any sounds of the road and any sounds the men might make as they surreptitiously attempted to free themselves from their bonds. Once off road, Alice exited the car in order to cut the chains off a gate. Once through the gate, the Rover bounced over the ruts of the road, its headlights illuminating oil derricks. Kathy looked at Alice in alarm and wondered where they were and why they were here. Alice was looking for something, and when she found it, she turned the vehicle around, backed it up a ways, then braked and turned everything off. Kathy followed Alice to the back of the Rover when she finally got out.

"Okay, get out!" Alice told the first man, cutting the ties on his feet, so he could walk. "Ladno ubiraysya," she repeated her command in Russian. "You stay there," Alice pointed with her knife at the other terrified man, the one whose legs were still tied together. "Ty ostan'sya tam," she added in Russian for effect, proving to everyone that she knew the language, albeit imperfectly. Alice had examined the ties and saw where the wire had cut into the men's arms causing them to bleed. She couldn't see any blood in her SUV, but she knew that didn't mean a thing. She was concerned about leaving DNA evidence behind, which was why she also examined the plastic to see if either had gotten off it. She closed the back of the Rover, leaving the second man inside as she led the first man towards one of the derricks. Before Kathy could ask where they were going, Alice threw out her arm to stop her wife from taking another step forward. The man was not so lucky. He hadn't seen Alice stop Kathy and kept walking forward where he fell, quite abruptly, disappearing from sight. They heard a splash, but it was far away and muffled. They only heard because it was dark, and the sound carried.

"Whaaa–?!" she began, but Alice grabbed her again and pulled her back before she fell in another hole.

"Be careful! This place is full of holes, and if you aren't vigilant, you could fall in too," Alice told her.

"Did he just fall in an oil hole?"

"Sorta. It's probably more like a maintenance hole. They are all over the place, and they are never checked. Most are covered, but this one wasn't and probably hasn't been for years. We were closer than I thought," Alice admitted. "It's been years since I was out here. I thought they would have covered it up by now."

"Have you used this method to dispose of enemies before?" Kathy asked, and when Alice didn't answer, she had her answer. Alice hadn't told her much about her past kills, and she really didn't want to know more. Together, they returned to the SUV and got the second guy out of the Rover, heading back towards the hole. He struggled, worried when they returned so quickly without his partner. Alice smacked him repeatedly, unsettling his equilibrium when she struck his ears. Despite the wires cutting into his arms, he had thought to fight her, but all thoughts of fighting vanished as he went down on his knees. Alice drove her booted foot into his spine and sent him headlong into the hole. Both women turned away, so they didn't hear him hit bottom. Alice pulled the plastic from the back of her SUV, rolled it into a tight ball, and flung it into the hole after the men. The smell of oil was strong around them, and the mighty derricks were endlessly pumping, coaxing the life blood of this area to rise and make some company rich.

They both got back in the Rover, and Alice started the engine and drove away. She stopped just long enough to close the gates behind her and place the chain around the posts with her gloved hands, so it wouldn't arouse suspicion. They were strangely silent on the ride home, both seemingly enjoying the music. As they turned down their street, they saw their watchers' car, only tonight, one of the men was on the side of the road, back about ten feet in the weeds, peeing. Alice turned her Rover, aiming straight for him. Her headlights clearly highlighted his body as he dove out of her way. They both laughed at his discomfort as Alice expertly pulled the Rover around the waiting car and into their driveway. She peeled her gloves off before stuffing them beneath her seat. Kathy followed suit, still chuckling.

Alice finally got to remove her brace on the same day Kathy went in for a full checkup. Kathy hadn't used a doctor in years, so she didn't know this general practitioner. Dr. Lenoir was quite thorough and ordered further tests after asking several pertinent questions and listening to Kathy's lungs. A mammogram and x-rays would make Kathy's life very interesting over the coming week.

Alice was busy. She and Kathy had been to several of Artum's properties in the past few nights while setting things up. She'd had to search far and wide to obtain everything she needed and avoid arousing suspicion. Her shopping list was rather...eclectic, you might say. She parked the Rover in city parking and boarded a train going downtown. Their watchers were either too lazy to follow or didn't have direct instructions to follow her on foot, so they had no idea where she went on the train or what she carried in the boxes and bags she brought back. Some of the packages couldn't be seen since she wore a backpack to keep her hands free in case she needed to act quickly. Downtown Los Angeles was not the best neighborhood, even in the light of day.

So far, they hadn't had to openly kill anyone, but she knew it was only a matter of time. She didn't count the two in the hole in Long Beach. She was certain they had either died during their fall or would eventually die of starvation in the hole, and she didn't care which. But she realized their disappearances might have some in the organization rethinking their choices. Her nights were filled with plans and shaking the men that Ken Edwards had assigned to follow her had proven difficult. Either his instructions had changed, or these were a better caliber of watchers.

Her plans had to be put on hold temporarily when Kathy began her tests. Alice's days were now filled with concern about Kathy as she waited with her for the mammogram results, x-rays, and other tests Dr. Lenoir ordered.

"She must think there is something wrong if she's ordering all these tests," Alice worried.

"Well, I haven't been checked out in years, and I think she's just being thorough." Kathy dismissed Alice's concerns, but she was worried too. Dr. Lenoir had poked and prodded and some of it had hurt.

"Mrs. Weaver, please come in with your wife," the nurse suggested from where she stood in the doorway. Alice would have come in anyway, but she stood immediately, pleased she didn't have to balance on the brace anymore. Her leg felt thinner and much lighter without the cast and brace. It also felt weaker, so she was being cautious; her gait was still a bit awkward.

"What do you think she wants to tell us?" Kathy whispered. "Maybe I'm pregnant?"

"Lucy, you've got some 'splainin' to do!" Alice said in her best Desi Arnaz impression. "Could you imagine…at our age?"

"Our baby is nearly grown up," Kathy admitted with a smile, remembering Emily as a baby. She had filled out so much in the last year, and it was good to see. Kathy looked at Alice with a critical eye too. She had also filled in a little this past year, and it looked good on her.

"Mrs. Weaver? Kathy?" the doctor came in, closing a folder she had been reading. She shook both their hands. "I'm glad you could come in. I have your test results here," she said as she took a seat. The nurse sat down in front of a computer on the other side of the small examination room and waited. "I need to run some biopsies, but this," she pulled an x-ray from the folder, "needs to be looked at by another doctor." She held the x-ray up to the light for a quick glance, then put it on the lightboard on the wall and flipped a switch to illuminate it for all to see.

Both Alice and Kathy were shocked. The x-ray showed several spots across Kathy's chest. In fact, it showed many, many various sized spots.

"Is something wrong with your tests?" Kathy asked, looking at the odd x-ray.

"No," the doctor responded firmly.

"Is it cancer?" Alice asked.

"We don't know yet. We need to run more tests."

"What in the world? How did they get like that?" Kathy asked. She had felt the mass that Alice discovered in her breast, and she knew there was another in her other breast. Now, she could clearly see both those masses on the x-ray, but there were numerous others of various sizes. They almost looked like pencil-sized dots all over the x-ray. Did she have measles?

"These are inconsistent, and I want to biopsy this one," she said, pointing to the mass in the right breast. "That will allow us to draw it out and get an idea what we are dealing with. I also want to do a full body scan since these," she pointed to spots that were visible at various points above her skeleton on the x-ray, "also don't make sense."

"So, what is it? Breast cancer?" Alice asked, trying to bore holes in the x-ray with her eyes.

"That's just it, we don't know. These spots are too erratic, too random. They aren't behaving like normal cancer cells or masses."

"So, lymphoma?" Kathy asked in a small voice, feeling ill at what she was seeing.

Again, the doctor shook her head. "I don't know, and I want you to see one of our oncologists as soon as possible. The pattern is too random, and it doesn't seem to be targeting one specific system. This is too spread out too. Something..." she murmured, thinking aloud as she looked at the x-ray again. "Have you been working with asbestos? Maybe you were refitting a house and inhaled something?"

Kathy immediately shook her head. "No, we haven't done anything like that." She didn't count the warehouses they had visited in the past few nights because she hadn't inhaled any of the smoke they caused, but she had certainly coughed a lot from the activities they were involved in.

The doctor questioned her extensively about her travels and any other activities that might have caused what they were seeing on the x-ray. She asked about foods she might have eaten, all kinds of arbitrary questions, but both Kathy and Alice could see she was grasping at straws. She was attempting to find the cause of these erratic growths that didn't exactly look like cancer cells. Kathy agreed to undergo the fine needle aspiration biopsy procedure. Alice held her hand as she watched the needle being inserted into her wife's breast. The doctor pulled it out after she hit the mass she wanted to aspirate. Alice could tell it hurt Kathy because her hand tightened. but even more painful were the thoughts playing on her mind about what this could mean.

"How long until you get the results of that?" Kathy asked, pointing at the needle the doctor had labeled.

"A few days," she admitted, looking sadly at Kathy. "Can you come in tomorrow for the full body scan, so we can see if that tells us anything about what we are dealing with?" Dr. Lenoir made it seem quite urgent, and both Alice and Kathy were reeling, but they agreed to come back the next day. They were mute during the drive home in the Rover. Alice reached out and held Kathy's shaking hand.

"I'm going to lose my hair," Kathy said.

"I could shave my head again in solidarity," Alice said, trying to lighten the mood...and failing.

"Oh, my God. I never thought about cancer," Kathy said quietly, starting to cry.

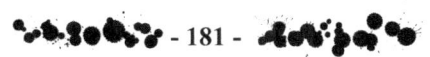 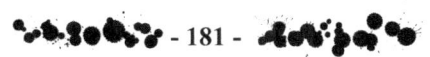

Alice pulled over to the side of the road and parked, pulling Kathy into her arms while she sobbed. It was a long time before she stopped, and Alice's shoulder was completely soaked with her tears. Just as Kathy began to breathe normally, they heard a knock on the passenger side window And saw a Los Angeles policeman was standing next to the car. Kathy sniffed, and Alice handed her a tissue before she rolled down the window.

"Can I help you, officer?" Alice inquired politely.

"Is everything okay, ma'am?" he asked, looking at the two women closely.

"My wife just learned some devastating news, and I was comforting her," she told him honestly. She hoped he wouldn't give her a ticket or hassle her; she wasn't in the mood.

"Ah, I see," he said, noting Kathy's puffy eyes and seeing her dabbing at her nose with the tissue. "Please be careful when you get back on the road," he said as he gave a mock salute and backed off, returning to his vehicle.

"Well, he was nice," Kathy said in a raspy voice. She was obviously still quite upset.

"We weren't doing anything wrong," Alice pointed out.

"For a change," Kathy added, and they both chuckled. "How are we going to tell the kids?"

"Do you want to tell them before we know the results of the tests? You know, this is going to scare them."

Remembering how many times they had been scared by their other mother's faux deaths, Kathy decided to wait and tell them when they knew what they were dealing with.

"If you don't want to go out this time, we can wait," Alice offered when she saw how upset Kathy was feeling that evening. The kids sensed something was up with their parents but didn't want to ask. At the same time, they were both pleased with how often their parents had gone on date nights, or so they thought.

"You know, I really want to go out and destroy something," Kathy admitted eagerly.

Alice smiled slightly. These trips to the properties Artum owned under various pseudonyms to hide his assets were becoming routine. They'd destroyed several buildings now, and he couldn't possibly have traced it to them...yet.

"Okay, but this should be the last one," Alice stated with a gleam in her eye. Kathy laughed. She knew this might be just the beginning of the war. She realized that Alice had planned the invasion of Sebastian's old warehouses with military precision. Alice didn't do anything halfway. She had been calculating, thorough, and given the amount of time she'd held back due to her broken leg, she had been very, *very* patient.

"Maybe we should rethink this location," Alice stated when she saw this warehouse had guards.

"Do you have an alternate warehouse on your list?" Kathy asked, wondering if their night out was ruined. She needed something to get the tests and their possible results out of her head. She coughed slightly, feeling defeated.

Not wishing to disappoint Kathy, Alice leaned back in the SUV and began to fill their packs with the supplies they would need. Each of them carried a gas can that had been blackened, so no one could see the telltale red color of the plastic containers. Alice had thought about getting jerrycans for the SUV, so no one would question why she was carrying so much gas if she got stopped, but this was not the time to think about accessories for her Rover. She'd parked down the street and hoped no one jacked the expensive SUV. She thought about getting another vehicle for this kind of trip and was reminded of the vehicles she had sold from the storage units.

They waited for the security guard to pass before sneaking into the warehouse. Alice went one way and Kathy the other, both splashing gasoline on the floor and onto the boxes on the shelves. They had no idea what was in the boxes, but they could guess. Leaving the gas cans in the shadows by the foot of the stairs, they climbed together to a loft-like section of the warehouse where the offices were located, ducking down to avoid being seen. Alice began to wire the office with detonation cord. Kathy had seen that the highly explosive core of the cord was wrapped in a reinforced, drab olive-gray plastic coating. Alice explained this would transmit a detonating wave, which was perfect for their efforts.

As Alice wired the cord to a throw-away phone—one of several she and Kathy had purchased at random gas stations—Kathy wandered to the desk, keeping low and away from the windows that surrounded the office. Just as Alice finished her work, Kathy hissed, "Alice, look at this!"

Alice crept next to her wife, watching that her head didn't rise above the windows where they might be seen by the guards in the warehouse below. She looked at the accounting books Kathy had found, her eyes opening wide in shock at the various amounts and names she saw listed there. She glanced at Kathy, who nodded to confirm she had seen correctly.

"What are you doing in here?" a man's voice asked gruffly. Both Kathy and Alice turned towards the door where Richard Pasternack stood.

He recognized them instantly. Alice ran to shut him up, but it was too late. He yelled, and the nearest security guard was already running up the steps. Alice wrestled with Richard, and he was shocked that she would attack him. This worked in her favor, and she was able to stun him by striking his head against the frame of the door. He went down when she struck him a second time, using his head as a bouncy ball. By then, the security guard had arrived and was trying to cuff Alice. He grabbed her wrist, but she twisted away. Alice adroitly grabbed the cuffs from his hands, wrapped them through her fingers, and used them as brass knuckles, slugging him in the jaw and shocking him with the ferocity of her attack. He couldn't believe this petite woman could best him, but he went down when she kicked him in the head and knocked him out.

"Help me," Alice ordered Kathy as she shut the office door. Kathy wheeled the office chair over and helped her wife pull a stunned Richard up onto it.

"He...isn't...very...light...is...he?" Kathy huffed and puffed.

Alice grinned as she cuffed Richard to the chair with the security guard's cuffs, then found a second pair for the other wrist. When they were done, they wheeled him back to the desk.

Alice hog-tied the security officer with his own tie and dragged him further into the office. She hoped the commotion hadn't attracted anyone else's attention. So far, it seemed quiet down in the warehouse.

"Do you want to explain this, *Dick*?" Alice asked Richard when he was able to focus. Seeing Alice and Kathy Weaver standing before him in black outfits, he realized they must be the ones that had started the fires at Artum's warehouses and house!

"I'm not telling you jack," he asserted stoutly, then swallowed reflexively when Alice pulled a hunting knife from the sheath on her leg down by her ankle. It matched her outfit perfectly, and he hadn't noticed it earlier. She held the blade to his neck.

"Do you know what it feels like to bleed to death?" she asked him in a quiet voice while gesturing to the ledgers. "You might want to explain who these companies are...quickly!" she threatened. She could hear people moving around in the warehouse below, so she kept her voice low. She knew that Richard's silhouette could be seen through the frosted glass of some of the windows. She made sure he wasn't visible from the clear windows intended to allow anyone in the office to look out over the vast warehouse, rolling him to the side of the desk away from those windows. She knew the people below would expect to see one shadow, not two or three. She gestured to Kathy to stay low. "Go through the drawers," she whispered to her wife.

Kathy, her heart pumping wildly at this turn of events, obeyed instantly. Her eyes bugged out at the cash that spilled from the drawers when she opened them. "Look at this!" she hissed to Alice, trying to contain the excitement in her voice as she showed her wife the bundles of used bills. Then, she came across bundles of bills in larger denominations that had been shrink-wrapped. They looked brand new, and she wondered if they were real.

Alice tilted her head and said, "You better start talking, *Dick*," letting him decide if she was referring to his name or a certain body part.

"I am not telling you–" he began, and Alice turned her knife without hesitation, plunging it through his hand secured to the chair. His body jerked automatically, but the handcuff around his wrist kept him in the chair. Anticipating his scream, she clamped her other hand over his mouth, and that was when she smelled gasoline and realized the scent must be coming from her glove.

Kathy's eyes almost bugged out of her head when she saw her wife stab their neighbor. She quickly turned back to the desk drawers, opening them one at a time and placing the cash she found on top of the desk.

"Richard...Dick...you got something you want to say to me before I kill you for refusing to say jack?" Alice asked conversationally. She

pulled the knife from his hand, watching his eyes flare as she stabbed the knife faster and faster into the wood of the chair between his fingers.

Richard had never been so frightened in his life. Sandi told him she had seen Alice Weaver at Sebastian's, but he hadn't believed her. He had refused to go along with his wife's plans, even after Carmen had gotten in trouble at school. He was disappointed he hadn't been able to buy the Weaver estate from bankruptcy, but there were other properties. They already owned several they had acquired through various deals. Working with Sebastian, and now, his heir Artum, had proven quite lucrative. The pain in his hand was excruciating, but the smell of gasoline had him worrying about what they might have done with gasoline in the warehouse. Alice's normally polite demeanor was nowhere to be seen. Who was this person before him? Her eyes were frightening. He nodded to let her know he did have something to say to her, and as soon as she removed her glove from his mouth, he began explaining about the companies and people in the ledgers before him.

Kathy was aghast! He spilled information for quite a while. Alice just studied him to ascertain if he was telling the truth. She was also listening in case any of the security guards came to see where their co-worker had gone. When the guy on the floor started making groaning noises, she stuffed crumpled papers in his mouth to shut him up. When that hadn't worked, and Richard had faltered in his recitation, she kicked the guy in the head again, silencing him. She gestured for Richard to continue, and after that display, he sped up.

"Wait, so they manufacture some of the chemicals here in *this* building?" Alice interrupted to ask.

Richard nodded, hoping if he kept talking, it would buy him time, and someone would come and rescue him from the predicament he found himself in. He thought of screaming but knew that was a bad idea. The look in Alice's eyes told him she'd silence him permanently before she was done.

"Is that all you have for us?" Alice finally asked when he seemed to run out of steam.

He nodded reluctantly. They had gone through most of the pages of the ledger before him.

"Kathy, put that and that," Alice nodded towards the various ledgers, "in your pack. Leave the cash; we don't need it."

"But Alice..." Kathy began. She knew there were hundreds of thousands of dollars on the desk now.

"We don't need it!" Alice stressed. "There is blood on that money plus cocaine and other drugs," she told her wife, who pulled the ledgers out carefully with the tips of her fingers once she realized what they were dealing with. When they heard a slight noise near the door, both Kathy and Alice looked up and were horrified to see Emily opening the door slowly, her eyes wide at the sight before her.

What Emily saw was her mothers wearing black outfits. Alice was holding a knife at the ready, and Kathy was stuffing a ledger into a bag. There was a strange man hog-tied on the floor before her, and Carmen's father, Richard, was handcuffed to a chair in front of a desk filled with cash.

"Emily!" Kathy gasped, seemingly frozen in time.

"What in the world are you doing here?" Alice asked, shutting Richard's gaping mouth with her glove before he could say anything.

"I snuck into the back of the SUV and hid under that lap blanket you carry," Em confessed, her eyes wide.

"Quiet!" Alice hissed, hearing what she thought was movement in the warehouse below. They all froze. Kathy and Alice exchanged looks, and Emily continued to take in the scene before her. She was shocked! She'd heard Alice's story about Kazakhstan but seeing her at work with Kathy helping her was beyond anything she could have imagined.

"How long have you been in here?" Kathy whispered, frozen in place next to the desk where she had finished packing up the ledgers they were taking.

"I saw you two go up the stairs and waited to follow. When they didn't return," she gestured at the security guard and Richard Pasternack, her eyes flaring as he recognized her, "I worried that you might need help."

Kathy and Alice exchanged looks. There was nothing they could do now since Emily had seen what they were up to. Alice slowly released Richard's mouth with a hissed warning, "Be quiet or else..." She didn't need to finish her sentence. They both knew what 'or else' meant. She looked around the office, nudging Kathy as she picked up another bag she'd found. "I had another thought," she told Kathy and began stuffing money into the bag.

"I can tell you where there is even more money," Richard began, trying to bargain for his life. He proceeded to tell the two women a fount of additional information as they listened. Alice shoved a cleaning rag she had found lying about the office into his mouth when she realized he was finished. Emily's eyes looked like they were going to bug out of her head as she watched. "Shhh," Alice said, touching her fingers to her lips. She'd heard something from below. It was probably one of the other guards. She gestured to Kathy that they should go, realizing they'd been there far too long.

"What about the phone?" Kathy asked, gesturing to the wire that lay unconnected.

"Too late. We don't have time," Alice answered as she handed Kathy the bulging bag of cash after swinging the pack over her shoulder.

"Mmm hmm," Richard tried to speak around the rag. His hands gripped the chair as he struggled, but Alice ignored him. He was no longer important, and she had to get her family out of here.

She grabbed Emily by the arm, touching her finger to her lips to signal the teen to be quiet.

They eased the office door open, but instead of going down the same stairs they had used to come up, they went farther along the corridor. Slowly, they opened other office doors until they found another stairwell, which they climbed down cautiously. Alice was worried. They had been in the warehouse too long, and the guard and Richard could be discovered at any time, along with the gasoline and unwired phone they had left behind.

They came out into a space filled with plastic. Plastic covered the doors, the windows, and the walls. Inside this space, women were working in their underwear, and Alice saw one man guarding them with a machine gun. She glanced around to confirm there was only one guard, then she snuck up on him. Gesturing silently, she signaled that Kathy and Emily were to stay back. Alice rose behind the guard, and when he sensed someone was near and began to turn, she whipped her knife across his neck. He went down. She wrenched the gun from his hands before he could pull the trigger and slipped the safety on. The women stopped working. They were shocked and froze where they stood. The glazed looks on their face told a tale. The violence before them was not even penetrating their consciousness.

"Get out!" Alice told them in English. "Leave and save yourselves!"

They stared blankly at her. Looking at their appearance, she switched to Spanish. "Sal de aquí!" she said but received no response. Finally, she tried Russian, "Vykhodi, ty svoboden!"

This last command they understood. The women exchanged looks. She'd told them they were free. She waited only a moment before gesturing with the machine gun. One of them hesitantly reached for her clothes and began to leave. Alice nodded encouragingly, and the others followed suit. They were moving slowly, looking over their shoulders at Alice in fear. "Bystreye! Bystreye!" She told them to hurry.

Kathy watched as the women left and wished she could help them. A couple looked as though they'd been beaten, and she could only imagine the conditions they had worked under in this factory. She surveyed the area where they had obviously been sorting cocaine, diluting the pure substance with other chemicals to increase their profits before placing the final mixture into little packets.

Alice was frisking the guard and found a pack of cigarettes and lighter. He hadn't dared to smoke around all these chemicals. The place was toxic, and she whispered to Kathy and a wide-eyed Emily, "Don't breathe any of this crap, if you can help it."

They were tempted to leave by the same door the women had used, but they had something to finish first. Alice put down the gun and made her way out of the factory.

"What are you going to do with that?" Kathy whispered, gesturing to the cigarettes and lighter. She knew Alice didn't smoke.

"This will make a great fuse," she replied as she handed them to Kathy. They walked out another door and right into the path of another guard, who was holding a gun. He raised his gun, the sound of it being cocked back eerily loud in the quiet of the warehouse.

"Hold it right there!" he shouted, so he would alert his fellow guards to come to his aid. He only saw women intruders, but there might be more. He didn't recognize any of them from the crew that worked in the plastic room.

Alice raised her hands and Kathy and Emily followed suit. Kathy was looking to Alice for some sign of what she should do. She had an urge to cough but suppressed it. In one hand she held a bag filled with money, in the other she held the cigarettes and lighter handed to her by Alice. Her pack with the ledgers hung from her shoulders and over her

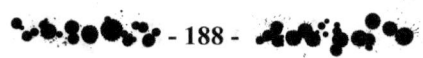

back. Emily shifted uncomfortably as she also raised her hands, wondering what her parents would do.

"What are you doing here?" he asked while he waited for others to come. Surely, someone heard him.

"We're here to destroy your boss's operation," Alice told him, surprising all of them with her bluntness. She indicated she was going to lower her one arm, holding out her hand to show him she had nothing in it. She'd returned her knife to its sheath on her leg after she'd killed the man in the factory. Suddenly, she realized where they were standing. Her nose told her how near they were to the goods, but apparently, he couldn't smell the fumes.

"How are you going to do that?" he sneered, not believing a word she said.

"Mind if I smoke?" she asked, again flexing her fingers to show there was nothing in them.

He nodded, wishing he could have one as well. He guessed it couldn't hurt to let them smoke while they waited. He held his gun confidently, knowing they had nothing better to do than wait. *Where the hell were the others?* he wondered.

Alice took her time pulling a cigarette from the pack that Kathy handed her, then lit it and inhaled deeply to get a nice red glow on it. Alice was looking at it thoughtfully and watching the guard across the glow. Taking it in her fingers, she looked at it once more, making sure the guard's eyes were focused on it and on her, then she cocked her head as she flicked it towards the puddle of gasoline next to them. At the same time, she body-slammed Kathy and Emily, pushing them away and out of his line of fire. There was a flash as the gasoline fumes ignited. Alice continued pushing Kathy and Emily towards the exit door as the guard, distracted by the fire that was spreading rapidly along the gasoline trails, yelled in consternation. They made it out the door of the warehouse just as he started to fire his gun, but it was too late. They were out of his line of sight, and the flames had started his clothing on fire.

"Ah, ahh, ahhhhhh!" he screamed as he desperately tried to extinguish the flames.

"Come on," Alice said, running for the SUV and holding Kathy and Emily each by an arm. Dropping her hand from Emily when they reached the street, she reached into her pants' pocket and started the vehicle remotely, unlocking it as they got closer. Finally, she released

Kathy. They all jumped into the SUV, and she slammed it into drive, pulling quickly away from the warehouse. In the rear-view mirror, they could see the flames were already licking out the open door.

There was an explosion behind them, and they looked back in time to see the office go up in flames. Turning back to the front, Kathy screamed, "Look out!" and Alice swerved just barely missing the six Russian women. She breathed a sigh of relief; she had almost clipped one of them. Alice slammed on the brakes, stopped abruptly, then opened her window. Grabbing the bag of cash from Kathy's lap, she threw it at the women's feet. The bag fell open, and the cash spilled out. Alice sped off, watching in her rear-view mirror as the Russian women stopped to gather around the bag.

Alice stopped only once on the drive home to throw their gloves in a storm drain. The smell of gasoline on the gloves was overpowering.

"Now, what are we going to do with you?" Alice asked Emily, looking at her in the rear-view mirror. The pale teen glanced at Kathy, who was recovering from a coughing fit before she could turn in her seat and face her daughter.

~The End~

❦ MACHIAVELLIAN MALICE ❧

BOOK 29

When your life is a mess, and you are surrounded by enemies, how do you combat the overwhelming odds against you? Alice and Kathy must face down more than health concerns; life concerns and a litany of grievances are stacked against them.

Alice sat up suddenly. She'd been dreaming, and the nightmare that had nearly taken her away was of Emily standing in front of one of the buildings they had burned down. It took her a minute to realize she was home in their bed, and Kathy was asleep beside her.

Kathy. Jeez, the day hadn't gone well as the medical staff poked and prodded her, took x-rays and scans, and drew blood. They couldn't figure out why she was having so many problems, and her breathing was becoming more and more ragged as they argued about what course of treatment to give her. She hadn't been sleeping well, mostly because they had stayed out late in order to take the war to their enemy. Last night had been too close.

Alice lay down again as she thought over the warehouse fire. They'd taken out a drug factory, and she knew Artum would make someone pay for that. They had thrown hundreds of thousands of dollars in cash at the women, and she hoped they would use it wisely, but she also wondered how many of those six women were addicted to the drugs they had been packaging? How many of them would really escape the plight she was certain they hadn't asked to be thrown into? One or more of them would most likely go back into the only life they knew, and they would certainly point a finger towards the two women they had seen with the teen.

God, Emily had seen so much last night. There had been no answers from the shocked teen about what they should do with her. Alice had reluctantly driven them home, stopping at a big box store to dispose of some of the evidence in the SUV, stowing it in various garbage bins far from the scene of the crime and in places she knew there were no cameras. Kathy and Emily wanted to help her, but Kathy was coughing too much and would draw attention to them, and Alice was so angry about Emily, she waved her back into the SUV. She would normally have taken the rest of the evidence to the house in the valley but didn't want to take Emily there.

She thought about the threat that man Iggy had made against their daughter, her Emily, the daughter of her heart. She loved Kit too, but Emily was her blood. She knew without a doubt that this was her child from her and Kathy's unique mixing. She wouldn't have allowed her beloved daughter to be taken into prostitution and end up like those women, virtual slaves to.... And that was when Alice thought of the clinic that had saved Emily. She nearly sat up again to wake Kathy. They must take her to see Doctor Wilkerson.

"I don't understand why these people were in there, but this was definitely a front for a drug lab," the crime scene investigator stated, pointing back at the smoldering ruins of a once large warehouse. "Why was that one handcuffed to a desk?"

The Los Angeles Police Department, the Los Angeles Fire Department, the Drug Enforcement Administration (DEA), and a few other acronyms, including the FBI, were all very, very interested in this fire—even above all the other suspicious fires they had been investigating lately.

"You think Alice Weaver is involved in these suspicious fires in LA?" someone brought up as they discussed their current caseloads.

"Why not?" he shrugged. "She's not doing much online," he pointed to the computer that was monitoring the stocks Alice was buying on the internet, at least the ones they could find. Things had been rather quiet for a long time. What they didn't know was those were dummy stocks, and their own computer was giving them false information. Alice had no reason to invest anymore if she didn't want to. She had enough money to last the rest of her life, enough even to last the rest of her children's lives. If she wanted, her money would last several lifetimes for several generations. The amount of stocks she bought were small in comparison to what she already owned, which provided a legal income she could claim on her taxes. She'd bought a few things just for a write-off. She'd also bought a few stocks just to bring monies into the country that she could now claim.

Artum was convinced it was Alice Weaver setting the blazes that were costing him so much money. It was right after her ask and his refusal that these things started happening to his properties, so he started investigating her. Reading about the house she had purchased in Malibu, which was already on the market, didn't interest him. But the house in Palos Verdes fascinated him. He even found the original listing that read:

A private estate located in the prestigious Palos Verdes Estates offers resort style living at its best! This secluded estate boasts sensational panoramic views of the Pacific Ocean from almost every room of the home. A total renovation was designed and completed by the famous architect Don Hendrickson during the last three years. This renovation is a perfect balance of refinement and resort style living. This estate will exceed all your expectations, from the grand curb appeal and a huge lobby to a spacious living room and formal dining room. Also includes a great master suite, gourmet kitchen, fantastic library, multi-function media/family room, two staff quarters with their own kitchen/ laundry/ dining facilities, N/S tennis court with ocean views, wine /cigar cellar, fantastic semi outdoor gym with its own bath and two separate garages with space for a total of 9 cars! The park-like grounds are lavishly designed and surrounded by 3 sides of parkland. This is one of a very few contemporary styled architectural estates on the hill, with big windows filled with sunlight and views! Please do not miss this grand estate, which has so much to offer!

He would have sent his guys to watch the house but didn't want them to get too interested in it yet. He knew the address as Alice had even given it to them to rescue Kathy, which they had failed at with her refusal. He had to play it cool. He couldn't let anyone know that a woman was besting him. And then, he was informed that one of his holding companies had suffered another loss, one of their biggest to date. The lab had gone up in flames with Richard Pasternack and several of their guards inside. No mention was made of the women they had working in the lab. How in the hell had anyone found out that he owned that building? It hadn't been on Sebastian's rolls. He had owned it under another company name. Did Alice Weaver have people investigating him? He recalled things Sebastian had told him, how she had come into his homes, wherever he might be. Was she the cause of all these problems? He had higher-ups that he had to make payments to; he couldn't afford this embarrassment. The people he reported to would want answers…no, they would *demand* answers.

He couldn't fathom that this petite blonde was capable of the things he suspected. She had to have someone working for her. If he could prove she was behind these setbacks, he would destroy her and her family. If Alice could have read his thoughts, his life would already be in jeopardy.

"We've identified the body that was handcuffed in the office. The dental records indicate it's one Richard Pasternack. He lived in Palos Verdes Estates with his wife, a nurse that works in hospice care. She hasn't been working, but they also own..." the voice droned on in the meeting. Those listening were falling into a stupor until they heard, "her daughter was involved in a scandal at school. Remember those pictures that were circulating of Alice Weaver's daughter, Emily?" Several people perked up with that information, exchanging looks as notes were rapidly made on that information as well as on the report the speaker was reviewing. It would be passed up the chain of command in the police department, the DEA, the FBI, and eventually, the CIA since Madelyn Korbel had flagged anything with Alice Weaver's name on it. Then, he casually mentioned, "They lived down the street from Alice Weaver's estate in Palos Verdes." That had many in the meeting scrambling to connect the dots.

Kathy agreed they should go see Doctor Wilkerson, but she was already feeling depressed about the many tests that Doctor Lenoir had ordered for her. However, Wilkerson had been able to cure Emily, and Alice had the utmost faith in him, so it couldn't hurt to go see him and get his opinion on the many tests ordered.

"Alice and Kathy, it is so good to see you," he said in greeting.

"Doctor Wilkerson," Alice returned, shaking his outstretched hand.

"Surely, you aren't here to talk about the dividend paperwork that just went out? The quarterly–" he began, but Alice cut him off.

"No, we are here for you to examine Kathy," she nodded towards her wife.

Kathy smiled and would have let Alice continue, but Alice stayed strangely quiet, letting her wife tell the doctor what she had been feeling: the fatigue, the cough, and what Doctor Lenoir had found.

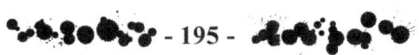

"So, you thought they were speckles or like the measles?" he asked after a while as she described the x-rays she had seen.

"Yes, the dots were very prevalent," she noted, and Alice nodded in agreement.

"But you haven't been working with any chemicals, asbestos, or similar substances prior to this?" he asked astutely, taking notes as he listened.

Alice and Kathy both thought about the gasoline they had played with in the past week and shook their heads. Everyone knew that too much gas might be a carcinogen; however, this was too much and too soon. The spots inside Kathy's body were older than her exposure to that flammable material. Kathy briefly remembered Alice telling her that she could have put a match out in the gasoline, that it was the vapors that burned, not the fluid itself. It had seemed funny at the time.

"I'm going to need the other doctors to send over their tests results, so if you would sign here," Doctor Wilkerson produced an authorization paper, "…unless you want to go through those tests again?"

Both women shook their heads. Neither wanted Kathy to be subjected to a battery of duplicate tests.

"Do you think it's cancer?" Kathy asked him, sounding almost hopeless.

"I won't know until I see the results. I'll send this off immediately," he said, handing the signed form to a tech who worked for him. "Send that to L.A. Medical and then, follow up in half an hour with a phone call. I want those results immediately," he told the woman, who nodded as she hurried off. "I may have to run a few tests of my own," he warned Kathy, then patted her hand. "We'll find out what's going on and get you the appropriate treatment," he promised.

They both felt strangely relieved as they left the high-tech lab of Doctor Wilkerson. He had pulled off a miracle for Emily, but they both hoped that whatever was wrong with Kathy wasn't anything like that.

They started packing for Kit's graduation at Stanford. The four of them would be flying up to San Francisco and renting a car to drive in. Kit was so excited that she was graduating with honors, and Alice had

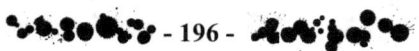

teased her for not being valedictorian. The young woman explained because she had changed her major and gone to school one year too many, she wasn't eligible for that honor. The fact that she had been accepted to Harvard for her master's program was honor enough.

"I won't promise to be valedictorian there either," she teased Alice when she told her.

"Happy, healthy, and well-educated...I couldn't be prouder," Alice told her sincerely as she gave her a bear hug, remembering the young, frightened girl that had come to live with her so long ago. Her heart squeezed painfully seeing how much the girl looked like Kathy. She was reminded of her own sister's graduation from this same school so long ago. Kathy and Connie had been here together, along with Portia and Andie. Only immediate family were asked to the graduation ceremonies and even for family, four tickets was the max.

Kathy cried unashamedly as Kit's name was called and she walked across the stage to receive her diploma. Sean snapped pictures with the digital camera. They had been asked not to clap or whoop to prevent the ceremony from dragging on too long and to allow everyone's names to be heard. At the end though, after the last graduate had been called, the students had all thrown their caps into the air and whooped and hollered. The audience rose to cheer and stomp along with the graduates.

After the ceremony, Alice took the family to one of the best restaurants in San Francisco to celebrate. As they reminisced, she was so pleased to see her family together and felt herself tearing up. Near the end of the night, Kit took her aside and asked about Kathy's cough.

"Oh, it's nothing. We took her to the doctor, and they haven't found anything," she told her daughter airily, having agreed with Kathy that they would tell this story to their children for now.

They all helped Kit load up her vehicle the next day. Alice realized everything wasn't going to fit, so she went to go get a U-Haul and trailer. They repacked what they could in the small truck and put the car on the trailer, so Kit could drive it back east. She had a small apartment there that Alice had bought for her, so she could intern that summer and then go to school at Harvard in the fall. She could have stayed in the dorms but felt it was too much to put up with the underclassmen and their antics at her age. Neither mother saw any signs of the boyfriend Kit had mentioned, and they decided not to ask. They would wait for her to tell them about him when she was ready.

After everything was loaded, Kit went out for another meal with her family. She was sad to say goodbye to Stanford. It had been such a big part of her life for so long.

"Did you say goodbye to your friends, honey?" Kathy asked, putting her arm around Kit's shoulders as she gazed at the building the young woman had lived in these past years.

"Yeah, we had a party the other night to say our goodbyes. I didn't think some of them would even make it to graduation," she grinned, pleased she'd had the experience. She'd been one of the lucky ones. Alice had ensured there were no outstanding student loans for her to repay, and the generous allowance had made things easier for her than many of her fellow students. Now, she had a nice, solid car she was towing back east and a place to live when she got there. She knew she had it good.

"You know, if you need anything, you can just call," Alice said, looking at the woman who was now taller than Kathy but still looked just like her.

"Always, Momma A," she said as she let Kathy's hand fall from her shoulders to envelop the smaller woman in her arms. Alice had always been there for her; she barely remembered the time before Alice had entered her life. She deliberately erased the thoughts of when Alice had been missing for a time while she was in college.

Alice slipped her an envelope with cash and a debit card, and she whispered, "Call if you need more."

Kit grinned. Alice already paid her credit card off every month. She didn't need more, and she wasn't greedy.

Everyone waved as Kit set off. She wanted to get to at least Sacramento or even Reno before she stopped for the night. She had plenty of cash, a credit card, and a debit card as well, all thanks to her parents.

"You know, we never got to go on that vacation with the RV because of that internship Kit got," Sean commented.

"Ah, but that is where you are wrong...sorta," Alice told him with a smile, looking up at her strapping son with pride. He towered over all of them. The football practices gave his muscles ample opportunity to grow, and with his voracious appetite, he seemed to never stop growing. Alice was certain his long legs were hollow. He was a fine-looking specimen of manhood, growing out of the pimples that had plagued him and into a man she was proud of. He wasn't very attractive but had rugged looks and a steady look in his eye.

"I am? How?"

"Well, rather than camping, how about we drive from here and go see Mount Shasta and the area around it? Maybe we could go up to the Redwoods too? No one has to be back for school," she added, since they were out for summer, "and your Mom and I would like to take you up there."

"Oh boy," Emily enthused. She'd been quiet for a while now, ever since the night she had snuck into her mother's SUV and been transported to the warehouse where they proceeded to burn it down, killing all who were in it. She realized Richard Pasternack had been a bad man, but she hadn't expected her mothers to kill him in that way. She'd heard that the Pasternacks had a funeral for him, but of course she couldn't go. She was conflicted about her feelings for Carmen. The girl had been so nasty to her. She hated her, and yet, at one time, she had been her best friend. This vacation sounded good. "I didn't pack enough," she informed her mothers.

"That's why I repacked your bag after you were done," Kathy laughed, coughed, and looked at Sean with a grin. She'd repacked his bags too.

Alice was sitting on the bench along the bluffs, looking out at the Pacific Ocean. She was waiting for Kathy to join her when she heard smaller footsteps and looked over to see Emily.

"Mom, I have questions," she stated unnecessarily.

Alice sighed. She'd been expecting this and knew that the teen had been very patient, waiting for punishments that never came. With the graduation and other events in their lives, she had wondered when Em would take the time to make sure they were alone and could talk. Kathy and she had both waited, wondering if the teen were shell shocked and would need therapy. "I'm sure you do," she said mildly.

Em grinned, then that turned into a grimace. "I really don't know how to say this…" she hesitated, clearly uncomfortable.

"I'm sure there is a lot you've been thinking about," Alice understated. She wouldn't start the ball rolling. The teen had to ask all by herself; she wasn't about to volunteer information.

"Mr. Pasternack…" she began. "I heard what he said. He was a bad man?" She felt foolish putting it like that, sounding like a child, but Alice intimidated her sometimes. She'd heard what he told Alice about where to find money. She hadn't understood it all, but it was enough, and with what happened later, she understood that he was laundering money for someone. She hadn't told Alice or Kathy that she'd heard him talking before she entered the office too, having listened unashamedly before making her presence known. She couldn't understand it. When she had hung out with Carmen, her father and mother had been so kind, charming even.

Alice nodded. She could hear the little girl in her teenager. Just in the time since Alice had come home, Em had grown as she healed from the blood disease. She had caught herself eyeing her daughter, speculating about her time and again, wondering at the woman she was about to become.

"Did he have to die? Did he deserve to die?"

"I sometimes think some people are born to die," Alice said cryptically, parroting something she had heard in an old western. At the teen's startled look, she clarified, "Some people choose to be evil…some are born that way."

"Do you think Mr. Pasternack was born bad or chose it?"

"I think he got caught up with all the money made by the drugs. That business wasn't about the wholesale goods they imported, it was about the drugs they brought in and distributed. I didn't even know about the drugs until he told us."

Em thought for a while and then asked, "Did he launder the money for them?"

Alice was surprised by how astute and how calm the teen was. They were in this picturesque part of California, and the park was absolutely beautiful. They were parked near a cabin she had rented; within a half hour of the mighty redwoods they would be seeing again tomorrow. Now, they were just relaxing. At least she had been relaxing until her daughter decided she needed answers. "Yes," she nodded, "he laundered money and more. He obviously knew what he was doing. He invested funds for them. He knew where the money was coming from and where it went."

"There was a lot of cash in that bag," the teen mused. "Why didn't you keep it?"

"Because those women needed it and deserved it," Alice replied, wondering what else the teen would ask. She certainly hadn't wanted any of those funds. She also didn't need them but wouldn't tell the teen that.

"Do you think they will share it or…get caught or…" the teen wasn't sure what she was asking, and she was obviously being influenced by the TV shows she had watched over the years.

Alice smiled, showing off even, white teeth that had all been replaced over the years. "Some might be smart enough to get out of there. Some might get caught, and they will mention the women who freed them. You can never talk about this…" she began, wondering if this was too much to burden her daughter with. The child already had several secrets she had been told to keep for her parents.

"I know how to keep a secret, Mom," the beleaguered teen said in a tone that had Alice smiling again.

"I know you do, honey, but it's a habit of mine to remind you."

"How do you know the women weren't there voluntarily?" Emily asked, surprising Alice with the question.

"I suspect they were taken prisoner in Russia and transported here, then their passports were confiscated, or something like that. If they weren't useful in prostitution, they had to be useful in other ways."

"Even with masks on, I bet they inhaled that stuff," Em stated astutely, remembering the scene in that horrible room where the women were working in all the dust. Even she knew what it was.

Alice nodded sagely. "I hope you never have to see that stuff again," she stated, a warning buried within the statement.

"Don't worry, Mom. I don't like drugs," she assured her.

"Oh really?" Alice asked, wondering at the meaning in the teen's statement.

"Well, after what Carmen and her friends pulled last year, I don't want anything to do with drugs or alcohol."

Alice nodded. That made sense.

"I mean, maybe when I'm older and I know what I'm doing, I might like a drink or something," she continued, "but nothing in excess like that ever again." She shuddered at the memory of seeing her vulnerable self in those photos and hearing what people had said about her. So many lies. She hated Carmen for that!

"Well, when you are an adult, you will have a lot of decisions to make for yourself. I just hope you are responsible about them," Alice advised. She too remembered the photos of her daughter and the rage she had felt against the teen who had taken them. She had worked so hard to erase those photos, although they seemed unending as people stored them on their private computers and shared them occasionally. The only thing that had helped her feel better were the pictures she had posted that contained viruses and would destroy people's hard drives if they were stupid enough to download the whole picture. This conversation wasn't going at all as she had thought it would.

"What if I was one of those women?" the teen asked suddenly, after a long period of quiet reflection while gazing out at the beautiful view before the sun set.

"Which women?" Alice asked, confused and glancing around hoping to see who Emily was referring to.

"Those women in the drug factory..." the teen began.

Alice suddenly understood, and her face changed. She wasn't about to tell Em what the men had said about her. It could so easily have *been* her. "I'd have been very sad for you. It can't be an easy life when they are addicted to that stuff. And if they get too old for the work, are they done away with?"

"I bet those men who use them don't care. They are just after the money."

Alice nodded. This teen was right on the mark, but she wasn't about to ask how she knew. She obviously had thought this out.

"Did Mr. Pasternack deserve to die?" the teen wondered aloud again.

"I think he did," Alice said softly and watched the teen nod. "Are you feeling bad for him, honey?"

"I think I feel bad for Carmen. Despite what she did, he was her father, and he loved her."

Alice understood. Carmen had been Em's best friend for a while. It had been a setup from the get-go, but the teen hadn't realized it until it was too late.

Em leaned into Alice. It was a bit cool here on the bench looking out over the water. The fog was rolling in, and neither of them had a jacket or a sweater. "Do you know how many people you have killed?" Em asked in a subdued voice.

Alice froze momentarily but not so long that the teen would notice. She had been thinking how nice it was that her daughter still wanted to cuddle and had put her arm around her. She remembered the little girl who had put her head into Alice's neck with her arm slung across her chest and around the other side of her neck. It had been an endearing habit of the little girl. Alice had relished those moments alone with her daughter. Now, Emily was on the cusp of womanhood and demanding answers that Alice wasn't so sure she wanted to or should answer. "No, I didn't keep count," she admitted honestly.

Emily thought about that, wondering how many people her mother had killed. She'd heard about Kazakhstan from her mother's own lips. Now, having seen what she did to Mr. Pasternack, she wondered that she wasn't shocked about it.

"I don't just kill willy-nilly," Alice downplayed, looking at her semi-horrified, semi-fascinated daughter. "I need to justify any killings in my mind. I need to know there is a purpose…a reason."

Emily nodded. She too had felt that Mr. Pasternack deserved to die, but she wondered why she felt bad for Carmen, who had hurt her so badly. "Are you a psychopath?"

"No."

"How do you know?"

"A psychopath lacks empathy. I don't kill randomly; I only kill if it's necessary."

Had it been necessary to kill Mr. Pasternack and that guard? Thinking about the gun the man had held on them reminded her of the men who had broken into their home and touched her. She shuddered slightly and Alice felt it.

"Cold?" she asked, wondering if they should head in. She wanted Emily to stop asking questions, and at the same time, she wanted to answer whatever questions the teen might have. She instinctively knew this wasn't the end of her questions.

"Yeah, but I don't want to go in yet. I never knew Mom was your accomplice," Emily told her.

"Accomplice?" Alice asked, feeling a challenge to the word.

"All this time, I thought she was just your housewife. You know," she added, seeing Alice's expression, "keeping the house straight, raising your kids, washing the laundry?"

Alice chuckled. That was why they had a housekeeper. Kathy did whatever the heck she wanted, had unlimited funds, and loved her.

This child of their love couldn't understand, not this young. "Your mother," she began carefully, unsure if it was fair to speak for Kathy, "is not a murderess. A true murderer deludes themselves that the killings were justified or deserved. There is only one reason to kill: to protect yourself and save innocent lives."

"Is that why you killed?" she asked.

Alice nodded, and added so the teen would hear her, "Yes. I believe I have saved people with my actions." She didn't add that some killings were for revenge and to prevent the people from doing again whatever it was that had pissed her off.

"Then, by your own definition, you are a murderer," the teen stated. Alice's facial expression changed slightly. "You have deluded yourself that the killing was justified or deserved," she quoted.

Alice chuckled. She'd have to be on her toes with this child of hers. The teen was very quick, and she had both her mothers' brains.

"Are you going to kill Mrs. Pasternack?" the teen asked.

"Do I have a reason to?" she asked in return, hedging. She was beginning to suspect a lot about Sandi Pasternack. Alice was certain she was a killer acting under the guise of a healthcare worker who helped in hospice. The look in the woman's eyes was enough; Alice recognized another killer. She'd seen her own eyes and read what they told her.

The teen shrugged. "I just wondered if she, you know...was on your hit list?"

Alice laughed and shook her head. "I don't have a hit list."

"Oh," the teen sat back, cuddling into the warmth that Alice's body generated. She sounded almost disappointed.

"Have you ever killed a child?" she asked and felt the tension in her mother's body, even though she tried to hide it.

"Not that I know of," Alice answered honestly and then turned the questions on her daughter. "Do you want me to kill Carmen?"

"Would you?" Em sounded both horrified and fascinated at the idea.

Without hesitation Alice answered, "No." Nothing more, no explanation, just a simple, 'No."

"Why not?"

"Because I am holding onto the belief that there is hope for that girl," she lied. Based on her observations, that kid was seriously screwed up and would only continue to hurt others. "I don't kill children," she finished quietly.

"But after what she did…" the teen began defensively.

"She deserves to be punished, but not a final punishment, and not by me."

"What if she came at me to kill me?"

"Then, I would defend you to the best of my ability," Alice told her and hoped that was the end of the conversation. It was making her distinctly uncomfortable.

Emily waited a while and then asked, "Do you think you and Mom will ever break up again?"

Alice could sense a lot of meaning in that one question. She knew the last few years had made them all a little uneasy. "Your Mom and I have come a long way. We've worked hard to make this lifelong commitment. It's not what everyone thinks it is. It's not waking up early every day and making breakfast, so we can eat together. It's not even cuddling in bed until we fall asleep together. It isn't the clean home, which I might add Mrs. Fernandez contributes to," she teased, and the teen grinned. Kathy had taught them all to clean up after themselves, so Mrs. Fernandez didn't have to do everything. "It's about someone who steals the covers and snores like a chainsaw. Sometimes it's about the slammed doors, words we didn't mean to say, and even the silent treatment we give each other as our hearts are trying to heal. The most important thing to learn from all that is to forgive. If you don't come back to forgiveness, then there really wasn't a relationship in the first place." She let the teen digest all that before she continued, "I love coming home to the same person. Your mother knows that I love and care about her and about all of you. All our anger and all our foibles make us who we are. It's about laughing together over something hilariously funny or even something we did that was stupid. It isn't about finger pointing or assigning blame but about helping each other become the best we can be. That goes for your mother, for you, your brother, and your sister. All of you. I didn't leave because I wanted to leave. I left because your Mom needed that time apart. I hadn't planned on leaving for quite that long though," she finished wryly, and Emily chuckled.

"I don't know that I'll ever have what you and Mom have," she stated sadly, and Alice immediately felt a sense of foreboding.

"Why do you say that?" She wanted to tell her daughter she was too young to feel that way but didn't want to dismiss or belittle her feelings at such a tender age.

"I can't imagine trusting anyone that much."

Alice felt bad about that. Carmen had betrayed her on so many levels. She wondered if Emily had had a crush on the little twit and that was part of the hurt. "Living with the person you love is amazing. It's an experience I hope you have someday, and you will find it was worth the wait. It might not come when you want it, but if it does come, I hope you are open to it. I didn't think I'd find it either," she confessed, and the teen looked at her, startled. "I was alone a long time, dating but not looking for a long-term relationship...and then, your mom came along."

"Why did you marry Mom? She's nothing like you."

Alice smiled, remembering the night she had proposed to Kathy. "Have I ever told you about the night I proposed to your mom?" she asked the teen.

Emily shook her head.

"Maybe this should wait? It's getting cold out here," Alice offered, but the teen shook her head vehemently, snuggling in closer to Alice's warmth.

"No, I want to hear. Please tell me," the teen pleaded, wanting a confirmation of the love between her two mothers.

"Okay, but I'm only going over the highlights," Alice told her and began to tell her story. "Remember the gazebo in our backyard?" At the teen's nod. she continued. Kathy had gasped as they arrived at the gazebo. Dozens of flowers—roses, lilies, and many she couldn't even name—were in pots, planters, and vases all over the gazebo. A bottle of champagne stood in a large champagne bucket with two glasses sticking up out of the ice. "What's this?" she asked in wonderment as she turned to look in the amused eyes of Alice.

"This is a celebration," Alice responded, adding *I hope* in her head. She let go of Kathy's hand to reach for the champagne and step into the gazebo. To her satisfaction, Kathy followed her, as she had hoped she would.

"A celebration of what?" Kathy looked around, amazed at all the flowers and admiring their beautiful bouquets. The odor alone was almost overwhelming, but the sheer mass of blooms took her breath away.

Letting go of the champagne, Alice turned and grasped both of Kathy's hands. She got down on one knee and saw the apprehension begin in Kathy's face.

"Kathy, I'd like to make this official. Will you marry me?"

Kathy just stared at her for the longest time.

For the first time in a long time, Alice felt nervous. Fear was almost clutching at her heart. The longer Kathy took to answer Alice's question, the more Alice felt like she was strangling. She tried to wait patiently, but the silence was beginning to kill her. She realized she had never felt this way before, at least not from this side of the situation.

Kathy finally blinked after what seemed like ages. She realized Alice had set the stage for this proposal and how truly romantic it was. She swallowed as tears welled in her eyes at the incredibly romantic gesture. She was having trouble speaking as she started to nod, blubber, and say, "Yyyyes, I'll marry you, Alice," and yanked Alice into her arms, burying her head in Alice's neck as she sobbed.

For once in her life, a woman's tears didn't confuse her. She understood the emotions Kathy was experiencing right now. If she could have, she would have cried with her, but life had long ago killed the thing inside her that allowed tears to fall. She could only hold Kathy tightly and hope she understood she felt the same emotions as she rocked her.

Slowly, and after a long time, Kathy's tears of joy stopped, and she pulled back, her face a mess. "This is so beautiful," she hiccupped.

Alice smiled as she reached in her pocket for the ring she had searched for that morning. "Then, will you accept this as a token of my love for you?" she asked formally, remembering some movie that had used those same exact words.

Kathy gaped at the beautiful diamond she saw in her love's hand. It was flawless, as far as she could see, and the ring her husband had given her was half the size of this incredible stone. She held out her left hand, and Alice slipped it on her ring finger. It fit perfectly, and she stared at it a long moment before taking Alice in her arms once again and hugging her tight. "Thank you. I love you sooo much!" she sobbed once again.

It was a long time before they sampled the champagne and made toasts to each other and a long life together. They talked over plans of having a small ceremony. It had become legal once again in the state of California for same-sex couples to marry, so their plans wouldn't have to wait. They made several trips to carry the containers of flowers into the house, placing them all over the house and filling it with the delightful aroma of roses, lilies, and other varieties of flowers that Alice's romantic proposal had wrought. But before they brought everything into the house, Kathy had insisted on taking pictures of the gazebo filled with the flowering bonanza. She had then called Mrs. Fernandez to take a picture of the two women amongst the flowering blooms. The three of them carried armloads of blooms into the house and placed them on every available flat surface.

"This is going to make the house smell like a flower shop," Mrs. Fernandez teased as Kathy showed her the ring. She was pleased for the couple. She didn't understand their relationship, but she liked weddings. She and Kathy excitedly made plans.

Alice watched and laughed at their excitement. She hoped Kit would like the idea too.

"Kit told me she was just so glad you two would be together forever, but she never shared all the details of your engagement," Emily said to her mom, delighting in the story. She had seen the pictures of course, and she had always wondered at them. "She loves calling you Mama Al," she teased, knowing it was funny.

Alice smiled.

"I didn't remember it all quite like that," Kathy suddenly spoke up behind them. She'd come up very quietly on the path, intending to tell them to come in as it was getting cold with the fog rolling in. Hearing Alice tell the teen about the night she had proposed had halted her progression, and she was pleased to hear her wife tell it so well.

Alice turned, wondering how long her wife had been there. She was looking a little bit frail to Alice's knowing eyes. She smiled, not letting on in the least how concerned she was for Kathy's health.

Kathy looked at Alice. Those amazing eyes captivated as much today as they had so long ago. They looked at her and made her feel beautiful, and that was all that mattered.

"Mom, you two are lucky to have found each other," Emily said succinctly.

Kathy nodded and looked at her daughter as she got up from the bench. "We are indeed. Yes, we are indeed," she answered as Alice came and slipped her hand around Kathy's waist to walk her back to the cabin. Being shorter, she couldn't quite rest her head on Kathy's shoulder comfortably, but she could breathe quietly into her ear as she whispered, "I love you."

Kathy squeezed where she was holding onto Alice as she walked with her daughter and wife.

"Spouses can't testify against spouses," he pointed out.

"Does that apply to same-sex spouses?" someone asked.

"What do you mean?" Madelyn interjected, looking up from the paperwork they had been previewing and fixing the speaker with an intense look.

"Well," he looked uncomfortable to be asked such a straight-forward question in the group meeting, "it's not like it's a *real* marriage, you know, between a guy and some chick."

There were quite a few muffled laughs, and Marilyn looked at the man like he was insane. "So, you are saying two women or two men married to each other could testify against their companion because a marriage between same-sex partners isn't real?"

"Yeah, something like that," he answered, and he sounded earnest.

"You," she said, pointing at the man, "go…leave. You're off this task force!" She pointed at the door.

"*What?* What did I say?" he asked, spreading his hands in confusion.

Madelyn rose so she was towering over the table. Leaning forward on her hands to make her point, she replied, "If you have to ask that question, you're too stupid to be on this task force." She gestured to the paperwork everyone had brought to the meeting, "We don't want you here if you are so narrow-minded you might miss things. So, I'm asking you *nicely*," she said in a menacing voice, "to leave." She gestured at the door once more.

He looked around at the other agents, mostly the men. Several avoided his look, but a couple stared at him with incredulous looks. Gathering his notes, he stood up.

"No, you won't be needing those," Director Wolf told him quietly from his seat in the corner where he had been observing. Gesturing at the paperwork, he said, "Leave that."

Embarrassed now, he made his way around the long table and exited through the door, being careful to close it gently behind himself.

There was silence in the room for a full thirty seconds before Wolf looked over at Madelyn and asked, "Doesn't that only matter if it wasn't in furtherance of a crime?"

Since there wasn't any proof that Alice Weaver had actually committed any crime, that was a moot point. Madelyn's eyes narrowed as she contemplated what Wolf might know that she didn't know before answering, "Well, unless we can prove a crime was committed, there is no way we could apply any pressure on Kathy Weaver, even if she *would* testify against Alice. Furthermore, due to the length of time they've been married, I doubt she'd give her up." She didn't add that Kathy probably knew what side her bread was buttered on, but she had met the mouse, saw the way she looked at Alice adoringly, and knew in her gut they would never be able to convince the woman to testify. Kathy would plead the fifth, and she had enough money to hire an army of the best lawyers to keep her out of trouble. Thinking about it, Madelyn knew there was no way Kathy could have been involved in any of Alice's wrongdoings.

"So, it's cancer then?" Kathy asked despondently as Doctor Wilkerson finished telling them what he had found after he did a few more tests on her.

He nodded after glancing at Alice as though asking for her permission. He licked his lips before continuing, "Yes, and it's an aggressive form of cancer that does not have any of the more obvious marker signs to show what kind of cancer it is or what kinds it is developing into."

"Kinds?" Alice asked, narrowing her eyes at the word.

He nodded again, gulping at the unwelcome news he would have to impart, but he knew better than to keep anything from their generous benefactor. Alice had invested in them when no one else would. For the sake of their company, he couldn't afford to piss off her or her wife. "Yes, it's mutating rapidly, and we can't tell you what kind it will become next, but it's already in her lungs, breast, and the lymph nodes."

"Upper or lower?" Alice asked, seemingly ignoring the indrawn breath of her wife, who had gasped at the idea of breast cancer.

"Both," he answered, realizing she might know more about cancer than he thought. "I can pinpoint where it entered the body, but I can't figure out where it's going since it's mutating so rapidly. Just in the week since Dr. Lenoir took these," he indicated the tests that had been sent over, "and mine here," he indicated the other folder, "it's spread and grown."

"Wait! You can tell *how* it entered my body?" Kathy asked, surprised.

He nodded.

"How?" Alice asked, almost angrily. She was holding Kathy's hand, as though to keep from striking the man as they waited for the information to come from his mouth.

"There is a striking array of cells that are focused around her hand and move up her arm to her lungs. From there, I believe it went to her breasts and lymph nodes..." he began, pointing at the upper body x-rays to show the small white dots, but Alice and Kathy had exchanged a look, and then, Kathy looked down at her hand, the one clasped in Alice's.

"What can we do about it?" Alice asked practically, controlling herself...but just barely.

"We will start an aggressive form of chemo to halt the growth but I–"

"What if I do nothing?" Kathy asked suddenly, shocking them all.

Recovering first, Doctor Wilkerson said sadly, "Then you will most certainly die."

Alice turned to Kathy inquiringly, but she wouldn't look at her. Kathy was focused on the doctor. "How long?"

He swallowed. "I'd say about four months, maybe five, but I have to advise you to fight. It will be a horrible death otherwise, and I believe you will smother," he gestured to her breasts and the lungs beneath them.

"Kathy, you've got to fight," Alice almost pleaded with her, looking at her intensely.

Kathy looked in Alice's amazing eyes and was surprised to see tears welling up. This made her want to cry as well. She nodded almost absentmindedly. She would fight. Oh yes, for this woman she would fight.

The ride home was particularly tense. Alice pulled over at a cliff overlooking the Pacific Ocean and looked out at the view before

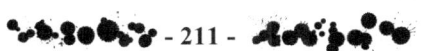

turning to her wife and pulling her into her arms. She sniffed her hair, luxuriating in the familiar smells of Kathy's body wash, shampoo, and conditioners. A hint of her perfume was so welcome now.

"I don't want to die," Kathy said in a frightened voice. "I want to live," she said as she pulled back to look at Alice. Her eyes were awash in tears, and Alice's tears were welling up but unshed.

"Then we fight!" Alice responded.

"Do you remember that pin prick I got in the lawyer's office from Sandi Pasternack's ring?" Kathy asked casually, watching Alice's reaction to head off what she thought might be a potential problem.

Alice remembered that incident in a flash. She too had been about to shake the woman's hand, but with Kathy exclaiming in pain, she'd refused. She remembered the look in Sandi's eyes...had that been disappointment? "You think that's when–?" she asked, but she agreed as Kathy nodded.

"It is concentrated in this hand," she indicated her right hand and looked at it as though it should be cut off. "But without proof..." she continued, looking up at her wife and seeing her eyes narrow in contemplation. She knew she was starting something she might not live to see. "We don't have proof," she almost pleaded.

"Then I will get the proof," Alice promised her. Her mind was already working on a plan to get into the Pasternack's home down the road from their own.

Angrily, Alice drove them home, cutting off an idiot who was driving too slowly. The next light halted her, giving the man she had cut off time to pull up next to them. He looked at them angrily and Kathy, on the same side he was on, shrugged and held her palms up in a helpless gesture. He indicated she should roll down her window. Stupidly, she complied.

"What the fuck is wrong with you, lady?" he shouted past her to Alice, ready to get out of his own car.

"Look, mister, my wife suffers from PTSD. She didn't mean anything by it," Kathy tried to explain.

Alice had turned when Kathy opened her window since the excellent air conditioning in the Rover gave her no need to open her window. She wondered if Kathy had passed gas or something, and then she saw the guy in the car next to theirs. She was ready to get out of her SUV in answer to his tone. Kathy reached over and put her hand on Alice's leg, squeezing warningly.

"Then she shouldn't be driving!" he shouted across the roar of the engines. Alice had put hers in park and was revving her engine, ready to put it in drive and speed away from this moron. At the feel of Kathy's hand on her leg, she put it into drive.

"I agree, but then, what am I going to do. Please forgive her," Kathy said sweetly and saw him calm down slightly.

Just then, the lights changed, and Alice roared off angrily, leaving the man coughing in her exhaust. She outdistanced him easily with the powerful engine of the Rover.

"Why'd you appease that moron?" Alice asked.

"Why'd you antagonize that moron?" Kathy countered saucily.

Alice started to laugh at the incongruity of their conversation. They'd had a bad, tension-filled day. She'd made it worse, and Kathy had told the man she suffered from PTSD in order to defuse the situation. That was probably true with everything she had been through, but it was also funny. Kathy joined in, enjoying laughing with her wife.

Kathy started chemo, and the first dose, administered through an IV in her arm, seemed easy. It felt cold as it entered her vein. Doctor Wilkerson had offered to put a shunt in her chest to make it easier to administer the drugs. In fact, he had encouraged her to do so, but Kathy had refused.

"No, I won't have one of those things stuck in me," she indicated her chest where they wanted to implant the shunt. "You can use my veins; they're healthy," she said, holding out her arms to show the veins at the V in her arm.

"I don't think you understand what this will do to them—" he tried to explain, but Kathy cut him off.

"I know," she countered sadly. "They will scar and shrink, and you'll have to use other veins sometimes," she said resignedly, gesturing to her other arm. "I don't want a shunt."

He sighed quietly, not willing to argue. This treatment, while experimental, should help slow the growth and might even stop it. He'd called around to see who was in the latter parts of their studies doing clinical trials on humans and made sure Kathy Weaver did not

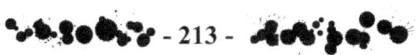

get the placebo. He shuddered to think if they failed because Alice was one of their most vested benefactors.

"That's cold," Kathy complained as the liquid entered her arm. It looked odd, with a pale pink tint to it. They put warming blankets on Kathy as Alice sat quietly by waiting for her, willing to fetch her anything as they watched the first bag of poisons drain into her body.

"Now, you are going to start feeling nauseous, and I want you to take…" Wilkerson droned on, prescribing various drugs that Kathy would have to take to counter the effects of the drugs they were pumping into her body to kill the cancer cells.

Alice went to the drive-thru at the pharmacy to fill all the prescriptions, and they waited. "How are you doing, babe?" she worried, looking over at Kathy, who was taking slow, cleansing breaths.

"I'm good. I think the nausea is starting, but maybe I should get something to eat?"

"Did you eat today?"

"Yes, I started with a banana and then, half an hour later, I had cereal, so I wouldn't have an empty stomach for this," she lifted her arm to show the spot where they had inserted the needle. It was covered by a small patch of cotton, and Kathy had been holding it in place rather than having tape applied. She claimed the tape ripped her skin, and she'd rather hold it herself. She gently removed it now with her fingertips, and it had stopped bleeding. It already looked like it was going to bruise.

"Then, we'll stop for lunch," Alice promised, looking back as the pharmacist's voice came over the tinny-sounding speaker.

"These prescriptions are for you?" he asked, looking at Alice with her punk rock hairdo, the blonde hair sticking up.

"No, they are for my wife," she said, indicating Kathy, who leaned forward so they could see each other. She raised her hand as though she were a schoolgirl in class.

"I'm going to need some identification. Some of these are pretty strong," he said disapprovingly.

Kathy mumbled under her breath about jackasses as she fumbled in her purse for her wallet and held up her driver's license.

"Please put it in the drop box and send it through," he intoned, squinting at her.

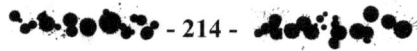

Alice took it and dropped it in, shoving hard on the receptacle so it went through with a bang. She saw him back away slightly as it shot through. She looked back innocently when he looked up, then he picked up the license and examined it carefully. He looked from the picture to Kathy, who was still leaning forward, comparing her with the photo. He looked suspicious as he examined both, then put the license back in the drawer and added some papers he had printed off and a pen.

"You need to sign for these," he told them as Alice gathered the things together. She handed everything to Kathy in case he was going to be a stickler about that.

Kathy sighed as she retrieved her license and began looking through the paperwork, all of it mostly for insurance purposes to prove they were receiving the drugs.

"That will be sixteen hundred and eighty dollars," he said as he bagged everything up after she returned the paperwork.

"Doesn't our insurance pay for all that?" Alice asked, hearing Kathy gasp in the background at the amount. The blonde was getting annoyed.

"Yes, they will reimburse you for this–" he began, but Alice interrupted.

"The normal procedure is to give the patient the meds they need and bill the insurance company," she clarified.

"Yes, but some of these may not be covered by–" he began, but she interrupted again.

"Then, you tell me which ones aren't covered, and we will get the insurance company and the doctor to iron that out. Meanwhile, my wife needs these meds to survive." She pointed at the bags of medicines they had watched him fill. "She has just started chemotherapy, and I don't think the doctor would be happy if she didn't comply by taking all the medicine he has prescribed." Alice looked behind her vehicle and saw a line of cars was forming behind her SUV. She could see the man behind them was becoming impatient.

"Ma'am, I don't set the–" he began again, but Alice was becoming impatient too.

"I'm not here to tell you how to make your policies or how to go about billing, but I'll wait while we straighten this out, so my wife can get the medicine her doctor clearly wants her to have," she said in a deceivingly polite voice.

He couldn't bluff her, and he too could see the line of cars forming behind her SUV. He turned off the microphone and looked towards someone else, discussing it with them. The person shrugged. He made a quick phone call while Alice watched him, a smile plastered on her face.

"Do you think he–?" Kathy began, but Alice shushed her under her breath.

"He's probably listening to us through that," she said in an aside, nodding slightly towards the microphone.

After what seemed an interminably long time—the guy behind them had started tapping on his horn, earning a glare from Alice—the pharmacist began putting the bags into the drawer, and he clicked on the microphone again. "We will bill your insurance company, but you are legally liable for any of these they don't pay for," he told them again in a disapproving voice.

"Thank you," Alice replied in a sugary, saccharine voice as she gathered the many bags, handing them to Kathy. As soon as she could, she drove away, tapping on the brakes to alarm the idiot behind her, who had rushed to fill her spot even before she drove off.

"Jeeze, how am I going to remember what to take and when," Kathy put in, looking at the many bags of medicines that Doctor Wilkerson had prescribed.

"We'll set up a medicine chart, maybe get one of those plastic pillbox things for daily doses or whatever. I think we might want to change our pharmacy though," Alice put in as she maneuvered around some traffic.

"You noticed the attitude too?"

"Oh yeahhh," she answered with a grin.

"I feel like having Carl's Jr.," Kathy mentioned.

"Grease?" Alice asked, concerned.

"Just the hamburger, no fries. A Dr. Pepper sounds good and maybe a salad?"

Alice would give her anything she wanted. She knew Kathy had to be feeling ill after all that poison was pumped into her veins, but she was hiding it remarkably well. Going through the drive-thru at Carl's was a lot less stressful than the one at the pharmacy. They parked in the parking lot to eat their lunch.

Kathy dug into her Western Bacon Cheeseburger sans cheese with gusto. "Mmm," she said as she took a sip of her ice-cold soda.

"You may regret that later," Alice said as she laughed at her wife's expression.

"I don't care," she returned, watching as Alice bit into her own hamburger and licked at the western sauce around her mouth enticingly. How could she feel like crap and be aroused by her wife at the same time?

Kathy enjoyed her meal, and she did regret it later. As soon as they were home, she snuck the many bags of medicine up to their bedroom and went right into the bathroom to throw up in the toilet. Everything she had just eaten came back up, along with anything she hadn't yet digested from breakfast. It took a long time before she finally had the dry heaves and then, she rinsed her mouth out with water. Immediately, she had to turn quickly and pull her pants down to sit on the throne and evacuate her bowels. It was horrible!

Alice stood by helplessly as her wife was sick in the bathroom. There was nothing she could do about it, so instead, she turned on a fan in the bedroom and opened a window, hoping her wife would appreciate the gesture and not be insulted. She headed down to the kitchen for some crackers and white soda. "Make sure you have lots of this on hand," she instructed their housekeeper as she hefted the packet of salted crackers and the soda she'd poured into a glass with ice.

Mrs. Fernandez nodded and said, "Yes, Ms. Alice." She wondered what was going on but didn't ask; it wasn't her place. A lot of odd things had happened in this house over the years that she pretended not to see or hear. It was a good job that paid well and even offered health insurance. She would do this job for as long as she was able.

Kathy had turned on the water in the shower and was washing her sweaty body and rinsing the acid from her backside. Despite the hot water, she was shivering and feeling miserable. It took a while before she turned off the water and wrapped herself in a fluffy white towel.

"Need help?" Alice asked from where she was standing by the door, feeling helpless.

"I need my robe," Kathy answered, her teeth chattering despite the heat and clouds of steam in the bathroom.

Alice handed her the fluffy robe she rarely used. Alice preferred the satin one but knew Kathy needed more than the thinness of that right now. She wasn't trying to be sexy; she just wanted to get warm. Alice helped rub her hair dry and tuck her into bed with her sweats on.

"Jeeze, how bad is this going to get?" Kathy mumbled as she carefully ate a cracker and sipped at the soda. "Thank you for this," she murmured, gesturing with the glass.

"Don't ask," Alice mumbled back with a smile, watching her. She'd done some research and knew it might get really bad really fast.

"Wonder if I'm going to lose my hair?" Kathy mused miserably as she looked at the long tendrils hanging over her shoulder.

"Think of the wonderful hats you can wear. You can even get a wig if you want." Alice tried to smile, making it sound like fun.

"Well, there is that," Kathy answered, burping ungracefully from the soda.

"Feeling any better?" Alice laughed at her wife who was usually much more polite and discreet about belching.

"Yeah, and I'm finally getting warm." She pulled a leg out from under the covers to cool down a little. "We're going to have to tell the kids," she stated, looking at Alice.

"How much of it do you want to tell them?"

Lowering her voice, Kathy asked, "How much have you found out?"

Lowering her own voice, Alice answered, "That twit is still pulling stunts, but her computer isn't hooked up to her mother's, and the mother's computer is not on a network. I'm going to have to figure out some other way to get the information I need."

Kathy knew the twit Alice was referring to was Carmen. They were both of the same opinion on that girl. She was bad news and heading for worse. What she had pulled on their daughter was enough to set any parent off, and while they'd sued the Pasternacks and reached a settlement, this disease Kathy was fighting was not pleasant and certainly wasn't worth the money they had won and put in trust for their daughter. Furthermore, if Sandi's ring was the cause of this cancer, she had a lot to answer for.

"Are you dying?" Emily asked, her voice sounding like a little girl, not the teenager she had become. Sean looked on worriedly where his two moms were sitting on the couch explaining what was going on.

"I'm not gonna lie to you, Em. This is a going to be a rough road, and I could die," Kathy told her, wanting to take her in her arms but also knowing it had to be on the teen's terms. She could tell Sean was trying manfully not to cry, holding it in but looking devasted.

"But you're not old. You can't die," the teen continued.

Alice exchanged a look with Kathy. They had to remember this teenager was still young in many ways.

"I assure you, I can. I have before," she tried to joke but regretted it when the teen blanched. She'd been very young when Kathy had been taken before. Alice had just returned last year after being away, and they'd also thought she was dead. "But this time…" she continued, trying to forget the look on her daughter's face, "I'm going to fight." Alice took her hand to remind her wife she was there. "We," she amended, "are going to fight…together."

"Why didn't you tell us when you found out?" Sean asked. His voice was suspiciously odd.

"This all happened rather suddenly," Kathy told him. "Doctor Wilkerson had to find an experimental treatment to help me."

"He's good at that," Emily said resentfully.

Both of her parents looked at her. "Yes, he is. Thank goodness he is," Kathy agreed, remembering her fears for this youngest daughter of theirs. First, she had worried if she would be able to have her, and then later, she had worried if she would lose her to a mysterious blood disease. She looked at Alice, who squeezed her hand reassuredly. It was Alice's blood transfusion that had saved their daughter. "The cancer has spread fast, but he found a study that he believes may help me."

"What happens if it doesn't work?" Sean asked.

Alice studied her only son. He was trying to think things through logically and asking all the right questions. He was so close to being an adult. "Then we try something else," Alice answered quietly, drawing their kids' attention to her.

"Isn't there something we can do? Donate blood? Platelets?"

Alice shook her head. She wished it were that easy.

Kathy smiled. "We're going to follow Doctor Wilkerson's orders for now. I just wanted you two to know, since there is a good chance I will lose my hair and my appearance will be altered."

It was this revelation that had Emily getting up from her seat to take Kathy in her arms. "Oh, Mommy," she sobbed.

Alice exchanged a look with Sean and would have gone to him, but he fisted his hands and rubbed at his eyes as he rocked slightly. Her heart melted at his anguish. Their children had been through so much in their young lives. She looked at Kathy who was comforting their daughter, and Kathy released her hand and nodded towards Sean. Alice got up to put her arms around the young man, and he rose, brushing her off.

"I'm okay, Mom. I just…I just…need time," he said, sounding devastated. "Is there any more?" he hesitated as he looked at Kathy, who shook her head. "Then, may I be excused?" he asked respectfully of both women. Kathy nodded. Then, he looked down at Alice, and she looked sadly back at him for a moment before adding her nod to Kathy's. He immediately left the living room and headed for his bedroom.

Alice exchanged a look with Kathy and then, hearing a noise, whirled to see Mrs. Fernandez crying unashamedly as she listened to their conversation. She went to her and took the older woman in her arms as she cried, the first time she could ever remember such an exchange with the woman.

The Skype phone call to Kit was just as bad as they watched their eldest daughter cry unashamedly.

"Are they sure? Maybe I should come home?"

"No, darling. I want you to stay at school," Kathy told her oldest daughter. She took Alice's hand in hers and rephrased that, "We both want you to stay at school. Momma A is taking good care of me. I don't want you to lose time from your studies." Alice had her arm around Kathy and rubbed her shoulder reassuringly.

"I haven't even started. I'm still getting settled," Kit told her, gesturing to the luxurious apartment behind her that Alice had purchased. Alice bought it through an agent, who had taken her on a video tour, and she hadn't quibbled on the price as she bought it from afar for their daughter. The agent had been surprised, amazed, and pleased by turns as Alice asked questions, knowing the area from her own time at Harvard.

"How's the job?" Alice asked, trying to turn the conversation away from the cancer. The first part of the conversation had been so sad that both her wife and daughter had cried.

Kit shrugged. "It's okay," she answered, sounding nonchalant. Then she grinned, "I'm loving it, learning a lot, and making great contacts." Then she sobered. "But that isn't anything compared to what you are going through," she said, directing that last comment at Kathy.

"You don't worry about me. We're fighting this, and you have a life to live. You enjoy that job and apartment. I think Momma A overindulged you though," she said, waggling a finger at her daughter and giving Alice a look.

"*What?*" Alice asked, trying to look innocent and failing as she smiled. "She needed a place to live."

"But such a fine place?" Kathy asked, amused, as she looked through the camera of her computer and beyond her daughter to the luxurious apartment she could see.

"What?" Alice asked again. "It was a good investment."

Kit laughed at the byplay between her mothers. She was so happy to see them back together, and now, this cancer. Dammit! "Is there anything I can do?" she asked, trying to regain their attention.

"No, honey. I'll keep you apprised, but Doctor Wilkerson said I'll be going in once a week, sometimes twice a week, while we try this experimental treatment," Kathy told her, looking at her oldest earnestly.

"Twice a week? I thought cancer treatment was like once a month?"

Alice nodded as Kathy explained, "Normal treatment is once a month. This is an experimental treatment since the cancer is so aggressive and moving so rapidly. They can't wait for normal treatment, and the hope is this should halt its rapid advance."

Kit nodded as though she completely understood. "If you need...anything," she hiccupped, suddenly realizing the gravity of the situation again, "you'll call? Please?"

"I'll call every chance I get, and if I get your voicemail, I'll leave a message and let you know what's going on," Kathy promised. "I'm not going to call every day though."

Kit had been about to argue the every day comment but thought better of it. She exchanged a look with Alice, who nodded slightly. She wouldn't call every day either, but she would let Kit know if anything was amiss that Kathy didn't want to discuss.

They signed off soon afterwards, and Alice turned to Kathy. "I think you need to sleep now." She could see how exhausting this day had been for her wife.

"I concur," Kathy agreed, and they held hands as they headed for bed together.

Alice tried repeatedly to get through the firewall over at the Pasternack's. There was a lot she wanted to see on that woman's computer. She tried through the security company, but apparently, they too had a firewall, and it was first rate. She thought of contacting Simone in New York, who happened to own a security company too, but Alice didn't want to involve her in what she considered a family matter. It would complicate things, and things were already complicated enough.

Alice hadn't forgotten about the dear ex-senator, who still had his people regularly watching their house. She wondered why he bothered since both women knew they were there. She had relieved some stress the other night by sneaking out of the house with a handful of three-inch nails in her hand and making her way to the parked car where she propped nails up on both sides of each tire. Then, she made a 7-Eleven run for Kathy, who said she was craving a Slurpee. Alice sped out of her driveway, taunting the men, who trying to hide in their sedan, by driving fast and too close to their vehicle. They followed for about three feet until the spikes pierced their tires. Alice returned from the store in time to see the vehicle being dragged onto a flatbed with all four of its tires flattened. She laughed. She was prepared to do it again but hadn't seen the car in a couple of days since that incident.

Alice also hadn't forgotten the hornet's nest she had stirred up in the form of Sebastian's nephew, Artum. She wished he would just let things go, but knew she had cost him quite a lot.

"Why were you talking so heatedly with the gardeners?" Kathy asked, having watched her wife through the bedroom window. She'd been taking eight of her pills and seen Alice gesturing with the lead gardener.

"Oh, I don't want those foolish palms that grow forty feet high. He must have gotten some deal on them, and he wants to plant them up here. It would be like a beacon off the cliff," she gestured to the bluffs their land abutted.

"Yeah, I don't mind the squat ones," Kathy agreed with her, gesturing to the sago palms planted around their grounds, "but those others would be an eyesore out here."

Alice felt bad lying to her wife, but it was for her own safety. "You okay? You need anything?"

"No, you go play," she smiled, referring to Alice's attempts on the computer. She'd seen some of it when Alice showed her what she had found, which wasn't much.

"I think I'm going to take a swim first and work out," Alice told her.

"Mind if I watch?" Kathy asked alluringly, laughing at her.

"You stay out of the sun. Doctor Wilkerson said that stuff will make your skin extra sensitive," she warned, referring to the chemotherapy.

Kathy watched from the safety of the overhang that protected her with its shade. She also watched as Alice played tennis with their daughter on their private court. Alice was giving instruction but wouldn't let the teen win; she had to earn it. Sean joined them, and playing against the two kids made Alice sweat, although she gave as good as she got. The three of them ended up enjoying themselves in the pool afterward. The two teens tried to entice Kathy in, but Alice explained the chlorine was not good for Kathy's skin, which was extra sensitive now. The dryness was a side effect of the chemo. One good thing that came from having dry skin was the need for lotion. Alice eagerly caressed her wife's body, massaging it while rubbing the lotion into her skin.

"Will you look at this?" Alice said, bringing her phone to Kathy and showing her the video playing on the screen.

"What is this?" Kathy asked, frowning as she watched what looked like a four-screen video of some security footage. She could make out four young people in the videos. They were wearing ski masks that they had pulled up on their heads, clearly showing their faces.

"The twit and her friends are robbing my house in Malibu," Alice told her angrily.

"What?" Kathy asked, alarmed, and sat up on the couch where she'd been reading the newspaper.

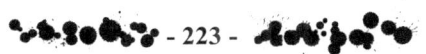

Alice left her phone with Kathy as she called the police on the house phone. She knew the alarm company was already on the way, but who knew how long that would take.

Kathy listened as Alice exasperatedly told the police in Malibu about the robbery in progress. She watched as they stole the television sets that had been left there to show the house, ripping the fixtures angrily from the wall. Then, with her heart in her mouth, she watched as the teens tore apart the rest of the house using the swords Alice had brought back from Kazakhstan, their razer-sharp edges making neat work of the furniture. The kids suddenly looked up and quickly exited to the beach, disappearing from the camera's view.

"Dammit!" Alice swore. The kids had not only taken the TVs and everything else of value, but also her swords. Some were seen leaving through the garage where they had loaded up a car, and the last of them were seen on the beach disappearing from view.

"Those swords are priceless," Kathy pointed out, looking up as Alice hung up the phone. "Why didn't you bring them home?"

"I forgot I'd left them when I brought the other things here, and when we put the house up for sale so quickly, I just...forgot," she finished lamely.

"You'll get them back," Kathy said confidently.

Alice looked up at her wife, who was resting on a couch in the TV room. It had taken a minute for Alice to find her when the spy cams had alerted her to intruders, and she realized what was going on at the house. Seeing who it was had instantly rekindled her age-old rage. Maybe she could not kill that *child*, but she could teach her a lesson. She thought she had already learned from her parents being financially liable for her acts, but obviously the elitist teen had not learned anything.

"I'm going to have to go into their home," she confided to her wife quietly.

"Didn't Emily say they had a security system?" Kathy worried. She sometimes liked it better when Alice did things without telling her ahead of time. She worried less that way. She wouldn't tell her wife that though. It had taken too long for them to get to the point where Alice confided with her.

"Yes, she did," Alice mused, wondering what kind of system it was since its firewall wasn't falling to her repeated attempts. It had to be a newer system, and it had to be secure because her techniques were rather…unique in their ability to thwart such systems. Her programs were state-of-the-art and illegal for the public to own…if anyone could even find them on her encrypted computers.

"How are you going to get past the security system? Are you just going in to look for the swords?" Kathy asked, confused. She was so tired, and she was starting to lose her hair. She hadn't told Alice yet, but she had seen hair on her pillow when she made the bed.

"I'm not sure. I'm going to have to scope out everything and make sure they have no night-vision cameras," she indicated her phone where the footage of the teenagers robbing her house had been clear.

"Why not just turn the kids over to the police?" Kathy asked, wanting to handle things honestly and above board for a change.

"Because the police won't get far. Sandi Pasternack will hire the best attorneys her husband's life insurance can afford, and she will get her daughter off again. That twit can't seem to grasp any of the lessons she is taught; she just amps up the ante."

"I can get you in," Emily said as she came into the room.

Both of her mothers jumped at the sound of her voice. They had been speaking low and hadn't heard her coming down the stairs.

"Dammit, Em! You have *got* to stop *eavesdropping*," Alice cursed her.

"I didn't *mean* to," she told them earnestly, looking between her moms and wondering why they wanted to get into the Pasternack's house.

Alice looked at her daughter. Just then, she looked exactly like Alice's sister Connie at the same age, and yet, when the teen grinned, she faintly reminded Alice of Kathy. She couldn't see that the child looked more like a young Alice, right down to the newly developing slant of her exotic eyes. There was also something so uniquely Em that Alice couldn't put her finger on yet.

"Those who eavesdrop never hear anything nice about themselves," Kathy said lamely, already too tired to cope with a misbehaving teen.

Alice turned to her wife with a questioning look, wondering about the sappy wisdom. Kathy grinned and shrugged. They both turned back to Emily.

"How much of that did you hear?" Alice asked.

"Something you wanted to get back from the Pasternack house?" Emily prompted, feeling a bit uncomfortable.

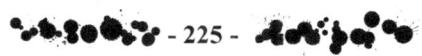

"You said you turned off their security system when you broke the windows," Alice began. She heard Kathy say weakly, "No, Alice," but ignored her. "Can you tell me how you did it?"

"I just punched in the code. I saw Carmen do it hundreds of times, and I guess I just learned the code from watching her."

Alice could have told her that those observation skills would come in handy. She noticed that Em was wearing sweats. She had probably been working on her karate skills in the weight room and overheard her parents talking. "What's the code?" she asked her daughter, watching her closely.

"I want to go–" began the teen, but both her parents interrupted.

"No!" Alice and Kathy said at the same time, then looked at each other and laughed.

"I don't want you getting involved in this," Kathy told her, quickly losing her smile. "This is something your mother needs to look into."

"Mom…" the teen started to protest, sounding a little bit whiny.

"Don't 'Mom' me!" Kathy answered quickly.

"Look, Em. You've already got a lot on your shoulders…" Alice began, holding up her hand to silence the teen's need to argue. "You have seen and heard some things I'd rather you hadn't. I don't want to add to that, if I can help it. I want you to have a normal life without complications."

"Come on, Mom. I can help…" she argued, despite the admonishments.

"No, you can't come with me!" Alice told her with a finality that the teen knew meant business.

"What if I don't give you the code?" Em asked saucily.

"Then, those long-awaited and long-overdue punishments will finally come to pass," Alice promised in a threatening tone that brooked no argument.

Emily stared at her parents. Kathy was looking ill, lying on the couch and holding Alice's phone. She was very pale, and against her dark hair, her skin looked even paler. Alice looked fierce. Her eyes were hard but were not changing color yet, and Emily knew better than to invoke that change. She crumbled in the face of such opposition and gave her mother the code. "What will you do?" she asked instead.

"I don't know," Alice admitted, much to the surprise of both her wife and her daughter.

"Shouldn't you have a plan?" Em asked, and Kathy turned expectantly to her wife, agreeing with the teen.

"Nope, gonna wing it," she said, smiling slightly at the amazingly similar facial expressions of her wife and daughter.

Alice waited a couple days; she was busy. She had to make a police report and explain what she had seen on the video, handing over the carefully doctored video of the break-in, which excluded the twit from the footage after she darkened it, so she wasn't recognizable. The others were immediately put on the police radar and would eventually be caught, but amazingly, they didn't give up their accomplice, Carmen.

Then, she took Kathy to another chemo appointment and fiddled on her phone while she waited for her to finish.

"Anything?" Kathy asked weakly from where she lay with the poison flowing into her veins. Today, it looked blue, and Alice teased her that she was now a real blue blood.

"No, I can't find what I want, and I don't dare put more of these invasive programs on a mere phone," Alice told her as she looked up, trying not to gasp at how white her wife had become. This was only the third session. She would be supportive of whatever the doctor wanted to do…until the end, and that was a real possibility. She made sure none of her thoughts showed on her face as she smiled at her wife.

"What are you looking for?" Kathy asked quietly, wondering what Alice was up to.

"I'm trying to get a handle on the senator's schedule. They've changed it three times since I tapped into their system, and I want to know why."

"The senator?" Kathy exclaimed, surprised. She had forgotten about him with all the commotion about the twit.

Alice, who had looked back down at her phone, looked up at her wife through her lashes and gave her a sardonic look in return. "You don't think I've forgotten what he has been up to, do you?"

"I thought you might, what with everything else," she gestured at the needle in her arm and thought about the other things that had occupied their attention a month ago.

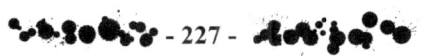

Alice lowered her voice as she put the phone down and gave her wife her full attention. "I have several things I'm looking into," she confided.

"Like what?" Kathy demanded.

"We'll talk in the car," Alice hedged, not sure she wanted to share what she had found with her wife but knowing she wouldn't lie if Kathy asked a direct question, not completely anyway.

"You think someone is bugging this office?" Kathy laughed.

Alice smiled, and just then, the nurse came in to check on her patient. Alice exchanged an 'I told you so' look with her wife.

"Okay, spill," Kathy teased as they drove away from the clinic.

"Which part?" Alice muttered.

"How do you know your car isn't bugged?"

"Because I sweep it after every time I take it out."

"Every time?" Kathy asked, surprised.

"Every time," Alice admitted, glancing at her wife before concentrating on the traffic.

"Have you found anything?"

Alice shrugged and shook her head. "Not yet, but you know, it would be just my luck that one time…."

Kathy had to admit she was right. "Don't think you are going to distract me that easily. What are you watching for on your phone besides the senator?"

Alice smiled. Kathy was more insightful about her hedging these days. "Before I start, is there anywhere you want to stop before going home?"

"Wendy's?"

"Why Wendy's?" Alice asked, surprised, changing to another lane, so she could turn off and head for the chain restaurant.

"I'm craving a Wendy's chicken sandwich and baked potato. Not the spicy one though; that would give me bad heartburn," she added, rubbing her stomach. She'd suffered from a lot of heartburn with the meds she was on.

"How about a chocolate shake?" Alice enticed her.

"Sold!" Kathy answered with a smile. She knew Alice would indulge her every whim. She just hoped she wouldn't throw up all her food. It was later in the day, and she had noticed she usually threw up after breakfast and the meds she had to take early in the day. A couple of the meds required her to drink milk with them, and a couple required

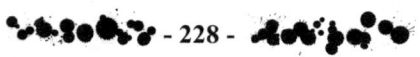

her to wait an hour before eating, but she always threw up after breakfast. She found if she ate a banana with some of the meds, the reflux wasn't as bad, and she could eat again. It was a horrible cycle; one the doctor had warned her about. She was also cautioned that she could easily become anemic.

Alice waited in the parking lot until Kathy was eating her chicken sandwich and digging her spoon into the chocolate Frosty she had decided to substitute for the shake. She bit into her own sandwich, a blissful look on her face as she tasted the lettuce, tomato, and fried chicken blending with the mayonnaise. "I'm trying to keep tabs on Artum and looking for Iggy. Then, there is Carmen and Sandi. I want to get in that house when they aren't home, but neither of them is doing things on a schedule." She said it as though the pair were deliberately doing this to inconvenience her, and Kathy laughed around her food, coughing slightly as something caught, then quickly sipping at her soda.

"Careful there," Alice warned. "Not sure you want me doing the Heimlich."

"I'm okay, just tried to swallow too much," she admitted as she chewed her food finer. "Are you finding anything?"

"More than enough to hang Artum, but Iggy is still being hidden. I'm beginning to wonder if he returned to whatever hole he crawled out of, or if they killed him for stealing from our house."

"What are you going to do?"

"For now, I'm just going to watch. Things were pretty hot with Artum, and I don't want to stir that hornet's nest if I can avoid it."

"Why not?"

Alice looked at her wife incredulously. "With you sick, I don't want to jeopardize our safety."

"How would that jeopardize our safety?" she asked naively.

"He could come to our house to take revenge, and he would probably kill me," she answered succinctly.

"What about me?" Kathy asked, almost sounding hurt that she would be excluded. "I mean, I did help."

"And Emily," Alice reminded her.

"That kid is starting to worry me with everything she knows."

"Me too," Alice admitted. She'd been watching the monitors and hadn't seen anything out of the ordinary with the teen, but with all she already knew, it was a wonder Emily wasn't in therapy.

Alice finally got a break when Carmen bragged in a post that she and her mother were going to a Broadway play that had come to town. She talked about how she had purchased a gown for the event, going on and on about it. Ignoring the obvious excitement of the obnoxious teen, Alice watched the comments and the girl's responses, gleaning far more than the teen would have ever expected when she posted. The child was a font of unintentional information, and Alice waited patiently as the night in question came, planning accordingly.

She waited until Kathy had gone to bed and she thought Emily was in bed. Sean was staying at a friend's house, which he seemed to be doing a lot with Kathy looking more ill by the day. She couldn't really blame the teen. Twice by turns, he'd thought he'd lost his parents, but this time was the first time he was actually watching it happening, and it was probably deeply disturbing to him. He wasn't talking much to his parents, and Kathy and Alice were sad about that. They both hoped he was getting what he needed from his friends and their parents. Alice had carefully vetted those parents and found them and their children to be decent people, so she wasn't concerned about their influence on her son.

As she prepared on the evening of the play, she dressed carefully to conceal her blonde hair, which she kept short and spikey. She thought of blackening her face but felt that would be too hard to explain if she were caught. Using her key, she slipped out her own back gate going along the bluffs until she passed her own estate and her neighbors' before cutting back and slipping out behind the car that was watching their house tonight. Fortunately, it was not parked as close as it had been previously. Just for fun and practice, she slipped up on the car and placed three-inch nails on both the back tires again, ensuring deep punctures and hopefully a flat tire or two when they moved. She added insult to injury by shoving a potato in the tailpipe, which made a slight noise, but the two idiots watching tonight didn't hear a thing.

It was dusk, and she picked her way onto the Pasternack estate, hoping they didn't have a dog. She didn't remember Emily stating they had one, and she thought people like Sandi and Richard, with a self-absorbed daughter like Carmen, were far too selfish to bother with pets.

She thought about her own family and determined they would adopt another dog, maybe even a cat or two. It was only right that their kids have pets. She wanted them to have as normal a childhood as possible.

She determined where the motion-sensor lights were by simply triggering them, one by one, and determining their range over the course of an hour. She knew that the Pasternacks had left over an hour ago and had timed her own appearance accordingly. It wasn't so dark that she couldn't make her way to their house using her night-vision goggles and see what she needed to turn off the security system with the code Emily had given her. She feared they had changed the code and shook her head at the laziness of human nature when it worked. Richard had obviously never changed it, and Sandi probably never thought of it after his death. As she made her way into the garage, she looked around with her goggles, determined not to turn on any lights until she had to. Nothing in the garage gave her the information she was seeking, and she turned off the security alarm and made her way into the house, noting that the house wasn't particularly neat and wondering if they had a maid or housekeeper. None of her research had indicated they did. She looked through their living room, noting the dining room was the most prestigious room of the house. The kitchen needed a thorough cleaning, with dishes stacked in the sink and on the counter. She checked through the windows into the backyard and saw no indication they had pets.

Next, she made her way upstairs to the bedrooms, realizing the master bedroom must have been the room she missed downstairs and cursing herself for thinking it was the den or office, which she was ultimately seeking. She noted that there were only two bedrooms upstairs. They were oddly narrow, and a long hallway connected both to an equally narrow shared bathroom. She checked for hidden rooms, wondering why such an oddly shaped house had been built in this expensive area of Palos Verdes. The guest room was stripped, and there was nothing to indicate it had any occupants, just a plain twin bed and desk, both bare and boring. There was nothing in the closet or under the bed as Alice's gloved fingers sought for anything hidden and dislodged some dust. She left that room and went to check out what she assumed was Carmen's room.

It looked like a tornado had hit the teen's room. The messiness she had noted downstairs was compounded by the used clothing thrown haphazardly about the room. Some clothing lying around had been folded, and she could only surmise that it had been clean at one point but never put away. The bed was unmade, the sheets were in a ball to one side, and the mattress was exposed. There were used dishes up here too, the remains of food congealed or caked on the dishes. Alice gazed at the dishes with disgust, her own fastidious nature finding the idea of attracting bugs like this abhorrent. She easily found the teen's computer. It was obviously well-used, and it was the only reasonably clean surface in the room. Alice found it still turned on and not password protected, quickly confirming her own findings that nothing was hidden. She'd installed a keylogger program through the virus the teen had experienced months ago, slowing things down until Alice could tweak it to her needs. She left the computer, her eyes adjusting once again to the gloom before she slipped her goggles back on and searched the room. She found her swords and would have taken them, but they were listed with the police as missing, and she wasn't sure how to use this information yet. She gave the messy room a once-over but found nothing she hadn't expected and left. She froze when she saw a figure coming up the stairs.

"What in the hell are you doing here?" she hissed at Emily, recognizing her daughter, who was also dressed in black jogging clothes like Alice.

"I thought I could help," the teen stated defensively.

"Are you wearing gloves?" she asked and confirmed that the girl was not as she grabbed the handrail.

Emily looked down dumbly at her hands, realizing she was leaving fingerprints in the home. "Won't they assume they are from when I was here before?"

"Not if they are fresh. This is one of the reasons I didn't want you here; you are leaving evidence," she hissed angrily.

Emily could hear the reproach in her mother's voice and winced. She had thought she was the best person to help her mother. She wanted to witness the revenge Alice would get on these people. She hated Carmen for what she had done to her, and overhearing that her parents wanted more information on this family after Richard's death, she felt she was the best person to help them. She made as if to wipe her hand down the rail.

"Don't do that," Alice warned her. "You're making it worse by spreading your DNA all over the scene." She took her own gloved hand and wiped down the entire banister as she went down the stairs with the teen following reluctantly behind. "Don't touch anything," she ordered angrily. "What else have you touched?"

"Just the garage door you came through," she admitted honestly, thinking hard on that.

Alice sighed, wondering if she could use the teen's help or should order her home. The chances of getting caught had increased with her presence. "Did the Pasternacks have anything like video surveillance or a nanny cam or anything?" she asked, figuring she might as well use her daughter's knowledge while she could. Sending her home would only increase the chances she might be seen.

"They didn't need a nanny cam–" and Alice lifted her goggles, so she could peer through the dark and stare at her daughter as she realized the stupidity of what she was saying. "Oh…" she finished.

Alice shook her head and rolled her eyes. "Did they spy on their guests or their daughter?" she asked, heading once again for the dining room. "Don't touch *anything*," she warned.

"I don't think so." She sounded like an unsure adolescent to Alice's ears.

Alice dug in her pocket. She hadn't brought much with her, but a pair of latex gloves surfaced, and she handed them to the teen.

"Put these on and stay quiet," she ordered, watching as the teen struggled into the gloves and held up her hands to show her mother when they were on. Alice didn't approve. She had never wanted to see her teen doing something illegal. Still, she had overheard so many illegal things Alice had done, and she had observed both her parents breaking and entering, not to mention Alice eventually killing several people. The fact that she hadn't broken was amazing.

Alice pulled her goggles over her eyes again and looked around the living room and dining area once more. She was looking for telltale items that could be used to conceal a camera or holes in the walls or ceiling. There was nothing. She'd looked before, but knowing she wasn't as quick or observant as she had once been, a second look never hurt. This time, she went into what she now knew to be the master bedroom, looking through things in the dressers, side tables, and cosmetics table the woman kept in there. She saw that Richard Pasternack's things were still in the walk-in closet. She went through everything, searching each pocket, looking but not finding anything of importance.

"What are you looking for?" Emily whispered, watching her mother for a long time, squinting through the darkness and trying to make out exactly what she was doing.

"Shhh," Alice replied, annoyed that the teen was watching her and wishing she could just send her home.

Emily subsided, but she wanted to help too. She looked around the room, peering into the darkness and wondering what Alice was looking for. She took one step towards the bed and heard her mother's voice.

"Leave it."

"What?" the teen asked, genuinely curious what Alice meant. Then, she wondered how Alice had seen her.

"Whatever it is, leave it," Alice said without even turning around.

Emily was annoyed. She wasn't eight years old anymore. She was old enough to help Alice search. She hadn't seen Alice find the sword box in Carmen's room, but if she had seen it, she wouldn't have understood Alice leaving it there. After all, Carmen had stolen it from Alice's home in Malibu. "Why can't we turn on the light or use a flashlight?" the teen asked, trying to see what Alice was fumbling for in the dark of the walk-in closet.

"Because people can see more in the light," Alice said shortly, annoyed to have to explain herself. Emily shouldn't be here. "It would give us away if we were seen through the window."

That made sense to the teen, but wouldn't it hurry things up if Alice could better see what she was looking for? "I brought along a penlight, and it should..." the teen began, fumbling with the light that she turned on in her hand.

Alice turned slightly, just in time to have the light flashed in her eyes. "Dammit!" she exclaimed, closing her eyes to its glare, which was magnified by the goggles she was wearing. "Turn that damned thing off!" she hissed at her daughter, angry now. "You've blinded me!"

"Sorry," Emily said quickly and scrabbled to turn off the small light, wondering why something so small could have her mother sounding so angry.

Alice recalled giving her daughter the penlight. It was cheap but effective, and now. she was blinded. She rapidly blinked away the white spots before her eyes. She sighed. She wished her daughter had stayed home, so this would go faster. She'd already been here too long and hadn't even looked through the office yet. She wasn't finding much here in the bedroom, and she had to be careful to put everything back exactly as she found it, so no one would be aware that she had rifled through their things.

She finally headed out of the bedroom and into the master bathroom, looking around at the opulence. It was rather nauseating and overboard; it bespoke of wealth…without class. Everything was gold-plated: the faucets, the edges of the mirrors, and even the toilet and bidet. It was over the top and gaudy, and it reminded Alice of pictures she had seen of other wealthy people who seemed to think that having gold on everything showed their wealth off splendidly. It didn't. There was no taste shown here at all. She found Sandi Pasternack had a taste for expensive name brand perfumes. They were overpriced and not nearly as fine as the ones Alice and Kathy used, which were custom made for them by Alice's perfumer. This woman had all the finest, top brand cosmetics, but extraordinarily little of the products was used. Alice finally saw the first thing that had her narrowing her cat-like eyes. She realized that all the fine cosmetics were there for show only. Behind the cosmetics was a false door, and Alice carefully opened it.

"Give me your penlight," Alice whispered to her daughter, pulling off her goggles with one hand and holding out her other hand expectantly.

"What'd you find?" the teen whispered back, suddenly excited.

"Never mind," Alice murmured, taking the light her daughter handed her and glancing around the glass-enclosed bathroom once she had turned it on. She aimed its beam into the drawer as she shielded the beam with her hand to keep it from flashing outside the box. She tugged slightly at the false door, pulling it open to reveal syringes and several vials. Her eyes narrowed at the Russian lettering, trying to wrack her brain and remember what Sasha had taught her so long ago. She couldn't make out what the substances were, but they all seemed to be the same. She slipped one into her pocket and carefully closed the hidden door, piling the makeup against it, then opening and shutting the drawer a couple of times to hide where she had been from her daughter.

"What is that?" Emily asked, curious.

"I don't know," Alice admitted, turning off the penlight and handing it back to her daughter. She thought about keeping the penlight but didn't want to encumber herself with anything in case she needed her hands free, and she had limited pocket space. Her jogging clothes weren't built for carrying much, and the bulge of the little glass vial was patently obvious to her. She grabbed the goggles again and looked around the bathroom some more, feeling under the sink cabinet for hidden spaces and anything else that Sandi or Richard might have reason to hide. Then she got up, hearing her knees crack with the effort as she headed for the office. She knew she should have gone there first but had relished the idea of leaving it for last. She would give it a thorough go-through and then leave, but with Emily along and watching, she would have to see what she could do despite the teen. She sighed at the inconvenience.

The office, or rather a den-like room, was the complete opposite of the display of wealth that had been so obvious in the master bedroom. This room was warm with dark woods that Alice could appreciate, but it also told her that Richard Pasternack had taste and his wife did not. The dark wood made it harder to discern if there were hidey-holes as it hid any telltale signs. She wished for a light but knew that would be a mistake of the highest order and could give away their presence completely. The shelf-lined walls held books in several languages, and her minimal knowledge of Russian proved useful as she realized they were versions of books like The Art of War by Sun Tzu and other classics: from Shakespeare in Russian to what she gleaned were The Harry Potter books, not in Russian but what she figured out was a similar language. With a name like Pasternack, she thought perhaps they were Ukrainian? She didn't know and would have to look into that another time. After looking over the various titles—few, if any, in English—for telltale signs of hidey-holes, she heard her daughter whisper.

"What are we looking for?" Emily was becoming impatient and bored. Whatever she had thought they would find and investigate, it wasn't Mr. Pasternack's collection of first editions or leather-bound, stinky books. Some of them were ancient, and she'd seen them all before.

"I won't know until I find it, will I?" Alice answered, amused. "You weren't supposed to be here, so be quiet and let me look," she admonished in a warning tone.

Emily subsided, chastised and annoyed. She wanted to help. After all, she was the one that had the code to the house, so why couldn't she… She took a step towards the desk and heard Alice speak without even turning around.

"Touch nothing. Just stand there," she told the girl.

"Why can't I help?"

"What are we looking for?" Alice countered, seeing something out of the ordinary and reaching for two books that had obviously been pulled out recently, if the telltale signs in the dust were correct.

"I don't know," the teen admitted and wondered if her mother was going to sit down and read as she reached for some books.

Alice was glad she was wearing gloves; her fingerprints would be obvious on these books since they were so smooth. The covers weren't leather though; they were some other material. As she opened the first book, she realized the two books were bonded together as one, and when she opened them to the center, it revealed a small box. She carefully put the books down on a side table, moving aside a large mound of paperwork to accommodate them. She pulled the box out but was unable to open it. It didn't have any signs of a lock, or even a hinge, and she studied it carefully.

"What is it?" Emily asked, unable to control herself.

"I think it's some sort of safe or something," Alice murmured, mostly to herself as she examined it. It was then she realized that some of the pages were thicker than others and moved. "Bring your light here but cover it with your hands," she ordered her daughter as she lifted the goggles to her head to peer into the darkness.

"Hey, that's cool," Em told her as she shined her penlight on the book that wasn't a book.

"Were you any good at Rubik's Cubes?" Alice asked her daughter, realizing there had to be a pattern to the page squares carved in the sides of the books.

"Wasn't that a Russian game?" Emily asked as she reached for the books, handing Alice the penlight, so she could touch the odd squares carved into the sides of the pages. It wasn't as easy as it would have been with bare hands, but she knew better than to take off the gloves.

"You should know that it was developed by a Hungarian," she corrected her daughter as she watched, amazed, as Emily adeptly pushed and prodded the cubes into place. They slid easily under her fingertips, or so it appeared to Alice's eyes.

Emily shrugged as she studied the cube and began to place her fingers on the thick slips of paper. "I just remember the craze; it wasn't very easy to get the nine squares on all the sides to match."

"You should learn the history of things too; that does become important," Alice advised, watching fascinated as her daughter figured out the complex slides that looked too complicated to her. Then, she too saw the pattern and pointed out a couple moves to her daughter, "Move that one there, and go up there," she advised, and the book suddenly released the box from its interior with a ping.

"Whoa!" Emily exclaimed rather loudly.

"Shhh," Alice told her as she reached for the box, which contained several wads of cash in both US dollars and English pounds. It was at the bottom of this small box that she found data sticks; those she took out.

"Aren't you going to take the money?" Emily asked, surprised.

Alice shrugged. "Why? I have enough," she answered as she put the money back and closed the box, quickly mixing up the sliders to hide the combination once again. She wiped the sides where Emily had touched the book, despite the fact she was wearing gloves, hoping that no one would notice it had been opened. Hearing a noise, she turned out the light, closed the books, and slid her goggles back on while returning the books to their shelf. She waited a while, listening to her daughter's breathing in the dark.

"What was that?" Emily asked quietly, barely getting the words out.

"I don't know," Alice admitted as she slid the books carefully back onto the shelf and looked towards the computer. Removing something from her pocket she replaced it with the data sticks.

"What's that?"

"Shhh," Alice told her as she carefully put some pea-sized cameras on the shelves, trying not to disturb any of the dust that had built up and leave any signs of their presence. Just as she was placing the second one, she caught her daughter's hand before she could touch the shelf. "No," she said quietly. "You'll leave evidence."

Emily hadn't thought of that. She'd been about to put her hand on the shelf as she tried to see what her mother was doing. She realized Alice must be quite good at this. She seemed to effortlessly examine things, and Emily had no idea how she saw things. She would have totally missed those books.

Alice next moved to the desk and began to rifle through the drawers, being sure to feel on the upper parts of the various inserts for hidden or concealed spots. In the last and biggest drawer, which was filled with paperwork she could not read in the dark, she found another data stick, and she slipped this in with the others.

"Why is that one blue?" Emily asked softly, noting the others had all been white.

"No idea," Alice admitted, shrugging but also a little pleased her daughter had also noticed the difference. Finally, Alice reached for the computer to turn it on. The computer was old, and the light from the screen was rather bright. Alice slipped her goggles onto her head and hoped that the glare and reflection on the window wouldn't give them away. She almost said something as Emily moved to the window and closed the drapes, then thought better of it.

A password prompt came up, but Alice had been prepared for it as she put her own stick into a USB port. The software rapidly scrolled through various combinations until it found the password. "Not too obvious," Alice murmured sarcastically as she realized the password was Pasternack, their last name. She took another data stick from her pocket and replaced the password stick in the port. She began to download everything from the computer onto it.

"Will there be enough room?" Em asked, watching Alice.

"I have no idea," she admitted as she began clicking on the history. The Pasternacks must have thought themselves smart as she found their banking information from several banks, smiling to herself at how easy they had made it by storing their passwords on the computer. Didn't they know you should *never* store passwords for financial information? She copied the links, then went to the password list and began copying those as well. What Alice was doing was second nature to her, and while she was thinking she remembered something she had wanted to check for in the house, but Em had distracted her. Before turning off the computer, she installed a keylogger program she had paid a lot of money for. It was so sophisticated that it wouldn't be detected without special equipment or programs. "Open the drapes. Leave them the way they were," she informed the teen as she looked about the desk, ensuring it was the same as when she started.

"Are we done?" Emily asked after she had reopened the drapes and peered out. It was too dark to see anything.

"You should be," Alice murmured, annoyed that she was answering to a teenager. She had to think beyond her own safety now, and it was causing her to slow down. She should have already been out of the house. "I have to check one more thing," she said as she looked around the library a final time, putting her goggles on to peer through the dark.

"What?" the teen asked, curious, as she followed Alice.

"Just stay quiet," Alice stated as she headed to the master bedroom again and began peering around.

Em ignored the mandate and asked, "What are you looking for?"

Alice sighed through her nose, exasperated at the teen's questions. "I'll know when I find it. Now, be quiet," she ordered.

Em subsided, wishing somehow, some way, she could help.

Alice began to look through the jewelry. She could recognize fine pieces, but most of this was fake, cosmetic, and gaudy. The woman's taste was not Alice's. "Do you know if they had a safe?" she asked the teen, then turned when Emily didn't immediately answer. She looked questioningly at her daughter.

Emily peered at her in the darkness, barely able to make out what Alice was doing, much less seeing. Then, seeing her mother's questioning look, she answered peevishly, "You told me to be quiet."

Alice sighed. "Now is not the time for hurt feelings or dramatics. Since you are here, help me. I didn't want you here; I didn't want you involved in any of this," her hands gestured around the house they had been searching.

"But I can help," the teen contended.

"You have helped. Now, answer my question. Did they have a safe?"

"I don't remember," she admitted. "What are you looking for?"

"A ring," she murmured as she turned back to the jewelry box, itself a cheap imitation wood, and rifled through things. "Mrs. Pasternack wore a ring the day we signed the paperwork in the lawyer's office, and I want to find it."

"Do you remember what it looked like?" Em asked reasonably, suddenly happy she might be able to help.

"No. Unfortunately, I wasn't looking at it in the office," she admitted, annoyed at herself. That wasn't like her. Normally, she was very observant. She closed her eyes for a moment to try to pinpoint that moment in time, to remember and focus. It took her a moment to get there, and she had to shush Emily once more as she concentrated. "I think it was like a signet ring. You know, one of those rings you wear when you graduate from high school or college?" she said to the teen. "She had turned it around," she said, remembering the incident now that she concentrated, and using her unique mind, she began to play it out. "Do you remember seeing anything like that?"

"Why would she turn it around?" the teen asked, confused, as she tried to remember ever seeing a ring anything like that on her friend's mother.

Alice was getting exasperated. She wasn't finding it as she rifled through the crap jewelry while trying not to get anything out of place. They were running out of time. "Because I think it has a needle in it, and she used it to hurt your mom!"

Emily drew back, horrified. She wasn't stupid, and her young, agile mind began to put the pieces of the puzzle together. "Do you think she made mom sick with whatever was in that needle?"

Alice immediately regretted becoming annoyed with her daughter. The goggles clearly showed Emily's face in the dark. "Yes, I do," she admitted honestly, calming her voice and putting the jewelry box back. She wanted to take Em in her arms and comfort her, but now was not the time or the place. They had to get out of here. "I think we're going to have to leave it for another time," she admitted as she went to the side table and looked through it again.

Emily was deeply horrified by what she had learned. If that were true, then Mrs. Pasternack had poisoned her mom! She looked around the dark room, trying to remember what she had seen during the times she had been here. She had no reason to come in here but had followed her friend when she came to borrow something. Mrs. Pasternack certainly wasn't as neat as her own mothers. "What about her medical bag?" she whispered to Alice, who turned around quickly.

"Where is it?" she asked, suddenly interested.

"She usually keeps it in the garage."

Alice returned the items she had rifled in the side table exactly where she had found them and closed the drawer. "Let's go," she said to the teen. The garage was on their way out. "What does it look like?" she asked as they headed for the door.

"Just one of those doctor's bags you see on all the old TV shows."

Alice nodded, unsure whether her daughter saw her or not as she gently opened the thick door. Looking around the three-car garage, she saw the vehicles that the Pasternacks drove, minus the one they must be using tonight. Along one side of the garage were shelving units with all sorts of junk piled on them. This must be Sandi's domain because everything was a real mess. Near the empty spot in the garage, there was one shelving unit that contained nursing items: masks, gloves, bandages, and a host of things that had Alice narrowing her eyes. She was wondering if they were stolen from the woman's employers or if she kept a supply of her own. The bag that Em had mentioned was sitting there in plain sight—at least plain sight through the goggles although outlined in green—and Alice eagerly reached for it, opening it and trying to peer into the black depths.

"Want my penlight?" Em breathed, staying close to Alice since she could barely see in the darkness.

"Yeah, but make sure you don't shine it anywhere near the door," Alice nodded as the teen flicked the penlight on and shone it in the bag, making sure her back was towards the door and the side yard out of the garage. The door had a big window in its center.

The bag was filled with syringes, meds, bandages, and other paraphernalia. Alice was careful as some of the syringes did not have caps. It proved that Sandi was not a very conscientious nurse.

"Jeeze," Emily said, sounding impressed and repulsed. She could see blood on some of the syringes.

Alice went very carefully, making sure she didn't get stuck as she rifled through the mess. At the bottom she found the ring she was looking for, and using a plastic bag from Sandi's own supplies, she dropped the ring inside and pocketed both.

"That's it?" Emily asked as she watched her mother.

"Yeah, let's get out of here and reset the alarm," Alice told her, sensing the teen felt the end was anti-climactic. They put the medical bag back on the shelf once Alice closed it up and headed for the alarm panel. Alice reset it with Emily's help, and they headed for the side door to make their escape. They put the code in just in time. Right then, the garage light came on, blinding Alice with its brilliance as it shone through her goggles. They both heard the garage door rising.

"Come on!" Emily gasped, realizing Alice couldn't see as she fumbled for the doorknob. Em grabbed her mother's arm and yanked her out the door into the dark just as the garage door rose completely.

"Shit!" Alice swore angrily, blinking rapidly to remove the spots from her eyes.

They headed for the path that wound down both sides of the road, the jogging path running behind the houses on Alice and Kathy's side of the block along the bluff. As they darted across the road, behind the car eternally parked there, they both looked back. Alice lifted her goggles to blink blindly in the dark at the house they had just left.

"Can you see anything?" Alice whispered, still unable to get rid of the spots. The light from the garage had gone right through the night goggles.

"Yeah, it's Mrs. Pasternack. I can't see anyone else," Emily whispered, sounding excited.

"Just get me home," Alice warned her. She didn't need to be caught now.

Emily led her along the bluff, noting that Alice was still having trouble. They were almost to their own gate when Alice finally freed her arm from Emily's grip. "Thanks," she murmured as she unlocked the gate, and they both went through. Alice relocked it with the key, and they crossed their lawn and entered the house.

"Where have you been?" Kathy rasped, looking at them both in consternation as they came into the kitchen together.

Alice looked up, surprised. Kathy had known where she was going, but she looked guiltily at her daughter standing beside her. Alice realized how that looked when Kathy asked, "You took Emily *with* you?"

"No, I–" she began, but Em interrupted.

"No, I followed her. I thought I could help," she admitted, looking as chastised and guilty as Alice felt. She bit her lip and leaned from foot to foot uncomfortably.

"You *followed* your mom?" Kathy asked, incredulous. She'd known Alice a lot of years, and that wouldn't have been possible in the past. She looked between the two faces to see if they were lying to her.

"Yeah, I know. I'm in trouble," the teen said, sounding rebuked.

"Do you know what would have happened if I had been caught?" Alice asked, putting her goggles down on the table. "And what if you had been caught?"

"What would happen?" Emily asked reasonably, her curiosity piqued.

"I don't think Portia could have gotten you out of the system," she answered ominously. "I probably would have gone to jail for trespassing, breaking and entering, and who knows what else."

"And they would have been on to us for finding out about their habits," Kathy added. She looked at her wife, feeling like she was about to throw up again. She'd spent an uncomfortable night trying to keep her meds down while wondering how Alice was faring. She asked, "Did you find anything?"

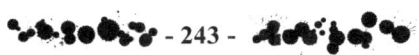

"I don't know yet, but we will see," Alice told her honestly, hoping her daughter wouldn't talk too much, or not at all.

Sensing that Alice didn't want Kathy to know what they found, the teen kept quiet. She didn't want to find out how much trouble she was in by reminding them of her presence.

"You aren't to speak about this night's escapade," Alice cautioned her daughter. "You might want to go to bed while I discuss things with your mom. And you are not to eavesdrop. Do you hear me?" she warned her ominously.

"I wasn't–" she began, then shut up. She knew she'd overheard and seen some things she shouldn't have, just enough that she wanted to know more. Wisely, she knew that now was not the time, so she backed down. "Yes, Mom. Good night, Mom," she said, leaning over to give Alice a peck on the cheek and taking a step to give Kathy one as well.

"Good night, darling," Kathy murmured weakly. She could feel her stomach roiling, realizing her daughter had probably experienced something she shouldn't have.

They both waited until they heard the teen's bedroom door close.

Kathy rounded on Alice. "Why didn't you bring her right home?"

"I didn't know she was there until I was about halfway through my search. That little twit kept my swords," she informed her wife, changing the subject.

"I don't care–" began Kathy, but a coughing fit cut her off as her throat was choking up from the bile. She went into the kitchen to get a glass of water with Alice following.

"Is there anything I can get you?" Alice asked, worried about that cough.

Kathy shook her head and waved her away.

Alice stood there weakly, not knowing what she could do for her wife. She wasn't as unobservant as Kathy would like her to be. She could see the bald patches where her hair was coming out in gobs. She had heard the choking coughs in the bathroom, the sound of her wife throwing up daily after she took her meds, and the repeated toilet flushing as her wife couldn't keep anything in or down from either end. She also could smell the severe diarrhea, and Alice had dutifully reported everything to the doctor.

Kathy continued to wave Alice away as she drank water and turned her back on her wife. She needed to cope with this part of her illness by herself.

Defeated, Alice went upstairs to change for bed, hiding the vial and the ring where she could access them tomorrow, then heading downstairs to her computers with the data sticks. Kathy found her there about an hour later.

"Anything?" she asked as she walked in carrying a large cup of water and eating salted crackers from a bag. She acted as though nothing had happened.

"That woman is pure evil," Alice commented as her computers went over the various sticks she had taken as well as the information she had downloaded.

"What about Richard?" she asked, curious. After all, he had confessed and was washing money for those drug dealers.

Alice shook her head. "It seems that Sandi is the brains of that outfit. She loved Dick," she grinned as she said that, referring to Richard. "He was only the accountant, but damn," she whistled, "he knew how to hide it." Alice showed the trail of how Richard had taken the drug money and funneled it through various enterprises ranging from fast food restaurants to some of the hospice care homes that Sandi worked in.

"What do you mean Sandi is the brains?" Kathy asked. That sounded odd to her.

"She directed where he worked and apparently, for whom. Sebastian was bad, don't get me wrong, but whoever his nephew is, or was back in the old country, he's brought an element in that I don't like," she waved to her computer screen. "That woman! I have to wonder if she's related to any of the people I met back in Mother Russia," she added, lowering her voice, so the children wouldn't hear if any were still awake.

"Sean is over at a friend's house," Kathy told her, reminding her that he spent a lot of time away. He couldn't cope with seeing Kathy looking the way she did. "I checked on Em, and she's asleep."

"Are you sure?" Alice asked. She'd checked too and wasn't so sure about that at the time.

"Yeah, this time I went in and stood there a while. There is no way she could have faked it that long," Kathy laughed. They both knew they had a handful in their teenaged daughter. She knew too much and was too strong headed. "What are we going to do with her?"

"I don't know," Alice admitted. There was just so much they could do. The teen really could hold what she knew over them, but at the same time, if she ever leaked what she knew, they were all in a lot of trouble. "We'll let my programs finish this up and go to bed. I'm tired," she admitted, stretching.

Kathy was pleased to see Alice get up and walk over to her, then take her in her arms and give her a hug and a squeeze. "We'll figure this out," Alice promised as she escorted her wife to bed.

Alice got up early, not needing as much sleep as her wife. She watched as Em headed off for summer camp where she was taking tennis lessons with some of her friends. She was relieved to have the girl out of the house, so she could work on her computers and go through the vast amounts of information the thumb drives contained. These sticks of information were invaluable. They told her things about Sebastian's vast network, which was now his nephew's. She hadn't known they were under so many different holdings, and she needed this information. She was sending out inquiries and waiting to read more of the information when Kathy came down the stairs.

"Are you going with me to the doctor's today?" she asked, sounding exhausted and looking pale and drawn.

"Yes. Is it at ten or eleven?" she asked to confirm.

"Eleven. We can pick up lunch afterwards?"

"Sounds good. I'll just finish up here," she indicated the computers she had cued up. She'd already pressed buttons to hide what was really on her screens, even from her wife. It was a long-standing habit of hers that she just couldn't let go of, even after all these years.

Doctor Wilkerson was pleased to get the vial. Even though he couldn't read the label, he was going to run some tests to find out what it was. He was even more amazed at the ring Alice handed him in the

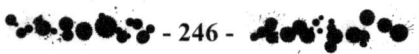

plastic baggie. When Alice showed him the needle in the false front of the ring, his eyes glimmered. He looked at it under a microscope and saw dried blood on its tip.

"I'll get right on this," he said.

"I want to know if that's Kathy's blood on there," Alice told him forcefully. "I also want to know if that's what caused this odd cancer in her body, if there is a cure, and if so, what that cure is," she indicated the vial.

"Of course," he assured her, wanting to get on that immediately, but he had to finish Kathy's treatment first.

Kathy was coughing from the lack of oxygen in her system, and Doctor Wilkerson quickly cued up the pure oxygen and put the mask on her face. Smiling kindly, he explained why her body was reacting the way it was.

Kathy remembered meeting him many years ago when she had wanted children, and Alice had arranged it for them. She still didn't understand how it was possible for two women to have children who looked like both of them, but she trusted this kind man. He was brilliant, and he had come through for them several times. She only hoped he could come through this time. She wanted to be here for her children. Hell, she wanted to be here for her grandchildren.

Alice kept her promise and took Kathy to her favorite fast-food restaurant after her treatment.

"If I tell you to pull over, pull over quickly!" Kathy warned after eating her hamburger and fries. It all tasted so good going down.

"Why?" Alice asked before thinking.

"Because I don't know how long that food is going to stay down, and I don't want to throw up in your nice SUV," she informed her wife as she sipped her soda, relishing the burps it produced.

Alice felt bad. She should have realized why without Kathy having to explain. She took her wife home; glad she didn't have to throw up but concerned as Kathy weakly made her way upstairs to take a nap.

Alice went downstairs to resume her study of the information she had stolen. There was just so much of it to sort through, and her eyes narrowed as she realized the enormity of it all and how she could use it.

Kathy got up later in the day when she heard Sean and Emily come in and head for the kitchen. While buttoning a new blouse, she saw Alice talking intently with a couple of the gardeners and wondered what that was about. The new gardeners had been doing a terrific job and were much better than the crew they'd had before the authorities dug up the yard. She wondered what had instigated the conversation they were now having.

One by one, the large, black Suburbans pulled up in front of the CIA building. There were ten in all. Four men and women got out of each one and headed for the front doors. Each was holding their identification badges in hand for security. Their presence overwhelmed security, and a button was pushed, but not before several of them got through and headed for the elevators, filling the first car as they headed upstairs.

Madelyn Korbel was notified of their impending presence before they reached the conference room where she was working with her team. Director Wolf was hurrying from his offices after getting off the emergency phone call he had just taken. By the time he arrived in the conference room, the first batch of agents, all wearing FBI windbreakers, had reached the conference room.

"Who is in charge here?" an authoritative voice asked as they entered.

"I am," Madelyn and Director Wolf responded simultaneously. They looked at each other, an understanding passing between them, and faced the blue-jacketed men and women, presenting a united front.

"We're here to gather all evidence on one Alice Weaver."

"You can't do that," several voices rang out, but Madelyn silenced her people with a simple wave of the hand.

"What's this about?" she asked, glancing at Director Wolf.

"All domestic information on Alice Weaver is to be turned over to the FBI," he told her, his expression warning her not to argue.

"ALL information," the man in charge of the agents spoke as even more agents were arriving behind him.

Wolf faced the man squarely, challenging him. "I'm sorry, some of the information is beyond your pay grade and will not be leaving this building."

The man made to interrupt, but Wolf continued, "Some of the information was received from international sources and will not be released unless I say so. As I wasn't asked beforehand about a cooperative sharing of the information, which we had been doing with the FBI–" he began, but the man had worked up enough courage to interrupt the director.

"You kept firing our agents and relieving them of their duty here–"

"Because they couldn't keep an open mind, and some of them–" began Madelyn, alarmed as several agents began to edge out around her own. She signaled her own people to begin covering up the boxes of information they had compiled, and a couple turned over the top pages on the piles of paperwork that were stacked all over the conference table.

"Ms. Korbel, I'm very well aware of the pissing match you have gotten into with several of our agents–" began the man.

"This isn't about that," Wolf interjected, "and if you're going to use that kind of language, I'm going to toss you out, then you'll have to get a court order for the information to be shared."

"Oh, *excuse me*," he stated in a sarcastic voice, glancing at Madelyn and the other women present. "I didn't realize you had sugar ears."

"Look, you gave us no notice you wanted to take over all the domestic aspects of this highly complicated case," Wolf interjected again. "So, if you give us a few hours I'm certain we can–"

"I'm here now, and I expect to take these boxes of information with us," he signaled his men and women, many who had arrived during the conversation.

"Take one step farther..." Director Wolf threatened, and the FBI agents all heard the cocking of shotguns behind them, not having noticed the large presence of CIA security that had followed them up.

The FBI agent in charge backed down immediately. "We'll wait here while you sort this...." His hands indicated the large piles of information on the conference table. He wasn't a stupid man— stubborn, yes, stupid, no.

Madelyn exchanged a look with Director Wolf, and he nodded slightly. She quickly began to give orders to her people, asking them to call in their assistants, who were assigned with helping to sort out the

piles and fetch more boxes. It took hours, and the FBI agents fidgeted as they waited. So many pieces of paper and so many piles and boxes that weren't given to them, which made them itchy to see what they contained. No one left the room except the assistants as they fetched coffee, paperwork, copies, and boxes. Slowly, the day went by as the standoff continued. The CIA security all stood at attention, looking over the heads of the FBI agents while the information was sorted, boxed, and stacked. Finally, Madelyn began nodding to Wolf that the agents could take the boxes they had separated. When the last box of paperwork was gone from the room, and the FBI agents had left with security following them out to the now loaded Suburbans, she and several others sat down with long overdue sighs. Madelyn got back up with a gesture from Wolf and followed him back to his private office.

"What the hell was that all about?" she asked once he had closed the door behind her.

"Someone has been investigating Alice Weaver and realized that the FBI didn't have all the data they felt they should have. As you weren't sharing as much as they felt you should, all domestic information about her has been returned entirely to the FBI." He held up a hand to silence her arguments. He already knew them himself. "You will continue working on the information that she provided us for the international aspects. That's a CIA prerogative," he smiled wryly. "I hope most of what you gave them," his thumb pointed to the cars that had left their drive rather abruptly, "were copies?"

Madelyn nodded and asked, "Who is creating such a hard line of authority between the agencies? We were cooperating with them."

He shrugged slightly. "I only got the order about three minutes before they arrived at our doors. Some really important senators are pissed that the CIA overstepped their authority and was handling *a domestic case*, as they saw it."

"It crossed over," she pointed out, and he nodded.

"Yes, it did, and someone in power got their knickers in a knot," he mused, wondering who. "Let's get the information we need on the money trail and earn our paychecks, okay?"

Madelyn nodded. She knew if someone in the senate oversight committee or some other powerful senator or congressman/woman was behind this, they could make things extremely difficult for them. A lot of what they did was, by necessity, secretive. Hell, she had so many

balls in the air, and juggling was just a small part of that. That they specifically wanted Alice Weaver's files made her very suspicious.

"You know, we are going to need something more from Alice eventually," he pointed out, not for the first time.

"Yes, I know," she sighed, wondering how she was going to get it. Alice Weaver wasn't known for her cooperation.

Alice was back at her computers before dinner when Emily came tripping down the steps, sounding every bit like the teen she was.

"Hey, Mom. Anything I can do to help?"

Alice looked up at her, and for a second, she saw her sister in the young face. It startled her. The eyes weren't quite hers though. They weren't her sister's either, and they certainly weren't Kathy's. Her eyes were reminding Alice more of a predator of sorts as she grew into the young woman she would be someday. Right now, she was just too...coltish. "No, and I want you to forget about doing *anything* to help anymore. We could have gotten into a heap of trouble last night, and your mom would never have forgiven me."

"She worries too much," the teen stated with the absolute conviction of youth.

"Your mother loves you very much and doesn't want to see you get hurt," Alice countered, pressing a button as the teen tried to walk nonchalantly behind the desk and see what her mother was reading. The screens changed, each displaying a different scene, but nothing that would give away what she had been scanning. To the viewer, one looked like stocks with the ticker tape rolling across the screen, another showed a news report, and yet another screen saver displayed scenes of Africa. It was an old trick; one she had used on Kit many times after she had come to live with them so long ago.

"Aww, Mom. Why can't I see?" she asked, realizing what Alice had done.

"Because I don't want you involved," Alice told her reasonably. "Now, go up and help your mom make dinner. I'm starving, and Mrs. Fernandez has the night off."

"Bet Sean wouldn't have had to help," she mumbled as she stomped off.

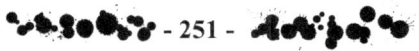

"Wait. Isn't he home?" Alice asked. She hadn't known her son wasn't home yet.

"No, he asked Mom if it was okay if he borrowed the Rav4. He said you told him it was okay?"

Alice hadn't said it was; she hadn't even seen her son when he got home from his friend's house. That would have to stop. She got up. "I'll help you make dinner," she said impulsively, annoyed that she had assumed Kathy, who was so sick, would make them dinner. How selfish of her. She'd have to make sure Kathy was better taken care of. She felt so helpless.

Kathy was surprised when she came downstairs and Alice was taking pan-fried steaks out and removing baked potatoes from the oven. The green beans made a great accompaniment, and she was pleased she was able to eat it all. Even better, everything seemed to be staying down.

Alice waited until she and Em had cleared the table, rinsed the dishes, stacked them in the dishwasher, and set the dishwasher to auto start before she sent the teen off to watch some TV. "Did Sean tell you I said it was okay for him to take the Rav4?" she asked casually as she pretended to wipe down the last of the clean counter.

"Yes. Didn't you?" Kathy asked, looking up at her wife.

Alice shook her head and tried not to smile at the trick their son had played on them. He didn't manipulate them often, but when he tried, they always caught him. He was normally an honest kid.

"Why that…" Kathy began, but her own grin belied her anger.

Alice was laughing at the incident when she caught a glimpse of someone coming over one of their fences.

"Kathy," she warned. "Go upstairs and grab an emergency bag for yourself. Get Em to take one too. You only have a few minutes." Her face fell at that moment when she observed the gardeners challenging the intruder, and she insisted, "Kathy, go! Take Em and go."

"What? Where?" she asked, concerned. "Alice, I need to help," she said, trying to make her wishes known as she rose, alarmed, and tried to see what Alice had seen.

"They are coming here. They are gonna trash the house," Alice said calmly, much more calmly than she felt. She looked up when she saw Em coming into the kitchen. "You! Go pack a bag. Enough for a week. Give me your phone," she said, holding out her hand.

"What?!" Em asked in consternation, holding onto her link with the world for all it was worth.

"You heard me. Now." She made a come-hither motion with her fingers. "Give me your phones NOW!" She indicated Kathy's as well.

"Alice," Kathy said warningly.

"No, Kathy. They are going to realize and come for us. Take her to the valley. You are not to go out." She held out her hand, and she looked so fierce they both complied, dropping the smart phones into her hand. Alice dropped the phones on the counter, putting her own next to them. Looking at her kid, she softened her face as she said, "Go upstairs and pack quickly. Do not call your friends, and don't even think of going on the computer." Kathy and Em had their backs to the kitchen window and didn't see that another person had jumped the fence and one of the gardeners had taken him down.

Emily immediately looked guilty, her thoughts betraying her. "But where–?" she began.

"Look, the family is in danger," Alice told her, grasping her shoulders and wanting to shake the teen into complying. "Those guys that looted our house are coming back. Remember how much we replaced around here," she gestured towards her computers downstairs but also towards the shelves where some of their knickknacks resided. "Please, do what your mom tells you," she indicated Kathy, who was looking concerned.

Kathy and Emily exchanged looks, scrutinized the deadly-calm-looking Alice, and headed quickly for the stairs.

"Alice–" Kathy began, but Alice put her finger over her mouth. She called out loudly, "Get packed. I won't warn you again!" They both heard Emily hurrying up the stairs. Alice took her finger off Kathy's mouth and said more softly, "You know this is necessary. Maybe they won't trash the house, but I want to keep you and the kids safe."

"I want to take the fight to them. That's what you are going to do, aren't you?" she asked.

Alice never changed expression, so Kathy wasn't certain.

"I need to help you with this," the brunette pleaded. "It's Artum, isn't it?"

"How can you help me?" Alice asked her reasonably, nimbly sidestepping the question. "I need someone to take care of the children. We have to–" she began, but Kathy interrupted her.

"They are my family too," she reminded her wife, looking at her fiercely.

"But what if something happens to us?" Alice asked.

"Alice, you know I love you. You know I love our kids, right?" At Alice's slight nod she continued, "I need to know I can protect them too."

"How are we going to keep them safe? With you there sitting on them…" she began, again trying to reason with her wife. "We can pick Sean up on the way."

"You don't think they'll listen?"

Alice gave her a look that had them both shaking their heads. No, their kids wouldn't stay put without supervision.

"Is there enough time?" Kathy asked, hearing noises from outside for the first time and turning to look. She was horrified to see several men jumping the fence and the gardeners apparently taking them down. "Alice, what…?" she began.

"Come on, there is no time. Physical objects can be replaced," Alice told her. "There is no more time. Get to the car, and I'll join you," she promised. She raised her voice and called, "Emily! Now! Come help your mother."

"But where are you–?" Kathy asked as Alice sprinted for the steps to the office.

"Just a backup on the computers. No worries," she said over her shoulder as she went. She'd been sloppy. If any of those men found those sticks, they would take them to Artum, and she couldn't have that. She needed bargaining space, and she wasn't sure how long the gardeners could hold the men off. She quickly executed a couple keystrokes and swiped the sticks off her desk, counting them as she slipped them into the safe. She set the traps and closed it up. Quickly, she headed back upstairs.

"Come on!" she said as she found her wife and daughter at the garage door. They'd wasted too much time as it was.

"What about my meds?" Kathy asked suddenly, alarmed.

"There's no time," Alice told her, pushing her towards the Rover.

"Alice, if we're gone for any length of time…."

Alice hesitated only a moment before turning and sprinting through the house and up the stairs. She ran into the master bedroom and into the bathroom. Seeing the line of pill bottles on the windowsill, she scooped them up. She saw more on Kathy's side of the bed and scooped them up too, grabbing a pillow and dropping everything in as she hurried back through the bedroom. She ran down the hall, nearly stumbling on the steps as she rushed, and into the garage where Kathy was already behind the wheel. She darted into the passenger seat.

"A pillow? I don't need a–" Kathy started, alarmed, and looking around for the pill bottles.

"They're in there. Just drive!" Alice shouted, glancing back to see if Em was buckled in.

The garage door rolled up, and Kathy stomped on the gas. The noise must have alerted their intruders as two of them were standing there as the door opened, and Kathy sideswiped one.

"Oh, my God!" she gasped, alarmed.

"Don't stop!" Alice shouted, turning the wheel, and hearing the bump of the other man against the SUV. She looked around as the car faced down the drive, and Kathy was putting it into drive. Several of their gardeners were fighting off men, and a couple of them were already down. Alice pressed a button, locking all the car doors at once.

Kathy stomped on the gas, and they all heard the squeal of the tires on the cobbled bricks of their expensive driveway. Several men looked up as she began to drive down the curved driveway. A couple broke away to cut her off. Kathy pressed the button on the visor to open the gate, not willing to wait for the gate to sense the car in the driveway.

Alice could hear shouting. Voices in Russian, Spanish, and English were yelling at them and at each other. Then, she heard the crash as Kathy ran into a car that suddenly appeared in front of them. They'd never seen it as they rushed down the drive. "Drive around it or through it!" Alice shouted.

Kathy tried. Her adrenaline was so high she was ready to take them all on. Her only thought was to get her wife and child away from these men. The crash slowed them enough that a man was able to smash the driver's window and slug her with a pistol. Everything stopped for her at that moment, especially when he slugged her again.

"Kathy!" Alice called, seeing how fast it had happened. She never saw the man coming to her passenger window, but suddenly, she was covered in glass. She looked up just as the butt of a rifle was heading towards her face. She turned, and it caught her on the side of her head. As she began to black out, she heard Emily's screams.

~The End~

❧ MALEFIC MALICE ❧

BOOK 30

Lessons on how to piss off a lesbian serial killer:

1) Hit her in the head with the butt of a gun.
2) Treat her with disdain and underestimate her abilities.
3) Involve her family!

Alice awakens to discover she has been taken prisoner. Flashbacks are instantaneous, and when she realizes that Kathy and Emily are there too, she is compelled to return them to safety. Alice doesn't want her family involved in this part of her life. She isn't comfortable with them knowing, much less participating, after all her years of hard work to keep them in the dark.

Paybacks can be deadly for those who don't realize how truly gifted Alice is. Follow along as Alice continues to triumph at what she does so very well...

"Didn't anyone analyze her computers when they confiscated them?"

One of the techs who had been analyzing data started to laugh.

"What's so funny?"

"Yes, they did analyze her computers, the only one they were able to get into. This report herrrre…" he said, dragging out the word as he searched for the report in question, "states that not only are the computers encrypted, but you have to specify which country or countries in order to be able to get into the computer."

"What does that mean?"

"It means she has a helluva computer setup, and the encryption is impossible to break unless you have one person trying hundreds, possibly thousands, of variations and making no mistakes to access the data. Even then, they have to declare the country she went through to obtain it or identify what country you accessed to find it."

"So, we can't read what was on her computers?"

"It was probably out of date anyway. She doubtless wiped it and then overwrote it just in case someone smarter than she got on them. I'm certain the police and the IRS tried a lot of things to get into them. This is a copy of the police report, and this one…" he pulled out a multi-page report, "from the IRS states that there was no way to break into these computers." He started to laugh again as he reread a section, "This one states they thought they had broken the encryption only to have the computer program start laughing loudly at them, the volume rising and falling and the voices calling them dirty names in various languages."

"Dirty names?" he asked, intrigued.

"I read that one," Madelyn put in, smiling at Alice's inventiveness. "Didn't the computer make seductive comments like, 'C'mon, baby, press my buttons some more' and 'Oooh, baby, did you have to bang my hard drive like that?' What about the one that screeched, 'What did you do to my floppy drive?'"

The group erupted in laughter.

"So, this Alice Weaver has a sense of humor?"

"Not only that. She obviously knew that someone would break the encryption at some point or think they had, and she prepared for it."

"She planned for it?"

Madelyn laughed as she nodded. They were finally getting the gist of the frustration she had felt many times while trying to investigate Alice Weaver years ago. They weren't going to find much. Alice was too good, too slippery, and now, she was certain she had the U.S. government by the short hairs. There was more that Alice knew and wasn't telling. Madelyn knew the powers that be might just get fed up and send in a team to capture Alice, and that would be fatal. She was certain Alice had planned for this possibility and had things set up in the event of her demise. They couldn't afford the bad press; it would give the government a pair of black eyes. They had to be careful and cooperative and hope Alice might give them additional information since they were literally coming up against dead ends. Almost all the players that Alice had given them were dead. Madelyn only hoped she could keep her superiors from losing patience.

They weren't going to get anything from Alice for the time being…she was a bit tied up.

Alice came to slowly, the headache forewarning her that she had been struck on the head. For a moment, she was back in that Central American prison, then confusedly, she was somewhere in Russia, but she realized that something was off. She started to focus. Looking about, squinting, she saw that she was in chains. Her wrists were bound to the chair arms, her legs to the bottom of the chair, and the ankle cuffs were painful where they rubbed against her bare skin.

She looked farther into the room. She saw Emily first, looking frightened and dirty, her hair down and bedraggled. Emily cast a stricken look at Alice and was relieved to see her mother conscious. Alice looked to the right and saw her wife, who was looking horrible. Kathy had a split lip, her skin pale beneath her dark hair, and she looked at Alice with bleary, tear-filled eyes, glancing at their daughter and back towards Alice.

"Alice Weaver?" a voice said in her ear, and Alice groggily looked up and focused on the too-close face of Artum. She smiled slightly, not surprised. "I see you are awake finally," he sneered. "I want my money, and I want it now," he said in what he thought was an intimidating voice. The man behind him shifted uncomfortably.

Alice swallowed, trying to stimulate saliva flow and blinking her eyes rapidly to not only focus but also try to calm her aching head. Instead, she found herself gagging and heaving as she tried not to throw up from the migraine she was experiencing.

Artum backed away in case she threw up on his expensive shoes, looking at the blonde woman in disgust. He glanced at the two men behind him in amusement before looking back at Alice. For such a petite woman, she had been a huge pain in the ass. He didn't believe everything Sebastian had warned him about, but he believed enough of it that he had developed a newfound respect for her. However, he had captured her, and she was helpless before him.

Alice had seen Artum's legs back away as she gagged. She glanced around the room, assessing it. They were in some sort of basement. It was made up to look like a dungeon. She wondered at that, betting it was the bottom floor of Sebastian's (now Artum's) mansion. The man lacked imagination. She'd seen that in all his operations she had studied and inventoried. He was a thug with no ideas of his own, living off Sebastian's carefully built empire and expanding in very obvious, patterned ways. Sebastian had been sophisticated and elite, and he kept his more unsavory business dealings separate from his legitimate business. Artum had completely blurred the lines separating the unsavory and legitimate. Alice finally raised her head, eyeing the man who was dressed to go out in a fine, pinstriped, double-breasted suit, cutting his figure close. She supposed he was handsome in his own way. She kept her eyes heavy-lidded, so he wouldn't realize how alert she really was. Plus keeping her eyes partially closed helped with the ache in her head.

"You have cost me a pretty penny, and I want the funds back," he hissed at her, leaning forward with one hand tucked inside his suit in the front, the other in his pocket. Alice supposed it was his attempt at looking debonaire.

"I don't know what–" she began, but he backhanded her, striking with the hand that had been in his suit front. Spit and snot flew as her head careened sideways. The migraine was excruciatingly painful, and she saw stars.

"Don't lie to me!" he spat in her face, grabbing her jaw and forcing her head up. "I know it was you who burned down my warehouse. The whores I caught told me!"

Alice smiled at him, allowing the humor to enter her eyes. She wasn't aware that her eyes had begun to change color, taking on an orange hue. She'd known that not all those women would get away. The drugs they had inhaled had probably inhibited their ability to flee. She wondered if any had escaped completely. She hoped so, for their sakes.

"You are going to replace every dollar you cost me," he informed her, "with interest!"

"I don't have–" she began, but he hit her again, not letting her finish. She glared at him. The orange of her eyes turned almost a shade of red, and he took an involuntary step back. "Takes a real man to hit a woman who is tied up," she told him conversationally, slurring it slightly around the blood flowing from her mouth.

"You are going to transfer twenty-five million dollars to me–" he began but was interrupted by the entrance of a Russian-speaking man.

"Kiev is on the line, sir," the man informed him, and Artum's head came up instantly. He unconsciously slicked back his hair as he straightened and neatened his appearance.

"Take over for me here. Get her account number and have her make the transfer," he told the man in Russian.

"Yes, sir," the man replied.

Alice watched the interplay in a mirror on one wall. It was obvious to her it was a two-way mirror...not a particularly good one at that. There was a light on inside the room, and she could tell someone was on the other side. She listened as Artum left, showing no sign that she understood what they had been saying. It had taken a moment for her to realize they were speaking Russian, but what Sasha had taught her came back quickly. The slang and dialect were easy for her to interpret.

"Unlock the shackles, and pull her up," the man ordered, standing in front of Alice to face her. He switched to English as he examined her and asked, "You know how to do a money transfer?"

Alice raised an eyebrow, this simple act causing her head to throb. She needed aspirin very soon. She played along and nodded, regretting the impulse as her head pounded.

"Good, I'll have a computer brought to you, and you will transfer the funds from your account to my boss' account," he told her reasonably.

"Why?" she rasped, allowing the blood that had pooled in her mouth to drool out as she wasn't willing to swallow it. The smack she'd received had caused one of her newer teeth to cut into her soft skin.

The man removing the shackle from one of her legs stepped back before the drool could drip on him. He looked at her disgustedly as he moved to the other leg, removing the heavy metal from around her ankle.

"I will treat you humanely, and you will be reasonable, no?" he asked.

"No," she answered agreeably.

He frowned. "You don't cooperate, and we will hurt you in ways you haven't even thought of," he threatened.

Alice laughed; he obviously didn't know her.

"You think this is funny?" He gestured to the other two men. It was then that Alice saw one of the men was Iggy, the man she had been looking for. He smiled at her when she noticed him, knowing full well that she had been seeking him. His companions had died, but he had been too smart for her. He approached Emily and stood behind her chair. The other man went directly to Kathy and pulled her head up, grasping at her long, brown hair. When her hair came out in his hand, he looked up, horrified, at the man standing in front of Alice and showed him the locks. "What is this?" the man asked, looking from his man to Kathy and back at Alice.

"Cancer," Kathy rasped out in pain, glancing at Alice and shaking her head. She could see the orange eyes even if these men could not.

Alice noticed her wife's bedraggled look, the wisps of hair hanging down and looking greasy and unkempt. She wondered how long they had been here and what the men had done to her wife and daughter.

"Doesn't matter," the man in charge said, nodding to the men.

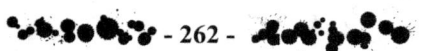

The man behind Kathy grabbed more hair, and although much of it came out in his grasp, some of it remained attached, and it hurt. Alice could see the pain in Kathy's eyes as he pulled her head up.

"Noooo," Emily moaned as Iggy began to feel her up, squeezing her tender, young breasts painfully.

Alice's eyes darted between her wife and her daughter, then up at the man in front of her. Her leg lashed out. He was too close, and the heel kick she had intended for his kneecap took him down instead of knocking him back as she had hoped. Too late, her knee came up and hit him in the crotch instead of in the face as she had planned. He went down like a shot, rolling away from her as he grabbed himself and moaned.

"Sergei!" the man holding Kathy called, alarmed.

The man on the floor held up his other arm, nodding. He was unable to speak but wanted to cut off whatever the other man was about to say.

"Nooo," Emily was saying again and again as she twisted and tried to pull herself away from Iggy's roving hands while he whispered in her ear. He reached down to pull her legs apart and began feeling at the apex of her jeans. Alice's eyes glittered as she watched the picture before her.

Sergei gently pulled himself up and called, "Iggy!" to distract the man. He had been able to hear the young man even if Alice hadn't.

Iggy looked up, unaware that Sergei had fallen to the ground. He let the young woman go and went to help Sergei up. Sergei grasped his arm tightly, and Iggy lifted him from his prone position. Slowly, Sergei straightened as he breathed through his nose, taking great cleansing breaths.

"Sorry about that. It wasn't intentional," Alice assured him, feeling a little better even though her head still throbbed. It must be the surge of endorphins helping to clear her head, but she still wanted to throw up and wondered how long she had been out.

"You...are...sorry?" he rasped out as the pain subsided slightly. Without another thought, he lifted his left leg and kicked between her legs. He was wearing cockroach killer boots, the ones with pointed toes used to catch bugs in a corner and prevent them from getting away. The only thing that saved Alice from real harm was the fact he used his left foot and not his right, which was still throbbing from the kick to his knee. He also hadn't measured the distance properly and barely grazed her leg and crotch area with his boot.

Alice pretended the blow had been substantial and leaned over as though in tremendous pain. It hurt, but not like she had been expecting; her head hurt way worse.

"You bitch!" he rasped out in Russian. "You fucking whore!"

"Sergei, don't forget what Artum wants," the man holding Kathy reminded him.

Sergei nodded, his hand waving away the concern. "I treat you with respect, and you attack me?" he said to Alice in English.

She looked up, trying to look at him innocently and failing. The orange eyes were mere slits, evidencing her disdain for him. She wouldn't be surprised if there was a cut in her jeans from the point of those boots. She was just grateful he had misjudged his kick, or she'd be in a world of more hurt than she already was.

"We will continue this soon," Sergei ordered, bobbing his head towards his two comrades and the door. Slowly, he hobbled toward the door as they joined him. The man that had been holding Kathy's hair released it, shaking his hand as the long strands came away and fell to the floor.

Alice watched the strands fall as she thought about their situation. Twenty-five million wasn't much by her estimate, but Artum didn't know what she knew about his operations, and she had the books Richard Pasternack had been cooking. Artum also didn't have the money he thought he did as she knew where it was. She wondered if he realized how much Richard had blabbed before he died?

"You okay, Alice?" Kathy asked from where she sat, her gaze taking in the gobs of hair on the floor as she also checked out her daughter, who was sobbing in her chair, and Alice, who was bent over.

"Yeah, I'll be okay in a minute," Alice told her as she took a deep breath and looked up. "How long was I out?"

"Two days," Kathy informed her.

"Two days? Are you sure?"

Kathy nodded, her head looking oddly mishappen where the hair had been bunched up and pulled out.

Alice glanced at Emily. "You okay?" she asked when she caught the young girl's teary eyes.

"He hurt me," she sobbed.

Alice nodded. "I know. I'm sorry. This is all my fault. I'll get–"

"How is this your fault?" Kathy asked.

"I should have gotten you all out of the house sooner. We shouldn't have waited. Where's Sean?"

"He went over to a friend's house."

"Yeah, but what happens when he comes home and doesn't find us there?"

"He'll go back to his friend's house, thinking he can," Kathy finished for her.

Alice nodded and closed her eyes briefly at another wave of pain.

"Headache?" Kathy asked, knowingly.

"Yeah," Alice managed to get out through clenched teeth.

"I'm not surprised. They hit you with a rifle butt."

That explained the horrific pain she was feeling. She wished she could raise her hand to feel her head. "How about you?" she asked her wife instead and glanced at Emily, who was still sobbing slightly but was trying to get it under control.

"I'm okay. They just grabbed me, but I couldn't understand what they were saying. Was that Russian?"

Alice nodded, regretting the gesture immediately as she closed her eyes and said, "Yes."

"Did you–?" Kathy began, and Alice again answered, "Yes."

"You understood them?" she managed to finish her question this time.

"Yes," the blonde said a third time, trying to get the pain in her head under control, taking cleansing breaths through her nose and out her mouth.

The door opened, and the man who had grabbed Kathy's hair returned. "I'm going to feed the three of you," he informed them, wheeling in a trolley. He left it in front of Kathy, untying her first before moving towards Emily, who flinched away, but he determinedly untied her. They both looked at Alice, who had opened her eyes. She nodded at them to indicate they should start eating. "I'll untie you after they have eaten," he told her, giving her a wide birth as he eyed her feet. Sergei wasn't happy and was icing his balls upstairs. Artum had gone out after the phone call.

Kathy pulled the cover off the dish of food and gestured at Emily to join her. It was pork chops in gravy, mashed potatoes, peas, and a side dish of apple sauce. Alice shook her head at the drink she saw Kathy reaching for, and her wife immediately pulled her hand back, brushing

Emily's hand aside as she reached for her own glass. Emily looked at her mother, then glanced over at her other mother, who shook her head slightly before closing her eyes again as she used meditation and cleansing breaths to try to lessen the ache in her head.

It took them a while to eat, and they were both still thirsty with nothing to wash down their food. They wondered why Alice wouldn't let them drink.

"Aren't you thirsty?" the man finally asked Kathy.

"We don't drink with our meals. It's bad for you to wash down a perfectly good meal," Kathy lied, knowing it was true but not something they practiced.

"I have to tie you up again," he told her, not unkindly.

"I...um...need to use the facilities," Kathy admitted.

"Pee in that corner," he said, pointing to the far wall. "There is a hole there that drains out."

"Seriously?" Emily asked. She too had to go.

"This isn't the Hilton," he said with a sneer. "Hurry up!"

Kathy exchanged a look with Emily, and they both glanced at Alice, who had a slight smile on her face but hadn't opened her eyes during their entire meal. Kathy shrugged and got up stiffly, heading for the corner. She was surprised to see a roll of toilet paper. They hadn't been fed since they got here, but that didn't mean she hadn't felt an urge to go in those two days; she'd just suppressed it. The thought of relieving her bladder suddenly made it harder to hold, and she quickly squatted, unfastening and pulling down her jeans. She was embarrassed when the man didn't look away and watched her. Hearing herself pass gas mortified her, and Emily, who had been following, turned around to give her mother some privacy. She glared at the man. The food had given her some time to overcome the humiliation of the other man's touch. She remembered him doing the same thing at Christmas last year too. She remembered him, and she wished him dead.

"Here...your turn," Kathy murmured to Emily as she wiped herself and got up, pulling her pants up and fastening them again.

"There's nowhere to wash our hands," Emily murmured in complaint.

"Do the best you can," Kathy told her as she stood in front of her fastidious daughter protectively, blocking the man's amused look at their discomfort.

In no time at all, they were tied up on the chairs again, and Alice was now allowed to eat. The metal cover had kept her meal warm, and she enjoyed the two pork chops and savored the gravy on her potatoes. She eyed the fork she was using, wondering if she could use it to kill the man fast enough but deciding to wait until her meal was done. She hoped the food would help with her headache. As the man leaned forward on the table, tired of waiting for the third prisoner to finish eating, she acted without waiting another moment.

"You ever seen this?" she asked, rapidly moving the fork in and out between his splayed fingers quickly and accurately, while just missing his fingers with the prongs. His eyes were captivated by the gesture, and before he could react, she turned the fork and deftly shoved it up the center of his nose, breaking the cartilage with the force of her blow and shoving the prongs into his brain. She thrust him backwards as she grabbed the edge of the dish cover and used it like a blade. As he went down, she sliced across his neck, hitting his jugular and jumping back before the blood spurted all over her. He was dead in moments.

"Holy shit, Alice!" Kathy said, losing her dinner. She was immediately followed by Emily, who also threw up at the sight of the dead man and the smell of her mother vomiting.

"Come on you two," Alice said, trying to keep her displaced humor in check. She quickly frisked the dead man, coming up with only a pocketknife. Alice untied them, using the knife when necessary. She threw each of the women the dainty cloth napkin that had been included with their meal, so they could wipe at their bile-speckled mouths.

"How did you know the drink was drugged?" Kathy asked as she wiped her lips. She just had gotten a glimpse of herself in the two-way mirror and was horrified to see the clumps of hair missing from her head. There was no way to hide the bald spots.

Alice shrugged. "Just a guess."

"Well, that was a meal well wasted," Kathy put in as she dropped the napkin on the wheeled cart. Emily followed suit, her eyes taking in the fork protruding from the man's face, the severed neck, and the blood leaking across the floor in a widening pool. She wanted to throw up again but restrained herself…just barely.

"I'm feeling better," Alice confided as she headed for the door and glanced out. No guards. She guessed they didn't think they needed guards in their own house. "Stay close and keep quiet," Alice cautioned in a whisper as she went out the door.

It was a beautiful basement with large paving stones holding up the walls. Their rounded edges made them look old and sculpted. Alice headed for a set of stairs also constructed of the paving stones, which led upstairs in a curving arch to what looked like a kitchen. She briefly wondered how the man had gotten the trolley down into the basement as she looked around the door and saw Sergei sitting in a kitchen chair with his pants pooled around his ankles and a large bag of ice held against his crotch. He was leaning back, facing the ceiling, and his eyes closed in relief. She nearly laughed. Instead, she turned, signaling for Kathy to stay back. She crept into the kitchen, trying to stay out of Sergei's line of vision.

"Iggy, is that you?" Sergei called out. His voice was slightly slurred, and Alice now noticed the wine bottle next to his hand. She wondered if the man had heard her or was just calling out drunkenly to his friend. She didn't pause as she reached the block containing several cutting knives and pulled out two. Hefting them in her hand, she balanced them, reversed them, and finally hurled one at the prone man. She was disappointed when she missed her mark. That was something that hadn't happened in years, but she wasn't going to worry about it right now. She let the second knife fly almost immediately.

Sergei heard the thump and felt the slight whiff of air as the first knife missed his throat by mere millimeters. The second knife didn't miss, and he looked up just as it struck him in the throat. He looked surprised to see Alice standing there. She was already reaching for another knife although she knew the second had hit home. He dropped the bag of ice he was holding to his balls as he lurched forward but made it no further as he fell to the floor. Alice took another knife anyway as she gestured to her wife and daughter.

"How did you–?" Emily began, but Kathy shushed her, grabbing her hand to pull her along. Alice looked around and found the back door, carefully unlocking it, then slowly opening it while gesturing for her wife and daughter to hurry up. She eased it open and looked around, seeing a backyard with a six-car garage and surprised to see her own Rover parked in the courtyard.

"Head for the car," she whispered to her wife. "I'm going to clean up in here," she gestured inside.

"No, I want to stay with you," Kathy stated, suddenly frightened.

"Me too," Emily answered, feeling argumentative.

"There are at least two men inside that I have to find, and with you along, I won't find them as quickly," Alice reasoned. "Get in the Rover and give me fifteen minutes. If I'm not there in fifteen minutes, start the car and go!"

"I'm not leaving without you," Kathy argued, weakly grabbing Alice's arm.

"Did you drink some of that stuff?" Alice asked, seeing Kathy's eyes were dilated.

"No, but I haven't had my meds in two days, and I bet some of them are giving me withdrawals," she said as she weaved on her feet.

"Shit," Alice mumbled, torn between helping her wife and avenging her loved ones.

"I'll get to the car," Kathy promised, suddenly realizing they'd be in the way, and Alice needed to hunt. These men couldn't be allowed to get away with what they had done to her family. She was feeling weak after the brief meal and the adrenaline surge that followed.

"I want to help," Emily tried to argue.

"Look, I need you to help your mom," Alice told her reasonably. "Please?"

Emily looked at Alice. Her mother had just killed two men and didn't even have a drop of their blood on her. Her actions had been cool, calm, and efficient. She realized that if she took care of Kathy, Alice would have free rein to search for the creep who had touched her. The filth he had murmured in her ears would haunt her forever. She nodded slightly as she realized Alice's eyes were practically glowing orange. She turned back to Kathy and took her arm, helping her down the back steps towards the Rover.

Alice breathed a sigh of relief as she carefully closed the door behind them, ensuring it made no noise.

They had waited five minutes. Kathy was in the driver's seat but feeling poorly. They had brushed off the seats before getting in as the broken glass from the windows was still covering them. Afterward, they sat down gingerly and waited. The food, the bile, and the lack of meds was catching up with Kathy. Sleeping in an awkward position last night while tied to a chair hadn't been good for her. Watching Alice and worrying that she wouldn't wake up hadn't helped things either. Kathy and Emily had attempted to talk but someone came in and threatened to gag them if they didn't shut up.

"Mom," Emily finally whispered, her hand pointing at a gas pump she noticed alongside the garage.

"What?" she asked just as silently, wondering what the teen was getting at.

"Let's cause some damage."

It took Kathy a moment to understand what Emily was talking about, but then, she got the idea. They both slipped from the car, and Kathy staggered a little on the cobblestones of the courtyard. She had to be careful; now, was not the time for a broken ankle. It was Emily who saw the basement window—maybe the window to the room they had been kept in—and she kicked the glass in. They looked around to see if anyone had noticed the noise, but when no one came, they proceeded with their plan. At first, they didn't think the gas hose would reach that far, but they found by unwinding all the twists, the nozzle just barely made it through the window bars. Emily wedged the nozzle between the bars and used a rock under the handle to hold it wide open. Kathy flipped the lever on the pump, and the liquid began pouring through the broken window. The air was soon filled with the odor of gasoline, and Kathy had a memory of the time Alice explained to her that it wasn't the gasoline that burned but the vapors. They returned hurriedly to the Rover.

"Here, you get in the driver's seat," Kathy told her, feeling the last of her adrenaline wearing off as she got in the back seat.

"Are you sure?" the teen asked, suddenly feeling even more excited at being entrusted with the driving.

"I can't drive," Kathy admitted as she lay down on the back seat. "Stay down and make sure the passenger door is unlocked."

Emily did as she was told, pulling the lever to let her seat down and keep her out of their line of sight if anyone came looking. She raised up just enough to see out, keeping her eyes glued on the back door they had emerged from and mentally wishing Alice would come through it.

Alice found the living room they had been in, the one where even now a few of the Weaver possessions remained on the shelves. She was tempted to retrieve them but resisted. They'd gotten their insurance settlement, and if Kathy had wanted to replace any of these items, she probably already had. Artum was welcome to these ones. She began looking for Iggy and Artum.

She found Iggy on the second floor in a room near the master bedroom where Sebastian had died. Iggy was watching television—porn—and masturbating to what he was seeing on the screen. He never heard the door open as he was in the throes, his penis hard and erect, but he definitely felt the pain when Alice cut off his member, covering his mouth before he could scream. He stared in horror as she lifted the penis and held it in front of his shocked eyes before quickly shoving it into his wide-open mouth. His hands came up to remove it, but she quickly stabbed through one hand, pinning it to the recliner he was sitting in. She used her weight to move the remaining hand back to the arm of the chair and pinned it with another knife. For a second, she watched as his fingers wiggled against the chair spasmodically, twitching as though in a fit. "You like little girls, Iggy?" she hissed, having witnessed him touching her daughter twice, the second time painfully. She glanced at the porn he had been watching and saw it was teenage girls, and she sneered at the castrated man with his blood oozing all over the expensive upholstery of the chair from between his legs. His pants were down to his knees, his middle fully exposed.

"No one touches my family and gets away with it. You may have hidden for a while, but everyone gets their comeuppance, you piece of filth. And don't think I didn't understand what you said to my daughter," she told him, her hearing excellent and her rage frightful. She repeated his words back to him in imperfect Russian, his eyes widening in horror as he had spoken to the girl in English, so she would understand what he planned to do to her. As he grew weak from blood loss, Alice finished her litany of his words and ended with, "And now, you eunuch, I will finish you!" When she pulled the pocketknife from her pants' pocket, he recognized it as his comrade's, and he watched in further horror as she cut off his balls, the sawing motion on his loose and bloody flesh causing excruciating pain. He screamed around the penis in his mouth. "Does that hurt, Iggy?" she taunted as she threw the flesh of his balls at the big screen where three men were pumping away at a girl. The blood splattered sickeningly across the screen.

Alice wiped the blade on his shirt, the blood loss and horror of watching himself being mutilated leaving him too weak to struggle against the knives pinning his hands to the chair. She smiled in his eyes as she deftly folded the dull blade of the pocketknife and slipped it into his shirtfront. Patting it, she departed, leaving him there with two kitchen knives fixing his hands to the chair, his lifeblood leaking out between his legs, his penis in his mouth, and his balls lying grotesquely on the floor where they had fallen down the big screen. His eyes were fastened on his balls, and he stared, not the big screen, but at the flesh on the floor as he died in the chair.

Alice saw guards outside walking the grounds as she looked out the windows, but Artum was nowhere to be found. That was…disappointing. She tripped no alarms as she searched the house, so they must have felt they were safe with just the guards. She made her way back downstairs, stopping on the first landing when she saw Sandy Pasternack picking up her handbag and leaving by the front door. Her eyes narrowed musingly as she quickly made her way to the back door through the kitchen and slipped outside. She got a strong whiff of gas just as a guard came around the corner smoking a cigarette. Alice had no choice but to take him down when his gun came up.

She ran at him, glancing up at the corner of a small porch and making use of the aluminum bar that held the roof out to shed rain. She swung up, the aluminum bar bending under her weight, and wrapped her legs around the guard's neck, quickly twisting and turning at the same time. His hands came up to fend her off, causing him to drop his gun onto the cobbles of the courtyard with a clatter. Alice's twist cut off his oxygen supply, and using her weight, she fell on top of him with her legs crossed behind his neck to keep the tension on and choke him. She winced at the pain as he fell backwards onto her legs, but she kept up the tension, not releasing him as he choked and thrashed, pulling unsuccessfully at her legs. She looked down at his flushed face and watched as he choked to death in her hold. She could feel herself weakening as he finally breathed his last.

"Mom, that was amazing," Emily gasped as she helped Alice up.

"Where did you come from?" she asked, letting the teen help her as her knee was badly bruised from the man's fall. "Do you smell gas?" she asked.

"Um, yeah. About that…" the teen began, helping a limping Alice towards the SUV.

Alice was surprised to find Kathy in the back as Emily helped her into the passenger seat. "Are you okay?" she asked Kathy worriedly.

"Nauseous. I need to get home," she answered. "Are you okay?"

"Yeah, just a bruised knee. How–?"

But Emily had closed the door, cutting off her question, and she was running around to get in the driver's seat.

"Oh, no…" Alice began, but the teen waved her protestations aside.

"Neither of you can drive, and we have to get out of here now!" the teen told her, her adrenaline riding high. Seeing Alice coming out the back door, she had quickly sat up in the seat, pulling the lever to bring it upright. Watching Alice attack the man that Emily hadn't even noticed, she had marveled at her mother's fluidity. This was nothing like the skirmishes she saw on television; it was better. She winced as the man went down under her mother's weight, then seeing the momentary look of pain on Alice's face, she had gotten out of the car. She nearly tripped on the cobblestones but had gotten there just as Alice finished the man off, so she could help her mother up. Emily had seen the glowing butt of the cigarette and the splashed gasoline, and she knew it was only a matter of time before the gas they had been pumping into the basement was found or the glow of that cigarette caused it to go up in flames.

Emily buckled her seat belt, reaching down to pull the seat forward, so she could reach the gas pedals comfortably. She told Alice to put on her belt as she started the car and slammed it into gear. As Alice began to argue with her strong-headed daughter, Emily quickly explained about the gasoline they had pumped into the basement. Alice had also seen the cigarette and smelled the gas, and she didn't need to be told twice. Emily was hesitant at first, but Alice encouraged her with, "Go, go, GO!" and they sped through the courtyard and onto the driveway, heading for the gate.

The gate was open, and Alice only briefly wondered if Sandi Pasternack had just gone through.

"Which way?" the teen fretted, worrying suddenly that they would get pulled over by the police. They'd never be able to explain away all the broken windows, and they didn't want any questions about anything else that had just occurred.

Alice pointed and watched as the teen uneasily made her way down one street and then another. The Rover rocked from side to side as the nervous teen drove carefully, ever conscious that her mothers were in the SUV with her. "Pull over here," Alice told her after a while, knowing there was no way Emily could cope with Los Angeles traffic at the moment.

Disappointed but also relieved, Emily deftly pulled over to the curb. She got out, intending to help Alice into the driver's seat, but her mother met her as she limped around the front. "You did good," Alice said, squeezing her arm as she painfully hobbled towards the open door. Alice got in, and they both buckled up just in time to hear the explosion and see the fireball from a couple blocks away. "Holy shit!" she murmured, unable to see it clearly with all the houses and trees between them, but she couldn't miss the smoke above the trees or the noise the explosion made. Just as they emerged from the hilly area of Beverly Hills, they met fire engines pulling onto the main drag. Alice pulled over to allow the fire engines and a line of police cars with lights flashing and sirens blaring to pass as they headed up the hill. Alice drove sedately away from the area, heading for home and minding her own business.

That night on the news, there was a helicopter's view of the fireball that had once been Sebastian's home. The devastation was absolute. The house had burned hotly, and there was an ongoing investigation into the explosion. The reporter stated, "I hope no one was in there," but Alice they knew at least three people had been in there, and she secretly wondered if the fire had burned too hot for them to find the bodies, briefly musing that ash might be all they found with that heat.

The Rover was parked in the garage. Alice had arranged to have the smashed windows replaced later that week. They'd gotten home early enough that she had been able to make a few phone calls. They'd all showered, Kathy had taken her pills, they'd eaten, and now, they were sitting in the master bedroom relaxing. After watching the news, Kathy had turned off the television, so they could just chat and try to calm down after the events of the past two harrowing days.

"So, our gardeners are assassins?" Kathy asked, wonderingly.

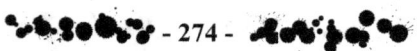

Alice nodded. After a few key questions from Kathy, she told her family what had happened. There were no signs of the Russian lackeys that had rushed their estate. "I got the idea from the Ottomans. They always employed gardeners who were assassins and usually mutes. Instead, I chose men I felt I could trust and who would keep their mouths shut despite anything they might see around here. I hired men who needed employment to get a green card, and this legitimized their work. Julio rotated his men."

"Who is Julio?" Kathy asked, forestalling Emily, who was listening avidly. She wasn't letting her mothers shut her out, not after what they had all been through. She was warm, dry, and wrapped in her cozy, velour bathrobe.

Alice shifted slightly, showing she was uncomfortable. The bruise on her knee was bad. She'd iced it, but she was out of shape for the moves she had made that day. She knew she would be sore for days. All the tension had washed away in the shower, and now, she was stiff. She was also listening for sounds that Sean was home. When they'd retrieved their phones from where they left them on the kitchen counter, she had called her son and asked when he was coming home. Getting back to her wife's question, Alice confessed, "Julio is a business acquaintance." She held up her hands in surrender at her wife's accusing glare. "He's only helping me out because he owes me."

"What exactly does he owe you for?"

"I gave him some of Artemis' business information, and he's been taking business away from the Russians."

"So, you are exchanging one drug dealer for another?"

"That's not how I see it," Alice admitted.

"But it's still drugs!"

"Yes, and eventually they will get caught!" Alice came back just as swiftly, feeling defensive.

"How?"

"Do you really want to know that?" she glanced from Kathy to Emily, who was watching, fascinated. Alice felt the young woman had a right to some of this information and to know she was safe. Alice was certain she *was* safe but felt better now that they were home and cleaned up. She didn't know how long they were safe though, and she was worried that Sean wasn't home yet. Artum had really stepped over the line by taking both Kathy and their daughter. For now, they were home, and they were safe, but Alice desperately wanted to go hunting. She also wanted to know all her family members were out of harm's way. She was considering where they might go…where they might *have* to go.

She looked at Kathy, seeing her normally pale color from the drugs was back. At least she was no longer pasty-grey, the slight withdrawals she had felt already in check after getting back on her schedule of meds and eating a decent meal. The bald patches were rather prominent on her head now. She'd tried a combover, which was failing desperately, but Alice affected not to notice.

Kathy glanced at Alice's eyes darting back and forth between them for a moment before sighing and shaking her head. "I guess I don't really want to know how they will get caught," she admitted sadly.

"I do," Emily put in.

Alice smiled, turning toward her daughter. "No, believe me, it's better if you have deniability." She saw the teen ready to argue and put up her hand to forestall her. "If you are ever taken in for questioning by the authorities, the less you know, the better."

"I'd never tell on you!" she insisted.

"I know you wouldn't, darling, but there are interrogators that are top-notch at their jobs, and they would trick you. You don't know how to pass a lie detector test or how to avoid their traps, and I don't want you to."

"But—"

"Please trust me. There is a time and a place for everything, and I understand you are impatient. I was once like you, and you have to learn patience."

"After what he threatened to do to me?" she suddenly sobbed, using tears to manipulate her mother and get her to tell what she was planning.

"I heard what he said he would do to you, and he paid for his audacity in saying that to you and for touching you," Alice promised her.

"Did you kill him?" Emily stopped crying, looking up and fixing Alice with eyes just like her sister, Connie's. But now, her eyes were turning a shade that neither Kathy nor Alice had ever seen before.

"I don't think…" Alice began, trying to reason with her daughter, and then, she heard the front door open and close.

"Mom?" Sean called from the front hallway.

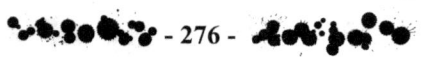

"We're up here!" Alice called back, anxious to see their son and assure herself that he was okay. To Emily she warned, "Not a word!" She glanced at Kathy, who nodded as she got more comfortable under the covers. She was exhausted. Alice unobtrusively covered her own bruised knee with her robe.

"Hey, thanks for letting me stay at Jeff's that extra night. I know, I know, it was a little much, but we…" he left off, seeing them all sitting on the bed and Kathy under the blankets. "Everything okay?" he worried. One side of Kathy's face looked a little red. He didn't realize the difference in her color, having not seen her for days. He also couldn't see that makeup was hiding the damage on both his mothers' faces.

"Your mom's been a little off, but she's feeling better," Alice answered truthfully, distracting him from looking too closely.

"Mom?" he asked Kathy, wondering if she was worse. She didn't look good to him. He could see her hair was thinning even more than he recalled, not realizing chunks of it had been pulled out.

"I'm fine. I threw up today, and it wasn't pleasant, but I just need a good night's sleep," she assured him.

He looked between his moms, wondering if they were keeping something from him, but he knew they'd always answer his questions if he asked. Right now, he didn't want to know the details about Kathy throwing up, and he wasn't sure he wanted to know anything else either. Her bodily functions didn't interest him in the least.

"So, are you some ninja warrior now with the video game?" Alice teased with her eyebrow raised.

"It's Warrior Call, Mom," he said in an exasperated voice as he grinned.

"Is that like Call of Duty?"

"Nope, completely different. You don't mind, do you?" he asked, not certain he wanted to stop playing the game even if she objected.

"Nope, so long as you keep up on your schoolwork and come up for air now and then. Don't let the gaming interfere with your sports either, okay?"

He smiled and leaned over to kiss her on the cheek. He moved to go over to Kathy's side of the bed, but the brunette waved him away. "I don't want you to get this if I have a cold or something," she warned him off. He was grateful.

"Hey there, squirt," he said, teasing Emily and poking her in the shoulder. Alice and Kathy saw her wince, but Sean didn't even notice as he made his way out the door. "I'm going to throw in a load of laundry. Anyone need anything washed?" he asked, hoping none of them did. He didn't want to see any blood from female periods or anything Kathy might have thrown up on. He thought women's bodily functions were kind of gross.

"Nope, we're good," Alice told him with a smile. He was so easy to read, but she was pleased that he was at least trying. She knew he was a good guy and hoped he would stay that way. She smiled at Kathy, who had probably been the one to teach the kid how to do his own laundry. The sports he was involved in probably caused a lot of sweat, and he stank often.

They all waited until they heard him head down to the laundry, and then Emily hissed, "I should know what you did to that guy."

"Geez, Emily. Are you still on about that?" Alice asked, exasperatedly.

"Yes, I need to know," she said tenaciously.

"Are you ready to tell your mother what he whispered to you?"

"How did you hear that? You were farther away from me than Mom."

"Let's just say I read lips."

"Do you?" the teen asked, suddenly horrified at the things she had been caught out on over the years.

Alice just smiled and Kathy smothered a laugh. "Get some sleep, Emily. You are going to be sore tomorrow, and I think we are going to have plenty to talk about in the coming days," Kathy warned her.

"But Mommm," the teen whined, trying to wheedle some more information out of them.

Alice laughed. "No, m'dear, that's enough for now. Your mom is *tired*," she said meaningfully, and Emily took the hint.

"Oh, all right," she said dejectedly, wanting to know more but hoping their talks in the coming days would give her the information she desperately wanted to know. She got up and gave Kathy a peck on the cheek, then came around to give one to Alice.

"Take some aspirin or ibuprofen before you go to sleep. It will help with the aches and pains you have now and the ones that are going to show up after you sleep in your bed."

Emily nodded as she turned and went through the door, closing it quietly behind her.

Alice looked at Kathy. "We won't be able to keep much from that one for long."

Kathy sighed. "No, we won't," she agreed. It saddened her how much Emily knew, or thought she knew, much less what the child had seen. She corrected herself mentally, *Emily was not a child. Not anymore.*

They woke up to earth-shattering screams coming from Emily's room. Alice leapt out of bed, opened their door and hobbled quickly down the hall followed much more slowly by an equally concerned and pained Kathy.

"What the hell?" Sean asked sleepily from his own doorway.

"I'm sure it was a nightmare," Kathy said as she came up. "You can go back to bed."

Alice was already in Emily's room. The normally neat room was a mess, and she looked about in concern, finally locating Emily on the floor, thrashing around and tangled in her blankets. She was screaming at the top of her lungs. As Alice caught her, she took a fist to her already battered head and winced as it connected in almost the same spot as the rifle butt. She'd hid her injuries from Sean, but careful concealer could only do so much, and she had probably rubbed some off in her sleep. Holding her daughter carefully—tightly but not in a way that she could construe as someone holding her down—Alice crooned to her. "Emily...Em...Em. Wake up, honey. It's Mom. Shhh, shhh, shhh." She rocked the teen as she gently woke her. The girl seemed unusually deeply asleep, and Alice finally shook her hard. "Emily, wake up now. It's just a dream, honey. Wake UP!"

Emily blinked up at Alice, suddenly realizing the sense of her mother's words and hugging her tight. "Oh, God! Oh, Mommy!" she sobbed into Alice's shoulder.

Alice winced at how tightly the teen was holding her, but she held on, rocking her and shushing her. "It's okay, Em. I've got you and nothing's gonna get you. I've got you, baby. Shhhh." She glanced up at Kathy, who was standing in the door frame and using it to hold herself up. She was crying at seeing her daughter in so much pain.

"He was holding me down. He was…was…" she couldn't continue and started hiccupping as she sobbed. It took a long time for her to calm down.

"We're going to get you the therapy you need, darling. We'll help you," Alice told her and then looked up at a horrified Kathy, who shook her head. What could Emily tell a therapist? If Emily told anyone what she had seen or heard, they would all be arrested.

"Alice," Kathy called to get her wife's attention after looking down the hall to check that Sean had gone back to bed. The door was closed, and she was certain he was soundly asleep again. That boy needed his sleep; he was growing so much. "You are going to have to tell her what you did, so she can rest easier. She can't see a therapist; we all know that."

Alice nodded, realizing the truth of her words but reluctant to tell the teen more of her misdeeds. Holding her close, Alice closed her eyes and wished that Emily was five years old again and just holding her would be enough.

Finally, calming down enough to release the tight hold she had on Alice, Emily pulled back slightly. Kathy walked forward and handed her daughter a wet washcloth she had fetched from the bathroom to wipe her tears. "Here is a tissue," she also offered, so the teen could blow her nose. "Care to tell us what the dream was about?"

Emily shook her head. She didn't want to remember it and live it all over again. Thankfully, some it was already fading.

"You never have to worry about that man again," Alice promised the teen. "I took care of him, and I made sure he suffered."

Her eyes still awash with tears, Emily looked up into her mother's eyes. "Can you tell me what you did to him?" she asked hesitantly, sure that Alice would refuse her.

Alice sighed as she let the teen go and helped her back up on the bed, her own bruised and battered body making her slow and stiff. Straightening the bed sheets and covers in her agitation, she wanted to avoid telling the teen anything.

"Cleaning won't delay it for long," Kathy quipped, and Alice laughed, looking up at her wife knowingly. There was no fooling Kathy after all these years.

"When I went back upstairs looking for Iggy," she told the teen softly, keeping her voice down in case Sean was still awake, "I found him watching porn on a big screen TV." She glanced towards the door, and Kathy shook her head. She'd heard Sean's snores when she went to the bathroom for the cloth. "The porn he was watching was pretty much everything he threatened to do to you. Before he knew I was there, I used one of the knives to cut off his cock." She watched as her daughter's eyes opened wider at the crude word. "I covered his mouth, so no one could hear his screams. Then, I shoved his penis in his mouth to gag him. As his hand came up to try and remove it, I pinned his hand to the chair with the knife, then I pinned the other hand with another knife."

"Wasn't he stronger than you?" the teen asked in awe as she visualized the man and what Alice was saying she had done to him.

"Yes, probably, but I had surprise on my side, and I'd waited until he was in the throes over watching what was on the screen." She had hoped she wouldn't need to get too graphic with her daughter and wasn't sure how much she already knew about masturbation or sex. "While he was pinned there and bleeding all over the upholstery, I asked if he liked little girls. I told him that no one touches my family and gets away with it. I also repeated exactly what he had said to you, only I said the words in Russian, and he stared, horrified, as he realized I had understood everything they had ever said. I could see the blood loss was affecting him. Next, I pulled out the pocketknife I had taken from the other guy and cut his balls off while he watched in horror. It was hard to do because that knife wasn't as sharp as the kitchen knives, but I managed. When I was done, I threw his balls against the big screen, leaving him to bleed to death. I also called him a eunuch," she smiled as she repeated that.

"What's a eunuch?" the teen naively asked.

"It's a man without a penis or sometimes just without balls," Kathy put in quietly, seeing how happy Alice was with what she had done on their daughter's behalf. Kathy was horrified but didn't feel as bad as she should have when she realized the man had threatened their daughter. "Exactly what did he say to you, Emily?" she asked, feeling sick.

Emily shook her head. She didn't want to remember. She was happy to know he was dead, but what Alice had done was horrifying, and she wanted time to think about it.

"Emily?" Alice asked, waiting for her daughter to look up. She realized she had been too graphic. She shouldn't have taken such pride in her work and repeated all the gory details to her wife and daughter. "Do I have your permission to tell Mom what he said?"

Relieved that she didn't have to repeat it, Emily nodded. "Just…not…now," she said in a voice that sounded exhausted.

Alice understood. She glanced at Kathy who nodded too. Looking back at Emily, Alice said, "I want you to know I'd do anything to keep you safe. I'm sorry they frightened you."

"It's okay, Mom. It's not your fault."

"Yes, Emily. This time it is my fault. I toyed with the man, and his minions came and took us. I should have handled it differently."

Emily looked up at Alice, surprised that she was taking the burden of this on her small, elegant shoulders. "It wasn't your fault, Mom. They decided what they would do, and they paid for it."

"Artum is still out there," Alice reminded her. "We have to be extra careful. I believe we are safe here…for now," she gestured at the house but wondered if they really were. The man's house had gone up in flames rather dramatically, and that might piss him off. He would want more than money this time; he was going to want revenge.

"Why don't we take a trip?" the teen asked, searching for ideas.

"Because the problems will still be here when we return," Alice pointed out. The teen was starting to think like her. She'd considered that very thing herself. *And we don't want him to think we're running,* she mentally added.

"And I need my medical treatment," Kathy reminded her daughter softly.

Alice and Emily looked up at Kathy, who looked almost skeletal with the skin stretched over her frame. Oddly, she also looked bloated, but they knew that was from the drugs she was taking. The bald spots looked especially bad with her bed head hair.

"Do you think you can sleep now?" Alice asked Emily, hoping her explanation of what happened hadn't made things worse for the teen. She couldn't have therapy, but Alice didn't know how to explain that without telling the teen one more thing she couldn't tell people. It was becoming ridiculous.

"Maybe," the teen told her placatingly. She had a lot to think about: everything that had happened; what Iggy had threatened her with; what Iggy had done; what her mother had done; and how she herself had blown up that house. She wasn't going to be able to sleep. "I'll try," she lied for both their sakes.

Alice knew it was a fib but was willing to give the teen her space. It was a lot to absorb, and she smiled as she tucked her daughter in bed, kissing her on the forehead. "I'm here if you have any questions," she promised. She got up with a pat on the teen's shoulder, noticing her wince. "Did you take some aspirin before you went to sleep?"

Emily nodded, wondering if it had done anything. She was still rather sore.

Kathy sat down to give Emily a kiss too. "We're both here, if you need us," she added.

"I know, Mom," Emily said sadly, seeing how ill Kathy looked and wondering how long she would be there for them. She wasn't stupid. Kathy looked horrible and was probably dying.

"Good night, darling," Kathy said as she got up and joined Alice at the door.

"Light on or off?" Alice asked.

"On," the teen said with a grimace.

Alice closed the door for privacy, and they walked back to their room.

"What did that man say to her?" Kathy demanded as soon as their bedroom door closed.

Seeing the look on her wife's face, Alice sighed but didn't hesitate to tell her. "He said he knew she was a virgin, that she *smelled* like a virgin," Alice told her. "Remember when you first got your period or the first few times you found 'come' in your underwear, and you realized you might have body odor from it?" At Kathy's confused nod, she continued, "He was playing on that and tormenting her with it. He told her he'd take her virginity from her, teach her to give head like a proper whore, and then she'd beg him to take her like a dog. He said he'd teach her to love anal, and then, he and two of his buddies would take her all at the same time. He told her they'd teach her to be their sex slave, and when they were done, they'd make money off the videos by selling them to men who love a good gangbang." She stopped, shuddering in disgust at the visual this man had given their poor daughter. "He was touching her and squeezing her breasts when he whispered all this filth in her ear. That's the kind of porn he was watching when I cut him, gangbangs."

"Good!" Kathy insisted, incensed by what Alice had told her. "He deserved it for filling her head with such filth! I hope he rots in hell! If you hadn't already killed him, I would kill him now!" she ranted, pacing about the master bedroom. "How dare he!"

"He was the one that threatened to sell her," Alice reminded her, surprised and strangely aroused at the tigress that was her angry wife. It was very inappropriate right now with Kathy as weak as she was, but Alice recognized that and stifled those feelings.

"How did you hear him? I couldn't…"

"You were busy with your own antagonist, but I was concentrating on what that bastard was saying to her, and despite my headache, I heard him, and what I couldn't hear, I read."

Realizing that Alice could still surprise her, she nodded. "What are you going to do about Artum?" Kathy suddenly asked, realizing he was the real threat to them. He gave the orders, and he had the money to pay these disgusting and dangerous men.

"I've begun to drain his bank accounts. I set the programs up while you were showering and after I'd started dinner," Alice confided. "I've already given some of his routes away, and the Mexican cartels won't be giving those back as they encroach farther and farther into his territories."

"How are you going to stop them?" Kathy asked, suddenly afraid that Alice was getting involved with those sort of people so close to home.

Alice didn't answer that question, deliberately deflecting. "Sandi Pasternack was at that house. She might have been behind that two-way glass," Alice told her wife, watching her become furious as she realized the implications.

"That bitch! How dare she!"

"I'm setting her up too, believe me," Alice told her wife, wanting to calm her as she saw how exhausted the anger was making the sick woman. "You have a doctor's appointment in the morning. You need to sleep."

"How can I sleep now that I know all this?" Kathy asked, enraged.

"Maybe I shouldn't have told you," Alice mused aloud.

"I needed to know, Alice. Don't you dare keep me out of the loop," she threatened, pointing a finger at her wife.

"I know, baby. I know," Alice said, taking her wife in her arms as Kathy struggled weakly. "I won't."

"You know that isn't the end with Emily, don't you? We're going to have to do something."

"I'll think on it," Alice told her. She knew that Em was going to need help. Psychological help at least, and she certainly wasn't qualified to help her there.

"What if Artum comes here again?" Kathy fretted, surprised when Alice kissed her hard and passionately. By the time Alice stopped, Kathy was out of breath and strangely aroused.

"Now, you need to think about something else," Alice told her quietly, not willing to slap the hysteria out of her as she kissed her repeatedly. "I know you may not be up to this but—"

"Don't you dare stop," Kathy threatened, pulling her weakly closer and wrapping her body around Alice's. She was relishing in the curves that had grown back from Alice's own emaciated state. The muscles that had come back were wonderful to feel under her fingertips and were exciting her.

Alice kept her mind strangely detached as she made love to her wife, noting the body that was losing much of the excess flesh she'd enjoyed over the years.

Nearly half an hour later, they were both satisfied—after a fashion—and exhausted. Kathy was gently snoring in Alice's sweaty arms. Alice thought about what she had just done, using sex to distract her poor wife, but she didn't regret it. What she regretted were the muscles she had used. She ached horribly. She gently tucked Kathy into bed, covering her naked body as she slipped into the bathroom to wash herself up and take some ibuprofen. The day was going to be hell with the lack of sleep, but at least Kathy was asleep, and she hoped Emily had managed to get some sleep with all the thoughts swirling around in her young head.

"We would need to know that Alice Weaver and all members of her family were out of the house for at least two hours."

"What about the housekeeper?"

"We would need the house completely clear, even the gardeners."

"That's rare. There seems to be someone around at all times." This comment proved that the house was under surveillance.

"It's those computers we need to get hold of. The history on them must be amazing."

"Remember when they confiscated the computers before? They found bupkis," someone reminded the team.

"That's because those were decoys. You don't think Alice Weaver would actually leave any incriminating evidence for us to find?"

"So, she deletes her history. Isn't there a way to retrieve stuff even if she erases it?"

"No, she does more than erase her history. She has programs that go much deeper than that, highly sophisticated programs. She encrypts her computers too, so just getting into them is impossible."

"Surely someone in our organization can get into them?"

"Yeah, we had our top people take a crack at her computers. That's how we know there is bupkis."

"They actually got a program that laughed at their efforts."

"What you mean it laughed at their efforts?"

"It was programmed with a computer-generated laugh track. was very annoying, and the laughter kept on and on. We had to pull the plug to get it to stop."

Several people chuckled at the story.

"Back to the bugging of her home. Can we get legal cause?"

"She's an international terrorist," someone asserted.

"That's unproven," someone else put in for clarity.

"She gave us information on Russian operatives, the mafia, even Kazakhstan."

"That doesn't make her an international terrorist."

"There is a treasure trove of classified information that she gave us, and how did she really get it?"

The debates were endless, and Madelyn was sick of it. Joint meetings had resumed between the FBI and the CIA, and they were fruitless. The discussions went on and on as they tried to think of ways to get probable cause, something a judge would sign off on, so they could bug Alice and Kathy Weaver's home again. Somehow, the bugs they had placed there in the past had all gone dead. The teams involved repeated their efforts, told the same stories, and came up with nothing. It was an endless loop, and people were becoming frustrated. Madelyn knew it was just a matter of time before she was pulled from this detail. The CIA didn't have anything to do with this kind of domestic research gathering. The only reason she was still involved was the American weapons found in Kazakhstan and the Russian mafia involvement. Eventually, it would be left to the FBI to watch Alice Weaver and try to charge her with something…*anything.* Madelyn had to wonder though…What was with the confiscation, and who was behind it?

Dr. Wilkerson took Alice aside before she could rejoin Kathy, who was getting pumped full of the drugs he had prescribed. Alice had stepped into the hall for a moment to take a phone call.

"Alice, do you have a minute?" Dr. Wilkerson asked as he saw her heading back to the room.

"Yeah, Doc. How's it going?" Alice asked distractedly as she put the phone back in her pocket and looked at him hopefully.

He shook his head slightly, pulling her away from the open room and out of Kathy's earshot. "That vial you gave me. How did you obtain it?"

"Why? What's in it?" Alice was suddenly very alert, her body tensed for whatever information the doctor had for her.

"That's just it, the contents have been forbidden in this country for decades," he said nervously, adjusting his glasses. Alice's intense look was making him nervous.

"Forbidden?" she asked, lifting a brow.

"Outlawed. The contents are a known carcinogen and contain some other highly questionable additives. We're reverse engineering it now, and I'm pretty certain it may be the cause of the effects we are seeing in Kathy's body." He nodded towards the room where even now the IV was dripping into the woman's arm.

"So, this substance might be the cause?" Alice clarified musingly, working to keep her anger in check as the doctor confirmed what she had already surmised.

"I don't want to say definitively it is the cause, but I'm starting to think it may be the culprit based on our tests. There was also microscopic residue of the same substance on that ring. Someone tried to wash it off, but they weren't as thorough as they thought they were. I have several people working on it, of course."

"All are sworn to secrecy?" she suddenly worried. Her multitasking brain filing the comment about the ring in its proper spot. She'd get angry about that later.

"Of course," he replied indignantly.

Alice waved her hand to show she meant no harm. "Just checking. Can you cure what it caused?" Her thumb pointed back at the room where Kathy lay.

He hesitated. "It's moving rather rapidly..." he began, but at her look he added, "I can only try. That's an experimental treatment, and while I know you got her in here fast, it's moving fast too."

Alice sighed and patted him on the shoulder, surprising them both at the touch. "I know you'll do your best." She looked around and then added, "She's getting so weak, and the bloating is upsetting her."

"I'm concerned at the bruising I see on her face and–"

Alice had forgotten about the slaps her wife had received, and who knew what else had happened while Alice was unconscious. Alice still had a mild headache from the slug she'd received. She'd covered up the bruising again with carefully applied concealer. She'd offered to do the same for Kathy and Emily again today, but the teen had opted to stay home instead. She nodded, "Yeah, she fell before I could do anything..." she began, realizing how lame that sounded but offering no other excuse. She didn't want the doctor suspecting she beat her wife and suddenly realized how perpetrators of that crime got away with it using just these kind of lame lies.

He nodded. "She must be extra careful. If you need a nurse...."

Alice almost flinched at that suggestion, thinking about Sandi Pasternack and her nursing skills. Her agile mind was focused on that woman in another area. She intended to get to the bottom of that situation and take revenge on the woman. "Thank you. For now, she's comfortable at home most of the time."

He nodded. "I'll let you know if the numbers get any better. Now, let's go see our patient, eh?" He smiled optimistically and led her back to the room where Kathy was receiving treatment.

"You know, I don't know how long I can continue to do that," Kathy said as they drove away from the facility later.

"Why do you say that?" Alice asked, worrying that Kathy was giving up.

"I think that nurse stuck me three times before she found a vein, and even then, she had to dig to find it." Kathy's veins were collapsing from the meds they were pumping into her body every few days.

"They did offer to put in a port," Alice pointed out. "They still could still…."

Kathy dismissed that statement with, "And I still don't want one."

"I know, babe. I know." She reached over to pat her wife's fragile hand. "Do you want Carl's Jr. today or Wendy's?" This had become their ritual.

"I'm craving Arby's actually. You know, they have that orange shake with cream? Reminds me of a Creamsicle."

"Arby's it is then," Alice smiled indulgently as she laughed.

They enjoyed these little 'picnics' as Alice called them, even if Kathy would throw up the food later. Heading home, Kathy said, "I want to shave off the remaining hair on my head. Will you stop at Mervyn's, so I can pick up a hat or scarf?"

Alice looked at her wife. The thick, luxurious, brown hair was so thin and straggly now that it looked greasy. The bald patches were evident all over, and she could see why Kathy wanted the hair gone. "You don't want a wig?" she asked instead.

"No, that would probably fall off and embarrass me. I'm going for a look," she teased her wife and smiled.

Alice nodded as she headed to the mall and the nearest Mervyn's. Alice didn't want to shop throughout the mall, her own aching body objecting at the walk around the store. They shopped for only a little while, picking out a straw hat that seemed summery and festive. Kathy also found two silk scarves that she liked, one red and one black. Alice smiled at these simple pleasures, hoping Kathy's ill health was only a temporary thing as she paid for her wife's purchases.

"Will you shave my head?" Kathy asked when they were home again.

"Are you sure?"

Kathy nodded and led her wife into their bathroom.

Alice fetched the scissors that Kathy had kept for crafting projects with the kids. They were heavy steel scissors and super sharp. She had Kathy sit on the toilet and lean forward as she snipped the remaining long, straggly strands from her scalp and dropped them into a wastepaper bin. When she was done, Kathy looked up and the women exchanged a look in the mirror. She looked horrible, and the cuts were choppy and uneven. Kathy reached into the shower for a razor and handed it to Alice. Gulping slightly, Alice reached for the shower wand. "Bend over a little," she told Kathy as she dampened the remaining hair on her close-cropped head. Once everything was wet, she took the shaving gel in her hand and rubbed it all over Kathy's scalp. Gently, she began to scrape the razor over her wife's head. Long, sure strokes took the short hairs away, and short, rapid strokes removed the stubble. Finally, Kathy's scalp was smooth and hairless. Alice rinsed off the last of the foaming gel, wiping her wife's head with a fluffy towel as she watched the suds go down the drain in the middle of the shower floor. She gulped as Kathy looked up, her bald head gleaming in the light of the bathroom. "Well, how do you like it?" Alice asked cheerfully.

Kathy looked at herself. "Well, it's better than it was," she said optimistically, but she could see that she didn't look good bald. Her head looked an odd shape to her. It was a shock. She felt the cold immediately, despite the heat of the summer day. "I don't think I would want to go out in public like this," she admitted, then laughed as she helped Alice clean up. A wave of nausea hit her, and she was forced to sit back while Alice finished up. "I did ask for it though," she admitted as she stared at herself in the mirror.

"Fortunately, it will grow back," Alice tried to console her. She didn't tell her wife how bad she looked; she would keep that tidbit to herself. Kathy's sallow skin and the taut look as her skin stretched over her bones were magnified by the bruising that was always faintly present. The bloated look from some of the pills she was taking completed the look, and it all made her look horrible.

"I'm going to scare the kids," she said with a smile.

"They know what's going on."

"I'm glad they aren't younger. This is scary," she answered, turning her head to and fro as she looked at the effects of her baldness.

"Maybe we should have waited for Halloween?"

Kathy laughed and got up, brushing stray hairs from her collar. Unbuttoning her shirt, she went to change into another. Tying a scarf around her now cold head, she looked at herself in the mirror, determining that the scarf looked stylish.

"Why red?" Alice asked, watching her as she tossed the towels into the hamper with the shirt Kathy had discarded.

"I'll wear the black one tomorrow."

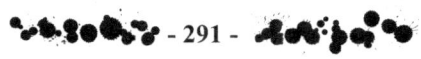

The kids were startled. Sean blurted, "Now, you really do look sick," before he put his hand to his mouth and said, "Sorry."

"No, you're right. I do," Kathy admitted, letting him off the hook and giving him a hug. "But I'm still here, and now, I'll save on shampoo."

He laughed as she had intended, but it was a hollow laugh. The kids couldn't help looking at her repeatedly through dinner as they attempted to make conversation.

"When is your next appointment?" Emily asked.

"Day after tomorrow. Why?"

"I thought I'd come along. Maybe I could get a new tennis racket?"

"You got a new tennis racket when you started lessons this summer," Alice pointed out, her eyes narrowing.

"I accidentally hit the edge and busted it," the teen admitted.

"Emily, I'm not made of money," Alice said exasperatedly. "You have got to learn to take care of your things."

"I hate to tell you," Sean said, bringing his parents attention to himself, "but I'm going to need new football cleats and a few other things."

Alice sighed, but deep down, she relished these common, everyday things. They were such a welcome relief from the more complicated things she had on her plate.

After they cleaned up the kitchen and the kids had gone off to watch television or play video games, Alice just held Kathy as they watched the sun set.

"What do you have planned?" Kathy asked, glancing at the ever-present gardeners, who even now were patrolling the fence line and planting some weird, fast-growing trees that wouldn't grow too tall and obscure their line of sight but would offer better privacy. They were working late. Given what she now knew, she realized they were probably here to defend the family against Artum or whoever else was out there.

"I've redirected most of Artum's money that I could find in Richard's books. I've also made Sandi penniless and put red flags on her credit, so she may lose her house sooner rather than later."

"What good will that do?" Kathy asked bitterly, gesturing to the bruise on her arm from the IV earlier.

"That will make her desperate and more amenable to other plans I have for her."

"Can you tell me what you have in mind?"

"My plans are not concrete yet, and I don't want to burden you..." she began, then seeing her wife's mutinous look, she glanced around to make sure they weren't being overheard. The bench they were sitting on overlooked the Pacific Ocean and was far from anyone walking on the path. In fact, they were alone. She began to tell her wife her plan, and Kathy's eyes opened wide as she realized how diabolical Alice's mind really was. Remembering what the doctor had told her about the ring, Alice's multi-tasking mind was thinking of other things she could do to Sandi beyond what she was telling her wife as she kept her temper carefully under control.

"Do you think it will work?" Kathy asked excitedly.

Alice shrugged her elegant little shoulders. "I don't know," she admitted honestly. "A lot of things will have to fall into place, and I don't want to get my hopes up. That's why I really didn't want to tell you; I didn't want to jinx the plan."

Kathy laughed at the superstition she could hear in her wife's admission. "I'm certain you can make it happen with just a few minor adjustments."

Alice looked around and stiffened slightly. "I think it's time we made our way back to the house."

Kathy looked around and saw two men at the end of the path. They were far from their house, but these men were out of place in this area and were not dressed for a walk by the ocean. She nodded and slowly got up as they casually walked back to their estate and unlocked the gate, being careful to relock it behind them as they went in. "Do you think that was Artum or his men?" Kathy asked fearfully.

"I'm certain it was them," Alice admitted and made a jerking motion with her head to one of the gardeners, pointing back where they had come from. The man nodded and put down his shovel, nudging another man to join him as they went to check out whatever it was that Alice had seen.

"Will this ever end?" Kathy wondered as they walked across the lawn. They were admiring their beautiful house, which gave them a feeling of contentment just seeing it and knowing it was their home for all these years. She didn't want to lose those feelings or the house.

"I'm hoping to bring everything to an end," Alice told her earnestly, worrying that there was too much stress for her wife. "I want it *all* to end."

They enjoyed a couple days of family time. Alice took both kids to get the gear they needed, and then, Kathy had her appointment. Emily opted to stay home again, chatting on the phone with a friend from school just like the old days. Both her mothers were relieved that she was able to find some sort of normalcy amidst the chaos that was their secret life. Sean had asked and received permission to go to Geoff's house for the night for a marathon session of video games with three other guys. Alice had supplied him with a big box of snacks and sodas, so Geoff's parents wouldn't be overwhelmed by the boy's appetite. As she gave him the keys to the Rav4, she cautioned him, "No drinking."

"Naw, I don't like the taste," he admitted. "The soda will be fine."

Alice smiled, not fooled. He had just admitted that he had drunk alcohol, and she'd follow up on that another time. She didn't want to ruin this evening.

"Let's go," Kathy said tiredly as she got into the Rover with Alice, and they headed to the clinic.

The sessions had become repetitive. One session in the week was one set of drugs, the other session another set. The deadly cocktail was showing no signs of being effective, and this was worrying Alice. Dr. Wilkerson seemed startled to see a now bald Kathy but hid his expression well as he greeted her and had the nurse insert her IV.

"I'm going to adjust Kathy's meds now that we know more about this," he indicated the chart he was showing Alice on the vial she had brought him, confirming the source of Kathy's disease.

Alice nodded in agreement, not even thinking about telling her wife of the change. She didn't need additional things to worry about.

"You know, I don't want to go to any of the fast-food places," Kathy admitted. "Throwing up that greasy food later hurts."

"Would you like a better quality vomit offering?" Alice suggested, and they both laughed.

"No, I have soup and crackers waiting at the house, and that's enough for me. I just want to get home and crawl into bed today."

"Are you feeling worse than usual?" Alice asked worriedly.

"No, I'm just tired and want to go home. Maybe a hot bath and crackers will make me feel better?"

Alice obliged her wife, taking Kathy directly home and offering her inane conversation that had them both chuckling. She delighted in thinking of things to make her wife laugh and smile.

Alice was so focused on caring for Kathy, she missed that none of the gardeners were about as she parked the Rover in the garage. Helping her wife slowly climb the steps into the house, she also didn't feel the ominous presence in her home. But when she saw Emily tied to a dining room chair in the middle of the living room, she froze, her hand on Kathy's arm tightening reflexively.

"Hello, Alice," Artum drawled as he gestured towards the two women. "Please, come in and be seated," he offered hospitably.

Alice was only startled for a moment. She realized now that she hadn't seen the gardeners on her drive up the driveway, which could mean only one thing: they were dead or had been removed. She assessed the room. The teen looked frightened but had a maddened glaze in her eyes, making them look an odd shade of green, and the gag in Emily's mouth prevented her from voicing her concerns to her mother. Alice saw Artum standing there looking victorious. Next to him was one of his goons and strangely, a third person that was a dwarf. Artum looked pompous, sporting his goatee and standing with his arms crossed. He was leaning on one leg, the other slightly bent in a cocky stance.

Alice didn't take Artum up on his generous offer of a seat. She gently pushed Kathy towards the couch as though they were obeying him, then she quickly turned and ran at him. Using his slightly bent knee to launch herself, she stepped up on his hip with her foot and took a leap over the length of his torso to his shoulder and kicked him in the head. He was unused to supporting that much weight, and the unexpected blow caused him to bend over. Alice allowed herself to jump down, then putting all her weight into her elbow, she smashed his cranium on her way down, knocking him out as they both fell to the ground.

"Son of a bitch!" she swore, wishing she could rub her now sore elbow. She was out of breath and slow to get up. She realized it had been a long time since she trained.

The second man, expecting conversation and startled by her attack, took a swing at Alice. She leaned back slightly, letting his punch go by her. Her arm then wrapped around his arm, pulling it at an unnatural angle, and they both heard the sickening crunch as she broke his arm.

Releasing the arm, she brought the heel of her hand up and crunched into his nose, pushing the cartilage back into his brain. She briefly thought, *This is becoming a habit*, as she pulled back, and he dropped to the floor, blood oozing from his nostrils.

The small man leapt onto Alice's back, thwarting her attempts to reach him with her lethal hands or feet. He clung on like a spider, and Alice could feel him attempting to wrap his hands around her throat. She twisted and turned, trying to dislodge him. Suddenly, she did a neat little flip forward and landed on her back where he was lodged. The blow knocked the air out of his lungs as her small body landed on his even smaller one. Alice made sure her elbow struck his solar plexus, and he gasped, trying to get oxygen into his lungs. Alice didn't give him the chance, striking repeatedly with her elbow. He had exhaled but couldn't draw in any air, and his face turned red then blue from the lack of oxygen. His hands grasped at his throat, then he reached towards his attacker in a plea for mercy. Alice pounded again and again and only stopped when his body went completely limp.

Crawling over to his prone body, she fished around and found a pocketknife in his front pocket. He sighed as his body relaxed and farted loudly. She wrinkled her nose distastefully as she found the knife, pulled it open, and slit his throat. She used the spurting blood and his handkerchief to rub her fingerprints from the handle.

Alice felt a blow to her head as Artum came to and attacked. She rolled with it. "You hit like a girl," Alice gasped, wanting to rub the sore spot, but there was no time. She rolled again to give her room to get away from the crazed man, who got in several well-aimed blows. He tried to stomp on her, but she rolled again, and then, reversing herself, she grabbed at the foot that was attempting to stomp her again. She struck at the back of his leg, unbalancing him, and he crashed to the floor. Alice wasn't about to let him get up again. She used her sore elbow on him, like what she had done to the small man.

"You...won't...succeed..." Artum gasped, his hands closing on Alice's neck as he tried to choke her.

She used her arms to try to break his grip. He was a strong man with a longer reach, and she was so much smaller. She saw stars when he squeezed her throat. She knew she didn't have a lot of time to do anything fancy. She was in a prone position, at a disadvantage, and unable to get leverage. She swung her head forward, using her forehead to butt against his chin twice. Her head hurt dreadfully. It was still recovering from earlier that week, and now, it was being used as a battering ram. Fortunately, it was effective. Artum loosened his grip marginally, and that was all Alice needed. Her arms broke his arms apart, and she rolled into a crouching position, ready to attack as the man got up. He was still bleeding from his lip where her forehead had smashed it against his teeth, and his jaw hurt from her attack. As he began to rise, was still unbalanced, Alice attacked. Her knee struck him in the eye, his head swung back, and he fell to the floor. Reaching in his jacket, he pulled out a gun and called her, "Schlyukha!" a whore in Russian.

Alice laughed as she responded in Russian and told him what she really thought of him. His eyes widened as he realized she not only understood what he had said but spoke the language. While she did not speak perfectly, it was adequate to make herself understood. He began to rise again; certain he had the upper hand now with the gun. Alice slowly approached him; her hands raised in surrender. Emily and Kathy looked on, horrified that Alice was going to be shot. As she got closer to Artum, Alice continued her insults of him in Russian, then she slapped the gun aside, painfully aware of her wife and daughter's location in the room, ensuring the gun wouldn't fire into either of them. She grabbed it from his hand and twisted that same hand to the point that it nearly broke his wrist. Using sleight of hand, she twisted the gun around, holding it steadily on him.

"What are you going to do now, whore?" he sneered, breathing hard at their exertions. He was shocked and surprised at how fast the woman had moved; that had been totally unexpected. Maybe there had been some truth in the stories Sebastian had told him. He had doubted so much of what he said and attributed it to the old man's admiration for the pretty woman.

"Kill you," she told him, focusing on him and pulling the trigger without hesitation. The thunderous roar of the gun was loud in the house, and she kept pulling the trigger until it clicked on an empty chamber. The first shots had taken Sebastian down, and Alice directed the remaining bullets to his heart, liver, and then, his head, continuing to fire deliberately and effectively. He was dead after the third bullet, but still she kept shooting, taking her frustrations out on his dead body.

"Alice. ALICE!" Kathy called, trying to get her to stop. Surely the shots would bring the police to their quiet little neighborhood.

Alice looked up, startled to see her wife and daughter in the room. The bloodlust was high in her, and she sagged in defeat as she dropped the gun and went to untie Emily. Kathy sank gratefully onto the couch, exhausted from her medical treatment and relieved that her wife was still alive.

"Go get those firecrackers and other fireworks I gave you and Sean for the Fourth of July. Hurry!" Alice told Emily to distract the dazed teen after she untied her.

"What?"

"We need to light them off now. HURRY!"

Emily suddenly heard her mother's words clearly and ran to get them. She was shaking so hard she fumbled and scattered them in her room. Alice was waiting at the bottom of the steps and took several from Emily as she returned. They went out on the steps and started lighting them off. One was a bottle rocket and soared into the air, whistling and whining until it went out with a pop. Alice hoped the distraction was enough to annoy the neighbors and allay any fears they might have had about gunshots. She slowly returned to the house with the teen after they lit several more fireworks over the course of about five minutes.

"If anyone asks, we are celebrating a milestone in your Mom's treatment."

"Are we?"

"No," Alice said sadly, shaking her head at the teen.

"Crap!" Kathy said, running her fingers along her bald pate.

"What? Did I miss something?" Alice asked, looking around and then up at her wife.

"He's bleeding," she gestured to where the men lay on the rug where Alice had downed them.

"Yeah...so?" Alice asked, confused and trying to see what was bothering Kathy.

"That's a real Persian rug. It'll cost a fortune to replace."

Alice looked to see if Kathy was sincere and started laughing. It took her several moments to catch her breath, and Kathy joined in after watching her wife lose her normally masterful control. Emily looked

on in consternation, not getting the joke at all. Finally, Alice wound down and wiped the tears from her eyes. "You realize we are going to have to burn that?" she pointed at the bloodstained carpet.

Kathy nodded, wiping her eyes on the sleeves of her shirt, then grabbing a tissue from the box on an end table and blowing her nose. "Just make sure you get all the ashes ground up."

"And composted," Alice agreed.

"Wait. What is going on?" Emily asked, completely confused about why her mothers had been laughing.

Alice looked at her daughter sadly. "This is about getting rid of this," she gestured to the room at large.

"Mom, you aren't going to report this, right?" the teen confirmed, perhaps more frightened than when the men had grabbed her and tied her up. She'd been on the computer, then suddenly, they'd appeared in her room. She hadn't heard them enter the house at all. Her music had been turned up loud with her mothers gone, and she hadn't thought to activate the alarm system, feeling complacent in their family home and used to the security that Alice offered them when she was around.

Alice shook her head, completely sober. She glanced at Kathy, then again at Emily, debating what to say to her.

"They'd throw away the key if they found out, wouldn't they?"

Alice nodded, waiting to see how Emily would react. She wondered what her daughter would say in the aftermath of this violence. She looked…dazed…confused…and frightened, as she should.

"You can't confess!" the teen suddenly blurted.

Alice shook her head, her eyes still their odd shade of orange, and she waited.

"This is justifiable homicide, Mom; you can prove that." Emily sounded almost as though she were pleading with Alice to hear her.

Kathy looked on, seeing the odd look in her daughter's eyes, and her heart was breaking slightly.

"Mom, I never want anything like this to happen again," she continued, sounding hysterical. "I don't want any of those…" she searched for the correct word, "thugs to touch me again!" She shuddered as she remembered how helpless she had felt when they asked her where her parents were, then tied her up and gagged her. She looked up at Kathy and saw how helpless her mother looked, and then, she looked at Alice standing there looking healthy. She had certainly kicked ass and that, above all, had made an impression on the young woman's psyche. "You have to teach me, Mom. I can't ever again let people like that," she gestured again, looking almost desperate, "get away with what they did. They were going to kill us all. They were determined to kill you." She waited for Alice to say something, and when she didn't, Emily added, "I won't tell anyone. Honest. But you've got to teach me to defend myself. You've *got* to teach me to cope…with this," she said hysterically, gesturing at the carnage in their living room.

"This isn't about me. This is about you and what you are willing to accept into your life. I am not a saint. I never claimed to be. And I don't want this," Alice gestured to herself and the first body on the ground, "for you…*ever*."

"Don't you see, Mom? I am in *this*," she returned defiantly, not afraid of Alice. She knew her mother loved her, would never hurt her, and would *die* for her. "I may be young, but I get that you are trying to protect me, and I understand you didn't ever want me to know about all *this*. But maybe I was meant to find out. Maybe, of all your children, I was meant to learn from you and right the wrongs." She saw the startled look in Alice's eyes. She didn't back away from the cat-like narrowing of her pupils or the fading orange tint she could still see in the iris. "I know you aren't a killer. I know you have compassion and reason and whatever it takes to defend yourself. Don't you think I deserve to know how to do that to the best of my ability?"

"I don't want you seeking out this…crap," Alice finished lamely. "I don't want this for you," she repeated, sounding devastated for her daughter, feeling helpless not knowing exactly how to help her.

"I don't want it either," the teen put in. "I stumbled across it, and maybe the fates wanted me to find out about you. Maybe these things," she gestured at the cooling bodies at their feet, "simply find certain people. Don't you think I deserve to know how to defend myself from situations not of my own making?"

Kathy was startled, and the reasoning of her teenaged daughter choked her up. It was obvious that Emily had been thinking this out. Kathy exchanged a look with Alice and surprised them both by croaking, "Teach her."

Alice stared at her wife hard. She was incredulous to hear her saying that. "Kathy, no…We agreed…."

Kathy shook her head and made a negative gesture with hand. "That was before. She's right. Things have a way of finding us. She needs to be protected, and Sean needs protection. We can't be there for them all the time. They're getting older. They'll be going out into the world, and they need to know how to protect themselves."

"You want me to confess to Sean what I am?" Alice asked, shocked and alarmed. She stared at Kathy, wondering if her meds were affecting her brain. Seeing the bald woman before her holding the straw hat and scarf in her hands that usually hid her now bare skin, Kathy looked almost alien to Alice.

"No, I don't want you to confess to Sean, but maybe he could use some combat skills. You know, maybe learn some defensive moves for life and for grace," she shrugged her shoulders, showing how thin she was becoming from the drugs being pumped into her body every week. Her face was round and swelling up, and it looked terrible with the taut skin in certain areas making it appear misshapen. The bones of her shoulder and collarbone were peeking through the shirt. "Maybe he might have need of those skills? I just know he needs to be home more and bonding with you before he's off to college next year. He needs to know you, Alice."

"Don't talk like you aren't going to be here," Alice demanded, determined to make Kathy see that this was not a good plan of action. "You're going to make it. Doctor–"

"Doesn't know if I will make it either," Kathy finished for her. "All we can do is try. All we can do is prepare our children the best ways we know how." She glanced at Emily listening to them, her heart breaking for her youngest daughter...her last child...her baby. "I'm sorry you didn't get a chance to keep your childhood a bit longer."

"Mom, that wasn't your doing," Emily told her, sounding older than her years. She put a hand on her mother's arm and gently squeezed. Kathy noted that Emily's hand was slightly shaking, and she was relieved that the child wasn't becoming cold-blooded about all this. "I think Carmen started that. It wasn't your fault that I overheard and saw what I did."

"I should have been a better mother," Kathy lamented, watching the last of Emily's childhood burn up before her. It was in the ether sphere, but she could feel it; it was almost tangible.

"You *are* a good mother," the teen insisted. She looked back at Alice. "What are we going to do with these?" she asked, glancing at the bodies.

"*We* aren't going to do anything," Alice told her automatically. "I'll–"

"No, Alice. She needs to know," Kathy interrupted, "the good, the bad, and the ugly."

Alice stared incredulously at what her wife was saying. "No, Kathy. She doesn't need to know."

"Yes, Alice. She might have need of that knowledge…someday."

"Your meds are addling your mind," she said aloud.

Kathy smiled, looking more like a Halloween decoration as her teeth showed prominently in her pale face, almost like horse teeth. "Probably, but then I think you addled my mind a long time ago," she teased. "Teach her," she repeated meaningfully. "Teach her to defend herself. Give her the confidence to go out in the world and not be afraid of such ugliness," her hands gestured at the bodies, one of which released a stream of gas in a long, drawn out hiss. "Teach her the good too?" she pleaded hopefully, almost crying at what she was asking Alice to do.

"No," Alice said, shaking her head, "I won't!"

"For me?" Kathy asked, hating herself for using her illness like this, but she was afraid of the madness she had seen in the teen's eyes. Emily had seen too much and experienced too much death and destruction at such a young age, and she had no outlet for it. The child couldn't see a therapist without sending her parents to jail, and neither parent was qualified to give her psychiatric care. There had to be an outlet, and the only thing Kathy could think of was having Alice teach her to stay out of trouble…the only way Alice knew how.

Alice sighed, wanting to cry as Kathy pleaded with her. "I'll teach her," she agreed.

They had to wait until dark, and in the meantime, Alice grabbed some plastic painting cloths from the garage. She rolled the bodies with Emily's reluctant help. It was obvious the teen was forcing herself, and despite Alice's initial reluctance to allow the teen to participate, she let her work through it. She could see by the way Emily handled the bodies that she was angry at them for forcing her to do this. Not angry at Alice or Kathy but at the men Alice had killed. It was their fault she had to help clean up their bodies.

Alice showed Emily how to clean the gun and put the men's fingerprints on the gun by repeatedly placing it in their grips. Using her own gloved hand to handle the gun, she pocketed it in the first man's pocket before rolling him up. The dwarf confused her, and she was surprised when she found his passport on his body. She stripped that from his body along with the large roll of American dollars she found.

"Shopping," Emily murmured, trying some humor.

"Charity," Alice swiftly retaliated, then softened her voice when the teen looked upset. "We don't need any of this money."

"I know," she said softly, helping to check the dead men's pockets before rolling them in the plastic sheets.

Kathy was unable to help; she had barely any strength left. One by one, Alice and Emily pulled, dragged, and pushed the bodies through the house and down the steps to the back of the Rover. In the garage, they were able to use a wheelbarrow to get the bodies into the vehicle. Stacking them in there, Alice had never been so glad about the size of their enclosed garage. She returned after they took the surprisingly heavy little man out to the Rover and found Kathy attempting to roll up their expensive Persian rug.

"I'll do that. Why don't you get a fire going in the fire pit? We'll have a barbecue, and later, we'll burn this."

Kathy nodded, exhausted. As she got up, she lost her balance slightly and nearly fell. She tried to hide it, but Alice saw and got up to support her. Taking a moment to give her wife a hug, she reassured her, "I'll take care of it." Alice could feel Kathy's bones against her during the hug. Kathy nodded, a little sob escaping her throat.

"I know you will." She went out and painfully put wood in the pit and threw the grate over the fire.

It was well after dark as they fed pieces of the rug into the fire. They'd cooked hamburgers on the grill, and Emily had been amazed that she'd been able to eat. The rug smelled funny, but they took their time and burned it slowly. Alice had cut the carpet into convenient squares, and her hand was hurting from using the knife so long. The rug had proved resilient to her attempts to cut it, and the bruise in the palm of her hand added to the large inventory of cuts and bruises she now sported on her body. She'd been on the phone a couple times during the evening, and Kathy quietly asked her about it.

"The gardeners were pulled off the job. Artum had set up a distraction with his men, and they'd gone to deal with it. I'm glad they aren't dead, but I gave them hell for leaving us unprotected."

"Why don't you let them deal with…?" Kathy gestured towards the house where Alice had Emily spritzing bleach and a combination of other chemicals to make the house smell clean and fresh. Mrs. Fernandez would return from her days off to a sparkling, fresh house. "Bleach would be a dead giveaway," Alice had explained to Emily, showing her the combination of cleaning supplies that would work on blood, body fluids, and DNA. She'd shown her how to clean the scene. She also showed her how well blood showed up under a blue light if they didn't clean thoroughly.

"I won't let them deal with cleaning the house because I don't want them to know Artum is gone. That wouldn't be good for business," Alice said meaningfully. This had happened so quickly. She hadn't been quite prepared, and it annoyed her. The phone calls had annoyed her as well. She'd kept them short, using a burner phone she had and afterward, throwing the phone in the fire with the damn carpet that was taking forever. It had been a large area rug. "So, what kind of rug are you going to shop for to replace this?" Alice asked in a forced attempt to be cheerful and change the subject. She used a poker to lift the lump of plastic that used to be a phone back into the flames and further destroy it.

Kathy laughed, as she was meant to. She also yawned. Her eyes were sunk deeply in the sockets of her head, and she looked terrible.

"Why don't you go to bed, love. I'll handle this," Alice gestured to the fire. It was going to take hours to burn all this, and she could see how exhausted Kathy was already.

"*We* will take care of it, Mom," Emily corrected and neither Mom was certain who she was addressing.

Kathy smiled wanly. She wished she could do more, but she knew she couldn't. She nodded and got up to head inside. Alice rose to help her. "Don't put any more on there until that is gone," she instructed the teen, nodding to the fire where even now the rug pieces were attempting to smother the flames. She noted grimly that it was a really good rug, even as it tried to thwart their attempts to burn it thoroughly.

Alice helped Kathy get ready for bed, washing her tenderly and lovingly, then tucking her in.

"Teach her," Kathy repeatedly weakly as she grabbed Alice's hand. "I'm sorry."

"I am too, baby. I am too," Alice replied as she patted her hand. Kathy was asleep in minutes, simply exhausted.

"Why don't we use gasoline on the carpet?" Emily asked Alice when she returned to the fire with another bundle in her hands. It had been at least an hour since she left to take Kathy to bed, and the teen had started to worry.

"Because it would leave a trace, and we don't want that," she replied as she saw the carpet pile hadn't gone down as much as she had hoped. She put her bundle down next to it and began cutting up the shirts, the pants, and the other clothing she had brought.

"What is that?"

"It's the clothes those men were wearing. I stripped the bodies," Alice admitted, talking in an undertone. Sound really carried at night, and it was very dark as they fed their fire.

"Is that to help prevent them from being identified?" the teen asked, and Alice nodded as she tried not to stare into the fire—it was tempting as sitting before a fire was a time for reflection. How dare those men break into her home again?

Emily had admitted she hadn't set the alarm and had turned her music up way too loud. They had taken her because she was distracted by her friend on the phone, and the music had covered the sounds of their entry. She was ashamed and vowed to learn everything Alice could teach her.

It was early morning but still quite dark before the carpet and clothing were all burned up in the fire. Now, Alice had had to find something to burn besides the logs and other wood they kept for this purpose. She'd broken up some wood shelving she kept in the garage, burning the particle board instead of the treated lumber. She explained her reasoning to Emily and wondered how much of it the teen would even remember as she yawned.

"Gawd, I'm tired," the teen admitted as they stirred the ashes of the fire, making sure it was down to almost nothing.

"We aren't done," Alice reminded her, just as tired and hurting. She was out of shape and older, not used to this type of activity.

"Oh…yeah," the girl replied, wondering what they were going to do about the now naked bodies in the back of her mom's Rover.

"Grab your fishing gear and change your clothes. We are going fishing."

"What? Fishing?" the girl asked, surprised. Alice made sure the fire was nearly out. Only a few smoldering pieces of wood were left, and she used the poker to move them to the middle, so they would burn together. They could see no further signs of the clothing and carpeting they'd spent the night burning.

Alice stretched as she changed into her fishing gear. It had been a long time since she'd taken the kids fishing or been out on a boat. She tried to remember the last time and couldn't. She was so tired, but she had to do this. The bodies had been in the back of the SUV far too long already. She packed the fishing gear in the back seats, and she and Emily got in the front. It was still very dark, but she could feel the air was clear and knew it would be a glorious morning when the sun came up. The missing windows meant they were cold in the SUV, and she cranked up the heat. Alice laughed at the ever-present vehicle parked down their street and the two men asleep in the front seats.

"Why don't they give up?" Emily asked her mother.

"They have a job to do. They are probably being paid very well to watch us."

"Not doing a very good job, are they?"

Alice laughed again and drove past without worrying about being followed.

"Do you own this boat?" Emily asked in a quiet, little voice as they drove into the marina. Alice seemed to know exactly where she was going.

"No, I rented this boat. That was one of the phone calls I made," she admitted as they started carrying their gear to the boat. "Get the covers off and fold them," she told the girl, pointing to the ones she meant. She hoped that anyone watching them would see their gear and stop watching, assuming they were just going early morning fishing. It was early even for fishing, but Alice wanted no witnesses as she hoisted the body of the little person onto her shoulder. The tarp she had brought along to cover the plastic sheet was hiding him from view. Her back protested, and she anticipated Artum and the other man causing her back even more pain. Thankfully, she found a wheelbarrow unattended and temporarily confiscated it to use for the other two bodies as Emily helped her get them on board. As they were loading the last body, they froze. Just as they had lifted Artum's body, they both heard a door open and shut somewhere along the marina, the sound carrying clearly on the early morning air. Finally, when everything was clear and all three bodies were hidden on deck, Alice stole a few chunks of concrete that some other boaters were using for weights. Emily returned the wheelbarrow as Alice readied the boat she had rented.

They sailed slowly out of the harbor, their lights leading the way. Alice had dimmed the lights immediately in front of her, so they didn't blind her and prevent her seeing their passage.

"Why that harbor, Mom?" Emily asked once they were on their way and Alice was showing her how to drive the boat.

"I used to have a boat. Do you remember that?"

The teen shook her head. "Is that what made you think of this way of getting rid of the bodies? Is that what you used to do?"

Alice smiled, the gesture pulling the skin taut on her face and showing her where there were more hurts on her battered body. Artum had landed a few blows. "Yes, I did this a time or two before, and we are going to use about the same area. There is a shelf here, and then, it drops off deeply. We will tie the bodies to those cinder blocks and throw them overboard."

"Good. Can we go home and sleep after that's done?" the tired teen asked.

Alice shook her head. "No, we need fish for our cover story, so we actually have to do some fishing."

Emily sighed and decided she better stop complaining or Alice might not teach her anymore.

They were out for hours. Alice showed Emily how to tie a knot to the concrete that wasn't about to come loose. She explained that fish would eat the flesh and even the bones of the bodies.

"Are you sure they can't trace anything back to us?" the teen fretted.

"No, but you should never be too sure of that. Always assume that you've left some trace, and they will find you. Be prepared."

"How do you live with that?"

Alice shrugged. "I'm good, Emily. I'm *really* good, and most of my life I've been *really* careful."

Emily realized the way her mother had worded that last sentence. "And now?" she asked, knowingly.

Alice grimaced as they dumped the unknown man first, watching him submerge and seeing the bubbles rise as he sank. Emily watched avidly well after he was out of sight. "I think I'm just getting old, and I hope I'm not getting careless. I just want it to stop."

"Well, you're done here, right?"

Alice shook her head. "No, there will always be a need for a cleanup on aisle three," she quipped.

"Huh?"

Alice smiled. "You need to learn obscure references, Em. It means that I will have to clean this up for a while; there are still some loose ends." She didn't tell her daughter about the senator or Mrs. Pasternack. She hoped she could leave Emily out of *that* distasteful business, especially with what had happened with that twit of a daughter the woman had whelped. Her eyes glittered as she thought of Sandi and the drug that Doctor Wilkerson was reverse engineering for her.

"I do pretty well in school," the teen pointed out.

"Yes, and we're grateful that you are a straight A student. Now, I want you to take more classes."

"*More* classes? I'm maxed out."

"I mean extracurricular classes."

"Like karate?" she asked hopefully, having asked for those a few times. She felt so foolish watching herself in the mirror as she imitated the karate she had watched on YouTube or other videos she had seen.

"No, not karate yet. I'll begin to teach you some of the martial arts, but I want you to take dance classes and–"

"Dance classes!" the teen cut her off, nearly shouting in consternation.

"Shhh. Sound carries over the water, and you'll draw attention to us," Alice warned her, looking about in the darkness. The lights of their boat were turned off, but who knew what or who might be out here. She could barely see anything with the curve of the Earth. They were well offshore as they tied a block to the little person's ankles. For a dwarf, he had a big penis, and Alice looked away.

Watching the little man slip under the waves Alice tried to remember the last time she had disposed of a body in this way and realized it had been an exceptionally long time. She was glad of that and hoped this would be the last time. She was so tired of it all.

Artum was the biggest of the men, and the multiple holes in his body had leaked blood all over the plastic. It was a good thing Alice had rolled him up in the plastic again after removing his clothes as it held in all the gory mess. She'd had a hard time removing his clothes. They'd been fine clothes too, despite the many gunshot holes. She'd been surprised to find he wore women's underwear but shrugged, knowing some men found them more comfortable, and who was she to judge? She was glad when Artum slipped below the water and was gone. She poured pure bleach where the bodies had lain on the deck of the boat, washing it down with a hose as the waste poured through the drain holes on the sides of the boat deck. She poured the last of the bleach on the tarps they had used, then using the last of the blocks she had brought for this purpose, she tied them to the plastic and tarps and threw them overboard. She watched to see they were weighted down enough to go below the surface and disappear, carrying any remaining DNA with them. Lastly, she threw the gun overboard, glad to have it gone.

"Let's go fishing!" Alice said brightly to the tired and now too quiet teen.

Emily had never felt less like fishing, but she was following Alice's lead and tried to wake herself as Alice fired up the boat and headed to a likely fishing spot.

They didn't catch much; they were simply too tired. Alice's weary body was protesting as she fought the line for her own catch. Emily's was bigger, which cheered the exhausted teen. "Why dancing classes?" the teen asked while waiting for a fish to bite the line that Alice had shown her how to tie and then, how to bait the hook.

"You are going to need poise and skills you aren't yet aware of. It will teach you the balance and grace that I can't teach you in combat fighting. It will give you all the things you don't know you need. I also want you to learn fencing, and we'll take classes together," she promised.

"You will?" the teen asked, suddenly sounding enthusiastic.

"Oh, yeah." Alice sounded pleased with the idea herself. "I want you to take languages at school too."

"Why?" the teen sounded dismayed as they brought in another fish, and Alice finally called it quits. She knew she was becoming dangerously tired and this could lead to mistakes…and mistakes were dangerous.

"Languages will teach your mind to use different pathways. Take Latin for the basics, which will help you with any of the other languages you choose. You need a well-rounded education, and I intended to speak with you about taking those anyway."

"How long do I have to study?" Emily sounded like a normal teen, whining at all the extra study and work Alice was requiring.

"The rest of your life," Alice admitted. "I only learned Russian a few years ago," she pointed out.

Emily quit whining as she thought about the things Alice wanted her to do and the reasons behind them. She didn't understand, but she knew if she asked, Alice would tell her. She just had to remember to ask the *right* questions. She didn't think Alice would mislead her, but she might not answer the questions completely if she didn't word them correctly.

Alice slept well into the afternoon, and Emily slept just as long.

"Is Mom sick?" Sean asked when he came home the next morning and saw she was still in bed. He looked at Kathy, wondering if she should be in bed as he watched her popping some pills.

"Naw, just a late night. You should have been here," Kathy told him brightly, secretly thinking, *Thank God you weren't here.*

"Yeah? What'd you do?"

"Your Mom grilled some hamburgers, and we made marshmallows and smores." *And she killed three men in the living room*, Kathy thought.

"Sounds good. Anything left?" he asked as he headed to the refrigerator to look for leftovers.

"No, sorry," she told him. "There is cereal though." She watched as he pulled out a mixing bowl and dumped a quarter of the cereal box's contents into it for his breakfast. She didn't say a word, although there was a time she would have admonished him for being such a

glutton. She finished taking her pills and took out a normal-sized cereal bowl for herself.

Alice looked worse for wear even after a second shower. She was wearing a lot of concealer on her face where she had suffered cuts and blows, and she walked gingerly from her stiffened body parts. She hoped to have the time now to rest her body from the past few days.

"Hey, Mom. Want to go out and play some tennis?" Sean asked when he saw her. She was looking old today, not as bad as Kathy, but moving quite slowly.

"Naaaw," she replied with a smile. "I feel like watching movies today and vegging on the couch. Maybe another time?"

"Yeah, sure. But you always say we've got to keep active..." he teased, enjoying the fact that he could turn her words back on her.

"Yeah, yeah," she waved off his teasing with a smile. "Want to watch movies with us gals?"

"Well, actually..." he began, seeing as he couldn't get a tennis match out of her.

"You want to go play video games? Here or with your pals?" she asked knowingly.

"If you don't mind? Coach has us scheduled every night next week, and I won't get another chance."

Alice exchanged a look with Kathy, who nodded discreetly, and she let the young man go. It was a relief as they could all be themselves after he left without trying to hide how badly they truly felt. Emily joined them on the couch, a cereal bowl held in her hands as she chewed dispiritedly.

"You okay?" Alice asked the teen, worrying that all this had been too much for her.

"Yeah, just tired," she admitted as she used her spoon to shovel in some cereal.

"Yeah, me too," Alice agreed ruefully, watching her daughter from the corner of her eye.

Kathy shook her head. This was such a weird situation to be in. Her wife and daughter were overly tired because they had disposed of bodies this morning! "Who cleaned the fish?" she asked, having seen the fillets in the refrigerator.

"Mom made me," Emily said sullenly as she took another spoonful.

"You caught the biggest fish," Alice grumped and her daughter looked up. They shared a smile.

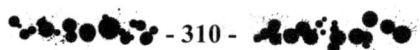

It took three days before Alice and Emily felt agile enough to walk without pain and stiffness. Emily went with them to Kathy's appointments, and Alice began to teach her how to stretch before practicing basic karate and other martial arts' moves.

"What are you doing?" Sean asked, seeing what looked like yoga moves.

Alice explained that she was teaching Emily some basic physical defense moves.

Of course, Sean had seen his mother work out in their weight room over the years, but she had never taught any of them her moves before. "She's not going to be able to do squat," he teased his sister.

"Huh, a lot you know. When Mom finishes teaching me, I'll be able to flip you!"

He laughed, but he looked at his mother and asked, "Would you teach me?"

"I don't know, smart guy. You're pretty busy with school sports."

"I'm not always there," he pointed out, wondering if she just didn't want to teach him.

"I could show you a few things, but you have to listen to me. No squirming out of things because you think it's sissy or something." She mentally chastised herself for using the word 'sissy' since it reminded her of something her father would have said. She didn't talk about her father…ever.

Alice took her children through the basic moves, correcting them when they tried to hurry through them, showing them time and time again until they could flawlessly achieve them.

"C'mon, Mom. We have done this five times already today," Sean complained after a week of moves he didn't think had any connection.

"Look, this isn't the Karate Kid with 'shine on, shine off,'" she warned him, looking up at the man that was her son. He still had some filling out to do, but she could see that football and other sports had really sculpted his young body. "You agreed," she warned him, and he nodded, sighing, and going back to the repetitive moves. "Once you learn these moves, they become instinctive. You'll see," she promised them both.

"How are they doing?" Kathy asked, having heard the kids' complaints when they thought Alice wasn't listening.

"Neither one of them is patient," she admitted, trying not to remember her own training. "I think Emily will have to go to a dojo

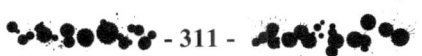

without me eventually. Maybe when Sean goes off to college next year."

"I don't want to think about that yet. It's a year away. Has he talked about any of the schools he might want to attend?"

Alice shook her head. Nowadays, she didn't talk to the kids except about the moves, slowly building on the foundation of what she had taught them step by step, which was hard as the kids wanted to be breaking wooden boards already.

And Alice wasn't teaching them all the time; she was doing other work. She'd let the gardeners go and placed others in their positions. Kathy had admitted that having assassins as their employees, even unknowingly, had unnerved her. Julio hadn't been pleased, but the routes that Alice had given them—and she hadn't given him all of the routes he knew—compensated him, so there was no resentment. He just liked knowing that people he brought into the country had a way to earn an honest living where he could get them green cards legally. He knew that Alice was right and leaving their posts had been dangerous. Now, he had to make other plans. Alice and he had reached an amicable agreement. The men and women who did their gardens now were part of a local service she had hired, legitimate and above board.

"What do you mean you aren't going to watch her house anymore?" former Senator Edwards asked the man standing before him.

"Look, we've watched her for months. We could watch her for years and nothing would change. She's cost me so much money in new tires it isn't even funny anymore. We have had nothing new to report to you in a very long time. What is the point? Why pay these men to do nothing but sleep in their cars every night outside the Weaver estate?"

"Sleep?" he asked angrily. "I don't pay your men to sleep!"

"It's a figure of speech," he lied, but he knew they slept because he'd caught them a time or two himself. "Enough already, Edwards. What are we watching them for?"

Ken Edwards wasn't certain why he wanted Alice Weaver and her family watched anymore, but he felt it was his decision to fire these people, and they weren't allowed to quit. Much to his chagrin, he had no choice in the matter when they walked off the job. He was furious but unable to do anything about it. He had already called in several old favors and had Alice investigated by the police and the IRS, and she'd gotten off. Now, the FBI was bungling the job, and it made him so angry he could choke.

"Hey, Ken? I have someone I want you to meet," his manager stuck his head in the room, so he could make the introductions. He'd been paid a lot of money under the table to make sure these two met, and he wasn't about to screw it up.

"I don't want to meet anyone," Ken waved him off, lost in thought as he took a drink of the whiskey he favored.

"Believe me, Ken, you want to meet this person," the man put in meaningfully.

"I'm tired. That was a long speech, and those questions were endless," he complained, hating the speeches he had to give, but they paid well, and he could only trade favors so far. Some things cost a lot of money, and he had a lifestyle he wished to maintain.

His manager wouldn't take no for an answer. "Ken Edwards, this is Sandi Pasternack," he said as he ushered Sandi into Ken's suite...

~The End~

⚲ About the Author ⚲

    K'Anne Meinel is the BEST-SELLING author of LAWYERED, REPRESENTED, SAPPHIC SURFER, DOCTORED, AND VEIL OF SILENCE as well as several other books including her first, SHIPS which was written in 2003 over the course of two weeks. She then played with it for several years before publishing it as an e-book and then was approached to publish it in book form. After that it was published on other sites as an e-book. In the meantime, she published some 50 short stories, novellas, and novels of various genres. Originally from Wisconsin, many of her stories have taken on locations from and around the state. A gypsy at heart, she has lived in many locations and plans to continue roaming. Videos of several of her books are available on YouTube outlining some of the locations of her books and telling a little bit more…giving the readers insight into her mind as she created these wonderful stories.

DOCTORED

If you have enjoyed **MALICE MASTERPIECES 6**
please look for K'Anne Meinel's novel **DOCTORED** from
Shadoe Publishing:
We have a chapter here for your enjoyment.

DOCTORED

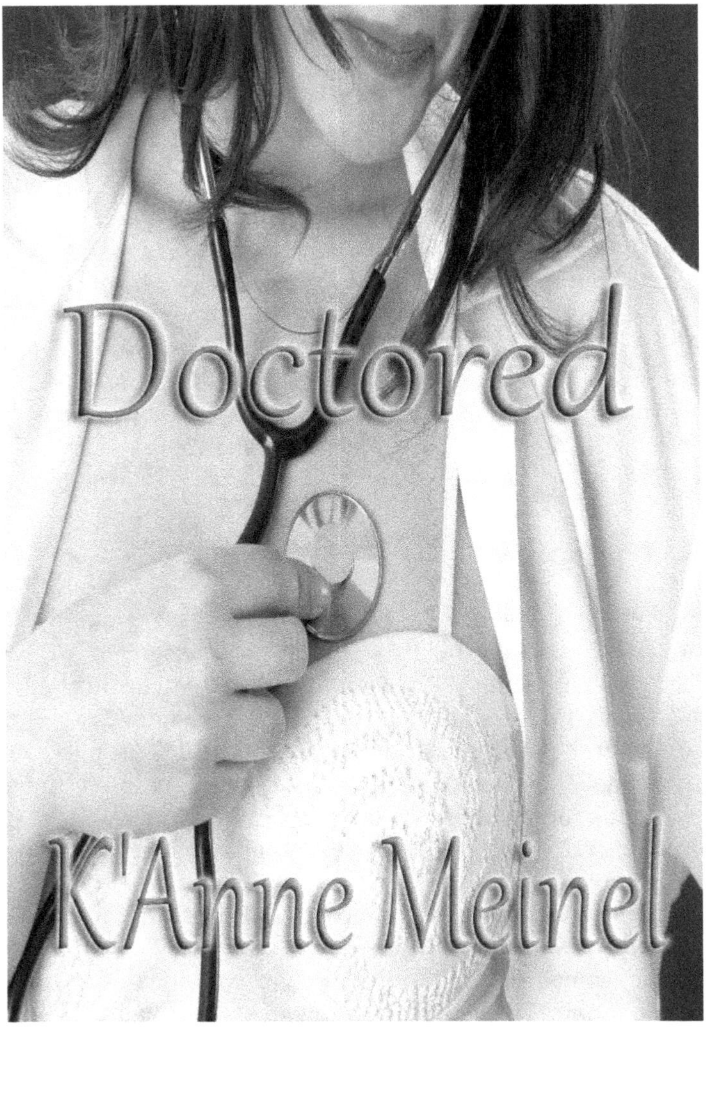

A brilliant child protégée, she dreams of becoming a doctor and a surgeon...and accomplishes her goals. Unfortunately, her youth and round, child-like face work against her. No matter how skilled she becomes, how knowledgeable, the old school, male-dominated medical hierarchy wants to keep her in 'her place.'

Deana has worked hard to become an expert in her chosen field, but few believe this 'child' capable. Specializing in infectious diseases, she travels the world—from the States to Europe to South America— honing her skills before winding up in Africa where her skills are desperately needed.

Meeting a nurse by the name of Madison MacGregor, she finds they share an insatiable curiosity and a love of helping others, but falling in love was not what she intended. Later, when she loses Maddie to a misunderstanding, she is haunted by the one that got away...

Ten years have passed and both the doctor and nurse have moved on with their lives, but fate intervenes when they find themselves working at the same hospital. Their friendship is revived...can their love be rekindled? Will the past haunt them or bring them closer? Will the secrets that both harbor keep them from realizing a future together?

CHAPTER ONE

"Hey! Where'd you get that huge bouquet from?" Bonnie asked her with a touch of innuendo and a sly grin.

"What? What bouquet?" Madison asked with a puzzled frown, looking around as though she could see them from her desk.

"The one at the nurses' station on the fourth. You didn't put them there deliberately?" she asked slyly, as though to get in on 'the secret.' She was actually hoping to ferret out more information.

"Why would I do that?" Madison stopped writing in the patient's chart and looked up.

"To show Tom that he isn't the only one interested? Payback for that bad date?"

Madison grinned ruefully at the ill-conceived idea of anyone being able to date Tom Masters. The arrogant asshole had told her equal

rights meant he expected her to pay for her half of the expensive date he had taken her on. She shook her head. Had he sent flowers to make up for it? "I didn't see them," she told her friend, truthfully.

"Well, Sheila told me that they couldn't fit them on or in your locker so they decided everyone could enjoy them. There is no card though," Bonnie confided, and that confirmed that she had looked.

Madison rolled her eyes. Having friends among the staff could be a little bit of a pain in the ass. She had to be careful as she was their superior. She finished up the chart she was looking at, closed it, and filed it as she got up from the desk. "Guess I'll go have a look," she told her impatiently curious friend.

"Mind if I tag along?" Bonnie asked, falling into step beside her.

"Don't you have patients?" Madison asked, looking down at the shorter woman and stopping to give her a stern look. Friend or no friend, the patients came first.

Bonnie sighed and turned away, hoping that Madison would share who the flowers were from. She was certain they weren't from Tom—he was too self-absorbed to think of anyone…especially someone like Madison. She looked back to see Madison escaping into the stairwell instead of taking the elevator. She admired the clean lines of her nurse's uniform, the sterile whites instead of the scrubs that everyone else wore. It made her stand out, but then as a nursing supervisor she needed to. Her looks alone would have had her stand out. It wasn't that she was really that attractive, she just kind of grew on you. As you got to know her, you realized she was beautiful, but not in an obvious way. It was her personality that made her beautiful.

Madison went up to the fourth floor nurses' station and was astonished at the bouquet sitting there. Alyson assured her they were for her and she stared in consternation at the many Birds of Paradise along with the long grasses in the bouquet. It was simple and yet striking at the same time. The quantity of them was staggering.

"Ah, so who are these from?" Alyson asked, trying to dig for information. The other nurses and a few of the doctors were all gossiping. "Are they from Tom?" she slyly slipped in. Rumors and innuendo fueled the gossip mill, in between caring for patients.

Madison looked up from the massive bouquet and shook her head, first to clear it from her own surmising of who the bouquet was from, and second to refute the question. Tom wouldn't pay for something so outrageous. He'd make a penny scream before he let it go. "No, not from Tom," she assured the triage nurse.

"Oh, is there someone else…already?"

Madison looked at Alyson again. "No, there is no one else, but it's not from Tom," she said with absolute conviction. She also didn't want that guy getting credit where credit wasn't due, and Tom definitely didn't need the credit.

"Are you taking the bouquet now?"

"I'll come back after my shift for it." She was already wondering if it would fit in her Prius. Those stems were kind of long…perhaps on the floor. It was going to look gorgeous in her small living room on the dining room table.

She was asked about the flowers all during the rest of her shift, repeatedly denying they were from Tom. The fact that she didn't have anyone else to name and her answers being vague might have kept the gossip going. She wasn't happy when it spilled over into the operating room when she was trying to concentrate on her patients and her job.

"So, Madison. I saw that bush you got, sitting on the fourth floor nurses' station," Doctor Traff commented, smiling behind his mask to show he was teasing. The twinkle in his dark green eyes might have given it away too.

"Yesss," Madison said tightly from behind her own surgical mask, glancing up from the tray for only an instant.

"Clamp," he requested, and saw that she was right on the money, ready and waiting. She often anticipated what he needed and that made her a good nurse. She also followed up on the patients as much as any of the doctors. Many of the doctors liked working with her—she went above and beyond, and was extremely conscientious—and it was appreciated.

"So, who sent them?" he asked, making conversation as he worked.

Madison looked down into the gut briefly and returned her eyes to her tray. They didn't need more hands in there, much less eyes, and her job was to keep the tools of the trade available to the doctors. She just wanted the conversation to stop. Her nurses had been asking all day. "I don't know," she answered honestly. She was never so relieved as when the patient began to pump blood and the surgeon's idle conversation was cut off. He could now concentrate on saving a life instead of Madison's love life, or lack thereof.

DOCTORED

"So, who do you think they are from?" Larry, another nurse, asked as they washed up after the surgery.

Madison rolled her eyes. The idle gossip wasn't going to stop. She was sick of it already and retreated into silence as she quickly changed. She glanced at the cleaning crew in the operating room and then checked off a few things on the chart before leaving.

Madison had a few more things to check, things she knew other nurses wouldn't check unless she followed up, but then she was thorough at her job. She changed into street clothes, not about to be seen in her nurse's uniform, and ended up on the fourth floor trying to carry the huge bouquet. There was no way she could easily walk it all the way down from the fourth floor, especially in the stairwell, so she pressed the button for the elevator. She saw many admiring glances and assumed they were for the enormous bouquet. It was really lovely, but she was embarrassed. Perhaps she should have left it at work, maybe divided it up and given it to a few patients. She wondered who it was from.

"Did you get in a fight?" Beth asked as she saw her maneuver onto the elevator with the bouquet, trying not to poke anyone in the eye with one of the sharp, pointy flowers or the long-bladed grasses.

"No," she replied simply, tired of the questions the flowers had engendered today.

"Are you seeing someone new?" Beth was determined to get more information.

"Nope," she grinned, hoping the doors would open again before further questions could occur to the woman.

The elevator stopped on the second level and a couple of people edged on, trying to fit in around the flowers. They eyed them warily...Bird of Paradise flowers could be used to maim, even unintentionally.

When Madison saw that one of the people who had gotten on the elevator was Tom, she seriously thought about using the flowers as a weapon. It would poke him quite nicely in the eye, one of which he was using to look at her suspiciously. She hadn't cheated. They had gone on one date only and that one had been a disaster. How dare he look at her like that! If she moved like so, it would accidentally poke him in the butt, but her humor wouldn't let her do the actual deed as the elevator settled on the first floor. He glanced at her and the flowers one more time before leaving the small box they were all in.

"You better go first," Beth offered generously. She had seen the look on Tom's face and couldn't wait to spread some rumors about it.

The flowers didn't fit well in her small Prius even if they were on the floor of the vehicle. They did, however, take up the whole dining room table and bring joy to her as she gazed at them over the wine she allowed herself after a full day's work. Who were they from though? That was the question she—and apparently many of the people she worked with—wanted answered. They were exotic and they were all over southern California, but this was a unique bouquet. Who had sent it to her?

Idly, she sat spinning the stem of her wine glass and gazing at the present she had received. She was trying not to read too much into it, but she couldn't help thinking about the who, the what, and the why. Her introspection was cut off as the children came into the house.

"Mom!" Chloe yelled with a smile. "Dad got us a puppy!" she said importantly as she came over for a hug.

Madison managed not to roll her eyes at Scott, taking her idea and going with it. It wasn't the first time…it wouldn't be the last.

"It's a shaggy beast," Conor said importantly, with all the dignity of an eight-year-old as he headed into the kitchen for a snack.

"A shaggy beast?" Madison nearly laughed as Scott came in and dropped off both children's backpacks.

"Hard day?" he asked as he saw her drain the remains of her wine. Then he saw the monstrous bouquet on her dining room table and turned to raise an eyebrow.

"No, not at all," she assured him, ignoring his questioning look. "A dog?"

"Yeah, we went to the pound after school. *Just* to look," he assured her. "Next thing I knew we had this shaggy, flea-bitten varmint."

She laughed, knowing the powers of persuasion her children possessed. "I'm sure you will adjust."

"It's going to cost me a fortune," he whined, trying to get her to see his side of things.

Madison was amused further. He had heard her suggestion that it was time for the children to have some responsibility and get a pet. He further wanted to be the hero and now had to deal with it.

"We went to Petco and apparently the dog needs one of everything," he lamented.

"Well, now you've done it," she assured him.

"Done what?" he asked, confused.

"You can't get rid of it now," she pointed out, knowing he wouldn't hesitate to take it back to the pound.

"Daddy, you won't get rid of Fluffy will you?" Chloe asked, sounding amazingly like her father with her whine.

"Of course not, honey," he assured her. "Now you go and play." He watched affectionately as she went off to the room that she shared with her brother in the tiny house.

Madison shook her head, knowing he'd backed himself into a corner and would expect her to get him out of it somehow. It really made more sense for her to have a dog in her small two-bedroom house with a yard than him in his small apartment, but she wouldn't rescue him, not this time. So many other times she had indeed gotten him out of his need to show off for the kids, but enough was enough.

"Here are your keys," he said as he handed over the keys to her minivan. She reluctantly handed him the keys to his Prius, preferring the smaller and more dependable vehicle to drive.

Madison was relieved when Scott left and she was alone with the kids. She needed her quiet time and sharing custody with him wasn't always easy. It was why she no longer wished to be married to him. He had needed so much of her time that it was like raising a third kid. She wanted a lover, not another responsibility. She wanted a partner, not someone who wanted to be taken care of, not someone who expected it. She sighed thinking about Scott and then her latest fiasco, Tom. Why the heck couldn't she meet someone nice who 'tripped her trigger' and could be a true partner? Someone who was adventurous and loving? Someone who didn't want something from her she wasn't prepared to give? She sighed again as she straightened one of the flowers and wondered who had sent her the absolutely outrageous bouquet.

TO BE CONTINUED...

~End Sample Chapter of DOCTORED~
For more go to www.Shadoepublishing.com to purchase
the complete book or for many other delightful offerings.

~ Because a publisher should stand behind their authors~

Discovering that you don't have everything you thought you wanted is a surprise. Getting a promotion, finding new friends, learning you are attracted to women....

Nia Toyomoto has worked hard all her life to prove she was the best; she graduated early from high school, college, and got the dream job in Manhattan. Becoming a partner at the tender age of thirty she thought she had it all until the law firm made demands about her personal appearance and a few other things that made her change her life for the promotion. Then she realizes having everything isn't all that it is cracked up to be without someone to share it with...

A successful lawyer in the big city, choices have to be made, sacrifices and surprises await this beautiful and talented woman...does she make the right ones though?

www.shadoepublishing.com

 *~ Because a publisher should stand behind their authors~*

What do you do when you meet someone who changes everything you know about love and passion?

Paige Harlow is a good girl. She's always known where she was going in life: top grades, an ivy league school, a medical degree, regular church attendance, and a happy marriage to a man. Falling in love with her gorgeous roommate and best friend Alyssa Torres is no small crisis. Alyssa is chasing demons of her own, a medical condition that makes her an outcast and a family dysfunctional to the point of disintegration make her a questionable choice for any stable relationship. But Paige's heart is no longer her own. She must now battle the prejudices of her family, friends, and church and come to peace with her new sexuality before she can hope to win the affections of the woman of her dreams. But will love be enough?

www.shadoepublishing.com

Coming out is hard. Coming out in the public eye is even harder. People think they own a piece of you, your work, and your life, they feel they have the right to judge you. You lose not only friends but fans and ultimately, possibly, your career...or your life.

Cassie Summers is a Southern Rock Star; she came out so that she could feel true to herself. Her family including her band and those important to her support her but there are others that feel she betrayed them, they have revenge on their minds...

Karin Myers is a Rock Star in her own right; she is one of those new super promoters: Manager, go-to gal, agent, public relations expert, and hand-holder all in one. Her name is synonymous with getting someone recognized, promoted, and making money. She only handles particular clients though; she's choosy...for some very specific reasons.

Meeting Cassie at a party there is a definite attraction. She does not however wish to represent her despite her excellent reputation. She fights it tooth and nail until she is contractually required to do so. In nearly costs them more than either of them anticipated....their lives.

www.shadoepublishing.com

~ Because a publisher should stand behind their authors~

In the male dominated sport of Formula 1 racing, Samantha 'Sam' Dupree is struggling to make her mark against the boys. She hears about a driver who is making a name for herself in NASCAR and goes to check her out. Little does she know that she's in for the race of her heart.

Addison McCloud wants nothing more than to drive. She doesn't care about fame or fortune; she just wants to be fast enough to get herself and her family away from her abusive father. Meeting Sam, changes her world and revs her life into overdrive.

When the two women meet, sparks flies like the race cars that they drive. Will they be able to steer their relationship into something more and win the race, or will their families make them crash and burn. The boys of Formula 1 are going to learn that Southern girls are a force to be reckoned with.

www.shadoepublishing.com

~ Because a publisher should stand behind their authors~

Carrie flees from the demons of her present, trying to protect the ones she loves.

Frankie hides from the demons of her past, and the memory of loved ones she failed to protect.

A modern day princess thrown to the wolves, Carrie's only hope is the rancher who had spent the better part of a decade in self imposed, near total, isolation. Frankie's history of losing those she tries to save haunts her, but this madman threatens her home, her livestock, her sanctuary. She knows she can't do it alone, has she still got enough support from her oldest friends?

 *~ Because a publisher should stand behind their authors~*

Amelia Gittens had the credit of being the first and only woman thus far in the United States military of being a sniper in combat, made possible by being in the Military Police unit of the crack 10th Mountain Infantry Division. After retirement she joins the City of New York Police Department, and suddenly finds herself involved in a suspect shooting incident which soon encroaches upon her entire life. In order to protect her therapist who has been targeted as a revenge killing, Amelia takes on the responsibility as if she was still in the Army, treating it as a tactical maneuver.

www.shadoepublishing.com